PRAISE FOR B

At First Light

"[In] this intense psychological thriller . . . Evan and Addie race to prevent more bloodshed. Hints of a romantic relationship between the pair enliven the story, and references to Beowulf and Viking history add depth. Readers will hope to see more of Addie and Evan."

—*Publishers Weekly*

"Brilliant Evan Wilding, with his goshawk and unusual friendships, will fascinate those who read for character."

—*Library Journal*

"*At First Light* is a winner."

—*Denver Post*

"A high-intensity thriller that will take your breath away . . . Barbara Nickless is an awesome talent."

—*Mysterious Book Report*

"The moment I finished this intelligent and pulse-pounding psychological thriller, I was ready for Book Two . . . Dr. Evan Wilding is one of the most interesting fictional characters I've met in some time . . . Author Nickless's prose is crisp and, at times, poetic. Her descriptions are vivid but balanced. I became immediately attached to her engaging and well-drawn characters. In some respects, *At First Light* is reminiscent of Dan Brown's *The Da Vinci Code*. I highly recommend this book to fans of fast-paced thrillers that include riddles, ancient languages, and literature."

—Claudia N. Oltean, for the *Jacksonville Florida Times-Union*

"*At First Light* is a stunner of a tale. Barbara Nickless has fashioned a deep exploration into moral depravity and the dark depths of the human soul in a fashion not seen since the brilliant David Fincher film *SE7EN*. This wholly realized tale is reminiscent of Lisa Gardner, Karin Slaughter, and Lisa Scottoline at their level best."

—Jon Land, *USA Today* bestselling author

"Barbara Nickless has crafted a dark, twisty thrill ride with a bad guy to give you nightmares, and a pair of protagonists you will want to come back to again and again. Lock your doors and curl up with this book!"

—Tami Hoag, #1 *New York Times* bestselling author of *The Boy*

"*At First Light* by Barbara Nickless is one of the best books I've read in a long, long while. With unique and unforgettable characters who match wits with a devious, sophisticated, and ritualistic serial killer, this complex and compelling story is as powerful as a Norse god and just as terrifying. I can't wait for the next book in the series featuring Detective Addie Bisset and Dr. Evan Wilding! Bravo!"

—Lisa Jackson, #1 *New York Times* bestselling author

Gone to Darkness

"A gritty, hard-boiled crime novel with breathless action and deep, sturdy characters. Detective Sydney Parnell and her partner, Clyde, a police dog, are a tantalizing duo, and the story's narrative and dialogue are authentic and witty and demand compulsive reading. *Gone to Darkness* is everything you want in thriller fiction."

—Robert Dugoni, #1 *Wall Street Journal* bestselling author of the Tracy Crosswhite series

"Nobody does atmosphere better than Barbara Nickless. With deft strokes, she draws impending doom within bleak settings and then colors them with vivid action and brilliant characters, both human and canine. *Gone to Darkness* is mystery and suspense writing at its best!"

—Margaret Mizushima, award-winning author of the
Timber Creek K-9 Mysteries

"Barbara Nickless's *Gone to Darkness* is another stellar entry in the Sydney Rose Parnell series. Even though she's now a Denver police detective, Sydney and Clyde catch a case involving trains, a unique milieu that Nickless masterfully evokes. Readers who enjoy an atmospheric setting, a kick-ass yet vulnerable heroine, solid police procedurals, fast-paced yet lyrical writing, and/or the closeness of a human-dog partnership should immediately buy or borrow every book in this series. (I stop short of suggesting stealing a copy, but if that's your only option . . .)"

—Laura DiSilverio, award-winning and nationally
bestselling author of *The Reckoning Stones*

"Barbara Nickless creates characters who matter—to each other and to the reader, who is fortunate to journey with them. With *Gone to Darkness*, Nickless expertly crafts a dark tale brightened with heart, humor, and humanity. It's a tightly woven, always-escalating, keeps-you-up-past-your-bedtime novel. And Sydney Parnell is my favorite kind of detective: a relentless empath on a mission to solve herself as well as the crime, navigating her demons to ensure justice for the victims of evil."

—Matt Goldman, Emmy Award winner and *New York Times*
bestselling author of the Nils Shapiro series

"In the fourth episode of her popular, bestselling Sydney Rose Parnell series, award-winning thriller writer and fan favorite Barbara Nickless leaves no doubt that she's on the fast track to A-list stardom. In *Gone to Darkness*, the action never slows, and the suspense ratchets up in every chapter of this delightfully twisted and energetic page-turning thriller from the mind of a budding superstar!"

—*Mysterious Book Report*

Ambush

"A nail-biter with some wicked twists . . . Fast paced and nonstop . . . Sydney is fleshed out, flawed, gritty, and kick-ass, and you can't help but root for her. Nickless leaves you satisfied and smiling—something that doesn't happen too often in this genre!"

—*Bookish Biker*

"*Ambush* has plenty of action and intrigue. There are shoot-outs and kidnappings. There are cover-ups and conspiracies. At the center of it all is a flawed heroine who will do whatever it takes to set things right."

—*BVS Reviews*

"*Ambush* takes off on page one like a Marine F/A-18 Super Hornet under full military power from the flight deck . . . and never lets the reader down."

—*Mysterious Book Report*

"*Ambush* truly kicks butt and takes names, crackling with tension from page one with a plot as sharp as broken glass. Barbara Nickless is a superb writer."

—Steve Berry, #1 internationally bestselling author

"*Ambush* is modern mystery with its foot on the gas. Barbara Nickless's writing—at turns blazing, aching, stark, and gorgeous—propels this story at a breathless pace until its sublime conclusion. In Sydney Parnell, Nickless has masterfully crafted a heroine who, with all her internal and external scars, compels the reader to simultaneously root for and forgive her. A truly standout novel."
—Carter Wilson, *USA Today* bestselling author of *Mister Tender's Girl*

"Exceptional . . . Nickless raises the stakes and expands the canvas of a blisteringly original series. A wholly satisfying roller coaster of a thriller that features one of the genre's most truly original heroes."
—Jon Land, *USA Today* bestselling author

"*Ambush* . . . makes you laugh and cry as the pages fly by."
—Tim Tigner, internationally bestselling author

Dead Stop

"The twists and turns . . . are first rate. Barbara Nickless has brought forth a worthy heroine in Sydney Parnell."
—BVS Reviews

"Nothing less than epic . . . A fast-paced, action-packed thriller-diller of a novel featuring two of the most endearing and toughest ex-jarheads you'll ever meet."
—*Mysterious Book Report*

"A story with the pace of a runaway train."
—Bruce W. Most, award-winning author of *Murder on the Tracks*

"Want a great read, here you go!"
—Books Minority

"Nickless is on my favorite writers list now."

—Writing.com

"Riveting suspense. Nickless writes with the soul of a poet. *Dead Stop* is a dark and memorable book."

—Gayle Lynds, *New York Times* bestselling author of *The Assassins*

"A deliciously twisted plot that winds through the dark corners of the past into the present, where nothing—and nobody—is as they seem. *Dead Stop* is a first-rate, can't-put-down mystery with a momentum that never slows. I am eager to see what Barbara Nickless comes up with next—she is definitely a mystery writer to watch."

—Margaret Coel, *New York Times* bestselling author of the Wind River Mystery series

Blood on the Tracks

A *SUSPENSE MAGAZINE* BEST BOOKS OF 2016 SELECTION: DEBUT

"A stunner of a thriller. From the first page to the last, *Blood on the Tracks* weaves a spell that only a natural storyteller can master. And a guarantee: you'll fall in love with one of the best characters to come along in modern thriller fiction, Sydney Rose Parnell."

—Jeffery Deaver, internationally bestselling author

"Beautifully written and heartbreakingly intense, this terrific and original debut is unforgettable. Please do not miss *Blood on the Tracks*. It fearlessly explores our darkest and most vulnerable places—and is devastatingly good. Barbara Nickless is a star."

—Hank Phillippi Ryan, Anthony, Agatha, and Mary Higgins Clark Award–winning author of *Say No More*

"Both evocative and self-assured, Barbara Nickless's debut novel is an outstanding, hard-hitting story so gritty and real, you feel it in your teeth. Do yourself a favor and give this bright talent a read."

—John Hart, multiple Edgar Award winner and *New York Times* bestselling author of *Redemption Road*

"Fast-paced and intense, *Blood on the Tracks* is an absorbing thriller that is both beautifully written and absolutely unique in character and setting. Barbara Nickless has written a twisting, tortured novel that speaks with brutal honesty of the lingering traumas of war, including and especially those wounds we cannot see. I fell hard for Parnell and her four-legged partner and can't wait to read more."

—Vicki Pettersson, *New York Times* and *USA Today* bestselling author of *Swerve*

"The aptly titled *Blood on the Tracks* offers a fresh and starkly original take on the mystery genre. Barbara Nickless has fashioned a beautifully drawn hero in take-charge, take-no-prisoners Sydney Parnell, former Marine and now a railway cop battling a deadly gang as she investigates their purported connection to a recent murder. Nickless proves a master of both form and function in establishing herself every bit the equal of Nevada Barr and Linda Fairstein. A major debut that is not to be missed."

—Jon Land, *USA Today* bestselling author

"*Blood on the Tracks* is a bullet train of action. It's one part mystery and two parts thriller with a compelling protagonist leading the charge toward a knockout finish. The internal demons of one Sydney Rose Parnell are as gripping as the external monster she's chasing around Colorado. You will long remember this spectacular debut novel."

—Mark Stevens, author of the award-winning Allison Coil Mystery series

"Part mystery, part antiwar story, Nickless's engrossing first novel, a series launch, introduces Sydney Rose Parnell . . . Nickless skillfully explores the dehumanizing effects resulting from the unspeakable cruelties of wartime as well as the part played by the loyalty soldiers owe to family and each other under stressful circumstances."

—*Publishers Weekly*

"An interesting tale . . . The fast pace will leave you finished in no time. Nickless seamlessly ties everything together with a shocking ending."

—*RT Book Reviews*

"If you enjoy suspense and thrillers, then you will [want] *Blood on the Tracks* for your library. Full of the suspense that holds you on the edge of your seat, it's also replete with acts of bravery, moments of hope, and a host of feelings that keep the story's intensity level high. This would be a great work for a book club or reading group with a great deal of information that would create robust dialogue and debate."

—Blogcritics

"In *Blood on the Tracks*, Barbara Nickless delivers a thriller with the force of a speeding locomotive and the subtlety of a surgeon's knife. Sydney and Clyde are both great characters with flaws and virtues to see them through a plot thick with menace. One for contemporary thriller lovers everywhere."

—Authorlink

"*Blood on the Tracks* is a superb story that rises above the genre of mystery . . . It is a first-class read."

—*Denver Post*

DARK OF NIGHT

ALSO BY
BARBARA NICKLESS

Blood on the Tracks

Dead Stop

Ambush

Gone to Darkness

At First Light

DARK OF NIGHT

BARBARA NICKLESS

THOMAS & MERCER

Text copyright © 2022 by Barbara Nickless
All rights reserved.

Published by Thomas & Mercer, Seattle

www.apub.com

Amazon, the Amazon logo, and Thomas & Mercer are trademarks of Amazon.com, Inc., or its affiliates.

ISBN-13: 9781662500817
ISBN-10: 1662500815

Cover design by Kirk DouPonce, DogEared Design

Printed in the United States of America

To the men and women who work long hours and risk their lives to return a nation's cultural treasure.

These are the things you are to do: Speak the truth to one another, render true and perfect justice in your gates, and do not contrive evil against one another. And do not love perjury because those are things that I hate, declares the Lord.

—Biblical scroll fragment discovered in the Cave of Horror, Judaean Desert, Israel, 2021

ONE—CREATION

"The Social Significance of Everyday Words"
Semiotics 300: Social Structures in Language
Dr. Evan Wilding, Professor of Semiotics, Linguistics, and Paleography
at the University of Chicago

Our days are filled with decisions, from what to have for breakfast to whether to drop a bomb.

But few of us stop to consider that each choice for something is a move away from something else. The word decide comes from the Latin decidere, which itself rises from the Latin de—meaning "off"—and caedere—meaning "cut." Every choice we make is a cutting off. It is a door closed. A road not taken.

It is of interest to note that the English word decide shares its suffix with homicide, genocide, and suicide. All of these words represent a cutting off. They refer to a choice we have made for ourselves. Or a choice another person has, with violence, made for us.

PRELUDE

When I thought about their deaths, which I did often, I knew it had begun in Jerusalem. First came the book. Then the hunt. Soon after, the violent, venomous arguments.

Much of what happened I could lay at my own feet. But the book had been the start.

I found the volume in Jerusalem's Christian Quarter. I'd ducked inside a squalid little shop after thinking I was done for the day and good for nothing more than a drink at the hotel bar. I glanced at my watch as I wound my way through the warren-like maze of shelves, past the touristy offerings of guidebooks and religious tracts, and to the back, where any literary treasures might be found.

Ten minutes, I told myself.

Nine minutes later, a cover caught my eye as I sorted through a teetering stack of old Hebrew tomes and Coptic hymnals. A dirty-cream background with a black cobra entwined around the title's gilt letters. The book, crushed in the middle of the pile, was in wretched condition. The cloth cover was creased almost to the point of amputation, the spine broken. The gold in the title was scratched. Tiny flecks of mold dotted the yellowed pages.

I ran my finger along the snake's sinuous coils and glanced inside at the copyright—1936. Written in English, the book was a purportedly scholarly volume released by a small university press. It had found its way—God alone knew how—across the Atlantic to this neglected shop. A throwaway title whose publication likely hadn't made the slightest ripple in academia before sinking into obscurity. The title bordered on the lurid: *Lost Treasure of the Jordan Valley!*

I turned the pages, which threatened to lift from the spine. The book concerned a collection of Hebrew texts—leather scrolls that had been found in the late nineteenth century before vanishing without a trace. I laughed softly. A story for the gullible. I reached out, intending to return the volume to the pile.

But as I stood in that dusty shop on that warm autumn afternoon, I felt the first intimation of larger things—hidden truths and the sanctity of place. Something had pulled me into this specific shop on this particular street, then guided my hand to this book.

A dizziness swept through me, and I braced myself against a wall.

"It's the heat," I murmured as I removed my hat and wiped my sleeve across my damp brow.

Steadying myself, I turned to the first chapter and read aloud in a low voice.

> Wadi Mujib near the Dead Sea during the eighth century BC.
>
> The scribe rested his back against the cavern wall, reveling in the cave's relative coolness, the relief from the iron anvil heat of the sun. In the smoky light of the lamp, he laid out his tools. The tanned hide of a goat. A reed pen. Ink. Carefully, he thinned the soot-black ink with a mixture of honey, oil, vinegar, and water. He had done this task many times. He knew what consistency of ink would serve his purpose.

Sounds and scents trickled in from outside the cave. The stench of the tannery, the voices of his fellow ascetics. His thoughts went to the far city of Ursalim and the events unfurling there. He and his small band were considered rebels. Heretics, even. The accusations had driven them from the city to seek refuge in the desert.

So be it. They knew the truth.

He rubbed his neck to ease the aching muscles; he'd been many days at this single task. Now he offered a prayer in the semidark and leaned forward to touch his pen to the carefully prepared leather.

"These are the words that Moses spoke, according to the mouth of Jehovah, to all of the children of Israel in the wilderness . . ."

I slammed the book shut. I knew what this supposed treasure was. A false text. A blasphemous deviation from the truth.

Again, I moved to return the wretched book to the stack. And again, something stayed my hand. Sudden rage—shocking and unexpected—burned through me. My fingers whitened as they gripped the spine. The threads tore beneath my nails.

And I became afraid.

Of what could happen. Of what I might do.

CHAPTER 1

Dr. Elizabeth Lawrence slowed, and flicked on the car's brights, looking for the turn in the dark. Incredible, the unexpected twists life can take. Her entire career reduced to two ragged fragments of papyrus that would set the antiquities world on fire.

Then blow it up when the truth came out.

She found the street and pulled to the curb outside Chicago's St. Paul Coptic Orthodox Church. At 10:00 p.m. on a Monday, the interior of the church lay dark beyond the arched windows. It was an odd place to meet, a street corner in a residential area next to a church. But she knew the location was convenient for Sam. And in the fashionable neighborhood of Logan Square, she felt comfortable.

Who would look for her here?

Plus, the church offered neutral ground. Sacred ground, even. Appropriate, given their business with each other.

Rain spattered the windshield, the first breath of a forecasted spring squall. The air seemed to swell with the damp. Elizabeth glanced at her watch. Sam should be here soon. She hoped the seller hadn't insisted on coming. The Egyptian, Hassan, had been demanding that she hurry with her assessment of the photos he'd sent of the ancient texts. Demanding that she commit to authenticating them or let him take his treasure elsewhere.

Now was the time to be painstakingly cautious lest the entire enterprise implode, taking them all down.

She reassured herself that the Sig Sauer handgun was under the driver's seat. Dr. Elizabeth Lawrence, doctor of ancient history and papyrology, head of the Chicago Institute of Middle Eastern Antiquities, onetime recipient of a MacArthur "Genius Grant," knew her way around guns every bit as well as she did around artifacts. Despite her appearance, she was no bespectacled denizen of academia's ivory tower. For forty years she'd been boots on the ground wherever her work required her to be. She'd rappelled down cliffs, fought off malaria and marauders, and lived alone in the desert among jackals and scorpions.

In a man's world, she'd gone her own way, and she had thrived.

A car drove past without slowing, its tires hissing on the wet asphalt. A black SUV. She watched until it turned a corner.

She had no way of knowing how many people were aware of the existence of the fragments. But there were plenty of other scholars, other institutes, even private collectors, who would pay millions for these ancient texts.

Some would be willing to steal them, should the opportunity arise. Even kill for them.

A wave of weariness swept over her, and she sank back in the seat, cursing her own weak body.

Maybe, while she was still able, she should end her subterfuge and ask for Evan's help. Tell him the truth about what she'd been doing. Not just the papyri, but everything else. He could serve as a surety that she still functioned—that her brain wasn't too badly impaired by her illness.

She fished a business card from her wallet and wrote *Dr. Evan Wilding* on the back. The cancer sometimes crowded out all but the most critical pieces of information. She'd been known to forget meals, forget her medications, leave the house wearing one shoe, walk into a blizzard without a coat.

She placed the card on the dash. She wouldn't forget to contact him.

A tap at the passenger window made her sit up straight. A figure bent down to peer through the glass. Samad Rasheed. Sam.

She hit the button to unlock the doors. Sam opened the back door and wedged a large basket into the seat.

"What the hell is that?" she asked as he closed the back door and slid into the passenger seat next to her.

"A gift from the Egyptian. To celebrate tonight and our upcoming success."

Elizabeth cast a wary glance into the gloom of the sedan's back seat. Had the basket moved?

"I'm not fond of surprises," she said.

"This one you'll like." He gave her a shy smile. His teeth gleamed in the outdoor lights of the church. It occurred to her that her son—had he lived—would be the same age as Sam.

She'd met Sam through his grandfather, Omar Rasheed, whom she knew from her many trips to Jerusalem. Omar was an antiquities dealer in the Old City, a kind and honest man who was as generous with his advice as he was at sharing his wife's sugary *basbousa* cakes.

Sam had his grandfather's thoughtfulness. But in him, kindness had softened to a reticence that made him an odd fit for the cutthroat antiquities business.

"Well," she said, "the moment of truth. Let's see them."

She turned on the overhead light even as she allowed herself a wry chuckle. What would her peers say if they could watch her prepare to examine scraps of two-thousand-year-old literature under a car's dome light?

Sam reached into his canvas messenger bag and carefully extracted two five-by-five-inch wooden frames labeled **HEB-PAPYR 03-09** and **HEB-PAPYR 03-10**. Or what she, and the others involved, called the

Moses papyri. Each frame held two squares of glass, and the papyri were mounted between the squares.

Tenderly, he passed over the first frame.

She saw immediately that the glass carried the bloom of soluble salts that partially obscured the paper, just as she'd noted in the photographs. A bloom like this was common, and unlikely to have harmed the artifacts. There was also adhesive tape of the kind used in the 1950s to repair fragile texts.

Together, the bloom and the tape suggested the texts were extremely old and had been poorly treated after their discovery.

"These are mounted in glass, not plexi," she said. "I thought you were going to have them remounted."

"You begged me not to," he answered. "And Hassan agreed. Did you think I wouldn't listen to the woman my grandfather calls Seshat?"

She smiled. In her first meetings with Omar, he'd spoken of her as a willful, spoiled American woman. Later, when they'd come to respect each other, he called her Seshat, after the Egyptian goddess of wisdom and writing.

She set the first frame in her lap and picked up the second. Her hands were shaking. There was the salt bloom again, but even through it, she could make out the Hebrew text *aseret ha-dibrot*, meaning "the ten statements." This was what had caught her eye when she'd first received the photographs. When she'd first learned of the appearance of the fragments in Jerusalem.

Carefully she lowered the second frame to join the first in her lap. Ten months she'd been waiting for this moment. Ten years, really, if she went all the way back to when the Old Testament had first caught her serious attention.

Would she live long enough to see it through?

A faint sound came from the back seat. She ignored it, her gaze transfixed by the tiny squares of papyrus.

"You understand that I can't authenticate them under these circumstances," she said. "I'll need to remount them. Does the owner trust me?"

"Of course, Seshat."

"Good."

Another sound behind her. Sam coughed into his hand.

"Well?" he asked.

"How long can I have them?"

"Two weeks? The Egyptian is eager to close."

Two weeks. She silently calculated the time to repair and remount, to analyze for indications of fraud. To begin the painstaking work of transcription and translation. To create the provenance of the papyri—the history of their ownership—which would add immeasurably to their value.

"All right," she said, surprising herself.

Sam's smile widened. "Good. Then you will get the Egyptian his money, and you will publish your findings, and everyone will be happy."

"Yes, Sam." Her smile felt fragile. "Everyone will be happy."

They shook hands awkwardly in the small car, then Sam peered through the windows before he opened the door and slipped out into the gathering storm. He leaned back into the car.

"The basket," he said. "It's a puppy. A Norwegian Lundehund like your old dog. The Egyptian said to consider it a gesture of goodwill. And a promise for our future together."

"Since when did Hassan turn sentimental?"

Another grin. "Since he received these papyri."

Sam closed the door and vanished into the dark and the rain.

She set the frames gently on the passenger seat, then turned around and perched on her knees. A puppy confined to a basket. Knowing Hassan, he'd probably drugged the poor thing to keep it quiet. She reached into the back and began to tug at the tightly woven ribbon that held the lid in place.

Even as her hands moved, she wondered, as she had before, if she'd underestimated the risk. From someone who wanted the papyri for themselves. Or from someone who—for their own reasons—would want them destroyed.

A car pulled up to the curb behind her, headlights off. She glanced up.

The thought flashed across her mind that perhaps she'd too easily trusted that the Egyptian's greed would protect her.

Not that it mattered now, she realized, looking down.

Now that the lid was off.

CHAPTER 2

The man sitting on the other side of Dr. Evan Wilding's desk in his office at the University of Chicago did not look like an archaeologist, despite introducing himself as such.

Ronen Avraham was tall and solidly built, midforties, clean shaven, with closely trimmed black hair. Blue eyes behind wire-framed glasses regarded him from an open, friendly face. But the friendliness didn't strike Evan as habitual—the lines bracketing Avraham's mouth suggested he spent much of his time frowning.

The squint lines around his eyes might have come from time in the desert, peering at pottery sherds. But if the Israeli spent most of his time outdoors—as he claimed—he must have damn good sunscreen. His complexion was pale, without the telltale tan line of a man who wore a hat. His fingernails were clean and unbroken. The only calluses were on his right middle finger and his left palm. The kind you get from trigger guards and slide stops—that is, the marks made by firing weapons, not wielding trowels.

His clothes—jeans and a black turtleneck, a charcoal-gray sports coat, black running shoes—didn't suggest a man who spent his days crawling in trenches or caves. On his left wrist was a black wristwatch of a brand that would refuse to fail even under the direst of circumstances. No dirt or scrapes disfigured the face of the watch or its nylon band.

Plus, the man had a gun. The bulge beneath his jacket might be invisible to the untrained eye.

But Evan's eyes were well trained.

So. There it was.

The man leaned back in the chair, steepled his fingers, and smiled. Evan could not have felt more under scrutiny if Avraham had rolled in klieg lights, placed a pair of pliers on the desk, and eyeballed Evan's molars.

He reread the man's business card. *Ronen Avraham, Israel Antiquities Authority.* Ronen, a name of German origin meaning "well-advised ruler." And Avraham—the Eastern Slavic form of the name Abraham.

Avraham was, almost certainly, descended from Jews who had fled to Palestine from Germany or Hungary or Czechoslovakia, back before Israel was a state.

A long road from there to the University of Chicago.

Evan leaned the crisp white business card against a stack of books on his desk and returned his gaze to the alleged archaeologist.

"You're searching for Dr. Elizabeth Lawrence," he repeated, mostly to annoy Avraham. He suspected the Israeli wasn't fond of idle talk.

On cue, Avraham sighed. "That is correct, Dr. Wilding. Dear Elizabeth, our mutual friend. When she did not show for our meeting, I naturally came to you."

Naturally? Evan hadn't laid eyes on Elizabeth in two months. And that had been for a quick and depressing lunch during which Elizabeth had confided her ill health and asked if he would continue her work after she was gone. Her news had required him to imbibe copious amounts of alcohol both during and after their meal.

Plus, in all the years he'd known her, no one had ever referred to Elizabeth as "dear" anything. Her subsequent tongue lashing would have reduced them to tears for being so presumptuous.

Evan said, "Of all the professors in all the offices in all of Chicago, you walk into mine?"

"Excuse me?"

"*Casablanca*," Evan said. "It's just my way of saying, why me? Why not speak with someone from her institute?"

Avraham's expression remained flat, his gaze neutral. But he shifted ever so slightly in his seat. Probably he hadn't expected resistance. Evan suspected most professors were pushovers when it came to giving up information.

Whether or not they'd seen the handgun.

"Elizabeth told me that if there were any problems, I should speak with you," Avraham said in his accented English. "And now I have a problem. The professor and I planned this meeting three months ago. But I was in the middle of an important dig, and only now could I leave the Judaean Desert."

"You're at Qumran?" Evan asked. The Judaean Desert was home to the caves of Qumran, where the Dead Sea Scrolls had been discovered.

Avraham gave him a hard look. "Qumran is one of eight caves we're excavating. We're doing our best to search as many caves as possible before more looters arrive."

"Have you made any finds?"

Avraham folded his arms. "Why do you ask?"

Evan heard the change in the man's voice—a hitch toward suspicion. He shrugged nonchalantly. "You mentioned the Judaean Desert, and I made the logical leap to Qumran. It's not exactly a secret that the Israel Antiquities Authority—along with damn near every biblical scholar everywhere—hopes to find more ancient texts."

Avraham made a small, noncommittal grunt, but his gaze sharpened in a way that made Evan glad for the expanse of his immense desk, which lay between him and Avraham. He wished his postdoc, Diana Alanis, were here in Chicago rather than off in the South American jungle. Diana's mind was a near match for Evan's own. But it was her physicality that left Evan in the dust. As it would almost any man.

Physicality that, depending on how the conversation went, might be required.

He glanced under his desk, where Diana's Pembroke Welsh corgi, Perro, lay stretched out on the carpet, working diligently to free a treat from his Kong. Perro made a poor substitute for his owner. The beast had barely looked up when Avraham entered the office.

Evan cleared his throat. "May I ask what your business is with her?"

"You don't know?" A black eyebrow lifted a millimeter. "I thought the two of you were close."

So, it was to be a chess game, with neither side able to take control of the board.

"Although she didn't mention you were a Brit," Avraham continued.

"All the way down to the Union Jack on my boxer shorts," Evan said.

Avraham ignored that. "Or that you're not very . . ." He raised a hand to the height of his shoulder, palm toward the floor.

"Tall?"

"Exactly." Avraham didn't blush or look away at the mention of Evan's dwarfism, which Evan appreciated. "She didn't mention that."

Bless Elizabeth for focusing on the important things, which didn't really include the fact that Evan stood four feet five on a good day.

"She's a woman of few words," Evan offered.

"True."

Avraham had been sitting in Evan's office in the Harper Memorial Library for just under six minutes. During that time, he'd surveyed the large room, noted and dismissed the dog, and appraised the professor.

In other words, Ronen Avraham looked and behaved exactly like the people Evan knew from the CIA and Mossad, and one gentleman from the Russian Foreign Intelligence Service.

Ergo, Ronen Avraham wasn't a student of human history and cultural artifacts.

He was a spy.

Evan pushed back from his desk. "I'm sorry I can't be of help. But if I hear from Elizabeth, I'll let her know you dropped by."

Avraham didn't stand.

"When do you expect to hear from her?" he asked.

Evan took a step toward the door. "I don't. Not really. I don't know how you came to believe Elizabeth and I are close, but the truth is, we rarely see each other. And when we do, our meetings aren't social. It almost always has to do with our work."

Evan saw immediately that his words had been a mistake. Avraham didn't move a muscle, but his focus narrowed until Evan seemed to be the only thing he cared about. It was as if the imaginary klieg lights had gone to full wattage.

Avraham said, "You discuss her work?"

Evan shrugged casually and resumed his seat with an audible sigh. "I'm familiar with a number of Semitic languages. Syriac. Amharic. Classical Arabic and Hebrew. Occasionally, Elizabeth runs a translation by me as a sanity check. I serve as another pair of eyes."

"When was the last time she asked for your help with something?"

"More than a year ago." Evan glanced pointedly at his watch, a badly banged-up Timex that had been his companion through multiple adventures across many borders. "I have a semiotics class to teach in an hour and was hoping to grab breakfast before then. So please, play whatever cards you can play or are willing to play, and tell me what this is about. Why does Mossad care about an American historian and papyrologist?"

"Mossad?" Avraham's laugh sounded practiced. "Is that what you think I am? A counterterrorist?"

"Or something. Covert ops. Intelligence gathering. Whatever you men from Tel Aviv are up to these days. What's your interest in Elizabeth?"

Avraham shook his head, still chuckling. "Mossad. That's a good one." The laughter ended abruptly. The klieg lights switched back on. "Do you think Elizabeth is involved in some sort of subterfuge?"

"I think nothing of the sort. But I suspect you're in a better position than I am to provide that answer. So why don't you tell me? Why are you so desperate to find Dr. Lawrence?"

In response, Avraham picked up a bit of pottery from Evan's desk. A sherd of pottery from Jerusalem—a forgery Evan kept on hand to show his students. "You have a brother."

Evan blinked. "How do you—"

"River Wilding. A good man. Fond of you even if he was raised here rather than in England. And a great archaeologist. He and I worked together recently in southern Turkey."

Evan found himself reeling. Had he completely misread Ronen Avraham? If the man was working with River, then maybe he really was what he claimed.

He found his voice. "I'll tell him you said hello."

Avraham's stare was pointed. "I doubt he'll remember me. But . . . I know much more about him than he does about me. You understand?"

Evan shivered. The words about River were a threat. The implication was as clear as if the man had carved the words on a stone tablet: if Evan refused to cooperate, there would be consequences.

What was Elizabeth involved in? And how the hell had Evan and River been dragged into it?

Avraham replaced the pottery sherd on the desk and stood. "I'll be back. Perhaps you'll know more next time. For everyone's sake."

Evan watched as the Israeli gracefully—and in near silence—crossed the large expanse of the office and vanished through the doorway. No footsteps rang from the hall.

Evan reached for his phone. He tried Elizabeth at her home, then pulled up her cell number from his contacts and hit the green icon to dial. It went straight to voice mail. Elizabeth had a single employee at the institute, if he remembered correctly. An assistant to help with paperwork and scheduling and whatever else needed to be done. But he couldn't remember the person's name.

He left a message at both of Elizabeth's numbers, then roused himself from his desk and went to stand in front of his floor-to-ceiling bookshelves, searching through the titles until he found the only two academic publications he owned that were written by Elizabeth—slim booklets she'd extracted from a journal and had bound.

The first was *Deuteronomistic History: Monotheism and Rewriting the Past.* The second, *Early Edom and Moab: Traces of Iron Age Settlement in the Levant.*

Hardly provocative. Or the sort of thing that would invite the interests of Israeli national security. None of her other works were provocative, either. He knew because he'd made a point, ever since Oxford, to read everything his onetime teacher wrote.

He placed the booklets on his desk.

The Institute of Middle Eastern Antiquities was Elizabeth's late-in-life passion project. She'd once told Evan that being confined to a desk and an office would be the death of her. But she'd changed after the loss of her son. She'd grown both fiercer—especially in her work—and more fearful. And who wouldn't? A blow like that would make anyone question their place in the world, their purpose in life. After Tucker's death, Elizabeth had taken her broad historical knowledge and narrowed it like a laser on her own personal search for meaning.

The institute she'd founded provided both funding and a way to channel that search.

Elizabeth specialized in a subset of the Middle East—Egypt, Iraq, Iran, Israel, Jordan, the Palestinian territories, and Syria. Her archaeological work consisted of finds that were routine and, to nonacademics, quite possibly dull. She sifted through ancient tax receipts, official correspondence, inventories, court records, and bills of lading. All the detritus of a society's mundane tasks. There might be a moment's elation at the discovery of a verse from the Greek poet Sappho or a bit of unknown writing from Sophocles. But those literary sparks were the exceptions that proved the rule: the engine of civilization was driven by an accounting of births and deaths, taxes and census counts, money and goods.

Thus was the life of a scholar, and it was not all that different from much of Evan's own work. He found the meticulous methodology soothing. He dove into it the way a chef would turn to familiar recipes—the simple pleasure of working the hands without greatly occupying the mind.

Crossword puzzles for the academic set.

But if Elizabeth was elbow deep in ancient tax assessments, how had she gotten tangled up with Mossad?

And why would her work drive Ronen Avraham to intimidate Evan by threatening River?

It was eight hours later in Turkey. Evan would call River in a couple of hours, when his brother would be done with the day's work and possibly the evening's drinking.

Evan crossed to the immense windows that overlooked the university's main quadrangle. Light filtered through the glass and its UV protective coating to slant gently onto the floor.

He'd lied about having class in an hour. His day was free, aside from the infernal and relentless need to grade papers. And his ongoing work on the Phaistos Disc, the early Cretan hieroglyphs, and more.

So much more.

He tried Elizabeth's cell phone a final time, then pocketed his phone.

It was a perfect morning to make the walk from his office to Elizabeth's institute on South Woodlawn. He generally wasn't comfortable walking in public—it meant contending with stares, some laughs, the occasional shouted comment. But today he decided to risk it. He needed the exercise. With his hawk, Ginny, in molt and thus flying poorly, he'd gotten bloody little fresh air. Plus, there was Perro. The little sausage needed the exercise more than he did.

He snagged Perro's leash from the hook near the door, and the dog squeezed out from beneath the desk and came running. Evan clipped on the leash, then shrugged into his coat and yanked up his hoodie. He reached into a desk drawer and removed a small key that hung on an Egyptian scarab fob.

"Ready to brave the masses?" he asked Perro.

Perro cocked an ear, then barked, an astonishingly loud sound for such a small dog.

"Very well, then," Evan said. "Let us join the madding crowds."

CHAPTER 3

Mid-March in Chicago was a striptease show in which the entire city flipped between winter and spring over the course of hours. It would cajole you into pulling on a winter parka in the morning, then flashing a little spring ankle and calf come afternoon. A day that started off in the twenties and spitting mixed rain and snow on weary Chicagoans could lift by the afternoon and offer a bantering warmth in the low fifties.

Today was one in which the weather gods hadn't yet made up their minds. It featured gloomy skies periodically punctured by brilliant stabs of sunlight and temps that toggled rapidly between the mid- and high forties. All accompanied by brisk wind gusts that still flashed winter's teeth.

Evan threaded his way through the campus. At the tail end of winter quarter, students were out and about. They whizzed past Evan and Perro in various fashion—skateboards, bicycles, and the simple running enthusiasm of youth. Now and again, a student called out a greeting, and Evan raised a hand in response. Even with the hoodie and sunglasses, it was impossible for a four-foot-five man to blend in.

As he and Perro strolled north on Woodlawn Avenue alongside elegant early twentieth-century homes, Evan recalled his first meeting with Elizabeth Lawrence.

While visiting from Harvard Divinity, she'd been a guest lecturer at Oxford, teaching a three-week class on the papyri stored in Oxford's

Sackler Library. Her enthusiasm for the fragments—discovered in the Egyptian city of Oxyrhynchus, and to date the largest repository of ancient papyri yet found—had been infectious. Seventeen-year-old Evan had stayed for the after-hours Q and A, then joined in the after-*after*-hours discussions at the Turf Tavern. He'd half fallen in love with Elizabeth Lawrence, a brilliant, prickly, demanding woman twenty-three years his senior. And he'd decided the best way to the heart of a woman like her was to be the smartest kid in the class. And so he had been. And it had worked. They'd developed a professional relationship that had, over the years, deepened to friendship—despite what he'd said to Avraham.

He waited for the light at 56th and Woodlawn while Perro sniffed at the ankles of pedestrians. Men mostly ignored the trespass, but the women gave delighted squeals at Perro's big-eyed charm—a charm that was mostly wasted on Evan, who contented himself with the required maintenance of food, water, brushing, and walks without feeling much for Perro beyond a slight annoyance. Diana loved the little beast, but to Evan, Perro looked like nothing so much as a bratwurst with feet.

The light changed and they plowed ahead.

Evan checked the address and stopped in front of a beautiful brick home with large windows and decorative black shutters. A path led from the sidewalk through a neatly trimmed yard that was brushed with the first green of spring. While Perro watered a bush, Evan stepped under the white portico above the door and read the small tasteful sign in the window. The sign informed all passersby that this was the Institute of Middle Eastern Antiquities and visiting hours were by appointment only. Another sign indicated that the building was under twenty-four-hour surveillance. He glanced up and spotted a camera.

He had no idea where Elizabeth had gotten the funding to buy this place, which must have cost over two million. Maybe it was a family inheritance. Maybe someone with money to burn had a passion for archaeology. It would be a good question to ask her, given

Mossad's apparent interest. She'd no doubt tell him to mind his own damn business.

He rang the bell. It chimed chirpily through the building, but nothing and no one inside stirred. The plantation-style shutters on the window nearest the door were slatted shut.

He pulled out the key he'd brought. Elizabeth had pressed it upon him at their last meeting. "In case I collapse and I speed-dial you by accident," she'd told him. "Better you find me than some innocent postdoc. There's a code, too." She rattled off a string of numbers. "Don't forget it."

Her nonchalance hadn't fooled him—she'd been terrified of what the future might hold.

He opened the door and followed Perro into the hallway, then closed the door behind them. While Evan punched in the code before an alarm sounded, then reset it, Perro scampered ahead to investigate, his claws clicking on the polished floors. The entryway was gloomy with the shuttered windows, and Evan flipped on the overhead light. A warm glow suffused the area; wooden floors, biscuit-colored paint, and a series of gold-and-brown framed papyrus offered a soothing visage. The papyri would be knockoffs; Elizabeth would never hang the real thing on walls. Rooms led off to either side—they'd once been the living and dining rooms presumably, but now served as office-cum-storage areas containing mostly unfilled bookcases. In addition to a closet door, which stood slightly ajar and revealed empty metal hangers, a second door on Evan's left held a small brass plate that read LEAH ZIELINSKI. Elizabeth's assistant. Evan tried the handle. Locked. He knocked; the sound returned a lonely echo.

He moved deeper into the house. The hallway doglegged past a staircase and disappeared toward the back. The stairs led to the second floor, which consisted of an open hallway with rooms on the back wall and a railing along the front, giving the space an airy feel.

Commanding attention at the top of the stairs was a large framed oil painting—a dramatic rendering of a partially nude Cleopatra. The Egyptian queen lay supine on the pillows, her eyes closed, palms up, and fingers slightly curled. She was presumably within moments of death, the fatal cobra visible in the painting's lower corner as it beat a hasty retreat from the bed of its victim.

Hell of a way to go.

"Hello!" Evan called. His voice rang hollowly. Perro came trotting back.

He thought he heard movement upstairs—a faint rustle and then a squeak, like a shoe on flooring. Perro cocked his head. A sudden sense of alarm for Elizabeth's well-being sent Evan rocketing up the stairs, Perro first at his heels and then ahead.

At the top of the stairs, Evan paused, but Perro didn't hesitate. The little dog spun right, jogged past collapsed wooden crates leaning against the wall, and darted into a room at the far end.

Evan hurried after him, skidding to a halt in the doorway.

The room was an office as empty of human life as the rest of the place. An immense desk, a chair, and a task lamp anchored the room's center. A wool coat hung on a peg as if Elizabeth had meant to be gone only a short time. Shelves lined the walls; they were stuffed with binders and books along with issues of several journals: *Near Eastern Archaeology, Journal of the Ancient Near Eastern Society, Dead Sea Scrolls*, and *Palestine Exploration Quarterly*. And the Army-issued Protestant Bible Elizabeth's father had received upon his enlistment during World War II. She'd once shown it to Evan in a moment of nostalgia.

When Evan walked around the desk, he spotted a scattering of framed photos, most of which featured Elizabeth at a younger age. The implements of document repair were strewn across her desk—an assortment of pastes and probes and scalpels, a box of disposable gloves—along with a magnifying glass clamped to the edge that would allow her to closely examine her work.

But whatever she'd been repairing was gone, leaving behind a cleared space amid the clutter.

Or perhaps the object hadn't yet arrived.

Oddly, there was neither computer nor printer. If Elizabeth had a laptop, she'd no doubt have taken it with her. And probably the printer was a wireless one kept in Leah Zielinski's office. There didn't seem to be an obvious place for it in Elizabeth's office.

Even more odd was the lone decorative item on Elizabeth's desk—outside of the framed photos. On the corner squatted an evil-looking dried toad that deserved, in Evan's opinion, the rude moniker of Butt Ugly. What had possessed Elizabeth to want to share space with a sinister-eyed and very dead amphibian?

Evan clicked his tongue at Perro, and the dog followed him out of the room. They searched the rest of the top floor—finding nothing more threatening than precarious stacks of empty wooden crates, flattened and unused cardboard boxes, and piles of books—then did the same downstairs, where an assortment of pottery, ceramics, and ancient weapons only partially filled the shelves. Elizabeth must be early in the acquisitions process.

Perro nosed into every nook and cranny, furring his nose with dust, while Evan opened closet and pantry doors. Nothing looked disturbed or out of place, although it was hard to tell in the chaos of a working institute/laboratory/gallery. Evan searched in the kitchen for keys, hoping to unlock the one door he couldn't look behind—to Leah Zielinski's office—but found only paper plates, plastic utensils, empty pizza boxes stacked near the back door, a coffee machine, and a few ceramic mugs with emphatic messages like **TALK TO ME AFTER I'M CAFFEINATED** and job-related ones like **I DIG OLD THINGS**. The refrigerator held creamer, a block of cheddar, a round of brie, and a bottle of sauvignon blanc, half-empty.

He went back upstairs to Elizabeth's office. Perro made a beeline for a patch of sunlight and, apparently considering his duties over, flopped down and promptly went to sleep.

Feeling mildly guilty, Evan searched the lone file drawer of Elizabeth's desk. At the very front was a note card she'd unfolded and tucked in a hanging file. Evan glanced at the opening: *Dear Dr. Lawrence, allow me to extend my heartiest congratulations* . . . His gaze dropped down to the signature line. The note was from an editor at the *Journal of Biblical Archaeology.*

Good for Elizabeth, he thought, returning the note to where he'd found it.

In the top drawer he found an elegant and formal letter with gold-embossed letterhead. The letter was written in French, and Evan spared enough of a glance to see that it was addressed to Elizabeth and sent by the Minister of Culture and Fine Arts in Cambodia. He returned it to the drawer without reading more.

Next, he found a folder of invoices, which he thumbed through, looking for anything that might pop out. The name Veritas Foundation appeared repeatedly, along with references to provenance. He also spotted a nondisclosure agreement from the same company. He narrowed his eyes. Why would a scholarly organization—which he presumed Veritas was—ask for an NDA from another scholar? NDAs were common in high-tech corporations where there were secrets to guard. But they were unheard of in the humanities, where the back-and-forth of debate was not only encouraged but desirable.

A closed appointment calendar lay on the desk. Reasoning that he should at least verify that Elizabeth had scheduled a meeting with Avraham, he opened the planner. Only a few dates had any notations, and they were almost all doctors' appointments, as if the calendar had been purchased for that purpose. The notations had begun six months ago, and the most recent appointment—marked as INFUSION—was for five weeks earlier.

Nothing since. Had she given up the struggle?

He flicked on the task lamp and looked closely at today's date, when she was supposed to meet with Ronen Avraham. There it was—penciled in and then erased—the initials R. A. next to the line for 9:00 a.m.

Interesting. Surely a meeting with the Israeli had nothing to do with Elizabeth's health.

He went through the pages more carefully, aghast at how appalled she would be if she learned of his snooping. He should close the calendar and flee the scene of his crime. But his unease—at Avraham's presence and Elizabeth's silence—drove him to pry.

His second search found only one other notation, this one from two days ago at 10:00 p.m.: **SR-pMoses I/II STPC**.

He scratched his beard, considering. *PMoses I* and *pMoses II* likely referred to papyri—it was a common form of designation for ancient texts. But he could make nothing of the rest of the entry.

He was closing the planner when he saw a business card tucked in the leather flap. *Chuma Hassan—Antiquities Dealer.* Evan knew the name. Chuma Hassan—often called simply "the Egyptian"—had a reputation for being willing to handle looted or stolen artifacts. What would Elizabeth have to do with someone like him?

Downstairs, a key jiggled at the lock on the front door. Perro raised his head and thumped his tail. Evan eased out the door and peered over the railing, wondering how he could explain himself if whoever was coming in the door wasn't Elizabeth Lawrence.

Or worse, how he'd explain himself if it *was* Elizabeth.

An ongoing unease made him snatch up a heavy book from a nearby box. Given his height and lack of mass, the book would allow him to do little more than get someone's attention.

But maybe a full-frontal attack would slow down an intruder, who would no doubt be doubled over, laughing.

You worked with what you had.

CHAPTER 4

The door opened, and a young woman strode into the front room of the institute. She was in her midtwenties, petite, with a mop of auburn curls she'd coaxed into a high, untidy bun. She punched in the alarm code, slid out of her green wool jacket and hung it in the coat closet, then pulled out her phone and typed something. An emerald ring on her left hand caught the light.

She glared at her phone.

Evan eased the book back into the cardboard box.

"Hello!" he called down from the balcony.

The woman startled and looked up. Her eyes went wide with alarm. "Who are you? Why are you here? *In* here? We're closed."

"I'm a friend of Elizabeth's. Evan Wilding. And you?"

She looked like she might flee out the front door. "You can't be here."

Evan held up the key with its pyramid fob. "Elizabeth gave me a key. And, as you can see, I don't pose much of a threat. Elizabeth and I have worked together in the past."

Perro trotted out of Elizabeth's office and came to stand next to Evan, ears perked, tongue lolling. The woman visibly relaxed—what self-respecting assailant would have a corgi as his partner in crime?

Perro had worked his usual charm.

The woman started up the stairs. "I'm Leah Zielinski, Dr. Lawrence's assistant. Is there something I can help you with?"

Zielinski. The name on the office downstairs. It was a cheerful-sounding word. Polish for *green* or *herb*.

Although, at the moment, the name's owner sounded more peeved than cheerful. She stopped halfway up the stairs. "What can I do for you, Mr. Wilding?"

"Right. I dropped by because I need to talk to your boss, and I can't reach her on her mobile. Or at her home."

"You're *Dr.* Wilding," Leah said suddenly. "The semiotician. Dr. El *has* mentioned you."

"Only told you the good things, I hope."

A faint smile. "She called you Sparrow."

"Some people do."

"She didn't mention—" She flushed to her roots. "She didn't say anything about your, you know . . ."

Amused, Evan waited.

"Your height," Leah finished. Her skin was now a vivid red that clashed with her hair.

"Well, it's easy to overlook. In a manner of speaking. So, Ms. Leah Zielinski, do you know where your boss is?"

She shook her head. "I've been in finals. Dr. El told me my study group could meet in the kitchen, so I've been pretty much camped out here every night. But she gave me the week off from work, and I've hardly seen her. Maybe she's just run out for coffee and croissants. Or maybe she's working from home."

If so, she wasn't answering her phone. "Any idea where her favorite coffee spots are?"

"As if! I was thrilled when Dr. El hired me. Being mentored by her will really help my career. And she's been generous with her teaching, even if she isn't super approachable. But her personal life?" Leah laughed. It was a sweet, delicate sound. "She'd sooner challenge me to strip poker than tell me where she goes for pastries. Or to lunch. Or dinner. Or how she spends her weekends. She's a *very* private person."

Evan nodded. No argument there.

"So," Leah said pointedly, "what do you need?"

"Just a couple of questions, if you don't mind." He headed back toward Elizabeth's office. Perro followed him, and a moment later Leah appeared in the doorway.

"What?" she said.

"This is where she worked?" he asked.

"Her cave, she calls it. Because she usually keeps the blinds closed." Leah frowned. "That's odd that the desk lamp is on."

Evan was fortunate he didn't flush as easily as Leah did. A quick glance at the appointment calendar assured him he'd replaced it exactly as it had been.

He gestured toward the empty space on the desk. "She's working on something here. Do you know what?"

Leah turned and gave a small cry as her gaze landed on the desk. She pointed at the toad. "That's an ugly thing, isn't it?"

"Any idea where it came from?"

The loose knot of her hair bounced as she shook her head. "Only that it wasn't here a week ago. Ugh."

Evan stared down at the mummified creature. Toads preferred the dark and the damp and thus often served as symbols of the night. In China, they were guilty of devouring the moon during eclipses; in European sorcery, they stood in for demons.

But if someone had given Elizabeth this toad, it was likely due to its connection to ancient Egypt. Egyptians had associated the toad with death.

A coolness touched his neck.

Then again, sometimes a toad was just a toad. Maybe Elizabeth had picked up the little fiend during her travels—it might appeal to her sense of the perverse.

Leah crossed to the desk and turned off the light. The toad merged into the gloom.

"I'm not really looped in on her day-to-day stuff," she said in a bright voice. "Mostly Dr. El has me working on a Greek papyrus so I can learn to do our conservation work myself. And she's having me learn not only ancient Greek but also Phoenician."

"Phoenician?" Evan asked. "By that you mean archaic Hebrew?"

That sweet laugh again. "Right. Sorry. We *have* been spending a few hours every week researching finds made during the nineteenth century by Britain's Palestine Exploration Fund—the PEF. Which means I've gotten used to thinking like a scholar from that period."

"Sounds fascinating."

"Oh, it is! The PEF started the first real excavations in the Holy Land. They referred to archaic Hebrew as Phoenician, although I'm not sure why."

They were now in Evan's area of expertise. "Because archaic Hebrew is classified with Phoenician in the Canaanite subgroup of the Northwest Semitic languages."

"Oh." Her dark eyebrows winged together. "I . . . see."

He gave the closed appointment calendar a casual glance. "Does *SR-pMoses-one-slash-pMoses-two STPC* mean anything to you?"

"Give me some context."

"It's something Elizabeth put in a text," he lied. "We were hoping to meet, but she had a conflict. This SR-pMoses one-slash-two STPC."

Leah slid one hand behind her back. "It doesn't mean anything to me. But, Dr. Wilding, if you're hoping to scoop some details from me about Dr. El's work, the answer is no. You'll have to wait until she gets back."

Her hand came back into view, and she folded her arms.

He nodded with approval at her loyalty. "Of course." He noticed a black-and-white photograph in the lineup on Elizabeth's desk—a European in Arab dress—and picked it up. "Lawrence of Arabia?"

Now a radiant smile. "I don't think it's any secret that she's on a T. E. Lawrence kick. She's interested because of her family."

"You'll have to explain."

"Dr. El's sister, Lillian, is a genealogy nut. She traced their family back to one of T. E. Lawrence's brothers. That caught Dr. El's interest, mostly because of Lawrence of Arabia's archaeological surveys—he worked for the PEF. And it's pretty cool, right? That Dr. El would sort of be following in her great-great-great uncle's footsteps. She's been reading up on his work in the Wilderness of Zion."

"Modern-day Israel."

She nodded. "Right. Although it's often called Zin, not Zion. It's where Moses is supposed to have gotten water for the Israelites by striking a rock during their wandering in the wilderness. That locale is right up Dr. El's alley—she did some work there years ago. She's pretty amped up about it." She laughed again. "And by *amped up*, I mean as excited as she ever gets. You know Dr. El. She doesn't get overly jazzed about anything. Keep calm and carry on. That's her motto."

Evan nodded absently. Could Elizabeth have learned something or discovered something in southern Israel that had brought her to the attention of Mossad?

"Has she traveled to Israel recently?" he asked.

"She goes a couple of times a year. But she hasn't gone in probably six months. The only trip she's made recently was a quick research trip to London."

He replaced the photo of Lawrence of Arabia among the other pictures on the desk. "Do you have another way to reach her, Ms. Zielinski? Maybe another phone number?"

"I did try calling her about signing for a delivery that's coming tomorrow. I got her voice mail. But I'll keep trying." Frown lines appeared on her brow. "I'm sure she's just busy."

Evan weighed how much to share. "A man came to see me a little while ago, claiming that Elizabeth had missed a meeting with him. He's an Israeli who says he works for the Israel Antiquities Authority. Did you know about their meeting?"

Leah pursed her lips, thinking. "Maybe she tried to cancel with this dude and couldn't reach him. Or maybe she forgot." A cloud passed over her face. "She's been a bit absentminded lately. She forgets to return phone calls or answer emails. Then she dumps it in my lap, and I have to make excuses for her."

Imminent death does tend to make the unimportant things drop away.

He turned back to the desk and gave the framed photographs a closer look. Lawrence of Arabia aside, the pictures appeared to follow a rough chronology from left to right. Evan lingered over a snapshot of Elizabeth with her teenage son, both looking radiantly happy against a backdrop of sea and shore. As far as he knew, there had never been a father in the picture. Not after conception, anyway.

Smack in the middle of the sequence was a picture of Elizabeth standing at an archaeology site with Ronen Avraham.

He reached over and picked up the photo.

The pair stood close to each other. Both wore sunglasses, and neither was smiling, but their postures were relaxed. In the background stretched a barren landscape of sand and stone, with rocky outcroppings just visible in the distance. Nearer by was the tumbled masonry of a prehistoric settlement mound. The site could be in the Negev desert. Or in the Judaean desert, where Avraham claimed to have been working.

Based on Elizabeth's appearance in the photo, her short hair still blond, her tanned face only faintly lined, he guessed the photo was maybe fifteen years old, when Elizabeth was in her forties. Ronen Avraham looked barely into his third decade.

Perhaps Avraham had been telling the truth about being an archaeologist.

Evan held up the photo for Leah to see.

"This man," he said. "Do you know him?"

Leah took the picture. "Maybe? If it's the same dude, he came by the institute about eight months ago. I remember because it was only a few days after I started working for Dr. El. The guy kind of weirded me out."

"Why was that?"

An embarrassed laugh. "He was just, like, super focused. I mean, all us academics are focused. We have our projects and our passions. And we can be mega competitive, too. But this guy was more like . . . it was more like he was being vigilant. I guess that's a better word. Taking in everything, checking out everyone who came in or went out, head on a swivel. Isn't that what they say in the military?"

"He struck you as a military man?"

"Maybe." Leah replaced the photo on the desk, lining it up carefully with the others. "I was still moving my stuff into my office, and sometimes I'd look up to see him watching me."

"Maybe he simply found you attractive."

This time, only a faint pink rose in her cheeks. "It didn't feel like that kind of watching."

Evan nodded. "He was in and out of here?"

"For a couple of days. I was too new to be comfortable asking Dr. El who he was. She just mentioned he was visiting from Israel. I assumed it was about some archaeological site over there." She ran a delicate finger along the top edge of the picture frame. "It's funny I never noticed the photo of him before."

"If he comes around here again, can you let me know?"

"*Is* he coming back?" Leah didn't look happy at the prospect of encountering Avraham again. "Who is he?"

"An answer we'd both like to know."

Evan's attention shifted to a stack of books on Elizabeth's desk. *Measuring Jerusalem: The Palestine Exploration Fund and British Interests in the Holy Land*. And another title, *East of the Jordan*. Leaning against the books was an index card on which someone, presumably Elizabeth, had jotted the phrase *God blasts those trees which try to touch the skies.*

"Not a cheery sentiment," he said.

Leah picked at the cuticle of her thumb. "Dr. El likes it. She always says ego is the enemy of good scholarship."

"Smart woman. And probably almost entirely alone in that sentiment."

"Yeah, maybe. Look, Dr. Wilding, I really need to get to work. I've got a lot of catching up to do. I'll probably be here all night."

"Of course. My apologies for taking up your time. Lovely ring, by the way."

She blushed and folded her hands, hiding the emerald. "Thank you."

Evan clicked his tongue at Perro, who had resumed his nap in the sunshine. The dog opened his eyes and blinked at Evan. "Let's go, Perro."

Perro hoisted himself to his feet. He and Evan followed Leah into the hallway.

At the top of the stairs, Evan stopped in front of the painting of Cleopatra.

"Beautiful and tragic," he said. "It seems like an odd choice for Elizabeth."

"Really?" Leah's voice held a hint of anger. "You're surprised she admires a woman who decided to take her own life rather than let herself be enslaved by the man who invaded her kingdom and destroyed her army?"

Evan stared up at the queen who had committed suicide at the hands—or rather fangs—of an Egyptian cobra. There was a lot of debate now about whether Cleopatra had actually committed suicide in that manner, or if she'd opted for the quieter and more certain method of an herbal potion. But the idea of the cobra held a certain power.

He said, "I expected Elizabeth to hate what artists and writers have done to the Ptolemy queen over the centuries. They took a woman with a lot of smarts and political astuteness, turned her into a sexpot, and accused her of using her feminine wiles to get what she wanted."

"There are those who say the queen died for love." Leah tipped her head. "But Dr. El says that's crap. She admires the *real* Cleopatra. The savvy politician. The woman who went out on her own terms. Not the image created in the minds of men with sex on the brain."

At the front door, Evan thanked Leah for her time. He felt her gaze on him as he and Perro made their way back down the walkway to the street. A moment later, the sound of a door closing echoed softly.

He'd left with more questions than he'd had when he arrived. So what was his next move? See if Elizabeth was at home? Wait to see if she responded to his messages?

If it weren't for Avraham's threats against River and his worry about Elizabeth's health, he'd drop it all until she decided to get in touch with him.

Speaking of Avraham . . . he pulled out his phone and punched in a number from memory.

Roberto Serrano had spent his entire career with the CIA, and he and Evan had worked together on three cases. Two had concerned forged documents. The third had been a complicated affair involving Interpol, a murdered French writer, and a missing Voltaire manuscript. Serrano had retired two years ago and claimed to have nothing on his docket but golf. But Evan knew that his old friend was never going to simply walk away from the business. Serrano would have his hand in something—consulting, perhaps some private investigative work. At the very least, he could give Evan a pointer as to where he might learn more about Ronen Avraham.

Serrano picked up on the third ring. "Don't tell me you need my help," he growled into the phone.

"Not at all. I was just calling to see if your golf handicap had improved."

"Bullshit. And no, it hasn't. Go ahead and start gloating."

"Me, gloat? Have you seen *my* golf game?"

"No." A pause. "Wait. Are we talking miniature golf?"

"You are fortunate we aren't meeting in person, Serrano."

Serrano laughed. "See, I'm still an asshole. Glad you rang me up?"

Evan tugged Perro back from the tire of someone's BMW and redirected him toward a small tree.

"You can absolve yourself of that insult," he said, "by telling me if the name Ronen Avraham means anything to you."

"Not a damn thing. Who's he supposed to be?"

"He claims to be an archaeologist with the Israel Antiquities Authority."

"But you think he's Mossad. Or from one of Israel's other security agencies."

"He's here in the US."

"Mossad, then."

It was Evan's turn to laugh. "You have a suspicious soul. Maybe he really is an archaeologist."

"Right. That's why you're calling me. Give me an hour. I have a friend who has a friend who knows a man who works in Tel Aviv. It's evening there. Post-cocktails. Maybe he'll be in a mood to talk."

"Thanks—" Evan began.

But Serrano had already disconnected.

Evan was about to phone the new love interest in his life, Christina Johansen—the brilliant and distinguished academic—hoping for a lunch date, when his phone rang out with the opening chords of Helen Reddy's iconic song of feminism, "I Am Woman."

That meant the caller was his best friend, homicide detective Adrianne "Addie" Bisset with the Chicago PD. She might be calling about a case—he occasionally consulted for the police. More likely, she was hoping to meet for dinner. Perhaps a foursome, if Addie planned to include her newest fling, a computer whiz named Jeff Minzer.

Evan had a smile in his voice when he answered.

Addie said, "We've got a body in a car parked in a dirt lot near the California stop on the Blue Line. I'd like you to take a look before the ME arrives."

His smile faded. "What are the specifics?"

"A woman dead from unknown causes. Looks like she's been here a couple of days. There's a suicide note with some odd notations at the bottom. And a business card with your name on it."

Evan stopped walking.

"Do you have an ID?" he asked.

"We can't touch the body until the ME gets here," Addie said. "But based on the plates on the car and her DMV picture, it's Elizabeth Kathryn Lawrence of Hyde Park."

Evan groped his way toward a low stone wall and hoisted himself onto it. Perro sat at his feet. "You're pretty confident?" he asked faintly.

"As confident as we can be at this stage. I take it this isn't good news for you. Did you know her?"

"Not as much as I would have liked. But yes. She is—she was—a friend. You mentioned a suicide note?"

"Looks like it."

Evan stared out toward the street, vaguely aware of passing cars. Cancer was brutal, no question. But Elizabeth had always been a fighter. He'd never known her to raise a white flag.

In his mind's eye he saw the entry in her planner from two nights earlier: **SR-pMoses I/II STPC**. He saw Chuma Hassan's business card in her planner. And Ronen Avraham.

Elizabeth told me that if there were any problems, I should speak with you, he'd said. *And now I have a problem.*

On the other hand, even the strongest warriors got tired.

Evan tipped his head back. Gray clouds scuttled through a bleak sky, and a chill wind rattled the bare branches overhead. Dead leaves cowered against the base of the wall. The afternoon had turned its back on spring and seemed to long for a return to winter.

Perro nudged his leg. Absently, he leaned down and scratched behind the dog's ears.

"I'm sorry, Evan," Addie said. "But right now, we're trying to determine if she really committed suicide or if it's something else. Since you seem to be involved in some way, I'd like your input on the scene."

Evan forced himself to his feet. "I'm on my way."

CHAPTER 5

Evan saw the police lights as soon as he turned his car onto West Medill Avenue.

The narrow street—which appeared to serve mostly as an alleyway for the residences to the south—had been blocked off on both ends of the crime scene, and crowds had gathered outside the two lines of tape. Per Addie, Elizabeth's car was parked on the other side of a twelve-foot concrete wall that—on this side—was beautifully muraled with blue skies, green growing things, and various planetary bodies. The wall was topped with a chain-link fence and razor wire.

The semiotician in Evan noted the mixed messages—beauty and boundaries.

He nosed his specially modified Jaguar into a narrow space next to an open field, as close as he could get to the scene. He considered leaving Perro in the Jaguar with the windows cracked. But a glance at the leather seats made him change his mind. Perro wasn't 100 percent potty trained, although Diana had assured him that any issues would stop once the corgi had gotten used to Evan and his new surroundings. But given where Perro had chosen to do his business—first on a sixteenth-century Berber rug and then on a stack of student papers Evan had carelessly placed on the floor—Evan wasn't entirely certain that Perro's indiscretions weren't personal. Plus, Diana had warned, the corgi needed to be kept busy. An idle pup was a destructive pup. He snapped on Perro's leash. The dog followed him out of the car and immediately lifted a leg against the tire.

"Don't they have cotillion school for dogs?" Evan growled.

Perro studiously looked away as he finished his business.

Outside the crime-scene tape, Evan approached the patrol officer standing guard, who balked at letting Perro in until Evan insisted the corgi was part of his investigative process. After a phone call to Addie greased the skids—"as long as the dog stays outside the inner perimeter"—the cop directed him and Perro to a pedestrian door set in the high wall. At the doorway, Evan paused and nodded toward an immense steel gate, now closed. The hinges were rusty, the latch padlocked.

"Is that the only automobile access to the site?" he asked the officer, who was still gaping at him. It wasn't every day you saw a dwarf at a crime scene.

"That's correct, sir."

"Meaning if it's a suicide, the victim opened the gate, drove in, then got out and closed the gate behind her."

"Presumably, sir."

"Then came back out through the pedestrian door and relocked it."

The cop shrugged. "Could be she didn't want to be found for a while."

"It looks like a heavy gate," Evan said.

A nod. "She must have been mighty determined."

As soon as he entered the walled-in area beyond the gate, Evan saw Elizabeth's old blue Prius. Two crime-scene techs moved around the car taking photographs; everyone else stood outside the tape, marking off the innermost perimeter of the scene. The Prius was parked at the far end of an empty dirt lot surrounded on three sides by the high concrete wall and on the fourth by a pair of two-story buildings that looked long abandoned and in bad repair. A few taggers had hit the wall on this side: mostly messages of the lewd variety.

Light and shadow played across the ground as clouds skimmed past the sun. The smell of dust and still-dormant grass hung in the air, intermingled with sweat and body spray and the surprising aroma of bacon from someone's half-eaten breakfast. A hubbub of voices bounced around the enclosed space—in addition to the techs taking pictures, he counted four more techs and five cops, none of them Addie or her partner.

Also in the air hung the distinct throat-clotting stink of death, though it was mercifully faint. The temps had been cold enough to slow decay.

In other words, it was like any crime scene.

Except this might be Elizabeth.

With Perro's leash looped around his wrist, Evan shoved his hands into the pockets of his coat. What a miserable place to choose to die. If, in fact, choice had been involved. Given Elizabeth's preference for privacy and her firm belief that one should not air one's troubles with the world, Evan found it all but impossible to believe she would have taken her own life here.

He heard Addie's voice before he saw her. She and her partner, Detective Patrick O'Brady, were just emerging from one of the buildings on the west side of the lot, their heads tipped toward each other as they conversed. Addie looked up and saw Evan. She said something to Patrick, then strode across the lot to greet Evan. He found his mood lifting, if only a little.

Addie had caught her dark curls in a high ponytail. Her mouth glowed with pink lip balm, and her normally pale skin held the first hint of an oncoming spring tan. She wore sunglasses perched atop her head and a small gold cross at her throat. Evan watched as her long stride ate up ground in a way he could never hope to match; her ease within her body was a small part of why Evan loved her. Opposites, as they say, attract.

When she reached him, she held out a hand as she always did when Evan arrived at a crime scene. It was the signal to everyone—including those who knew of their friendship—that he was here as Dr. Evan Wilding: police consultant, world-renowned interpreter for government agencies on the writings and symbols left by killers and terrorists, and a man known by the media as the Sparrow for reasons journalists thought were obvious, but which were entirely wrong.

Evan had once reflected that if his degrees and honors and accomplishments were written on Popsicle sticks and stacked atop each other, they'd be taller than he was. On bad days—which were rare—he knew he would trade away half the stack for long legs. On really bad days, he'd trade it all.

"Thanks for coming," Addie said as they shook hands. "I'm sorry to give you such awful news."

"One by one, the great ones fall," he murmured, quoting a history professor from his Oxford days.

Addie nodded. But then she glanced down and gave a sudden laugh. "This is your canine assistant? When did you get a dog?"

"I'm pet sitting. He belongs to Diana."

"He's adorable!"

Evan's bad mood deepened. "Can we stay on topic?"

But she held the smile. "He's a much better fit for you than he is for Diana. I think you should keep him."

"I'm most definitely not keeping him. He's a menace."

"But you two go together. You know what they say, right? Dogs and their owners start to look alike."

"I assume you're referring to Perro's keenly intelligent gaze and his genial expression, and *not* the length of his legs. Or the size of his ears."

"His obvious intelligence is exactly what I meant." But then she narrowed her eyes and leaned toward Evan. "Although now that you mention the ears, I can kind of see it."

Addie was one of only two people on the planet who could make a comment like that without risking Evan's ire. The other was his brother, River. The recently threatened River. Threatened by a man who claimed he'd had an appointment with a woman who was now most likely dead.

The wind gusted, and puffs of dust rose in the air. One of the techs shouted as the wind plucked up a paper bag and swept it away.

Evan gestured around the barricaded lot. "The car would be completely invisible from the street. Who reported it?"

Addie's expression turned serious again. "A tagger said he climbed the wall this morning. He spotted the car and got curious. When he saw the victim, he called us and then waited until we arrived. He had the spray gun and paints to back his story and a solid alibi for last night."

"What do we know so far?"

"Not much. The techs are taking photos while we wait for the ME, who is stuck in traffic. Was your friend suicidal?"

"She was dying of cancer."

"I see."

Evan pulled up an image of his last lunch with Elizabeth. They'd been at the Range in Lincoln Park, enjoying a table near the fire. He'd been delighted to see her. At least until he took in her ashen complexion, thinning hair, and gaunt form—and she'd whispered the word *cancer*. In typical Elizabeth fashion, she'd wrinkled her nose as she brought a glass of wine to her lips and said, "God, I even *smell* like death."

Evan forced himself back to the present.

"She was diagnosed six months ago," he said. "And she was still getting treatment, last I knew."

He gave Addie an abridged version of his morning. A visit from an archaeologist looking for Elizabeth. Evan's subsequent trip to Elizabeth's institute. He told Addie about the entry in Elizabeth's planner for 10:00

p.m. two nights ago—**SR-pMoses I/II STPC**—and his encounter with her assistant, Leah Zielinski. He left out a few details that might be irrelevant if Elizabeth had ended her own life—his belief that the archaeologist was an agent with Mossad, and the business card in her calendar of a man suspected of dealing in stolen artifacts.

It wasn't yet time to mention the worries crowding his mind.

"*pMoses* probably refers to ancient papyri," he said.

"Probably?"

"The letter *p* is commonly used by scholars in reference to papyri. Elizabeth used it herself." He rubbed his chin. "The only other possibility would be *parchment*, but that is generally abbreviated as *parch*. Either way, it suggests she was meeting someone about her work."

"You think it's possible that whatever happened in this meeting, combined with the cancer diagnosis, drove her to suicide? The gate is heavy enough to suggest she wasn't alone."

"Maybe. But Elizabeth didn't allow much to get in her way. Not people. Not gates. She was found in the driver's seat?"

Addie nodded, and he followed her gaze toward the car. A tech moved aside, and he saw that the driver's door stood slightly ajar. Glare off the windows kept him from seeing more.

"The door was open when she was found?" he asked.

"According to the tagger. After the ME takes the body, we'll tow the car to the police garage. Until then, all we have is what we can see through the windows—the suicide note and the card with your name written on it in the front. In the back there's a basket, a coat, and a canvas satchel."

"Is the note handwritten?"

"Typed."

That didn't sound like Elizabeth. She was fond of fountain pens and fine inks. But then, impending death might make a person efficient—a computer would allow for last-minute revisions.

Addie regarded him through softened eyes. "I didn't bring you here to look at the body of a friend. I just want you to get a general sense of the area before I hand over the note for your evaluation."

"It's all right. I should see her. In case it wasn't suicide."

He watched the debate dance behind Addie's eyes. She had never before tried to shield him from a corpse. It was his job to take in everything. His task to look for whatever indicators the killer had left behind—words or symbols or signs. Indicators that would reveal not only why he'd chosen the victim he had, but why he had killed at all.

"Addie," he said quietly, "let me do my job."

Another moment's hesitation, and then she nodded. He offered her the end of Perro's leash. Wordlessly, she took it.

He approached the car with a rising sense of dread, his legs turning weak as he walked. Most of the corpses he dealt with were ancient— long ago reduced to bone or mummified skin or mere dust. The bodies he'd seen as part of an investigation, on the other hand, remained with him, haunting his sleep.

And the body of a friend? That was on another level entirely.

Other than a thin curtain of dust on the tires and along the under- carriage, the Prius was clean. Tire tracks indicated that Elizabeth, or whoever had been driving, had pulled straight in through the gate and stopped with the car facing the blank cement wall on the north end of the lot.

He introduced himself to the nearest tech. "Any footprints around the car?"

The tech, a young Black woman who towered over Evan, let out an exasperated sigh. "Plenty. We've taken high-res photos and used an electrostatic dust-print tool to lift what we can. But the reporting party walked all around the damn scene."

"Was the engine running?"

"Not when we got here. But the keys are cranked."

"Aside from the driver's door, are the other doors locked?"

49

"Yep."

"Is it all right with you if I get closer?"

She took him in from her elegant height. "You're the Sparrow, right?"

"Evan Wilding."

"Well, Mr. Wilding"—she pointed at the ground with her clipboard—"just be careful to stay on the plastic sheeting. And wear this."

Evan accepted the blue paper mask she offered him. Then, before he could second-guess himself, he closed the gap to Elizabeth's car. He avoided the partially opened door and peered through the driver's-side window.

His friend sat slumped in the driver's seat, her head tipped back, her mouth open; he was grateful that her eyes were closed. She wore navy slacks, a pale-blue silk blouse, and a thin sweater. Rigor mortis had come and gone, and putrefaction had yet to start. But she was rigid, which put her time of death between thirty-six and forty-eight hours ago. There were no visible signs of insect activity, but the first flies would have already arrived. Elizabeth's left arm hung loosely at her side, mostly invisible from Evan's perspective. Her right hand and forearm lay in her lap, palm turned up, fingers curled. Unlike the rest of her body, the hand and wrist were swollen and purpled, suggestive of injury.

He closed his eyes and tried to remember: How chilly had it been two nights ago? Had Elizabeth felt the cold before she died? Had she been shivering when death came?

He forced his eyes open.

Elizabeth's short gray hair was mussed, her eyeglasses barely retaining their perch on the bridge of her nose. One navy-blue dress pump lay on its side in the footwell of the passenger seat.

Were these signs of a struggle?

Evan swayed with sudden grief; he bent his head against the momentary vertigo.

"Yo, Sparrow," the tech called. "You okay?"

"I'm fine."

"Don't you puke on our crime scene."

He straightened. "I won't."

He mentally overlaid the interior of the car with an invisible grid and began taking stock of what was there.

The sedan's keys hung in the ignition, half-cranked, the way they would be if someone were listening to the radio but not running the engine. Thin shards of clear glass flecked the floor mats, but he saw no broken bottle or other source. He noted the card with his name scrawled in black ink. And the purported suicide letter, lightly crumpled and placed on the passenger seat, the words unreadable from where he stood. In the back, Elizabeth's satchel, a much-used canvas carryall with a cracked strap, lay on the floor. The flap was pulled open, revealing an empty interior. Just visible beneath the satchel was a newspaper, folded to reveal a headline that read, *Moses Museum to Open in Chicago*.

A wool navy coat was folded on the back seat next to an empty, round wicker basket with a blue ribbon threaded through the weave. A conical lid lay in the footwell next to the satchel, draped by another ribbon.

There were no other personal effects that he could see. He forced his gaze back to Elizabeth. Death had softened the lines in her face so that she looked younger. Her hair—thinned by age or chemotherapy—still held strands of her youthful blond. He imagined her in her thirties and forties at digs in Israel and other parts of the Near East.

For much of that time, she would have been traveling with her son. Showing him her work with the hope he'd one day carry on. Until one stifling August afternoon when a drunk driver struck Tucker Lawrence in an intersection in Tel Aviv, killing him instantly.

From behind Evan, Perro loosed a volley of barks. A sound from inside the car—a distinct thump—drew Evan's gaze down to Elizabeth's feet.

For a single hopeful heartbeat, he thought that the police had been wrong. That Elizabeth, clinging to life, had managed to move. To kick out a protest. To announce that she was still, if precariously, very much alive.

A gust racked the car, and the door eased farther open.

He called out to Addie and leaned in.

And yelped as something near Elizabeth's feet moved in and out of his line of sight.

He backpedaled away from the sedan and promptly landed on his ass. The tech said, "Careful there." She was still laughing when a long black snake slithered out of the car through the open driver's door and plopped down on the ground in front of Evan.

The tech screamed, and he heard dirt scuff beneath her shoes as she fled. The other tech shouted, and Evan saw the man in his peripheral vision as he, too, bolted.

He kept his focus on the reptile. Any question as to the species of snake he was facing ended as soon as the snake reared, flaring its hood.

A cobra. An Egyptian cobra. *Naja arabica.*

The same creature Cleopatra had chosen for her demise.

CHAPTER 6

Evan froze, ass on the ground, elbows planted, his feet in the air.

The reptile swayed its head toward him and back; its black tongue flicked rhythmically as it scented the air.

Some part of Evan's brain noted the beauty of the beast. The soft black of its hood and upper body, its throat banded with a dusty desert umber. The soft yellow continued down its narrowing body to the sharply pointed tail.

He stared. More swaying. More flicks of the tongue. The reptile appeared as alarmed as Evan, which didn't seem like a good thing.

It hissed.

The sound was almost a growl, a rasp of sandpaper against sharkskin.

After that, Evan's mind went blank. All the advice River had given him over the years concerning snakes fled before the reality of a creature that could kill him with one strike.

Behind him, Addie said softly, "Don't move."

No worries on that score.

Faint footsteps sounded somewhere off to his left. Addie moving into position. A moment later, she made a clicking noise with her tongue, and the snake pivoted toward her.

"Back up slowly," she said to Evan. "No sudden movements."

Still on his ass, Evan carefully lowered his feet and used his heels to push away from the car, sliding on his rear.

The cobra pivoted back toward him.

The cobra pivoted back toward him.

"Stop!" Addie cried in a whisper-shout.

He froze. The snake continued to rock forward and back, like a baseball player preparing to throw a pitch. And what a killer pitch it would be.

Addie made the same sharp clicking, and the snake pivoted once more. Evan could see that the reptile was growing more agitated by the moment, uncertain whether he or Addie posed the greater threat. He scooted back another foot.

The snake swung back toward him.

Then Addie swooped in with a large plastic bin, the kind the crime-scene techs used to collect wet or bloody clothing. She dropped the bin on top of the snake and sat down on it. From inside came a series of frantic bumps.

She shot a grin at Evan, her expression half-relieved, half-maniacal.

"Can someone please call the zoo?" she said. "Tell them we've got a new exhibit for them."

~~~

"Remind me again what kind of childhood you had," Addie's partner, Patrick, said as the three of them stood together next to one of the abandoned buildings, out of the wind. Perro sat proudly next to Evan, chin up, ears perked, as if the small dog had been part of the rescue.

To give the corgi credit, he had barked just before the snake appeared. A warning, if Evan had heeded it.

"Your childhood," Patrick said again to Addie as he eyeballed the herpetologist, who was using a long looped stick to ease the snake into a clear plastic tote.

"My childhood was ruled by four perfectly evil brothers," she answered. "And I say that as a practicing Catholic. They used to take me with them when they went to trap water moccasins. I served as bait."

"Faith and begorra," Patrick muttered, crossing himself. For as long as Evan had known him, the tall, heavyset detective had made a point of embracing his Irish heritage. According to Addie, this love of all things related to the Emerald Isle came after a trip to the Old Country a mere few years ago and his marriage to a girl from County Cork.

Evan felt Addie's eyes on him. "Are you sure you're okay?" she asked.

He dabbed sweat from his face with his sleeve. "Splendid."

"Good thing it was you, doc," Patrick said with a sly smirk. "Been me, I'd still be pissing myself."

"TMI, partner," Addie said. She rested a hand briefly on Evan's shoulder. "I guess we know how Lawrence ended her life."

Patrick was scrolling through something on his phone. "This website says that cobras are shy. They'll retreat if they can. Lawrence had no guarantee that the snake would bite. Seems like a hell of a risk if she really wanted to die. Not to mention dramatic and painful."

"Not much room for a snake to retreat in a small sedan," Addie noted.

"Maybe the risk was part of the appeal," Evan said. "Leave it up to God. Or the fates." As far as he knew, Elizabeth was a practicing Protestant who believed the work she did was for the greater good. But he was unclear where she stood on matters of divine intervention. Or suicide. Not that it mattered now.

But the uncertainty struck him as wrong even as he said it. Elizabeth—at least the Elizabeth he knew—was precise and orderly about everything. She would turn up her nose at anything wishy-washy. Especially when it came to matters of life and death.

Do or do not, she'd once told him. *All the rest is rubbish.*

When the herpetologist had the cobra confined in the plastic tote, Patrick excused himself and crossed the lot to speak with her.

"Forget what I just said about risk being part of the appeal," Evan said to Addie. "Elizabeth was disciplined. If taking her own life was on her to-do list, she wouldn't leave it to chance."

"Then again," Addie said, "none of us know how we'll behave at the end."

"True. But she also hated making a fuss. Or being a bother, unless it had something to do with her work. She was a bulldog in that regard. But if she were to take her own life, she'd do it in such a way that no one would randomly stumble upon her corpse. She'd take poison or have the gun loaded, and then she'd call 911 just before she acted so that her body would be discovered quickly and by professionals. She'd even leave the door unlocked for them. So maybe . . ."

Addie's gaze went past him to the car. "Maybe not suicide."

"A cobra is flashy. Elizabeth wasn't." He said this even as the painting of Cleopatra rose in his mind.

Addie's gaze came back to him. "A snake is just as flashy for a killer as it is for a suicide victim," she pointed out. "And even more risky. If Lawrence saw her killer and survived, the cat would be out of the bag. Or the cobra out of the basket, in this case."

The clouds abandoned their hide-and-seek with the sun, allowing it to emerge in all its glory. Light swamped the scene, turning it into an overprocessed Polaroid. Evan blinked and dug out his sunglasses. Addie dropped hers back over her eyes.

"There's also a suicide note," she reminded him. "Written by those who commit suicide."

"Which I barely got a glimpse of."

"It will soon be all yours. Or rather a copy."

Evan found himself unwilling to meet Addie's gaze. What kind of death would he wish for Elizabeth? One done in her own time and under her own terms? Or as an act of violence against her?

Either involved despair.

Addie pressed on gently. "Does that seem like her? To leave a note?"

He nodded. Words had been Elizabeth's vocation and her playground, just as they were his. Deciphering texts written centuries ago, decoding the voices of people long gone. Elizabeth had loved it as much as he did. He couldn't imagine her exiting stage left *without* leaving a note.

He retreated into professionalism. "Once I have a copy of her note, I'll look for consistencies and inconsistencies with my own correspondence with her—I have texts, emails, a few letters. Any other writing samples you find with a warrant would also be helpful. This will allow me to make a reasonable determination as to whether she's the author."

Light struck off Addie's sunglasses, bouncing slivers of rainbows. "Any thoughts about the broken glass?"

"Papyri are often mounted between plates of plexiglass, but it's not unheard of for a less experienced person to use regular glass. Older papyri could also be mounted that way. If the shards are from Elizabeth's Moses texts, it should be possible to find traces of the paper itself or any contaminants, such as dust or salt."

"The broken glass could suggest an argument."

"Two papyrologists arguing over thousand-year-old texts would be the least likely people to cause any damage to the artifact. It could be nothing more than that the mounting was old and fragile. One slip of the hand would do it."

"Hmm." Addie sounded unconvinced. "Shall we see what the reptile expert has to say?"

Patrick was in an animated conversation with the herpetologist as they approached, his huge hands slicing through the air to make a point. The woman laughed at whatever he said.

"Detective Bissett," Addie said, offering her hand to the herpetologist. "And this is our consultant, Dr. Wilding. Thanks for coming to our rescue."

"Thank *you* for not simply killing this beautiful reptile," the woman answered with a lilting accent. "Most would have." She shook Addie's hand. "I am Yaa Mensah."

"Ms. Mensah was just entertaining me with a few facts about our fatal cobra," Patrick said. "Three hours to kill an elephant. As little as fifteen minutes to kill a human."

"Or even less," Mensah said. "In an older person or in someone who is ill, the venom would act more quickly. The victim might not have time to seek help."

Evan gulped—fifteen minutes. He could be dead by now. It could be *his* body destined for the medical examiner's office. Right behind Elizabeth's.

"Fifteen minutes?" Addie echoed. "Or less in someone ill or older."

"It is true," Mensah said. Her thick hair was oiled and braided and piled high. "It is also true that most antivenom is easy to come by in the United States."

Addie shaded her eyes. "Meaning any hospital would have it on hand?"

"Most would. Although a smaller clinic might have trouble accessing it."

"What should a person do if they're bitten?" Addie asked.

"Call an ambulance if they can," Mensah said. "That is first. Stay calm and remain as still as possible. Keep the bite below the level of the heart. After that . . ." She raised her palms. "Offer prayer."

"But a cobra?" Patrick scratched his long jaw. "Are those easy to get? Can you just walk into a pet store and ask for one?"

Mensah shook her head. Her gold hoops glittered in the sunlight. "To start, venomous snakes are illegal in Illinois. And it is a federal violation to buy, sell, transport, or own poisonous snakes."

Patrick's hand moved from his jaw to his neck. "How would this snake have gotten here, to the wilds of Chicago?"

"Unfortunately, it is not difficult. There are disreputable dealers and breeders who will sell a snake to anyone willing to hand over the money. Whoever purchased this snake could have done so online and had it shipped. But more likely, they bought the cobra at a reptile show as part of an illicit sale. You should know that most reptile owners and breeders are good people. But there are always a few of the"—she hesitated—"the rotten apples."

Addie crouched next to the plastic tote. The snake pressed against the side of the box, and Perro flattened his ears and growled.

"What would a snake like this cost?" Addie asked.

"Not that much. I would estimate four hundred dollars."

"And are cobra bites always fatal without treatment?"

"If it is not a dry bite—that is, a bite with very little venom—or if no antivenom is given, then yes, the victim will almost assuredly die. In the case of cobra venom, the method of death most often comes through respiratory failure when the diaphragm muscles are paralyzed."

"You're saying that, essentially, she suffocated?"

"That is probably the case." Frown lines bracketed Mensah's mouth. "Her death would have taken anywhere from a few minutes to perhaps several hours, depending on how much venom she received. Since she was in the car with the snake, she may have been bitten multiple times, which would put her death at the lower end of the range."

"But if she'd gotten help . . ." Addie let her voice trail off.

The frown lines deepened. "If she had been able to drive herself to a hospital, she would have received antivenom. At the very least, they could have placed her on an artificial respirator until the paralyzing agent of the venom wore off."

"Any advice for our medical examiner?" Patrick asked. "I mean, in terms of confirming the cause of death?"

"If you provide me with blood and urine samples from the victim," Mensah said, "I can run molecular and chemical analysis tests to confirm that venom is present in her blood. I will even be able to confirm that the venom came from this particular snake."

"That's impressive," Patrick said.

He looked half-smitten with the elegant Yaa Mensah. Evan recalled that Patrick was frequently besotted by smart, beautiful woman. And that he was also completely loyal to his smart, beautiful wife.

Addie stood. "We'll make sure samples are delivered to your office."

Mensah nodded. "Good."

The herpetologist handed out business cards, picked up the box with the snake, and headed toward the exit. She moved with a smooth elegance that matched the muscled grace of her charge.

After Mensah disappeared through the doorway, Evan retreated to the building where he and Perro could be out of the way while they waited for the ME. He watched the cops and techs as they stood in clumps, talking or looking at their phones. After a few minutes of conversation with another detective, Addie, trailed by Patrick, joined Evan out of the wind and leaned against the wall, propping one leg behind her, her foot flat against the faded timbers. Patrick took up the space on Evan's other side. The big man's face was flushed.

Addie asked Evan to fill Patrick in on what he'd told her earlier— his guess about the Moses papyri and the broken glass. When he finished, she said, "What did Lawrence's work involve, exactly? Start with generalities."

"She was a historian and a papyrologist. She—"

"Wait," Patrick said, holding up his hand like a traffic cop. "What is a papyrologist?"

"Someone who studies ancient texts. These manuscripts are often, but not always, written on papyri."

"And papyri are what?" Patrick asked. "Some kind of paper?"

"Papyri—singular, papyrus—is a plant that grows along the Nile. Strips are cut from the plant's stalk and pressed together to form a writing surface that is remarkably like paper. Elizabeth began her career in Egyptian papyri. She made a solid name for herself. But then she switched to Greek papyri, and then, about five years ago, she switched again, this time to ancient Hebrew texts."

"Meaning the Bible," Addie said.

Evan tipped his hand back and forth in a "sort of" gesture. "Meaning the Hebrew Bible or *Tanakh*, which is called the Old Testament in the Christian Bible. The New Testament was written primarily in Greek."

"Would her research be enough to sustain her institute?" Addie asked. "Where would the money come from?"

"Donors, mainly, as with any museum or institute. Probably she also did consulting work and took on conservation projects." He was thinking of the invoices in her desk drawer. The nondisclosure agreement with Veritas. The letter from the Cambodian minister. But those were just data points. The truth was, he had no idea what Elizabeth had been working on.

"And these Moses papyri, if that's what we're dealing with, they would be . . . what exactly?"

"They might be manuscripts that either refer to Moses or date from the same time. Without the actual papyri or any notes from Elizabeth, that's all I can offer. But we do know this. According to Elizabeth's assistant, Leah Zielinski, Elizabeth made annual outings to Israel and a more recent trip to England. Ms. Zielinski also said Elizabeth was researching work done by a group known as the Palestine Exploration Fund, the PEF, which is a British organization that used to operate archaeological expeditions in Israel. I believe it still does. Perhaps the Moses papyri—if they exist—are related to Elizabeth's trips."

Addie typed a note in her phone. "Sounds like talking to someone with the PEF would be a good place to start. Anything else she was working on?"

"That is as much as I know of her work, other than that her assistant said she was recently focused on her own genealogy. It's possible that Elizabeth is, or rather was, an indirect descendant of T. E. Lawrence."

Patrick brightened. "As in *Lawrence of Arabia* and Peter O'Toole? When I was a kid, I thought that movie was the most badass thing I'd ever seen. Fighting in the desert. Blowing up trains. Men getting sucked into quicksand."

But Addie frowned. "You think Lawrence's interest in Lawrence of Arabia could have something to do with her death? If it turns out she was murdered, I mean."

"Hard to see how," Evan said. "But never say never. T. E. Lawrence worked for the PEF during its early days. And he spent time in what is now Israel—the land that in his time was known as Palestine."

Addie made another note.

"There's one more thing," Evan said.

"What's that?"

"That archaeologist I mentioned. The one who came to see me this morning." Evan found Avraham's card still in his pocket. He pulled it out and passed it over to Addie.

"The Israel Antiquities Authority," she read out loud before reaching around Evan to give it to Patrick. "Another link to Israel. What is this group?"

"The IAA is a government-affiliated organization responsible for enforcing Israel's Law of Antiquities. They regulate archaeological excavation and do a lot of restoration work on artifacts."

"Lawrence might have been working with them?"

"If she was doing archaeological work in Israel, then almost certainly. There's a photo, maybe fifteen years old, on Elizabeth's desk of her with this archaeologist."

Addie tilted her head. "What didn't you like about him?"

She could read him like a menu.

"If you want my honest and semiprofessional opinion, the guy isn't an archaeologist. Or rather isn't *just* an archaeologist. He struck me as Mossad."

Patrick palmed his head. "The intelligence agency?"

"That's right. I should point out that Mossad, unlike our own intelligence organizations, functions completely outside the constitutional laws of the State of Israel. And they aren't always keen on informing local intelligence agencies of their activities. They are one of the most secretive organizations in the world."

Addie's gaze returned to the sedan. "Meaning that, technically, they are authorized to kill someone?"

"Meaning they can do whatever the hell they please and then submit an expense reimbursement request."

"What would Mossad's interest be in our victim?" Patrick asked.

"The IAA might have enlisted Mossad's help if something valuable was smuggled out of Israel."

"By Lawrence?"

"I don't think so."

He *didn't* think so, he assured himself. Elizabeth wouldn't do that. No.

Addie removed her sunglasses and wiped them clean on the hem of her blouse. "It would have to be an important artifact, right? For them to send a Mossad agent to Chicago. How sure are you that this Avraham is Mossad?"

"I'm not sure at all. I did say it was only an opinion," Evan pointed out.

"But you think there's a chance these Moses papyri were stolen?"

The thought made him cold. "*That* I'm not even going to take a guess on. Talk to her assistant. Maybe Leah will be more forthcoming with the police. And ask Mr. Avraham himself. Perhaps he, too, will be more up front with you."

Patrick's phone buzzed, and he stepped away. When he returned, it was to inform them that the ME was at least half an hour out.

"No need for you to stay," Addie told Evan. "I'll let you know what we find once we get the car to the garage and the techs have a go at it. In the meantime, no mention of Elizabeth's identity until we've reached her next of kin."

He nodded his understanding. "And one more thing. Elizabeth sometimes carried a handgun. The techs will want to know."

Patrick glanced at the sedan. "Not that it helped her much."

CHAPTER 7

Back at the car, Perro settled himself in the passenger seat and refused to move to the back. Maybe the corgi was worried about car-inhabiting cobras. Evan could hardly blame him.

He reached over and scratched Perro behind the ears. "It's okay, boy. No snakes here."

Perro offered a delicate bark, then spun in the seat to watch out the window and slobber on the glass.

Evan stared out the windshield, eyeing the Blue Line elevated train as it zipped past on the raised track—a metallic snake winding its way through the city.

Death by serpent. It was ancient, archaic, exotic.

And unending. A hundred thousand people died every year from snakebites.

Evan dredged up a list of famous people who'd met their deaths because of a snake—it was a bit of trivia he recalled from a long-ago college game. Ali Khan Samsudin—the Snake King—dead from the bite of a king cobra. The snake expert Joseph Slowinski died in Myanmar after the bite of a krait. The American minister George Went Hensley, struck by a viper while handling it during a sermon. And, of course, Elizabeth's icon—the Ptolemy queen, Cleopatra.

He frowned up at the "L" tracks. Then, after a time, he put aside the image of the victims and focused on the symbology of serpents. For if Elizabeth had been murdered, the cobra offered a dark and twisted passage into the mind of her killer.

To symbologists, snakes embodied the mysterious, whether it was the human psyche, the enigma of death, the libido, even the soul. In Egypt, Greece, Mesopotamia, and Mexico, the snake sometimes served as an instrument of evil and other times as a symbol of fertility and life. In Norse mythology, the sea serpent Jormungand wreaked havoc at the end of the world until it was slain by Thor. Even then, Jormungand had his revenge—Thor managed only nine steps before falling dead, victim to the serpent's bite.

There was the famous Ouroboros—the snake on King Tut's tomb, swallowing its own tail.

And the Greek Gorgon Medusa, who had venomous serpents in place of hair, a punishment from Athena. Her serpents represented the cycle of birth, death, and rebirth.

And what of the powerful and dangerous *naga*—the semidivine race of cobras who sheltered the Buddha? Or the serpents in the Hebrew Torah, used by God to punish the unruly Israelites in the desert.

In western culture, the most famous serpent was the one sent by Satan to tempt Eve, leading to man's downfall, after which God had condemned the snake to forever crawl on its belly and consume dust.

Which of these, if any, served as a motive for Elizabeth's death?

Or was there an entirely different meaning?

Evan stared at the thin film of dust on his windshield, carried by the wind. Over and over, he imagined Elizabeth's last moments. The coiled serpent and its needle-sharp fangs. Suffocation followed by another kind of darkness.

Who, if anyone, had been with her? Who, if anyone, had watched her die?

After a moment, he shook himself and reached for his phone. He dialed his brother in Turkey and was startled when a woman answered.

"You're not River," Evan said.

"You win," she said. "I'm not. River went to Istanbul for a couple of days. A big important meeting. Forgot his bloody phone, so I'm babysitting it. Can I help you?"

"I'm his brother. In Chicago. Do you have a number where he's staying?"

"Dr. Evan Wilding. It's a pleasure. I'm Theresa, chief bottle washer at our dig. You can ring him up at the Crowne Plaza, but you know he's not great on collecting his messages. When he checks in again, I'll let him know you called."

After thanking her, Evan disconnected and made one more phone call. This was to ensure that Chuma Hassan was in his office. To Evan's surprise, not only was the Egyptian available, but his receptionist scheduled Evan for a fifteen-minute appointment with her "terribly busy" boss.

"Forty-five minutes from now," she said. "Will that work?"

Evan checked the time, confirmed that he would be there, and pulled into traffic, watching in the rearview mirror as the walls shielding Elizabeth's body disappeared from view.

Hassan's office was on the ground floor of a limestone-and-granite art-deco building on the banks of the Chicago River. When Evan pushed open the door to Hassan's Galleries Extraordinaire—the name etched in gold on a bronze plaque outside the heavy wooden door—he found himself in a large, lavish reception area. Wooden floors topped with brown-and-gold woven rugs, walls the color of warm sand, and recessed lighting that made the room's many artifacts look lit from within.

Bronze figurines, medieval tray stands, and ornately carved columns filled the space; Egyptian funerary masks lined the walls, interspersed with framed paintings on papyrus that depicted everyday life in ancient Egypt.

Evan felt right at home.

A woman rose from behind a desk and crossed the floor to greet him. She was dressed in a skirt and matching blazer, both as neutral as the decor, and a cream blouse. A pale-yellow headscarf partially covered her dark hair. She walked gracefully in beige stilettos tall enough to challenge a circus stilt walker.

"Dr. Wilding?" she asked with a warm smile. "I'm Rana."

Doctor, not Mister. She'd done her research between his call and his arrival. They shook hands, then Rana's gaze went from him to Perro.

"He is so charming!" she cried. "Those eyes. They are like chocolate melting. You can see in one glance that this small creature has a great soul."

Perro sniffed the woman's ankles. Evan half expected the corgi to raise a leg. He gave the leash a tug, and Perro retreated.

"Such a good boy," Rana said.

Her gaze returned to Evan's face, but the warmth remained. If Evan had realized that dogs were such chick magnets, he would have long ago traded Ginny in for a fluffy white Bichon Frise. Hawks—fierce, independent, prickly—were most definitely not chick magnets.

"Mr. Hassan had to take a phone call," Rana said. "Please make yourself comfortable while you wait. Can I bring you anything? Water? Coffee?"

"I'm fine, thank you."

Rana retreated behind her desk and resumed her work on a desktop computer.

Evan settled himself in a wingback chair that looked more like a throne than everyday seating. No doubt, in its vastness, he looked like a child. While he waited, he pondered the newspaper he'd seen folded under Elizabeth's satchel inside her car. The headline had read, *Moses Museum to Open in Chicago*.

After a moment of poking around online, he found the headline in the *Chicago Tribune*. The accompanying article announced a decision by the billionaire Kelley family to open a Moses Museum. The not-for-profit museum would be dedicated to reviving interest in the Old Testament and showcasing the relationship between the three great Abrahamic faiths: Christianity, Judaism, and Islam, all of whom shared Moses as a prophet.

The museum was to be built in a yet-to-be-disclosed location in Chicago, with the head of the Kelley family—William Ernst Kelley—stating that they hoped to break ground the following spring. Several locations within Chicago and its suburbs had petitioned to be considered as the Kelleys' chosen site. The reporter noted that whatever site was ultimately picked would receive a great influx of cash for nearby businesses but also endure traffic headaches and the risk of residents finding themselves displaced by rising rents.

Evan lowered his phone and searched his memory. Sometime back—maybe two years ago—he'd gotten wind of plans for a museum that would celebrate the Old Testament. But that had been intended for the District of Columbia in Washington. A museum of this kind opening in Chicago—how had that slipped past him?

"You're stumbling, old sod," he said softly. "You used to be in front of things like this."

He searched for additional information. Controversy about the museum reigned within the close-knit community of biblical scholars—far outside his own areas of expertise—where snippets of worried buzz had arisen regarding the astonishing rate at which the museum was acquiring its artifacts—tens of thousands in a mere two years.

"You can't do a good job determining provenance when you're acquiring items at that rate," one specialist was quoted as saying in an article. *"It's*

simply impossible. And that means the museum almost certainly ends up purchasing stolen artifacts. Then we lose the knowledge about where the artifact came from and everything about its history. It's a terrible blow to biblical scholarship."

In addition to artifacts acquired by the Kelleys, the museum would include an entire floor devoted to exhibits provided by the Israel Antiquities Authority—the IAA. Ronen Avraham's supposed affiliation.

Evan frowned.

To handle the acquisition process and run the museum, the Kelley family had created the also not-for-profit Veritas Foundation. Evan's frown deepened.

Veritas.

The name on the invoices in Elizabeth's office.

An uncomfortable chill settled. Why would Elizabeth work for a foundation that was, essentially, her competition in the world of Middle Eastern manuscripts?

He read on.

There had been a few hiccups during Veritas's acquisition process. Eighteen months ago, the museum had purchased a sixth-century Coptic papyrus, which had proven to be a forgery. They'd also bought papyri stolen from a distinguished library in England—an incident that had led to the arrest of the thief, but no charges against Veritas.

Evan stared into space. Why hadn't the Kelleys been charged in the incident? Or at least given a wrist slap? Claiming ignorance as to the origin of well-documented papyri seemed weak. And anyway, in the eyes of the law, *ignorantia juris non excusat*: ignorance of the law excuses not.

Rana's gentle voice broke into his thoughts. She had returned silently to stand in front of him. "Mr. Hassan will see you now."

Evan tucked his phone away and followed Rana down a short hallway to a door, where she paused.

"Would you like me to watch your charming dog for you? Mr. Hassan is not overly fond of animals."

As if he understood, Perro brightened, looking from Evan to Rana and back.

With his thanks, Evan handed over the leash. "Just keep him away from your best carpets."

Rana smiled and opened the door. She waved him inside, then closed the door behind him.

Chuma Hassan, "the Egyptian," stood up from behind a vast glass-and-bronze desk. He was an immense man—tall and wide—and nearly bald. He immediately made Evan think of Sydney Greenstreet, the actor who'd played "The Fat Man," Kasper Gutman, in John Huston's film *The Maltese Falcon*. Hassan was in his fifties, with fleshy jowls and small curious eyes. He wore an impeccably tailored gray suit, and beneath his earthy cologne, he smelled of cumin and ginger.

"Dr. Evan Wilding!" he cried, apparently delighted.

"Thank you for agreeing to see me," Evan said.

Hassan walked around the desk with his hand out. He scooped up Evan's hand in his own and shook it with vigor. "So very happy to meet you, Professor. I've heard such wonderful stories about you and your work. I saw your articles on the Phaistos Disc. Brilliant. I do believe you'll be the man to crack the code."

"Well, I don't—"

"I am so rude. Sit. Sit. You would like tea, would you not? It's been ready since shortly after you called. The British and their tea, after all. And, of course, the Egyptians and their tea. Do you want mint? No? *Bdon sokkar?*"

"*Sokkar barra,*" Evan managed in his rusty Arabic. *Sugar on the side.*

"Of course. Here, sit. Make yourself comfortable. It will be only a minute."

Evan took the proffered chair on the near side of Hassan's desk. His eyes roamed the room while the Egyptian busied himself making tea on a bar off to the side. Like the waiting area, the room was filled with artifacts. But instead of the understated elegance of the outer vestibule, this space burst with color. Vivid paintings of the Nile, royal-blue carpets, a yellow accent wall. The effect should have been overwhelming, but Evan found it cheerful.

Apparently, dealing in looted and stolen treasures gave Hassan a sunny outlook.

"So." Hassan handed him a cup of steaming tea and placed a sugar bowl nearby. "What brings the great Dr. Evan Wilding to my lowly business? To what do I owe this honor? Here, have a *kahk*."

Hassan passed over a tray of butter cookies dusted with powdered sugar, each graced with a sliver of almond. He said, "My wife makes them. She's brilliant in the kitchen. Like all good women."

Evan had a fleeting thought of Addie offering to deck the man for his sexist comment. Then Diana offering her own fist, for good measure. He accepted a cookie, anyway.

"You are doing very well for yourself," Evan said with a nod toward the shelves crowded with statuary.

"Ah, you know the antiquities business. Always hopping. The rich get richer, and when they do, so do I." He beamed.

"The blue shabti in your lobby look almost—"

"Genuine?" Hassan gave a hearty laugh and returned to his seat behind the desk. "That's because they are. The rumor is that they are from Nefertiti's tomb, looted long ago. But surely that can't be. Still, they are wonderful. And stop looking so scandalized, Professor. All my business is on the up-and-up. I am a firm believer in the IADAA. I am a signature member. You know it, I assume?"

"The International Association of Dealers in Ancient Art."

Hassan bequeathed him a benevolent smile. "Of course you know it. You doubtless also know that I buy items in good faith, but that I am no man's fool. I double-check everything. You know what I mean? And I sell them the same way."

Did Hassan actually wink at him?

"Your reputation—" Evan began.

"Paugh. People are jealous. They talk. It is ridiculous."

"You've never—"

"Never. Well, almost never. Those of us in the business, we all get taken now and again, don't we? We can be fooled, same as anyone. But I will say for the record that business is getting very . . ." He paused and then pressed his palms together. "We are getting squeezed. All these regulations. These rules. Court cases and lawsuits. Such paranoia. If you ask me, all cultural objects should be allowed to circulate for the scientific and educational enjoyment of humanity. It is beneficial to all."

"But looters—"

Hassan waved his hands. "No, no, no. When the poor man needs to put food on the table for his family, that is the most important thing. What good is it to have some old thing buried under twenty feet of soil? Especially when the poor farmer can feed his children for a year by digging it up and selling it? And people the world over can enjoy its beauty. That is what I think about. Not, of course, that I condone that behavior. I want to stay in business. I follow the laws."

"I'm sure you do."

Hassan laughed. "You are skeptical, my friend. But it is a good tale that I tell. And I have had many opportunities to tell it. Now, what can I do for you?"

Evan had come up with a story he hoped would pass muster with Hassan and give him an in to ask the questions that were burning on his tongue. Namely, was Hassan truly willing to deal in illicit artifacts? And had Elizabeth been involved in any way?

"I'm here because I've been approached by the parents of one of my students. They have a few items in their possession." Evan lowered his voice. "Items they acquired during their travels to the Holy Land.

Regrettably, their restaurant is struggling, and they're looking for . . . options."

Hassan's expression turned flat. Evan was suddenly reminded of the cobra.

"I see," Hassan said. He planted his elbows on the glass top of his desk and pressed the tips of his fingers and thumbs together. His gaze narrowed while he waited for Evan to go on.

"The items will have provenance, of course," Evan said. "I am assured of this."

"I see," Hassan said again. "How is your tea?"

"It's quite good."

"And the cookies?"

"Excellent. Thank you."

Hassan leaned forward, resting his weight on his elbows. "You put me in an awkward position, Dr. Wilding. For I am thinking of two things. The first is all the work you do with the police. It's been in the papers. There was that Viking Poet case only a few months ago. Very dramatic. Everyone knows you are who the police call when they are stumped."

"They are rarely stumped."

Hassan's laugh was a ghost of his earlier good humor. "They are *always* stumped. They should have you working for them night and day. But that is not the issue in front of us today. The issue is that it is hard for me to know where your loyalties lie."

"If you're aware of my police work, then you will appreciate the delicacy of the situation I find myself in. My student's parents wish to keep their child enrolled at a prestigious and very expensive school. I wish for her to remain as well. She is a promising student with a good mind."

"And perhaps other good things," Hassan said.

Evan gave a vague wave of his hand and let the dealer think what he would.

Hassan continued. "And the other question is why come to me? Your friendship with Dr. Elizabeth Lawrence is also well known. Surely she is the one to help you."

That Hassan knew of his friendship with Elizabeth came as a surprise. It must have shown on his face.

"I am of course aware of this," Hassan said. "The antiquities business is not overlarge, and scholars and dealers must constantly—what are the words?—rub elbows. Can't she help you with this matter?"

No, Evan thought. *She's dead.* But he remembered Addie's caution. Elizabeth's name wasn't to be released yet.

"I don't believe Elizabeth would be interested in this particular kind of transaction," he said.

"Ah." Hassan leaned back. His chair groaned. "It's possible you misjudge our mutual friend. But that is her loss. What items are we talking about?"

Evan's heart sank at Hassan's implication. But he forged on. "New Testament papyri. I'm told they're very old, although I haven't seen them myself. Perhaps fourth century. Perhaps third."

"Then they would be listed with the government of the country of origin. Israel, I presume? Or rather, the West Bank?"

"I'm told that, due to an oversight, the texts were not listed in the dealer's catalog when the IAA came calling."

"That is not so easy these days, with all inventories computerized."

"Unless you know your way around computers."

"Interesting." Something very much like avarice gleamed in Hassan's eyes. "Do you have pictures?"

"I can get them."

Hassan's phone rang. He ignored it. He eyeballed Evan and tapped his fingers on the desk, clearly a man having an internal debate. After a few moments, he continued. "As for our mutual friend, Elizabeth and I have done business occasionally. It's a difficult world, the antiquities business. We all need our friends. And you shouldn't judge, Dr. Wilding. People like me, like your Elizabeth, we are doing the world a service. It is also true that, like your student's parents, even good and honest people can become desperate. This desperation, that's where I come in."

Evan nodded, ignoring the weight that filled his stomach.

Hassan stood. "Leave me your card. I'll be in touch."

CHAPTER 8

After leaving Hassan's, Evan decided to head for a late lunch at the Boonoon Bar & Grill while he waited for a copy of the suicide note and word from Addie about the contents of Elizabeth's car. The restaurant's owner was fond of Perro. And Evan, she said, wasn't half-bad, either.

A good plate of her jerk chicken would help him process the day.

The grill was a few miles from UChicago's main campus in an area of town that had once required an armored vehicle and an Uzi if you hoped to escape with your life. Or at least with your wallet. But gentrification, buttressed by decent government funding, had made the neighborhood safe as long as you beat feet before the sun went down. The owner, Cedella Brown, was one of the locals who'd benefited from the infusion of cash. She'd taken her share and poured it all into her Afro Caribbean restaurant, creating an establishment with some of the best food in Chicago—and live entertainment on the weekends to boot.

In the middle of the afternoon, between the lunch rush and the inevitable Happy Hour jam, the Boonoon was quiet. Even the usual barstool philosophers were absent. Cedella greeted him from behind the hostess's station and knelt to ruffle Perro's ears. Perro looked pleased with the attention. And what male wouldn't be? Cedella was as lovely as the lyrical trilling of her generous voice.

"Your favorite table is open." She straightened and smiled at Evan. He admired, as he did every time, Cedella's perfectly even, perfectly white teeth. She was a toothpaste advertiser's dream with her gleaming smile, which she tossed about with the ease of a Mardi Gras musician flinging beads.

She led Evan and Perro to a four-top table, then returned a moment later with something dark and iced in a tall glass, the drink garnished with a sprig of mint.

"It's white rum and a secret recipe. Don't bother asking what it is—I'm not saying. Now I got some specials. A tender oxtail with peas and rice. And a mutton curry hot enough to make even a man like you cry. Or"—she gave a dismissive roll of her eyes—"I can bring your usual jerk chicken."

"Perro and I will take whatever you recommend," Evan said wisely.

She sniffed. "And you will love it."

She strolled away. Evan absently pulled his appreciative gaze away from her sashaying retreat and sipped the drink. A good quality rum. Mint. Bitters. A simple syrup, probably from cane sugar. And something else that he couldn't identify. Cedella's secret recipe. He held the liquid on his tongue, savoring the combination.

But even as he enjoyed the moment, he was thinking how quickly life could change. For good or ill, each moment was a doorway into an unknown future.

His phone chimed with a text. Addie, informing him that Elizabeth's car had been towed and they were removing everything from it. They'd found the usual sorts of items—sunglasses, spare change, a box of tissues, lip balm, a tin of mints. No purse, but Addie texted there was a wallet in the console with Lawrence's driver's license, a credit card, and twenty in cash. And a phone, which they would do their best to unlock. They'd found the gun under the driver's seat. But no papyri.

A phone, Evan thought. Which suggested that Elizabeth could have called for an ambulance.

Unless she hadn't wanted to be saved.

Or someone had stopped her.

Next to arrive were a series of photos. Elizabeth's suicide note followed by pictures of several newspaper articles. The papers had been found folded under Elizabeth's satchel on the floor in the back.

Evan itched to start with the suicide note. To many profilers, the letter would seem like the logical place to begin. But when possible, Evan preferred to start on the outer edges of a case and work his way in, spiraling toward the answers at the center. That methodology allowed him to accumulate facts without prejudice or preconceived ideas.

He began with the newspaper articles.

The first article, about Veritas and the Moses Museum, he'd already researched. The second folded sheet was an inside page of the *Chicago Tribune*, dated two months back. One side was an ad for a furniture sale. The other side carried an article above the fold—a continuation of a piece on the front page about an ethics bill up for vote in the Illinois General Assembly. The third article announced that a local alderman was considering a run for the US Senate. Below the fold was an advertisement for an immunotherapy clinical trial for cancer patients. The trial was based at Johns Hopkins Hospital in Baltimore, but a Chicago address and phone number were provided at the bottom for anyone interested in applying. The study was looking for volunteers who met certain—unspecified—criteria.

If Elizabeth had applied and been turned down, would that have convinced her to take her own life rather than wait for the inevitable end? She had been a scientist at heart who believed in the power of rigorously acquired knowledge and the value of experimental trials. She would have been crushed to learn she wasn't eligible for a treatment that might extend her life.

The next photo Addie sent was a clipping from the English-language edition of the Hebrew newspaper, the *Haaretz*, dated two months earlier. This article, like the earlier one, mentioned the Veritas Foundation, which had purchased a rare Dead Sea Scroll. Absently, Evan tugged his beard. Such a purchase would have been quite the coup, as there were very few scrolls available to private collectors. Six months after Veritas purchased the fragment, it was identified as one sold by a smuggler. Which meant Veritas would have to relinquish its purchase to Israel and swallow the loss. The article included a quote from the Israeli prime minister expressing his anger at these brazen thefts and saying that his own family had been victimized by art thieves in the recent past.

Evan sipped his drink. Veritas wasn't showing a very good track record with its acquisitions.

His phone rang. Addie.

"Did you get the photos?"

"I'm looking at them now. You should know that there were invoices from the Veritas Foundation in Elizabeth's desk."

"What were the invoices for?"

"I didn't look."

"You're a terrible snoop."

"But one with a conscience that is only slightly tarnished. You can look for yourself when you have a warrant."

She sighed. "Talk to me about the Dead Sea Scrolls. Aren't those the oldest copies of biblical texts?"

"Right. They're religious texts written between 300 BCE and 100 CE. Which—translated—means before the Common Era and Common Era. Or what many refer to as BC and AD. The scrolls—written on a mix of leather, papyri, and even copper—were found by Bedouin tribesmen, mostly in the Qumran caves of the Judaean Desert during the 1940s and '50s."

"How is it possible that a Dead Sea Scroll was stolen?" Addie asked. "I figured all of them would be under lock and key in a heavily guarded location."

"Most of them are at the Israel Museum in Jerusalem," Evan said. "Others are in the Jordan Museum in Amman. The stolen fragment is probably one of a handful that made it into private hands before 1970, when the UNESCO convention—"

"What is UNESCO?"

"A United Nations agency that deals with the arts, among other things. They have a convention that forbids the sale of artifacts like these. Pre-1970 pieces still come up for sale now and again, and it's perfectly legal. Legal, that is, *if* they weren't stolen, as was the case with the papyri mentioned in the news article."

"You're saying any scrolls discovered *after* 1970 can't be legally sold?" she asked.

"That's right. Sold or even excavated. Not without permission from the Israeli government."

"Could the Moses papyri be Dead Sea Scrolls?"

"It's possible. Scrolls that either date from the original discovery or were found more recently. Pretty much as we speak, scrolls are still being found and excavated by the IAA."

"Then the question is, are Lawrence's papyri old discoveries or new ones? And what was she doing with them? Assuming she had them."

Something sharp and uncomfortable landed in Evan's stomach. The fact that Elizabeth was doing work for an organization that had been caught with its hand in the antiquities cookie jar, so to speak, wasn't good. He couldn't think of a single reason why she would do business with people like that. Unless it was before the news of the theft came out.

He wished he'd looked at the dates on the invoices.

"I don't know," he said finally. "If the Moses papyri are legally on the market, she might have been considering a purchase."

But he wondered if her pockets could have been deep enough for such a buy. Especially given that any pre-1970 fragments that came on the market were likely small, with little to offer a scholar. Buying one was more about owning a piece of history. It would be an expensive luxury for an institute as small as Elizabeth's.

Addie's voice broke through his thoughts. "How hard is it to tell if you're buying stolen goods?"

"You have to do some digging. Make calls, double-check the names and dates listed on the item's history of ownership. But even experts have been fooled by falsified bills of sale and faked letters indicating ownership. Every reputable institute must do its best to research and verify the origin of the artifact to ensure it was legally acquired. And to make sure it isn't a forgery."

"Is there a lot of that?" Addie asked. "Forgery, I mean."

"In biblical antiquities? It's one of the worst fields. So many people are desperate for proof of one thing or another, and they believe antiquities can provide those answers. Buyers can be easy marks for unscrupulous dealers looking to turn a quick profit. Worse, some of those dealers and forgers belong to transnational criminal organizations who care nothing about an artifact's cultural history. Elizabeth would have been an expert at sniffing out forgeries. But, as with stolen artifacts, even some experts have been fooled."

"Experts like you?"

"*Some* experts," he said.

"Would exposing forgeries have been part of her work?"

"Maybe. Certainly, she would have vetted anything she wanted to purchase to make sure it was neither stolen nor a forgery. She would have verified sources, conducted her own research, and probably sent an artifact to a lab to have it tested before making an offer on an item."

"Then how did the Veritas Foundation end up making bad purchases?"

"Like I said, even the best in the field have been tricked. It's also possible they were simply overeager and dropped a lot of cash without paying much attention to provenance."

"All right," Addie said. "Thanks for the crash course. Have you looked at the alleged suicide note yet?"

"Patience, young one. Greatness takes time."

She snorted and disconnected. Evan returned to the second page that had been found in Elizabeth's car—the one featuring several articles from the *Chicago Tribune*. There was the advertisement for the infusion therapy, the continuation of the article on the ethics bill, and a sidebar on the alderman's possible US Senate run; the article mentioned the millions required to campaign for national political office. Evan doubted Elizabeth had cared about either the ethics bill or the alderman. But in the interest of being thorough, he spent a few minutes with his phone drilling down on Alderman David Bakker.

Bakker was from a small town in northwestern Illinois. He'd attended the University of Illinois and earned his MBA there. He'd won his race for alderman and had proven to be an outspoken and dedicated conservative. Based on the articles Evan skimmed, Bakker knew how to win friends and influence people. Especially those with money.

But Evan couldn't find anything that linked Bakker to either Elizabeth or to her institute.

Although . . . maybe. He opened a map on his phone, stared at the screen for a moment, then leaned back and took a long swallow of Cedella's rum concoction.

Elizabeth's body had been found in Alderman Bakker's district.

He returned the glass to the table, the drink almost half-gone.

What might the geographic coincidence mean? *Did* Elizabeth have some connection to the alderman? Or had she simply been searching for an out-of-the-way place in which to retreat with the cobra and shuffle off her mortal coil? If that was the case, then reading the article about Bakker might have opened up a possible locale. Perhaps she'd even considered it a sign.

Unless, of course, her killer forced her to drive there. A killer who knew about a dirt lot tucked behind high walls and razor wire.

But why that specific place? Killers tended to use rivers and lakes— of which Illinois had plenty—or out-of-the-way rural areas as their dumping grounds. Places that minimized the chance of detection.

An urban dirt lot behind a difficult-to-open vehicle door didn't qualify.

Cedella's boisterous voice broke into his thoughts.

"Here it is!" she cried as she and a waiter approached Evan's table. "Fish Escovitch made from red snapper, a side of crispy bammy, and a bowl of Jamaican corn soup with pumpkin and potatoes. I prepared the Escovitch yesterday, so it has had exactly the right amount of time for the flavors to mature. You will love it, or I'll . . . No, of course you will love it!"

Evan wondered if the last statement was assurance or threat. He watched as she and the waiter set colorful plates before him, the plates heaped with equally vibrant food. He caught the aromas of onions and pimentos along with the sweet scent of coconut and the golden perfume of fried cassava root. When Cedella finished spreading the feast before him, she placed a dish of cooked beef and a bowl of water on the floor for Perro, who wasted no time tucking in.

Evan eyed the spread. "Cedella, it's wonderful. Truly! But where do you expect me to put all of this? I am but one man, and not an overly large one."

"You'll find a way," she said, and winked. "A bachelor like you, I don't want you to go hungry. And if you aren't quite man enough for it, then that is why we have takeout boxes."

Before he could summon a retort, she turned away. Left with no options but to give himself over to the abundance, Evan tucked in as well. The food was pure heaven, and for a moment he closed his eyes and imagined himself on a white-sand Jamaican beach, basking in the warmth of the sun as he listened to the gentle slap of waves and a distant Rasta band.

After a moment, he reluctantly opened his eyes and, as he ate, reread the news articles looking for anything that might link to the notation in Elizabeth's planner, **SR-pMoses I/II STPC**. But he came up empty.

Perro licked the last of the grease from his plate and hauled himself up on his hind legs to check out the spread on the table. Evan snapped his fingers. "When I want your nose in my food, you'll be the first to know."

The dog blinked slowly, first one eye and then the other—Evan could swear it was a wink—then disappeared under the table.

Evan was just finishing off the rum drink when Cedella appeared and set a folded sheet of paper next to his plate. "Your friend dropped this off," she said. "He said to tell you he's sorry he had to cancel."

Evan looked past her at the mostly empty restaurant. "Who?"

She leaned in. "You've been holding out on me. A handsome man who behaves like a gentleman. And no wedding ring! I hope you arranged to meet him here so that you could introduce us."

Wildly confused, Evan said, "Of course, Cedella. That's exactly what I had in mind."

"Good. Then you will arrange to meet him here again."

"What did he look like?"

Her eyebrows winged together in confusion. "He's *your* friend."

"I want the female perspective."

"Tall, dark, and handsome. Which isn't to say that short, dark, and handsome isn't good. A woman just needs some variety." She strode away to greet a four-top of newcomers.

Evan unfolded the note.

You're in danger. Meet me in half an hour at the establishment of our mutual friend Simon.

There was no signature, but Evan didn't need one to know that, based on Cedella's description, the note must have come from Ronen Avraham. Maybe Avraham had learned about Elizabeth's death and wanted to question him. Maybe he was ready to share why he'd had an appointment with her.

Evan refolded the note, which had been written on the back of one of Cedella's take-out menus and shoved it into the pocket of his hoodie.

You're in danger seemed rather theatrical. And why the drama of a note instead of a simple phone call?

Except . . . Elizabeth was dead. Possibly murdered. And Mossad had their own way of doing things.

He took a few more bites of the Fish Escovitch, then placed his fork on the edge of the plate and raised his water glass. As he did, he leaned back and took a casual glance around the room.

Only a few tables were occupied, two groups of four and a larger one of six. The smaller groups appeared to be coworkers, while the larger party was celebrating a child's birthday.

Only two people sat at the bar. An attractive woman in a navy suit and white blouse, wearing a pair of earbuds. Her drink of choice was something spritzy with lime, and she appeared deeply intent on a book spread open on the bar next to her. While he watched, she tapped her teeth with her pen, then wrote something on a legal pad.

The other person at the bar was a slovenly-looking man.

He sat at the short end of the L-shaped bar so that he faced Evan. Broad-shouldered, heavyset, and sharp eyed, he had a five-o'clock shadow and a greasy mop of dirty-blond hair. He wore jeans and a polo shirt and appeared to be paying no attention to anything other than his beer and the muted game on the television screen above the bottles of scotch and cognac.

Neither the man nor the woman looked like players in a cloak-and-dagger drama.

But Evan had felt the man's eyes on him earlier. He'd written it off as the usual stares he got everywhere he went. Now he wondered if the man's interest was more than simple curiosity.

You're in danger.

Thoroughly off his appetite, and full to the brim anyway, Evan pushed the half-empty dishes away. Cedella stalked by with a raised eyebrow, and a moment later, a waiter brought take-out boxes and the check. Evan handed the young man his credit card, then dialed Simon Levair, his friend and the owner of Levair's Used and Rare Books. Simon picked up immediately, and after an exchange of pleasantries, Evan asked, "Are you familiar with an Israeli named Ronen Avraham?"

"Ro?" Simon's voice held warmth. "Of course! Wonderful man. He's actually—"

"Hold on." Evan felt a momentary slip, as if the world had shifted underfoot. He hadn't expected Avraham to be telling the truth about his relationship with Simon. "You're talking about Ronen Avraham?" he asked. "Midforties, dark hair, looks like he'd be comfortable in a combat zone?"

"I can't say I've considered that before. But . . ." Simon sighed. "Now that you mention it, I suppose so, although I don't relish the image you have just put into my mind. Anyway, Ro stops by whenever he's in town to browse. Why are you asking about him?"

"I'm due to meet him there shortly."

"Ha! As I was trying to say, he's already here. And, sadly, he's my only client. It's an unusually slow afternoon. Ro is currently in the basement, browsing the used books. He wants any John le Carré I have on hand. Has good taste, Ro does."

"Can you let him know I'll be there in half an hour or so?"

"Excellent," Simon said. "I'll set out things for tea."

After they disconnected, the waiter returned with his card. Cedella hadn't charged him for half of what she'd brought, so, as always, he tipped handsomely. The waiter came by with a receipt and then placed the boxes in a paper bag.

Such a shame that it would go to waste.

Leaving the paper bag ostentatiously on the table as if he intended to return, he clicked his tongue at Perro and headed toward the bathroom. The same hallway led to the building's back door.

He hurried by the heat and noise of the kitchen, past the bathrooms, then eased the back door open just enough to allow him and Perro to squeeze through. He took up a position behind a dumpster and waited a few minutes to see if Polo Shirt emerged. But the man didn't appear, and Evan felt a little foolish for buying into Avraham's secretive routine.

Then again, only a couple of hours ago, he'd been eyeball to eyeball with a cobra. He couldn't claim to be in Kansas anymore.

CHAPTER 9

Downtown Chicago was bustling.

Evan found a spot in a parking garage off Michigan Avenue. From beneath his seat, he retrieved one of the puzzle toys Diana had given him for Perro and tucked it in his satchel. After a quick glance around for anyone who might be paying more than normal attention to a dwarf and his dog, he and Perro took the elevator down to the street. They headed toward the river, plunging into the glitz and glamour of Chicago's epicenter of retail therapy.

Tourists and locals alike were out to enjoy the breezy, semiwarm weather. The day had topped out in the low sixties, but already shorts and T-shirts were plentiful. Keeping a tight grip on Perro's leash, Evan dodged pedestrians, fellow dog walkers, and skateboarders. One of the advantages of being a person with dwarfism: if Polo Shirt had managed to track him from Cedella's restaurant, he would have a hard time spotting Evan in this crowd.

That was assuming the man had been doing anything other than enjoying his beer and whatever game was on the telly.

When they were a block and a half from the garage, Perro showed interest in one of the city's old-style streetlamps. While the dog watered the metal, Evan glanced casually around.

On the other side of the street, the man from the bar at Boonoon's stood on the sidewalk in front of a clothing store. He'd donned sunglasses, an unzipped navy windbreaker, and a plain white ball cap, but it was unmistakably him. He appeared to be fascinated by the collection of lime-green skirts and patterned blouses draped over mannequins.

With the way the light hit, Polo Shirt would be able to see Evan's reflection in the store window.

Perro finished watering the streetlamp and trotted forward, pulling on his leash. Evan followed, his heart drumming a staccato beat.

You're in danger.

He walked past Simon's bookstore, crossed at the intersection with the light, and plowed through the crowd until he was surrounded by people who were not vertically challenged. He ducked into a cookware place. A minute later, Polo Shirt walked by. Immediately, before the man realized he'd lost Evan and turned back, Evan hurried out of the store and jogged up the sidewalk to Simon's place.

Outside the elegant facade of Levair's Used and Rare Books, he spared a look over his shoulder. Plenty of shoppers thronged the sidewalks, none of them wearing a ball cap, navy jacket, and polo shirt.

When he turned back to the bookstore, he noticed that Simon's elegantly lettered sign read CLOSED. He had to smile—probably Avraham had flipped the sign himself. No wonder business was slow.

He slipped into the cool and musty scent of Simon's store, closing the door firmly behind him and locking it as a bell tinkled to alert employees to his presence.

Simon emerged from a back room. "Evan, my friend! How wonderful of you to come by! I let Ro know you were on your way. Tea will be ready in a jiffy." His gaze dropped to Perro. "You brought a friend."

Evan drew in a deep breath and willed his heartbeat to slow.

"This is Perro," he said. "He's Diana's creature. I'm merely dog sitting."

Perro looked quizzically up at him, and Evan felt a stab of conscience. The dog, after all, had tried to warn him about the cobra.

"Well, he doesn't seem to be hurting for a steady supply of good food," Simon noted.

"He's a glutton." Evan patted his own stomach. "And I just ate my weight in fish."

Simon grinned. "You went to see the lovely Cedella."

"I think she's fattening me up for something. Now tell me how you know Avraham."

Simon leaned against a table stacked with books on military history. "Ro has been coming here for five or six years, every time he's in town. Old archaeology books are a favorite of his. Last year I sold him a signed three-volume set—first editions, mind you—of Howard Carter's *Tomb of Tutankhamen*. I let it go for less than thirty grand, if you can imagine. The things I do for my friends."

"You're a generous soul."

Simon sniffed. "Do I detect mockery in your tone?"

"Perish the thought." Evan remained in front of the door, hoping that Simon wouldn't notice he'd turned the deadbolt. "Is anyone else here?"

"As I said on the phone, it's been quiet. I hardly know what to do with myself."

Evan thought quickly. He needed something to keep Simon occupied while he and Avraham spoke—Avraham had already pulled Simon in by arranging to meet here, and Evan was determined that his old friend wouldn't get any more involved.

"Perhaps I can help," he said to Simon.

Simon perked up.

"Didn't you mention not long ago that you'd gotten editions of a nineteenth-century journal from the Holy Land?"

"The *Palestine Exploration Quarterly*. Indeed, yes. An estate purchase from a man who inherited his grandfather's possessions but not his late grandfather's interest in archaeology. The journals date back to 1865 and were intended to provide readers with scholarly information about the Middle East—specifically the land of the Bible. I have yet to unpack them." He adjusted his spectacles. "Are you thinking Ro would be interested?"

"Actually, it's for me. I'm looking for anything by or about T. E. Lawrence. I believe he was published in the quarterly."

Simon's eyebrows rose. "Lawrence of Arabia? Is this a new interest?"

"Let's say it's a personal one."

"Ah. Fascinating." Simon glanced at his watch. "It will take me a bit of time to haul out the journals and catalog them."

Perfect. "Do you mind?"

"Not at all. A good afternoon for it, apparently." He gave the front door a forlorn look over Evan's shoulder. "But tea first, yes?"

"Maybe in a little while."

"Very well." Simon pushed away from the table, and Evan followed him through the front room. "T. E. Lawrence worked in the Wilderness of Zion, if I'm correct. The PEF published his and Woolley's work. I might have a copy."

"That would be wonderful," Evan said. "I'll take the journals and your copy of T. E. Lawrence's book."

"Of course."

Simon went up the stairs that led to his office and the small room he used for items he was in the process of cataloging. Evan waited until the bookseller had disappeared before taking Perro's leash and heading toward the basement where Simon kept the "ordinary" books—the novels and popular nonfiction titles that tourists flocked to.

Evan hesitated at the top of the stairs for only a moment before descending onto the first step and pulling the door closed behind him and Perro.

He saw Ronen Avraham as soon as he'd cleared the stairs and turned the corner. The man stood at the end of a row of overburdened wooden shelves. In his hand was, indeed, a John le Carré novel. *The*

Little Drummer Girl. He looked up when he heard Evan. Something like a smile touched his face.

"I was afraid you wouldn't come."

"I almost didn't." Evan moved farther into the room. "Why are we here?"

"I thought my relationship with Simon would convince you to trust me. Plus, what can I say?" He gestured toward the shelves with his free hand. "I like books."

"Spy books."

"Le Carré is a master."

"That's because before he was John le Carré, he was a spy named David Cornwell. A career I imagine you know something about. Are you the one who put Polo Shirt on my tail?"

"The guy who needs a shower, a shave, and a comb?" Avraham's eyebrows reached his hairline. "I'd figured it was the woman next to him at the bar. I must be losing my touch."

"I'll ask a different way. Why am *I* here?"

Avraham placed the spy novel on a shelf. "I'm getting desperate, Dr. Wilding. I'm very good at locating people, but I can't find Elizabeth. And now that my visit to your office has looped you in, people are following you. Or maybe they've been following you long before I came on the scene. I don't know who these people are, or what they're after. And," he added, "I suspect you don't, either."

Perro whined—a quiet sound like a throat clearing. Evan retrieved the puzzle toy, verified there was a treat inside, and set it on the ground for the corgi.

He faced Avraham.

"Let's leave me out of it for the moment," he said. "Why are *you* here, Mr. Avraham? Or is it Dr. Avraham? Should I assume you're involved with the IAA exhibit at the Moses Museum? But that wouldn't explain your likely connection to Mossad. Or your need to find Elizabeth." He played part of his hand, suspecting Avraham was already in the know. "Maybe you're here because of the Moses papyri."

"Moses papyri? Is that what Elizabeth is working on?" Avraham's voice struck exactly the right note of curiosity and ignorance. It was, in Evan's opinion, beautifully played. "Is that something she recently acquired? Something she shared with you?"

"No games, Avraham."

Avraham didn't move. He didn't so much as blink. But something in him shifted, nonetheless. Like a leopard dropping into a crouch in the dark of a moonless night.

The hair rose on Evan's neck.

"Are these papyri why you went to see Chuma Hassan?" Avraham asked.

"You followed me there?"

"I picked you up there."

"Then you tailed me to the restaurant. Why?"

"I thought you and I had something in common—our fondness for Elizabeth. I don't blame you for not trusting me—clearly she never mentioned my name to you. But when you wouldn't offer any ideas about where I might find her, I hoped you would lead me to her. Instead, you visit a man she detests."

"She might have—" Evan caught himself. "She might detest him. But she might also be working with him."

Avraham, however, didn't miss a thing. "You said *have*."

Evan debated only a moment, then took the plunge. "You're right."

"Meaning she's—?"

"Deceased. So why don't you explain to me how the very day you show up in my office looking for Elizabeth Lawrence, she ends up dead in a dirt lot?"

Avraham blinked. His face softened, as if the bones had given out beneath his flesh. Silence filled the room save for the faint jangle of

Perro's tags as the dog devoted himself to the puzzle toy and the treat inside.

"How?" Avraham rasped.

"She appears to have died from the bite of a cobra. Although that's only an educated guess right now."

"You saw her body?"

"Yes."

"A *cobra?*"

For an instant, Evan was back by Elizabeth's car, face-to-face with the snake. He recalled Perro's warning bark and felt a rush of gratitude for the corgi. "The medical examiner hasn't yet ruled whether it was murder or suicide."

Avraham staggered, his shoulder striking the bookcase. The le Carré novel toppled and plunged to the floor, breaking its spine. "Suicide?"

"You seem shocked."

"Aren't you?"

"Yes." Then Evan surprised himself by saying, "She left a note." Clearly, he was of two minds.

Avraham bent, picked up the novel, and carefully replaced it on the shelf. He came toward Evan, who braced himself. But the Israeli walked past and sank down on one of the stairs, using the railing to lower himself. He moved painfully, as if he'd suddenly grown old.

"What did the note say?"

"That's confidential."

"She didn't kill herself," Avraham said. "Not Elizabeth."

"Then tell me what happened. Tell me about the papyri."

Avraham turned his gaze toward the ground. Minutes ticked by while the man stared at the linoleum floor.

Evan waited.

After a time, Avraham settled his hands in his lap and lifted his head. His gaze was bleak.

"She was my friend," he said. "For many years, she has been my friend."

In his mind's eye, Evan saw the photograph on Elizabeth's desk at the institute. The one of her and Avraham standing next to each other in the desert in front of an archaeological site. Content in each other's company. The way old friends are.

Evan made his way to a nearby chair and perched on the edge. Perro picked up the toy and followed him, sprawling on the floor at his feet.

Evan leaned toward Avraham, who didn't move.

"Why don't you tell me what this is about," Evan said. "Tell me about you and Elizabeth."

Avraham opened his mouth to speak.

Then a sound from upstairs made him freeze.

Chapter 10

Avraham stood, his hand going under his jacket, reaching for a gun. He looked at Evan and pressed a finger to his lips.

Both men waited, listening.

After a moment, Avraham relaxed. His hand reemerged empty from his jacket. A teakettle whistled, and there came a gentle clatter of silverware. It was only Simon in the kitchenette above them. A few moments later, the floor creaked as Simon again retreated up the stairs to his loft.

Evan let out his breath.

"When you mentioned danger, I thought you were exaggerating," he said, wanting to believe that Elizabeth had not spent her last minutes with a murderer. Wanting to believe that everything happening was a terrible—and terribly sad—mistake.

But Avraham said, "The danger is real."

"Because . . . ?"

"Because Elizabeth was on the trail of something, some artifact or text that has brought attention from the kind of people you would call 'unsavory.'"

"The Moses papyri?"

Avraham shrugged. "She never mentioned these papyri to me. All she said was that she was close to acquiring some great artifact. When I expressed concern that others might want it as well—the word *cutthroat* applies easily to the illegal antiquities world—she told me I was paranoid. And now . . ."

Evan sensed that the Israeli was teetering on a precipice. He walked him back the same way he'd walk back an anxious or angry student.

"Let's start with what you do know," he said. "Tell me how the two of you met."

Avraham drew in a deep breath. "It was in Egypt."

He rose and brought over another office chair and placed it kitty-corner to Evan's so that he faced the stairs. He tucked the edge of his suit jacket back, making it easy for him to reach his gun. These actions—quiet, efficient—reminded Evan of every intelligence officer he'd ever met.

Perro yawned. He abandoned Evan and his toy and went to stretch himself beside the Israeli as Avraham began to speak.

Fourteen years ago, he and Elizabeth had both been presenting at an archaeological conference at the American University in Cairo. Elizabeth's talk was a broad-ranging discussion of archaeological sites in the Wilderness of Zion in the Negev Desert, where she'd gone seeking T. E. Lawrence's pre-WWI archaeological excavations.

So, Evan thought, Elizabeth's interest in Lawrence of Arabia began long before she knew of a possible genealogical connection.

But, Avraham said, her work had been stymied by an inability to get permits as war threatened to break out again between the Palestinians and the Israelis. Elizabeth wasn't indifferent to politics. But she'd found the entire situation maddening. And it was halting her work.

She wanted a better option.

After she finished her talk, Avraham went up to the podium to tell her how much he appreciated her lecture. They arranged to meet later. He didn't yet work for the Israel Antiquities Authority, but he had a few political connections. He offered to help her gain access to the remote sites she cared about. On one condition—that she take him with her.

"If you weren't yet working for the IAA, what was your interest?" Evan asked.

"Elizabeth was searching for the story of my people." Avraham's voice turned animated. "The story of the land is the story of the Jewish people. We *need* to find every piece of our history that we can. All of it, every bit of it, matters."

Elizabeth had agreed to Avraham's request, the only stipulation being, given his obvious comfort with firearms, that he not shoot anyone. Unless, of course, it was truly necessary. They'd worked together in the Negev for almost five years.

"They were fruitful years," Avraham said. "Both in terms of our discoveries and on a personal level. She was my mentor and saw it as her duty to teach me. Not just those tasks that related to archaeology but also less concrete qualities like persistence and faith. On school holidays, she brought along her son, who became like a younger brother to me." He looked up. "Did you know Tucker?"

Evan shook his head. "Sadly, our paths never crossed."

"He was a good kid." Avraham's smile was soft. "And those were good times. Eventually, though, duty called, and we went our separate ways. I accepted a position with the IAA, and Elizabeth returned to the United States. We were both busy with our respective jobs. For a few years, we didn't communicate much."

"But something changed."

Avraham pushed to his feet, his lean body unfolding with self-contained grace. His movement disturbed Perro, who woke and wagged his tail. Avraham squatted and ran his hand down the dog's back.

Evan wondered if Perro was as good at sniffing out human snakes as he was the reptilian variety. With Avraham, it was hard to tell.

"Yes," Avraham said. "Something changed. Some months back, she called me in the middle of the night, very excited."

"What was her call about?" Evan asked.

"She wouldn't tell me on the phone. She insisted I come see her in Chicago. She had opened her Institute of Middle Eastern Antiquities not long before. The institute had been a dream of hers—an idea the two of us hatched during our time in the desert and which she eventually saw to fruition. Naturally, I assumed she'd found something that would be of interest to us both. But all she would tell me was that she'd been in touch with her old friend, the Jerusalem antiquities dealer Omar Rasheed."

"Is he someone you know?"

"Only a little." Avraham gave Perro a final pat and stood. "Rasheed looks old enough to have been in the business since the time of Moses. His grandson is also in the business somewhere in the US. Rasheed's reputation is that of an honest man who is scrupulous about avoiding forgeries and looted artifacts."

"I sense a 'but' in what you're saying."

The Israeli nodded. "Unless you're a dealer with access to the kinds of testing that can be done on a big budget, it is almost impossible these days to protect yourself against forgeries. Rasheed might claim he has a nose for sniffing out fakes. But a man's instinct can only take him so far. And, of course, a gift for spotting forgeries doesn't protect you against buying stolen or looted goods."

"Have you talked to him since Elizabeth reached out?"

"I tried. He was congenial, but he gave up nothing."

Evan knew Avraham hadn't told him the full story. He knew this because even an agent of Mossad couldn't completely suppress the physical tells that reveal a deliberate muddying of the truth. The man's vagueness with certain details. His occasional reluctance to meet Evan's gaze. The way he smoothed his hair as he reached for words.

In Avraham, the tells were subtle. But Evan's job entailed reading subtlety.

Still, he accepted the gist of the man's story. Elizabeth and Avraham had worked together. He believed that they'd become friends—it would be difficult to fake the kind of distress Avraham had revealed at the news of her death. And she had found something of interest that she'd wanted to share with Avraham.

On the other hand, friendships fail. Or become secondary to other things—like great archaeological discoveries.

Evan leaned back in his chair. "What did you learn when you visited Elizabeth before?"

Avraham began to stalk up and down the bookcases, his voice floating back to Evan.

"She was chasing down a lead on a manuscript. A text she said was as valuable as the Dead Sea Scrolls and that would turn the world of biblical archaeology on its head. It would also, of course, be worth millions."

With her share of the proceeds, presumably enough to fund her institute for a long time. Evan said, "Assuming it wasn't a forgery. Or illegally acquired."

"Assuming those things. She would have to take possession before she could run the necessary tests."

"But she didn't tell you anything more about the manuscript?"

Avraham came to a stop in front of Evan and shook his head. "She trusted me, Dr. Wilding, as much as she trusted anyone. But she didn't tell me."

"So you have no idea if she—"

"If she found it. No."

"Or what it is."

"I've wondered if it's a Dead Sea Scroll," Avraham said, the doubt clear in his voice. "The scrolls align with her interests. And with the locations she's worked in. It would explain why she reached out to me. But then why would she be so secretive?"

Evan pictured Elizabeth's body. The shoe that had slipped off her foot. Her alleged suicide note. The flat eyes of the snake.

"A text that's worth millions would be more than enough justification for murder in the eyes of some," he said.

Avraham crouched so that he was facing Evan eye to eye. "I say she trusted me. And she did. Even with her life. But when it came to finding this text—whatever it was—I don't think she trusted anyone."

Evan worked to marshal his thoughts, which scurried about like bewildered ants. "A biblical text, something unknown, something that hasn't been documented and provenanced—that would mean something new."

"Probably."

Evan turned the corner he'd been avoiding. "Something likely looted. Or stolen. Otherwise, everyone would know about it. Did Elizabeth—"

From upstairs came the sound of footsteps. Simon moving into the kitchen. He turned on the radio—a jazz station—and a moment later a chair squeaked along the floor. He had apparently settled himself at the table.

"Never," Avraham said. "She never dealt with questionable artifacts. No matter the temptation."

Evan's thoughts cast back to his final lunch with Elizabeth. Her accounting of her illness. Her expression when she handed over the key to her institute—*In case I collapse and I speed-dial you by accident.* It had been an expression of studied nonchalance that hadn't fooled him. Time was running out—the time she needed to establish her institute, to make her mark. She must have been panicked.

Now the two men were so close to each other that Evan noticed something he'd missed before. Beneath the man's glasses—false, Evan saw—and his cool gaze lay a shadowed sadness. A grief that Evan suspected went past his personal pain at the loss of Elizabeth and toward something vaster. *The story of the land is the story of the Jewish people,* he'd said. Perhaps he felt grief at the loss of greater things. Land. Security. The simple right to exist in the world.

Surely the same expression would be mirrored in the eyes of Palestinian refugees around the world.

So much death and grief and betrayal over a tiny scrap of land.

"Just for the record," Evan said, "I don't support Israel's treatment of the Palestinians."

Avraham surprised him by saying, "Just for the record, neither do I."

"And yet you work for Mossad." He shifted the conversation. "When you stopped by Elizabeth's institute for your meeting, I have no doubt you let yourself in. Did you by chance leave a dead toad on her desk?"

Avraham laughed. "A what?"

"It was something new, according to her assistant." Avraham looked bewildered, and Evan waved a hand. "Never mind."

Avraham regarded him another moment, then stood and walked the length of the nearest bookshelf. "You must know *something*, Evan. What about these Moses papyri? Or another text she might have mentioned?"

But Evan cupped his chin in his hands and shook his head. "Elizabeth never said anything to me. The Moses papyri were just something she scrawled on a note in her office."

He chose not to mention the rest of the entry in her calendar. Not yet. Not until he knew more.

Avraham went on as if he hadn't spoken. "You do know something. Or else she trusted you to figure it out. That would explain why she told me to go to you if there were any problems. And"—he stopped and turned back—"I would say the fact that Elizabeth is dead is one hell of a problem."

CHAPTER 11

Perro sat up suddenly. Avraham fell silent.

The corgi trotted over to the stairs and cocked his ears. He gave a low growl.

Both men got to their feet. This time, Evan didn't need Avraham to warn him to be silent. He was straining to hear whatever had alerted Perro. But no sound trickled down to the basement.

Who could say what Perro might growl at? A corgi that urinated on a man's sixteenth-century Berber rug might growl at anything. Or nothing.

But the silence, broken only by the faint strains of jazz from the radio, felt ominous.

Worried, Evan mouthed *Simon* to Avraham, who nodded; the bookseller was blissfully unaware of any danger that might arrive. Avraham touched his own chest, then held up one finger. He then pointed at Evan and raised two fingers.

The message was clear: *I'll go first.*

Evan wasn't going to argue. If it came to hand-to-hand combat or—God forbid—a shoot-out, Avraham was imminently more qualified to handle it. Evan looked around for something to use as a weapon and spotted a hammer next to an open box of nails. Simon had probably been doing some repair work on the shelves. He snatched up the hammer, looped Perro's leash around the bottom banister, and followed Avraham up the stairs.

Perro whined.

"Hush," Evan whispered.

Perro cocked his ears but fell silent.

The Israeli moved with the tread of a ghost. Evan tried to match the man's soundless, gliding steps but failed miserably. Every stair groaned beneath him. Avraham shot a glare over his shoulder, and Evan shrugged. What could he say? He wasn't cut out for espionage work despite having played tenth fiddle in a few national-security operations.

At the top of the stairs, Avraham hesitated with his ear to the door. After a moment, he turned the knob silently, eased the door open, and slipped through.

Evan tiptoed after. When he peered around the edge of the half-open door, he barely spotted Avraham before the man melted into the shadows that fell between the table lamps. He followed slowly, willing himself into invisibility.

The large room lay quiet. Gentle lights gleamed on manuscripts and artifacts locked inside glass cabinets. Rows of books marched like much-loved but war-worn soldiers behind high cabinets, also locked. A stray bit of sun found its way through a high narrow window and glowed on the hardwood floor.

A door banged off to their left, in the direction of the small kitchen. Avraham lifted his head like a Maasai warrior stalking a lion and swiveled on the balls of his feet. He pivoted soundlessly and ran to the hallway that led to the kitchen.

He vanished.

Evan hurried after him, holding the hammer in a tight grip, the head of the mallet toward the floor. At his height, kneecapping someone was his best option.

In the doorway to the kitchen, Evan paused. The back door stood open, thumping against the wall as the wind gusted. Avraham was nowhere to be seen—presumably he'd gone outside.

Evan followed.

The door opened onto a narrow paved alley lined with garbage cans. For a moment, all Evan saw was asphalt, the backs of nearby buildings, and—high above—a strip of blue sky. Then he heard a groan and spotted a pair of polished loafers on feet attached to legs clad in an expensive suit. The rest of the man was hidden by a dumpster.

Simon.

As Evan reached his friend, Simon groaned again. The bookseller was sitting upright, but he looked dazed. His forehead bore a vivid red contusion above his right eye.

"Ro went that way." Simon waved a weak hand westward. "In hot pursuit of my attacker."

Evan crouched next to Simon. "What happened?"

"I'm not entirely sure." Simon cleared his throat. "A man approached as I was throwing out the trash. He said good afternoon, asked if I was the bookstore owner. When I offered my own good afternoon and told him that, yes, I was the proprietor, he hit me across the back with something—surely a fifty-pound weight. I went down like the proverbial sack of potatoes and smacked my head. Embarrassing."

"What happened after he hit you?"

Simon's voice was faint. "It appears I lost consciousness."

"Simon—"

"As you can see, I'm perfectly fine. After a time, the man reappeared briefly here in the alley and then ran off again."

"Did you get a good look at him?"

"A *good* look? No. He had blond hair. And he was wearing a ball cap and a ghastly gray-and-pink polo shirt under a cheap coat. Utterly without taste, which should come as no surprise."

Evan glanced uneasily up and down the alley; at the moment, he'd love nothing more than to have Avraham close by.

"Can you stand?" he asked.

"Of course I can stand. He didn't break my legs." Simon's voice sounded stronger. "But I could use a little assistance."

~~~

In the kitchen, Evan helped Simon lower himself into a seat at the table. He closed and locked the back door, then got a clean dish towel and dampened it with warm water before pressing it gently to Simon's forehead.

Simon's hand drifted to his own shoulder, and he winced. "I feel just as I imagine a man would if he was unfortunate enough to get between a rhinoceros and its favorite fruit. Or is it favorite grass? Whatever it is rhinos eat."

"Do you have a penlight?" Evan asked.

"In the utility drawer. Under the phone. Whatever for?"

"Hold this," Evan said, indicating the dish towel, then fetched the penlight. He shone it in Simon's right eye, then the left, then back and forth.

"Do you even know what you're looking for?" Simon asked.

"I'm making sure your pupils are responsive," Evan said, trying to sound confident. He'd seen a doctor do it on an ER show.

"And?" Simon asked.

"They're perfect. But to play it safe, I'll drive you to the hospital."

"Nonsense. When we're done here, you can call Sophie for me. She used to be an ER nurse. She'll make me stand on one foot and recite the Declaration of Independence backward. Then she'll bring me home and take me straight to bed."

"A terrible prospect," Evan said, one eyebrow raised.

The bookseller gave a sly grin. "Dreadful."

Simon removed the dish towel, frowned at the dabbing of blood, and returned it to his forehead. "What I would like is for you to look around and see if my assailant took anything. Why else would he have knocked me down in such an uncivilized manner? Or in any manner, really?"

Evan took another dish towel and filled it with ice. He passed it over to Simon. "I'd rather not leave you."

Simon rolled his perfect-pupil eyes. "That's what Sophie is for."

~~~

Evan brought Perro up from the basement, and the pair did a rapid circuit of the main floor, looking for anything obvious like broken glass or gaps in the shelves. Nothing looked out of place.

Upstairs, though, was a different matter.

The storeroom was closed and locked. No disturbance there. But Simon's office had been searched. Desk drawers were pulled open, and their contents riffled. The laptop that was normally on the desktop was gone. And the surface of the library table where Simon did much of his evaluation work on newly purchased books was as clean and clear as a field of virgin snow.

It reminded Evan of the vacant space on Elizabeth's desk.

When he returned to the kitchen and gave Simon a report of the damage, the bookseller turned a furious scarlet.

"How dare he?" he cried.

"Was your laptop there?"

"Yes. But it's password protected and encrypted. Everything is backed up. I'm not worried about that, outside of the inconvenience. What the bastard took were the journals I'd pulled for you. The ones from the Palestine Exploration Fund. I had them spread out across the library table."

Evan took a seat at the table across from Simon. "You found something on Lawrence of Arabia?"

Simon nodded, then winced. He raised the ice to his forehead again. "I found the PEF's 1914 publication of T. E. Lawrence and C. Leonard Woolley's work in the Wilderness of Zion. And now it's gone." He brightened. "But at least I still have a copy of a later publication of their book. Or presumably I do. I hadn't pulled it yet."

A car backfiring a block away made them both jump.

"Where is our good friend Ro?" Simon asked. "I thought he'd be back by now, culprit in hand."

"Aren't you going to call the police?"

"I would," Simon said, "under normal circumstances. But nothing about this seems normal." He gave Evan a penetrating look. "Before I call them, I have to know. What are you mixed up in?"

"I'm looking into the death of a friend. And I'm working with Addie. It's all aboveboard. At least on our side of things."

"I'm sorry, Evan. Is it someone I know?"

"Elizabeth Lawrence. She ran the Institute of Middle Eastern Antiquities over by UChicago."

"I do know her!" His face fell. "Or rather, I did. She came into the store a few times, although the only thing she ever bought were 1950s mystery novels. If you and Addie are looking into it, then I assume the poor woman was murdered."

"The medical examiner hasn't made a ruling yet."

"But you believe she was."

Evan longed to push away the thought. "It's possible."

"And you think the theft of the journals might be related?"

"It's probable."

"Oh, dear." Simon rose and shook the ice out into the sink, waving Evan away. "Perhaps bringing in the authorities would be best. Especially since I lost something valuable."

"Not to mention the assault."

"There is that."

"I'll fill Addie in on what happened. But when you talk to the responding officer, maybe leave Avraham out of it for the moment."

"What?" Simon's eyes searched Evan's. "I always suspected there were hidden depths to Ro. Very well. He can go to the police himself if he wishes. But I admit, I'm getting a bit worried at his absence."

"I'm confident Ronen Avraham can take care of himself."

Simon called the police, then rang up his lady friend, Sophie. Both promised to get there as soon as possible. When he'd hung up, Simon turned again to Evan.

"I did manage to do a little research while you and Ro were talking. The work of T. E. Lawrence and Woolley was actually a cover for their military mapping operation. Both men were with Military Intelligence in Cairo before the first printing of their field work in Zion."

"Did the two of them actually do any archaeology?"

"They did. And you'll find that copy of *The Wilderness of Zin* in the front room, in the Near East section. Feel free to take it with you, along with anything else you find there that might be of use. Just do try to not spill any tea on it. Or"—he shuddered—"any of those vile alcoholic concoctions you toil over like you're one of Macbeth's witches."

After first Sophie and then a police officer arrived, Evan gave a statement to both Simon's girlfriend and the officer, leaving out a few details that he decided wouldn't be of particular value to either party. He asked Simon to let him know if he heard from their mutual friend; then he and Perro headed out.

It was nudging toward evening, and the skyscrapers cast the streets in shadow. If anything, the crowd had thickened as diners made their way into one or another restaurant. If Polo Shirt was still about, Evan couldn't see him. Nor did he see anyone who looked the least bit sinister.

Still, he didn't draw a deep breath until he and Perro were safely ensconced in his car. As he exited the garage and then waited on the light at West Ontario, he glanced over at the book he'd taken from the store, Simon's copy of *The Wilderness of Zin*. The front of the dust jacket showed an Arab dressed in the local fashion of long, loose robes, standing atop a crumbling wall of stone. He flipped the book over. On the back was a snapshot of T. E. Lawrence with his fellow archaeologist, Woolley, in their very British tweed suit coats and white button-down shirts.

He set the book down and watched pedestrians stroll across the intersection.

Lawrence of Arabia. Oxford graduate. Archaeologist. Spy for the British Empire.

Ultimately, the leader of the Arab revolt against the Ottoman Empire.

Evan stared out at the deepening shadows. He had not missed the fact that Avraham's surprise over the Moses papyri seemed feigned. Nor had Avraham pressed Evan for details about the papyri, even as he asked about Elizabeth's work. Was it possible the pair of them had found something in the desert? Something Elizabeth had gone back for?

Evan double-checked his phone for a call from Roberto Serrano, his CIA friend. Nothing yet. It was the middle of the night now in Israel.

The light turned green. Evan touched the gas.

"What were you up to, Elizabeth?" he said aloud as he nudged forward in traffic. "What did you think you'd find?"

CHAPTER 12

Addie phoned while Evan and Perro were on the Kennedy Expressway, stuck in traffic.

"Have you analyzed her suicide note?" she asked without preamble.

"I've been delayed."

"By what? What are you doing right now?"

"Driving home." He gazed out at the sea of brake lights. "Although the term *driving*, which suggests forward motion, might miss the mark."

"Can't you multitask?" Addie growled.

When Addie was working a case, trying to get her to respect the notion of work-life balance was a lot like asking a grizzly bear to go vegan. As a man who was used to dealing with historical objects that stretched back thousands of years, Evan sometimes found her impatience insanity inducing. But her dedication while on an investigation was also one of the many things he loved about her.

"What about you?" he asked as the car in front of him eased forward. "What have you learned?"

A horn sounded over the phone. Apparently, Addie was also enjoying Chicago gridlock.

"I'm learning that nothing in police work moves quickly," she said. "Strike that. I already knew detective work can be glacial, and yet I continue to be surprised."

She gave him a summary of the day's events. The crime-scene techs had found blood on one of the shards of glass in Lawrence's car. It would be a few days before they knew whether it was Lawrence's. Patrick had learned that Lawrence had applied to the cancer-treatment program mentioned in the newspaper and had been turned down because she was too far along with stage 4 colon cancer. Addie hadn't been able to confirm whether Ronen Avraham worked for the Israel Antiquities Authority or whether the Palestine Exploration Fund was familiar with Elizabeth's work—she'd try again in the morning. She'd also left a message for the attorney mentioned in the suicide note—a name Evan would be familiar with if he'd even bothered looking at the letter. Ralph Raines, attorney-at-law, had gone out of town for the week and was expected back in his office tomorrow.

"Leah Zielinski wasn't much help," Addie said. "She told us she was hired to type and file reports, handle the phone, conduct small research projects. If someone else has a key to the institute, she doesn't know about it. Their security cameras aren't yet operational. A technician is supposed to come by next week to take care of the cables and wiring. Lawrence was gone a lot, according to Ms. Zielinski, so her job was mostly to be a warm body in case someone dropped by. And no one ever did. Which worked well for her because it gave her time for her studies."

Evan was thinking he'd like a job like that when Addie said, "Where things got interesting was when it came to the illegal reptile market."

The car in front of Evan slammed on its brakes. Startled, Evan did the same. Perro scrabbled for purchase in the seat as the car screeched to a stop. Evan tried not to think of the leather.

"What did you learn?" he asked Addie, once his heart slowed.

Her anger came clearly across the connection. "I had no idea the reptile market could be so corrupt. And violent. Who knew that hot snakes are a thing?"

"Hot as in illegal?"

"Hot as in venomous. *And* illegal. Humans are smuggling some reptile species from their homes before scientists have even been able to give them a name. And sometimes"—Addie's voice hurtled forward with the fury of an avalanche—"the drug traffickers and reptile traffickers work together. Like the time somebody decided to hide bags of cocaine inside live boa constrictors. It did not go well for the boas."

Evan sympathized with her anger. "How does Elizabeth fit into this?"

Addie growled, still fuming. "She'd made inquiries about acquiring an Egyptian asp at one local pet shop. Maybe more. Of course, no one I talked to confessed to selling her a snake. As for reptile shows like the ones Yaa Mensah mentioned, the last show in Chicago was almost a year ago. So that seems an unlikely source. Online is another matter. There's a guy in Florida who will sell you anything. Probably his sister if he thought you'd make an offer."

The final rays of sunlight slanted through the Jaguar's windows as the traffic broke up. Evan pressed the gas pedal, and the car gained speed. He glanced in the rearview mirror at the Chicago skyline shrinking behind him; it resembled a child's set of building blocks.

Was it possible? Had Elizabeth planned so far ahead and with such intricacy for her own death?

"I'm sorry, Evan," Addie said. "Patrick talked to an agent with the US Fish and Wildlife Service. We're considering the possibility that she may have gotten tangled up with the wrong people. And by wrong people, I mean the Mafia. Like *The Godfather*. These aren't people to mess around with."

"If Elizabeth bought a cobra from the Mafia, why would they want to kill her?"

Addie huffed a sigh. "Why would the Mafia want to take a rare, beautiful creature out of the jungle and insert cocaine in its anus?"

"I see your point. When will you hear from the herpetologist about tracing venom in Elizabeth's blood?"

"Mensah says she'll finish running all her tests by tomorrow afternoon."

He nodded to himself and pulled around a tractor trailer.

"What about you?" Addie asked. "Since you didn't get to the suicide note, what were you doing?"

He heard the accusation in her voice, and it almost made him smile. He should get a COPS ON THE CASE T-shirt for her.

He launched into an account of his day, leaving out his visit to Hassan and summarizing his thoughts around the newspaper articles and a possible link between Alderman David Bakker and the location where Elizabeth had been found. He mentioned he'd made a phone call to a friend "in the business" in the hopes of learning more about Ronen Avraham, and then the surprising news that Avraham was a longtime patron of Simon's bookstore.

"Avraham claims he never heard of the Moses papyri, but he thinks Elizabeth was on the trail of a rare manuscript," Evan said. "And that she drew the attention of several interested parties, mostly of the criminal kind. If he's right, then it's possible she ran afoul of these less-than-honorable people."

He could almost hear Addie perk up. "She meets someone, takes possession of these papyri, and then her killer comes along, cobra locked and loaded?"

"There's a struggle; the glass holding the papyri is broken."

"And if we're lucky, the killer leaves behind a few drops of blood before abandoning her in the dirt lot. Then tell me, Dr. Wilding, who are we looking for?"

"The same men and women who always show up when there's money to be made from possessing a valuable artifact. Buyers, sellers, restorers. Auction houses and gallery owners and outright thieves." He summarized the events at Simon's, including Polo Shirt and the disappearance of the Palestine Exploration Fund journals. And the story

Avraham had told him about meeting Elizabeth long ago and their ensuing friendship.

"Do you believe him?"

"He's lying. But not about everything. I haven't sorted out the truth from the falsehoods. Not yet. Anyway, he went after Polo Shirt and didn't return."

"And what about you? Are you okay?"

"Not a hair on my head was touched. Unlike poor Simon."

"Is it possible Avraham staged it all? Maybe he had Polo Shirt assault Simon; then he and Polo Shirt make off together with the goods."

Evan took the exit off the expressway. "No need for that. Simon would have sold Avraham the journals, if that was his interest. Simon would have sold them to Polo Shirt, for that matter. The violence was completely unnecessary."

"Do you have a theory?"

"I assume Polo Shirt followed me to Simon's store despite my efforts to ditch him. When Simon went outside, leaving the back door unlocked, our bad guy disabled him and slipped in to take whatever he assumed I'd asked for. Maybe he thought that if I intended to purchase the items, then stealing them was his only option. When he spotted the PEF journals, he must have seen a connection with Elizabeth's previous work in Israel."

"You think he was following you because you might lead him to whatever Lawrence was after?"

"It's the only theory I have at the moment."

"Can't say I'm crazy about the idea of you being tailed by a violent criminal."

"It's not on my bucket list, either," Evan agreed. "But I suspect that's the last we'll see of him. He thinks he got his answer in those PEF journals. And maybe he did. Which makes it imperative I get another set of them."

"You have no idea what this man's intentions are," Addie said. "Maybe you should . . . maybe you should stay at what's-her-name's place for a couple of nights. Until this is over."

He heard the hesitation in her voice and wasn't surprised. He'd gotten the distinct sense that Addie wasn't thrilled by his relationship with Christina. Which made no sense. He was happy. And usually, when he was happy, Addie was happy.

"You know the security setup at my house," he said. "I'm safer there than anywhere."

Another silence, which Evan took to mean he'd won the argument. Finally, Addie said, "What are you doing tomorrow?"

"I'm at your disposal."

"I was hoping you'd say that. I'd like to have you present when we search Lawrence's home and business. I'm meeting Patrick at the institute at ten thirty a.m. The judge is appallingly slow, but everything should be good to go by then. In the meantime, patrol is driving by every couple of hours to keep an eye on the place."

"Count me in."

"Thanks. If you're not going over to what's-her-name's, do you have plans for tonight? Other than working on the suicide note, I mean."

He hesitated, then said, "Christina is coming over."

"Oh."

"Aren't you doing something with that Minzer fellow?"

"Sure. Later. Jeff got tickets to a show at the Laugh Factory. He tells me I need to laugh more. I tell him okay, be funnier."

Jeff Minzer was the latest in a seemingly infinite string of tall well-off men who had caught Addie's intense—if inevitably temporary—attention. She swore each man was the real deal. And they were, Evan mused, for a week or a month. All of them fell by the wayside, while Evan, until recently, had waited patiently on the sidelines, hoping Addie would notice him.

She hadn't. Not in that way. Best friends, but friends without benefits. Friends without romance. So he'd packed up his hopes for a future with her, and when Christina gave him a call, inviting him to dinner, he'd said yes.

"Do you think Jeff is right? Am I too serious?" Addie sounded plaintive.

"'A day without laughter is a day wasted,'" Evan said, sidestepping the question by quoting Charlie Chaplin. In truth, it seemed as though Addie had laughed a lot more back when they'd first met over spilled drinks at an art opening. That was two years ago, shortly after Evan moved to Chicago. Maybe the job was getting to her. Murder and violence, day in, day out. How could it not?

"If it's true about wasted days," Addie said, "then I've pointlessly burned through a lot of time. Can you meet me for breakfast after you've flown Ginny?"

"Won't you be breakfasting with the sidesplitting Jeff?"

"Jeff is a slug. He never goes anywhere before noon. Perks of being self-employed. Meet at the Wildberry Cafe? The Water Tower location?"

"I'll see you there at eight thirty."

"Eight," she countered. "No, seven forty-five."

"Eight fifteen."

Addie sighed her agreement and disconnected.

His phone immediately rang again. Christina Johansen.

"I'm stuck in traffic, my love," she said.

He smiled. "You and me and all the rest of Chicago. How close are you to the house?"

"If the traffic breaks, a mere fifteen minutes. I have a shaker of dirty martinis. I'm hoping to mooch dinner off you."

His smile deepened. "I happen to have a mutton cassoulet in the refrigerator, ready to pop in the oven. And a loaf of rustic bread."

"I've had my fingers crossed that you'd say something like that. It's one of the many reasons why I find you fabulous. I'll hop off the expressway and pick up a bottle of Marcillac if they have it. Otherwise, a malbec. I hope you're in the mood for a woman who's been deprived of sex for almost twenty-four hours."

"Strange coincidence, the same amount of time for me."

Her laugh was downright wicked. "See you soon."

Dear God, let it be so.

~~~

It was almost an hour later by the time he pulled into the garage at the Aerie. The whimsically named house, on lease to him by a retired professor, was a Tudor cottage set on generous grounds that included deciduous and pine trees, a topiary garden with a small maze, a guest-house, and a mews for Ginny. He spotted Christina's Lexus in the circular driveway.

No time to dawdle.

Perro, once freed of the back seat, disappeared into the house, no doubt looking for a new target to rival his destruction of Evan's Berber rug.

Evan found Christina in the gourmet kitchen, pouring cocktails. Of medium height and lithe, with cropped black hair and a generous assortment of tattoos, wearing a burgundy dress, fishnet stockings, and combat boots, Christina looked more like the lead singer for a punk band than a brilliant scholar.

He loved the dichotomy.

He paused for a moment outside the arched doorway, watching her before she noticed him. She hummed off-key as she stared into the middle distance, her bearing buoyed by an untapped energy that made her seem taller than she was. Christina had what social scientists called "presence." With her confidence and her intense intelligence, she took over every room she walked into. Given what she had taught him about

Viking Age beliefs, Evan was partially convinced that her aura came from insights he could barely glimpse.

They'd met four months ago, when he'd been called in to consult on the Viking Poet case. Christina, a professor of Viking Age studies at the U of C, had been an invaluable resource as the Chicago PD raced to find the killer. Their relationship had begun in the usual simple way of physical attraction—she'd made it clear early on that Evan's height was immaterial to her. She was drawn to his thick, curling hair and the eyes she called as green and dazzling as the lakes of her native Sweden. And, of course, his mind wasn't exactly a drawback.

They'd dated casually for a few weeks and then exclusively as their relationship deepened to one of mutual respect, shared interests, and a love of stimulating conversation.

Not to mention their compatibility in bed.

He flushed at the thought just as she turned and saw him. She offered a wide smile, holding out a martini glass filled with pale-green liquid and garnished with a skewer of olives.

"I heard the garage door," she said. She held her own glass in her other hand. A delicate curve of red from her lipstick showed on the rim.

He walked into the room and took the glass; they clinked a silent toast before he took a sip followed by a healthy swallow.

He closed his eyes for a moment. "Just what the doctor ordered."

Her fingers brushed his cheek. "I could tell by your voice you've had a day. You want to talk about it?"

Like a child, he shook his head no. He did not want to let work seep into his relationship with her. Plus, the profiling he did for the Chicago PD operated under a nondisclosure agreement. Even though his current case was personal, he couldn't talk about it with her.

"I'm sorry," he said.

"No worries," she said, accepting it.

When he looked again at her, she was giving him her bedroom eyes. Heat rose from her like a magnetic field, shimmering along her skin, pulling him into her space. She leaned down and kissed him on the lips, her dress falling away from her neck. He swallowed.

It was a long, lingering kiss.

When she straightened, he murmured, "My day just took a turn for the better."

"Glad I could help." She grabbed the shaker from the countertop and topped off his drink. "I hope it's all right that I went ahead and fed Ginny. And raided your refrigerator for brie and fig jam."

"I tasted the evidence of the jam." He touched the corner of her mouth.

She turned her head and licked his finger.

He froze, two different hungers raging with him—hunger of the everyday variety for simple nutrition. And a desire for this woman that was more like a volcano poised to explode.

Best tend to the volcano, he concluded.

Evidently, she agreed.

Later, they left the tangled sheets and returned to the kitchen.

He slid the cassoulet into the oven; then Christina trailed behind him as he went into the converted dining room, which served as indoor space for his hawk. He pulled on a leather falconer's glove and lifted Ginny from her stand and onto his fist. The goshawk squeaked her joy at his presence. Perro reemerged from wherever he'd been hiding and, as always, refused to acknowledge Ginny's presence. The hawk returned the favor. While the casserole warmed, the four of them went into the backyard to sit near the gas firepit and enjoy the chilly evening. The trees hadn't yet budded, but the pines murmured as the sky deepened from pewter to periwinkle and finally a velvet black, creating a beckoning darkness beyond the gently hissing flames.

After dinner, with Ginny locked away for the night in the mews behind the main house, Christina took his hand and again led him to the bedroom. When Perro trotted after them, Evan closed the door firmly in the dog's disappointed face. For the next hour, there was no Elizabeth or Avraham or venomous snakes.

Only Christina.

~~~

Afterward, Christina slipped into sleep. But Evan lay on his back, staring through the darkness at the ceiling. A faint glow came from the outdoor lights, illuminating the bedsheets and Christina's quiet form. He checked the time on his phone. The night—technically speaking—was still young. Addie was probably just leaving the comedy show.

He hoped she'd had a good time. He hoped she'd found plenty of reasons to laugh.

He puffed out a sigh. Why was he thinking of Addie while Christina lay next to him, her skin still damp from their lovemaking? What kind of louse was he? Not to mention certifiably insane.

He leaned over, breathing in her scent. She murmured in her sleep and turned away.

He slid out of bed, padding over to the dresser to retrieve sweatpants and a T-shirt. When he left the bedroom, he closed the door softly behind him.

~~~

Perro trotted after him into the two-story library, Evan's favorite room and the crown jewel of the Tudor house with its floor-to-ceiling bookshelves, generous display cabinets, dark-wood trim, leather club chairs, and an immense stone fireplace.

The corgi used the miniature ramp Diana had provided to reach a footrest and from there scoot into Evan's favorite chair, where he made himself comfortable. The chair was now covered with clumps of Perro's hair and host to an assortment of the dog's puzzle toys.

Evan cleared a space on his library table, moving aside the wooden puzzles he loved—maybe he was more like Perro than he wanted to think—along with books on Minoan culture, several unbound folios, and a notebook filled with printouts from a recent case in which he'd consulted for the FBI. That reminded him he still needed to write up his final notes on the case for his own records.

He flipped on a task lamp and shrugged into the polar fleece jacket hanging on the back of the chair, then printed a copy of Elizabeth's suicide note from the photo Addie had sent him and set it on the table's cleared space. He remained standing while he read through it quickly, then again more slowly.

> To Whom It May Concern:
> My name is Elizabeth Kathryn Lawrence, and you find me here of my own free will. To confirm that the corpse you see is really that of E. Lawrence (assuming, as I hope, that I am not found until nature has run its course), you may confirm my identity through my dental records, which are in the care of the estimable Dr. Donald Nelson, DDS, of Arlington Heights.
>
> While I'm on the topic of official business, you will find my will and all my intentions for the disposition of self and my worldly goods—including the Institute of Middle Eastern Antiquities—with Ralph Raines, attorney-at-law, also of Arlington Heights. If some time has passed between my disappearance and the discovery of my body, it is my hope that these papers will make my wishes clear.

I am taking my life for all the usual dreary reasons. Impending pain that will lead unavoidably to an excruciating and possibly protracted death. The loss of my son whom I miss more with each passing day and who I believe is waiting for me. And finally, a crushing setback in my life's work—that toil and passion that gave me life when family no longer could.

As to my work—let us say I had immortal longings. And I still do, to my shame. But I have been humbled, and the substance and nature of those longings has changed. I should have remembered: God blasts those trees which try to touch the skies.

Still, I offer no apologies for what I have done.

Elizabeth Kathryn Lawrence

N216C109

Evan sat back, the words swimming before his eyes. *I offer no apologies for what I have done.*

And what have you done, my friend?

He blinked and lifted his head; his gaze landed on Perro. The dog had been snoring contentedly, but now he shook himself awake and thumped his tail cheerily at Evan. Evan rose and went to the chair, pushing aside toys and wedging himself in next to the corgi's bulk. He ruffled Perro's ears and was rewarded with a look of adoration.

He stared out at the darkness that yawned beyond the mullioned windows.

He wondered what he would have done if he'd known Elizabeth was contemplating suicide. Would he have talked to her, tried to stop her? Offered to keep her company in her final hour?

How long had she deliberated death by her own hand? Did the horrid toad squatting on her office desk symbolize her determination to choose her own death?

Suicide had a long and even noble tradition. It was suicide that launched ancient Rome after the abused Lucretia took her life and the men around her were spurred to overthrow their foreign king and create the Roman Republic. Suicide was woven throughout the Bible—Samson, Saul, Jonah, and others. And thoughts of self-death wound their way into Shakespeare, then down through the ages and into the modern writers—Sylvia Plath, Virginia Woolf, David Foster Wallace.

Elizabeth would have seen all these examples as a demonstration that suicide, while not a first option, had its place.

But its legacy did not give the survivors any comfort.

He gave Perro a final pat, which raised a cloud of fur, and returned to the table. He sat down and pulled over a notepad and pen. Jotting quickly, he made a list of his first thoughts.

1. Frequently found in *falsified* suicide notes are mentions of feeling crazy or cowardly, or verbiage intended to indicate a state of mental confusion. No such language is found in this note.

2. Verbiage found in the letter is common in suicide notes:
   a. Formal language
   b. Disposition of belongings
   c. An apology (or, in this case, a determination not to apologize; I make note that this kind of refusal is typical of Dr. Lawrence based on my personal experience with the deceased)
   d. Mention of loved ones
   e. Mention of ill health and fear of a painful death

3. The letter is grammatically correct and properly punctuated, as would be expected of someone with Dr. Lawrence's education and attention to detail.

4. The author of the note makes a point to provide help with identification of the body. This is very much in keeping with Dr. Lawrence's personality.

5. Two of the reasons offered for suicide—an impending painful death and the loss of her son—are known facts about Dr. Lawrence.

6. The third reason offered—that the author of the note has suffered a professional blow—seems to contradict what little we currently know of Dr. Lawrence's work: that she was hunting for something important and had possibly found or was close to finding it.

7. Unusual for suicide notes, the message is typed rather than handwritten. Dr. Lawrence's signature at the end of the note is computer generated. The paper is of a common printer variety—surprising given her specialization in antique paper.

8. The phrase *Let us say I had immortal longings* is paraphrased from Shakespeare's *Antony and Cleopatra*, a line uttered by Cleopatra after she has held the snake to her breast and allowed it to bite. Dr. Lawrence's interest in, and possible affinity for, Cleopatra is evidenced by the painting that hangs in her institute, by statements made by her assistant, Leah Zielinski, and by her possible choice of snakebite with which to end her life.

9. Dr. Lawrence mentions her hope that she will not be found until "nature has run its course." This suggests she intended to die somewhere other than a busy neighborhood in Chicago; still, her body was discovered behind locked doors (auto and pedestrian) and a high cement wall, although the driver's door was ajar. Of note—the large car gate was locked from the outside, possibly

suggesting that Elizabeth had returned outside and locked it herself.

10. The meaning of *N216* and *C109* . . .

Here he paused and powered up his laptop. A quick search revealed that *N216* was a designation for both ball bearings and a Bell 427 aircraft. *C-109* was the designation for a variant of the B24 Liberator. It was also an industry standard for testing the compression strength of cement mortars.

"Why so maddeningly vague, Elizabeth?" he asked of the chill quiet air.

He reasoned that a better option was to suppose that the alphanumeric strings were biblical verses. He looked up the verses in Nahum, Nehemiah, and Numbers—all books from the Hebrew Bible. And then he turned to C—Chronicles, Colossians, Corinthians. He didn't include every possible verse, although he made note of them in an appendix to his report. He focused on the most likely and added them to his earlier list.

10. The meaning of *N216* and *C109* are likely biblical. Options include:
    a. Nehemiah 2:16 "The rulers didn't know where I went, or what I did. I had not as yet told it to the Jews, nor to the priests, nor to the nobles, nor to the rulers, nor to the rest who did the work."
    b. Numbers 21:6 "Yahweh sent venomous snakes among the people, and they bit the people. Many people of Israel died."
    c. 1 Corinthians 10:9 "Neither let us test the lord, as some of them tested, and perished by the serpents."

Evan pondered the choices. The serpent references were obvious. But the other verse, the one about not telling everyone of Nehemiah's intention to build the wall of Jerusalem, also bore consideration. Perhaps Elizabeth—or her killer—had been deliberately vague with *N216* because she—or he—intended both Nehemiah 2:16 and Numbers 21:6.

He turned away from the computer, picked up his pen, and swiveled it between his thumb and fingers.

His first reluctant thought was that the note was genuine. The only unusual aspects were the choice of paper and that the note had been typed. Maybe, Elizabeth had done so because it was easier to make edits. She would be particular with her words.

He turned once again to his laptop and typed in the phrase from the last line of the note, *God blasts those trees which try to touch the skies.* It was the same line she'd printed on an index card in her office. But Google had nothing to offer.

He leaned back and stared at the high beamed ceiling.

If an attorney were to ask him in a court of law whether he, as a professional semiotician, believed Elizabeth's suicide note to be written by her hand, he'd have to say yes.

He could imagine it. A woman who has lost her only child, who is in a great deal of pain from terminal cancer, decides to make her exit at a day and time of her choosing. She finds a quiet, out-of-the-way spot, leaves a note explaining herself and offering assistance to the powers that be, and takes the same dramatic exit used by her heroine, Cleopatra.

Still, as with the paper and the computer printing, there were things that didn't add up.

The location, for starters. To the best of Evan's knowledge, the place where they'd found Elizabeth's car had nothing to do with her, or her family, or her work. A link with the alderman mentioned in the newspaper, David Bakker, seemed remote. And if she'd been alone, how had she managed the gate? He'd told Addie that Elizabeth didn't let much get in her way. But determination could only take a person so far. Plus, Elizabeth being Elizabeth, if she'd decided to die in a place where some random innocent could find her, she would have apologized in her note for causing a shock.

He turned his mind to homicide. Murderers who'd planned a killing tended to either lure their victim to a remote spot or have a location in mind to leave the body once the dreaded deed was done. While the first requirement for the chosen site might be to minimize the danger of discovery, some killers were deeply particular about their geographic options. Ted Bundy, as just one example, had called his killing fields "sacred ground."

Location mattered.

At a sound from outside, he lifted his head. The wind had risen and now breathed hard against the windowpanes like a fairy-tale wolf, huffing and puffing. He glanced over at Perro, who dozed on, then watched the trees sway for a moment in the outdoor lights before he returned to his work.

If Elizabeth had been murdered, then why—in addition to choosing a risky dumping site—had the killer opted for such a difficult and unpredictable weapon? One that could be wielded *against* him as much as *by* him. One that might not even perform as expected.

Snakebite was poison, and poisoners had their own profiles. They were typically men who targeted older men and women of their own race. Since poisoning required subterfuge, poisoners were often cunning and creative. But they were also socially immature and inclined to take what they wanted.

Snake *handlers* were something else entirely: bold, daring, often adrenaline-fueled types who courted risk.

How to juxtapose these opposing personalities?

He stretched his neck and scratched beneath his chin. The intricacies of the human mind often led a profiler down myriad bewildering paths.

Putting aside serpents for the moment and satisfied that there was nothing more he could take from the note itself, he pulled up and printed his and Elizabeth's email correspondence. There wasn't much, but what little he had he laid out on the table. Next, he emailed himself their entire exchange of texts over the last two years—since he'd moved to Chicago—and sent those to the printer as well.

While Perro rose and circled and resettled, Evan once again leaned over Elizabeth's words and began the laborious work of making a list of similarities between the emails, the texts, and the suicide note, paying close attention to her preferred turns of phrase, her tendency toward formality even in the texts, and her near disdain for abbreviation. Her "linguistic fingerprint"—that is, her way of using written language— was amazingly consistent across all forms of communication.

Another indication that Elizabeth had written the note, even if she hadn't yet intended to use it.

His glance landed on the book from Simon's shop. *The Wilderness of Zin*. He flipped through the prefaces and introductions from various editions to land on T. E. Lawrence's own introduction to his work. T. E. Lawrence apologized for his and Woolley's lack of expertise in Semitics and their need for working in haste—their presence was often required elsewhere.

Elsewhere, Evan was sure, had something to do with the German presence in the region and the looming war. Like Ronen Avraham, T. E. Lawrence was a spy.

On impulse, he dialed the number from the card Avraham had given him. A momentary connection showed on his screen.

"Avraham?" he whispered.

The connection ended.

He startled when a voice sounded behind him.

"Hard at work in the middle of the night?" Christina asked.

He turned. Christina watched him from the doorway; she looked sleepy but was dressed in clothes and coat, a bemused expression on her face.

He went to her. "Did I wake you?"

"Only by your absence. What are you working on?"

"Nothing, really."

But she laughed, glancing past him at the papers, the open laptop. "I can see that it's nothing. I'll let you get back to it. I just missed you when I woke up and decided I'd head on home. I have an early day tomorrow."

"I'm glad you stayed as long as you did," he said. "Dinner tomorrow?"

"The party, remember? I want you to meet a few of my friends and coworkers."

He nodded as if he hadn't completely forgotten. "I can hardly wait."

"You're lying." She trailed a finger through his curls. "Don't worry, they'll love you."

He kissed her fingers. "Are you sure you have to leave right now?"

"Tomorrow, my love. Now get back to work. I'll see myself out." A lingering kiss, then she glided away from him and vanished down the hall.

A bell chimed softly from the laptop, and he turned back toward the library table. The laptop screen now showed an exterior view through one of the cameras the homeowner had installed. It was part of an elaborate security system, and Evan had never asked the owner why she'd gone to such lengths to ensure her privacy and safety. He was certain she had her reasons, and the system had occasionally proved useful, even if it sometimes made him feel like he was living in a gilded cage.

He bent over the laptop.

Sensors had detected a car pulling up to the locked gate. The car was still there, headlights on, engine running. From what he could see, it looked like a dark SUV. But no one rolled down the window to try the intercom.

He couldn't read the license plate through the glare of the headlights.

A shiver made its way down his back. He heard the front door open and close and suddenly knew he didn't want Christina going through that gate after everything Avraham had told him.

He glanced again at the screen. The SUV was still there. He sprinted across the library and down the hallway toward the front door, yearning for longer legs.

"Christina!" he yelled as he flung open the front door.

She'd started the engine of her Lexus. He ran outside barefoot and grabbed the door handle on the passenger side as she was putting the car into gear. She saw him, and with an expression of alarm, hit the brakes. He opened the door.

"I really need you to stay," he told her. From the doorway behind him, Perro added an affirmative bark.

Christina arched a seductive brow. "Why, Dr. Evan Wilding. And I thought your last entrance was dramatic."

~~~~

After Christina had fallen asleep for the second time, Evan returned to the library and the laptop. The camera now showed that the street beyond the gate was empty. All the doors and windows were locked, the security system assuring him with banks of green lights that all was well.

He tried reaching River again, this time at the Crowne Plaza hotel where River's assistant had directed him. He was rewarded with his brother's gravelly voice.

"Evan!" River cried. "It's the middle of the night there. What are you doing?"

"Checking up on you."

"Right. In the middle of the night. Is Mother okay?"

Evan refrained from saying River was more likely to know how their mother was, despite the fact that she and Evan lived only a few states apart. River had always been her favored child.

"She'll outlive us both," Evan said. "Just to spite us. No, I'm calling because I'm wondering if you know a chap who reached out to me."

"Another emergency, I take it." Now there was a smile in River's voice. River, who spent a third of his time chasing bandits and armed looters, another third battling floods, wild animals, and treacherous dealers, and only a third getting any work done. River slept like a dog, ate like a horse, and lived by the maxim *carpe diem*. He always seemed to find it amusing when his big brother got into hot water. Or, compared to River's, more like lukewarm water.

Evan felt the smile in his own voice despite his concerns. "We can hope it's not an emergency."

He told River about Ronen Avraham's visit and Elizabeth's death. He kept certain details to himself, even with River, out of respect for the investigation. But he knew whatever he told his brother would remain between the two of them.

Evan finished with a question. "Do you know Avraham?"

"Never heard of him. He's with the IAA, you say? I did have someone from there stop by a few weeks ago. Name of . . . Hold on, let me see if I've still got his card around here." The sound of drawers opening and closing banged through the connection. Then, "Yup. Guy by the name of Levi Hoffman. Told me he's with the IAA's Unit for the Prevention of Antiquities Looting. He wanted to know if I'd been approached by anyone working for the Veritas Foundation."

"Veritas?" The organization founded by the Kelley family. And the name on the invoices in Elizabeth's desk. "You're sure?"

"Yup, pretty sure. IQ of a hundred and sixty. That's me."

"And have you? Been approached by them?"

"Twice. A French American by the name of Timothée Chablain. Or he called himself French. Didn't have a trace of an accent. Came by eighteen months ago and again last fall. Making the rounds, he said. Told me he was head of acquisitions for Veritas. Dressed like bloody

Indiana Jones, right down to the bullwhip. Put me off before he even opened his mouth."

"What was he looking for?"

"Artifacts related to the biblical world. Said his boss was putting together a museum and wanted artifacts from the land where Abraham lived before being anointed by God. I asked him if he'd ever heard of the UNESCO 1970 Convention."

"What did he say?"

"That of course he'd heard of it. He was just wondering if I knew of artifacts that were sold out of Turkey before 1970. As if. I told him to take a flying leap. You would call him a cheeky bastard. I prefer the more refined term *asshole*."

"You think he was looking to make illegal purchases?"

"I think he would have stolen the ground I was standing on if he'd had a way to take it with him."

They chatted for a few more minutes, River assuring him that he could bloody well take care of himself and not to worry but that Evan should be leery of "this Avraham fellow." Evan then dialed Omar Rasheed's antiquities business in Jerusalem, the one Avraham had told him about. But it was still early there, and no one picked up.

Eyes blurred by fatigue but with his heart at a nice trot—tired but wired—Evan spent more time deep-diving on the Veritas Foundation. He found a year-old *Forbes* interview with William Kelley, the head of Veritas, in which Kelley discussed his dreams of opening a museum to highlight archaeological evidence revealing the literal truth of the Bible. The Moses Museum Evan had read about in the *Tribune*.

Evan appreciated Kelley's goal, even if he questioned the man's ability to succeed. But information he found in other newspapers and magazines alarmed him. He dug up more tales of the sudden run on antiquities fueled by the Kelley family's billions. And a striking lack of concern for origin or provenance.

He closed his laptop. "What were you thinking, Elizabeth?"

When he returned to bed, Christina sensed his presence and turned toward him without waking. He brushed her bare shoulder with his fingers, then closed his eyes, willing sleep.

Whatever Elizabeth had been up to, he had been drawn into it without knowing a single thing about what mysterious treasure she might or might not have found.

He rolled onto his back.

Despite the seeming accuracy of the suicide note, he struggled to believe that she'd chosen to take her final bow. Not yet, anyway. Someone had sent her into the next world prematurely. Someone with access to her computer and her files.

He'd tell Addie to take another look at Leah Zielinski.

A moment later his eyes popped open, the name *Rasheed* circling in his brain. He returned to the library and his laptop, conducted a few searches that concluded with images from Google Maps, then closed the laptop again with a satisfied nod.

Addie would be pleased.

CHAPTER 13

"I think the suicide note is real," Evan said to Addie.

She nodded. "I read your preliminary report this morning."

They sat across from each other at a table near a window at the Wildberry Cafe, two weary death investigators surrounded by the cheery hubbub of chatting diners, clanging cutlery, and cooks calling out, "Order up!"

Because life went on.

Evan had risen at the crack of dawn. He'd checked the cameras, then wakened Christina, who had departed after extracting his promise he'd be at the party. He'd taken Ginny for a quick flight, grabbed a shower, and arrived at the café a few minutes after Addie.

Now, groggy from the short night, he filled Addie's coffee mug and then his own.

"Of course you read it." He smiled an apology.

Addie picked up her coffee, set it back down. Reached for the cream. "It's a thorough report, Evan. I appreciate it."

"Your disappointment suggests you're hoping she was murdered."

"I'm a detective." Addie poured cream until the coffee threatened to overflow. "I like to detect."

"Well, don't give up hope." He wrapped his hands around the coffee mug, drawing solace from the warmth. "Elizabeth's linguistic fingerprint—the way she used written language—is a match between the note and her other correspondence. But there are a few inconsistencies I didn't include in the report because I'm not yet sure what to make of them. The fact that the note was typed, as I've already mentioned. The choice of paper and the oddness of a computer-generated signature. And I don't like her deliberately cryptic reference to what I suspect are Bible verses."

"Why not?"

"I've never known Elizabeth to be unclear."

"I see." Addie pressed her palm to her forehead as if warding off a headache. "So what am I supposed to make of these contradictions? Did she or did she not write the note?"

"I think she wrote it, but she wasn't planning to use it. Not until the cancer got worse."

Addie looked up. "Meaning someone found the note on her computer and added the Bible verses?"

"It's possible, right?"

"Sure. Did you notice a computer in her office?"

"No, but I imagine she carried a laptop back and forth."

"Then I'd guess not many people would have access to it. A narrow pool of suspects makes it risky for a killer."

"Risky like a cobra?"

"There is that."

"I'm also having trouble with the timing. She was close to finding an important artifact. Close enough—and excited enough—that she urged her friend Avraham to fly here from Israel."

"Maybe her search didn't pan out. That's what she implied in her note. It could have been the final blow for a very sick woman."

And finally, a crushing setback in my life's work, Elizabeth had written.

"That could also have been added by her killer," he pointed out.

Addie nodded. But she looked skeptical.

And rightfully so. Why couldn't he accept the idea of Elizabeth's suicide? Were the questions badgering him mere reluctance to accept his friend's defeat? Or was there something in her note that suggested to his subconscious a particular falsehood?

He went on. "Also, the location is an odd choice for Elizabeth, who was deliberate about everything in her life. The lot is semipublic. And insignificant to her. Why would she go there to die?"

"Maybe because we only think it's insignificant?"

He sighed. "Agreed. But one more thing. Knowing Elizabeth, if she'd expected to be found before her body decomposed, she would have included an apology in her note."

Addie's expression shifted from skepticism to pity. "Evan, the one thing we will never be privy to is her mental state. Let's talk about the Bible verses. Why would our theoretical killer have added those?"

"Elizabeth was looking—as far as we know—for biblical texts, which the killer could have been aware of. Or maybe he added the verses because he is himself observant and wanted to let us know that Elizabeth died for her presumed treachery."

"Only we don't know what treachery she committed."

"If we figure that out, maybe we'll have our killer."

Addie topped off her coffee. "Then assuming it wasn't suicide, we're looking for a religiously motivated killer who knew about her search for ancient, secret texts and who had access to her computer. And to a cobra. What about Leah Zielinski?"

"Leah might meet at least two of those conditions. But scholars and dealers both likely visited the institute. Given the size of the egos in this business, any one of them could have felt betrayed."

The waitress came by for their orders, but Addie waved her away. "Give us five." To Evan she said, "I need a minute until the caffeine kicks in."

"Bad night?"

"Bad enough." She added sugar to her coffee, then stirred it and sat back, adjusting the jacket of her charcoal-gray pantsuit. There were faint smudges under her eyes, and she'd parted her hair unevenly. Presumably, she hadn't slept well, either. Had it been Jeff Minzer or the case?

She drank half her coffee, then closed her eyes. Evan adjusted his own jacket—a twenty-year-old tweed thing that he loved and which at least eight women had told him to ditch. Maybe that was why his romantic relationships fell apart. He was too much a bachelor, set in his ways.

"Okay." Addie opened her eyes. "Let's continue."

"I might have cracked the code in her calendar. According to Avraham—"

"You've heard from him?"

"Not a word. But according to what he told me yesterday, Elizabeth had been in touch with an antiquities dealer in Jerusalem named Omar Rasheed. Avraham also said that Rasheed has a grandson in the business here in the US. I ran a search on the name, hoping the grandson is also called Rasheed. There are around three thousand with that name living in the States. Two in Illinois. And only one in Chicago."

"You think that—?" Her phone pinged with a message, and she glanced down. "It's information coming in from the techs. Let me read it, and I'll share."

Evan watched as she read. Detective Adrianne Marie Bisset was, indisputably, his best friend. They laughed at the same jokes, loved the same movies, shared the same interest in art, and only rarely quibbled over each other's taste in music. And always, they had each other's backs. Or—he squirmed—he'd had her back until the last twenty-four hours. Until his concern for Elizabeth had driven him to conceal things. Like his visit to Hassan and the fact that he'd told Avraham of Elizabeth's death. His concern had made him a liar, not to put too fine a point on it.

Addie's fingers flew over her phone's screen as she answered the text.

He noticed how the morning sun caught the auburn flashes in her hair, one long curl falling free to frame the left side of her face. The dimple in her chin. An endearing crease between her lively eyes as she typed.

A sudden heat of shame flushed his skin. What a wretch he was, rising from the bed of one woman and promptly ogling another. If there was a cad hall of fame, he deserved a place in it.

Both liar and fickle lover. What contemptible behavior awaited him next? Worshipping idols? Coveting his neighbor's new sports car? Who knew what nefarious behaviors lay on the slippery slope that led to—say—a sudden urge to host loud, drunken parties?

Addie replaced her phone on the table. "We have an estimate on time of death. Elizabeth died late Monday night or early Tuesday morning. Best guess is between eleven p.m. and one a.m."

He nodded, but it startled him to hear the news. To learn of facts and data points now placed around Elizabeth's death, making her absence more real. Diners at the next table burst into laughter over a shared joke, and he turned to stare out the window at the bright-blue sky. A dog-walking pedestrian paused and turned her face up to the sun, soaking in the warmth and light.

For Elizabeth, there had been only the darkness of night in her final moments.

Addie went on. "Her bladder voided, either at or near the time of death."

He turned back from the window, and again he nodded. Nothing unusual in this.

"But it gets interesting," Addie said. "The crime-scene techs found urine in the passenger seat. Also in the driver's seat, but less. The amount on the driver's side is consistent with transfer stains—the urine on Elizabeth's clothes transferring to the fabric on the seat. That supports a scenario in which Elizabeth relocated to the driver's seat *after* her bladder had voided."

"Meaning she was moved?"

"That's the most logical explanation."

The world shrank until it encompassed only this single fact. "Which means she was murdered."

Addie picked up her coffee. "Again, it's the most logical explanation. She might have even believed her killer was driving her to get help."

"So she moved to the passenger seat . . ."

". . . and he moved her back to the driver's seat after she died. To make it look like suicide."

The waitress returned and took their orders. A stack of banana-coconut-cream-pie pancakes for Addie and strawberry-almond french toast for Evan. He wondered if he could stomach it.

"You okay?" Addie asked after the waitress left.

"Sure."

"That was a stupid question. I'm sorry. Can we circle back to the Rasheed you found in Chicago?"

"Of course." He pushed away the news of Elizabeth's indignity and cleared his throat. "Samad Rasheed lives in the Chicago Lawn suburb. Social media indicates he's young, has a lot of friends, is interested in antiquities, and prefers to be called Sam. Not a lot to go on, but it got me thinking. Maybe *SR* in Elizabeth's calendar stands for Samad Rasheed. If this Sam is in fact Omar's grandson and thus in the antiquities business, it's possible he has a connection to Elizabeth."

Addie gently drummed her fingers on the table. "You're making some big leaps, but let's run with it."

"That allows us to break down the notation in Elizabeth's calendar, 'SR-pMoses I/II STPC.' We're assuming, reasonably, that *pMoses* refers to ancient biblical papyri. *SR* could stand for Sam Rasheed. And if so, then maybe *STPC* is a location. If we assume that Elizabeth wasn't killed where she was found—"

"—because it's hard to imagine her killer luring her to a dirt lot in the middle of the night."

"Or for her to have reason to go there on her own. If we also assume the killer didn't want to drive around the city with a woman dead or dying from a cobra bite, maybe STPC is close to where her body was found."

Addie leaned over the table as Evan pulled up a maps app on his phone and showed her his discovery.

"St. Paul Coptic Orthodox Church," she murmured. "STPC. How far?"

"A mile from where Elizabeth was found."

She looked up from the map. "Any link between Sam Rasheed and St. Paul's?"

"Maybe, maybe not. One thing I could see on Sam's accounts is a picture of him standing next to a sign for DePaul University. The university's Lincoln Park campus is ten minutes from St. Paul's."

"DePaul is a Catholic university. Why would Rasheed, presumably Muslim, attend a Christian school?"

"Your cultural suppositions are showing. If Sam is related to Omar Rasheed of Jerusalem, then he's probably of Palestinian descent. Worldwide, there are nearly one million Palestinian Christians. A sizable proportion of those are Catholic. Ergo, we have a man of Palestinian descent at one of America's largest Catholic universities."

"And a young man interested in antiquities who attends a school near Lawrence's last possible location before her death."

"Do I get a gold star?"

"Let's see what else we can learn about Mr. Samad Rasheed first."

Addie picked up her phone again. After she obtained Rasheed's address from the DMV and learned he drove a white 1999 Toyota Corolla, she checked to make sure he had no outstanding wants or warrants, then asked someone in CPD to check the city cameras for the night Elizabeth was killed. The officer would look at the streets between DePaul University and the church, plus the area around St. Paul's and again near where Elizabeth's body was found. She also sent patrol to check if the young man was currently in class or at his Chicago Lawn address.

The waitress brought their pancakes and french toast while she was on the phone, and when she hung up, Addie dug in. Whether it was the coffee or Evan's news, she looked fully awake now.

"Okay," she said. "Verdict returned. The gold star is official. This is good, Evan." She sighed with pleasure at the food, then poured more coffee for them both. "As for your friend, Ronen Avraham, he's MIA. We're checking flight manifests and hotel registries, but no trace of him so far. And no luck with the Israel Antiquities Authority. They told me they're not in the business of giving out information about their staff. Also, no one is answering the phones at the PEF."

"I have a call in to someone with connections. I'll let you know what I learn."

"Who are you talking about?"

"I'm not talking about anyone."

She rolled her eyes at him. "You and your shadow network." She'd never been impressed by his contacts within the intelligence community. Maybe because the police and the Feds were often unimpressed with each other. "We've got people talking to Lawrence's neighbors and friends—not that she seemed to have a lot of the latter. Mostly what we hear is that she kept to herself. We're waiting for her phone records. Once we can get inside her home and the institute, we'll turn over any computers to forensics and see what they can find. Her note, hopefully, and when it was last edited."

"Any luck reaching her sister?"

Addie nodded and spoke around her last bite of food. "We can release Lawrence's name. Which means the news of her death will be all over the media. But we're holding back the potential cause of death."

"No snake?"

"No snake."

The waitress came by to take their plates and leave the check. Addie insisted on paying.

"If Elizabeth was murdered," she said, placing her credit card on the table, "then in terms of means and opportunity, all we have right now are gaps. Let's talk motive. The Moses papyri. Yesterday you mentioned less-than-honest dealers, looters, and forgers. Are these the kind of people who are capable of murder?"

"You mean outside of the fact that the antiquities business is often a cover for international criminal networks involved in billions of dollars' worth of racketeering? Not to mention a source of funding for terrorism? The legal market was worth forty-five billion dollars last year. That number doesn't even touch the value of the illegal market."

"Oh," Addie said, her fork halfway between the plate and her mouth.

"I'm not suggesting Elizabeth was deliberately working with criminals. But maybe she—and the Moses papyri—got scooped up in something."

He told her what he'd learned about the Veritas Foundation, their purchase of antiquities and their search for a Chicago property where they could build the Moses Museum. And the fact that one of their representatives had come sniffing around River's excavation in Mesopotamia.

"They've gotten in trouble buying millions of dollars' worth of items with unverified provenance," he said. "Some of the items were smuggled into the country under false labels and using go-between countries to circumvent that UNESCO 1970 Convention I mentioned. The one forbidding the removal of artifacts from the country of origin."

"Do you think Veritas could be part of an international criminal network?"

"Maybe not willfully." Evan drank the last of his coffee and rested his hands, palms down, on the table. "What do you know about the owner of the Veritas Foundation, William Kelley?"

"Not enough. I'd like to hear more of what you learned."

He drummed his thumbs against the laminate. "Kelley made his fortune in the food-and-beverage industry, including a growing chain of fast-food restaurants and contracts nationwide with some of the top corporate event planners in the country. He caters business dinners, international conferences, and owns the contract for several large school districts on the East Coast."

Addie nodded her understanding, and Evan continued.

"Outside of the antiquities business, Kelley has never gotten into trouble. He's a happily married family man who claims to live by his Christian values. So maybe describing him as more eager than wise would be reasonable. Of course, his acquisitions people might not be as scrupulous as their boss. River said Timothée Chablain, Kelley's head of acquisitions, was in Turkey sniffing around for biblical artifacts. He didn't seem to care much about provenance."

"People like that give good Christians a bad name," Addie said. "Based on the Veritas invoices in Elizabeth's office, could these questionable sales—willfully illegal or not—be related to her death?"

"If Elizabeth had a lead on something valuable, whether it was the Moses papyri or something else, then Veritas would be very interested in her work. Or maybe she had reasons of her own for questioning some of their acquisitions. I found a letter in Elizabeth's office sent to her by the Minister of Culture and Fine Arts in Cambodia. I didn't read it. But it might give us insight into what kind of work she was doing. After the fall of Pol Pot, Cambodia became a hot spot for self-proclaimed archaeologists who looted artifacts dating from the Khmer regime. Some of our finest museums, including the Metropolitan Museum of Art in New York City, have these artifacts on display. There's been pressure from the Cambodians to return these relics."

"If Lawrence was hassling museums to return the goods, that would make some people unhappy. But murderously unhappy?"

He shrugged. But the thought gave him hope—he wanted Elizabeth to be wearing the white hat in this scenario.

"There's the other elephant in the room," he said. "Although maybe it's more like an aardvark."

"An aardvark?" Addie burst out laughing.

"I'm working on my metaphor. Aardvarks are elephants' distant cousins."

Still laughing, she said, "Okay, what aardvark?"

"That link I mentioned last night—that Elizabeth's body was found in Alderman Bakker's district."

"I think we just went from aardvark to—I don't know—a platypus? Her body had to be found in *someone's* district."

"True." He added cream to the last of his coffee. "And platypuses, just FYI, aren't related to elephants."

She laced her fingers beneath her chin. "You think Alderman Bakker had something to do with her death?"

"I just think we should consider all the facts. It wasn't an easy place to leave a body."

"What does your semiotics say about dirt lots and muraled walls?"

"Nothing. It's just that if the location didn't make for an easy dump, then it had meaning to the killer. He chose a difficult death for Elizabeth. And a location that isn't ideal in terms of either convenience or anonymity. There are messages here."

"Then what are they?"

But he shook his head.

Addie's phone lit up with a string of text messages. She excused herself and thumbed through them. When she looked up again, she wore a smile of satisfaction.

"We got the search warrant for Lawrence's home and the institute," she said, shoving the phone in her purse and reaching for her jacket. "You have enough coffee in you? Let's get rolling."

CHAPTER 14

Evan's phone jangled as he and Perro were about to get into his car. It was Roberto Serrano, his retired CIA contact.

"You have interesting friends," Roberto said. "Aside from me, I mean."

In the bright spring warmth of the crowded Chicago Loop, unease tightened along Evan's spine as if someone had yanked a rope. He froze with his fingers on the door handle.

"What have you got?" he asked.

"I'm not going to name names," Roberto said. "For obvious reasons. Our mutual friend once worked as an archaeologist. But he has no association with the antiquities organization you mentioned."

Meaning Avraham wasn't with the Israel Antiquities Authority.

"According to my contact," Serrano said, "he's a friend to Israelis at the highest echelons. The very highest, if you get my drift. His actual employer is one known to operate as part of a certain agency's bayonet."

The noise from the jostling crowd turned suddenly faint and far away as Evan braced himself against the car.

Bayonet. Roberto meant the Kidon, otherwise known as the tip of the spear—Mossad's assassination unit. A group known for its brazen daylight killings, often conducted deep in enemy territory. Their directive came from the Hebrew Talmud—"If someone comes to kill you, rise up and kill him first."

Evan straightened and glanced around at the pedestrians strolling past, reassuring himself that the world hadn't really turned dark and quiet. "How good is your source?"

"Better than good."

Of course. "Anything else?"

"Is that not enough? You need to watch your back, my friend. And all your other parts."

Perro strained at his leash as a woman walked by, a tall, smartly dressed brunette wearing oversize sunglasses and an air of distraction.

The corgi had good taste.

Evan pivoted to watch the woman as she strode past, her head nodding to whatever she was listening to on her earbuds. Something about her seemed familiar. Or maybe it was only Roberto's words, casting shadows.

Evan said, "Aren't we and the bayonet on the same side?"

"That depends on their agenda."

The woman reached the end of the block and turned north, disappearing around the corner of the Water Tower Place skyscraper. Perro gave up straining at his leash and sat at Evan's feet.

Roberto said, "I thought you were going to rest on your laurels, my friend. Focus on deciphering ancient texts. On your students. I thought you were getting out of this business."

Evan palmed the back of his neck and stared at the empty space where the woman had been. "So did I."

~~~

Forty minutes later, Evan stood with Addie and Patrick in Elizabeth's office at her Chicago Institute of Middle Eastern Antiquities.

"Fork it," Addie said.

They were staring at the historian's empty desk. The books that had been there yesterday—the volumes about turn-of-the-century Brits in

Jerusalem—were gone. So were most of her files, including the invoices and the letter from the Cambodian minister. Gone, too, were her calendar, the congratulatory note from the journal editor, and the PEF quarterlies.

Only the toad remained.

"Damn Friedberg," Patrick muttered. Evan assumed the curse was directed toward a judge who had been in no apparent rush to issue warrants.

"Maybe the thief didn't get everything," Addie said, flexing her gloved hands. "Let's dig deep."

While Addie and Patrick began searching the shelves, Evan recalled Elizabeth's tendency to stuff all kinds of things, important and unimportant, in her pockets. She'd always preferred pockets to purses and had once whipped out a pre-Islamic alabaster votive figurine from a pocket of her cargo pants. He turned to the coat he'd noticed yesterday, still hanging on its peg by the door.

"We need to search her jacket," he said.

Addie replaced the books she'd been peering behind and turned to him.

"She could have gone a week on what she carried around with her," he said.

The pocket on the right yielded tissues, reading glasses, mints, floss, and a compact mirror. The one on the left held a pack of gum, a ballpoint pen, and a crumpled grocery list.

From the lone inside pocket, Addie retrieved a small, unsealed manila envelope. She pulled it free, holding it by the edges, and held it up for Evan and Patrick. Scrawled on the outside in a precise hand were the words *MS? See Finch.*

"Does this notation mean anything to you?" Addie asked Evan.

"Given her field, *MS* is most likely shorthand for *manuscript*. As for the rest, Dr. Allen Finch is the manager of the conservation lab at U of C's Oriental Institute."

Addie held the envelope gingerly. "Could this be one of the Moses papyri?"

Evan shook his head. "She'd never be careless with something so old and valuable."

Addie gently pressed the sides of the envelope until the top gaped open, and then peered inside. She tilted it toward Evan, who leaned in.

The first envelope held a second much older manila envelope, this one creased and brittle with age.

Coiled at the bottom was a scrap of thick leather, blackened and stiff.

He felt the same odd distancing that Roberto's words had elicited. As if the world had gone quiet and dim. He braced himself on the desk. There was no indication, inside or outside the envelope, of what Elizabeth thought the scrap could be, what manuscript it might belong to. But, in detecting as in fisticuffs, you worked with what you had.

He said, "Old Hebrew scrolls were often written on leather, typically from sheep or goat hides. Maybe this scrap *is* related to the Moses papyri."

"You said she wouldn't be that careless," Addie pointed out.

"She wouldn't." Unless she was profoundly desperate. Or in a hurry. Or if the piece was simply meaningless. But then why send it to Finch? Evan frowned at the fragment; from what he could see, the leather looked as though it had taken decades—even centuries—of abuse.

After a moment he shook his head and said, "It's quite odd."

Patrick had abandoned his search and joined them. "What would they test for at a lab?"

"If it's an actual artifact, they'd evaluate it for age. They'd also look for the presence of stains and especially ink to determine if either stain or ink had bled into the cracks in the leather—which would suggest a more recent forgery on an ancient strip of leather."

"You're saying there's writing on there?"

"Impossible to know from our angle."

Patrick reached for it with his gloved hands. "We'll turn it over to our lab."

"No." Evan stepped between the two detectives. "Have you heard of the James Ossuary?"

Patrick didn't lower his hand. "The box presumably holding the bones of Jesus's brother?"

"Yes. The police badly bungled the forensics. The Israel Antiquities Authority finally declared the box a modern forgery. But with the poor forensics, we'll never know the truth of whose bones are in that ossuary."

"Maybe our techs are smarter than their techs," Patrick said. But he'd lowered his hand.

"Our labs won't be able to process this kind of evidence." Addie removed a plastic evidence bag from her purse, filled in a description, and held the bag open. After Evan dropped it in the envelope, she sealed the opening with tape and dated and initialed it. "I've given you custody in your sworn position as a qualified officer of the court," she explained. "The conservation lab is accredited, which means they're approved to hold evidence. Can you deliver this to the university's director and either stand over his shoulder while he does the work or make sure he's intimately familiar with chain of custody before you sign it over to him?"

Evan nodded and slipped the plastic bag into an inside pocket of his canvas jacket. The envelope created an eerie feeling of warmth against his chest. As if it held a message from Elizabeth.

He waited in silent speculation while Addie and Patrick finished their search of the room. Then Addie propped herself against the desk and opened the notes app on her phone. "Yesterday, Polo Shirt stole the journals of the Palestine Exploration Fund from Simon Levair."

"Right," Evan said.

Patrick leaned against the doorjamb and thrust his fists under his arms. The cuff of one sleeve rode up, revealing part of a tattoo—words from a poem by his fellow Irishman, WB Yeats, whom Patrick was fond of. *For the world's more full of weeping than you can understand.*

"And Lawrence of Arabia worked for the PEF as an archaeologist," Addie went on. "They published some of his work."

Evan nodded.

"And," she continued, "Elizabeth was also interested in Lawrence of Arabia."

"According to Leah Zielinski, it was part of the genealogical research she was doing," Evan said. "A possible familial relationship. But if Avraham was telling the truth, Elizabeth was interested in T. E. Lawrence long before she knew of any family connection."

Addie's brow wrinkled. "Dr. Lawrence the archaeologist is following in the footsteps of Lawrence of Arabia, also an archaeologist. Except you've told me he wasn't really an archaeologist."

"If I said that, I wasn't being fair. He *was* an archaeologist. But he was also much more."

"For one thing, he led the Arab revolt against the Ottoman Turks," Patrick said from the doorway. "According to the movie, anyway."

"That's right." Evan stared unseeing at Elizabeth's desk, searching his memory. "Before Lawrence of Arabia *was* Lawrence of Arabia, he was T. E. Lawrence, the illegitimate son of a British baron and a governess mother. He studied at Oxford, then went on his first archaeological expeditions near the border of Turkey and Syria. There, he was recruited by the British military to participate in a so-called archaeological expedition in a part of Israel known as the Wilderness of Zin, or Zion. He spied for the British in the months leading up to war with the Ottoman Empire and the opening salvos of World War One, spending much of his time making military maps. Ultimately, as Patrick said, he encouraged and led the Arab Revolt."

Evan scratched his beard. Archaeology as a smoke screen for spying was a common enough occurrence that sometimes real—and entirely innocent—archaeologists were arrested and tortured as spies.

In truth, spies and archaeologists blended rather well together. There was Lawrence of Arabia and his partner in crime, Leonard Woolley. Gertrude Bell in Egypt. And several others who had worked for the OSS, the forerunner of the CIA.

But it seemed nonsensical to imagine Elizabeth turning to spy craft. And if she were a spy, who was she spying on? And for whom?

As if she'd read his mind, Addie said, "If this Avraham is, as you think, working for Mossad—"

"He is. I heard from my friend."

He watched Addie chew over this bit of information.

"Then, could our Lawrence also have been a spy?" she asked.

"Wait, what?" Patrick pushed up from his slouch in the doorway. "You think that's why this Mossad fellow is interested in her? She was a *spy*?"

Both detectives looked at Evan. He looked at his feet. If Elizabeth had been a spy, it had been the least of her work. Otherwise, she could never have built the institute.

An unpleasant thought drifted across his mind—where had the money for the institute come from? Could Elizabeth have begun spying on illicit dealers and middlemen?

Or—he wanted to turn away from the thought—helping them?

"I don't know," he finally said.

The search of the rest of the institute and then Elizabeth's home proved fruitless. Leah's office contained textbooks, school papers, office supplies, a landline, and an unused memo pad. At Elizabeth's house, they found nothing related to her institute. No files, no paperwork, no envelopes holding mysterious scraps of leather. Elizabeth had left behind a neatly made bed, dishes washed and drying in the side sink, and a coffee machine ready to go for a morning that would never come.

While Patrick left to attend the autopsy, Addie invited Evan to go with her to talk with William Kelley, the head of the Veritas Foundation.

"I had to impress upon Kelley's guard-dog receptionist that when the police want to talk to you, it's good PR to make yourself available." She looked at her watch. "But we're going to be late unless you have some pull with the traffic gods."

Evan and Perro followed her out the door. "Only the kind that brings a harvest of traffic jams and a bounty of red lights."

~~~

The Veritas Foundation was headquartered in an imposing steel-and-glass office building located a few miles from the Chicago River. On the drive over, Addie peppered Evan for more information on Kelley.

Evan expanded on what he'd touched on just before Addie had gotten the call about the search warrants. He summarized the profile he'd read in *Forbes* magazine in which Kelley spoke of a vivid dream he'd had that led him to the idea of a museum dedicated to the first five books of the Bible—Genesis, Exodus, Leviticus, Numbers, and Deuteronomy. Kelley created the Veritas Foundation as a charitable institute whose purpose was to acquire and donate biblical antiquities to his envisioned Moses Museum. He said in the article that an important tenet of his faith was that everyone know that the books of Moses were dictated by God and written down by his prophet.

Addie double-checked the address, then pulled into a parking spot marked **VISITOR** and killed the engine. "Go on," she said.

"Not long after," Evan said, "Kelley announced he was in the market for Old Testament artifacts as well as other relics dating from roughly 2000 BCE to 500 BCE. His announcement has triggered one of the largest artifact grabs in history. The Veritas Foundation bought Egyptian papyri, Persian pottery, Roman glass, ancient oil lamps, and clay jars. Within a year, he'd spent more than ten million dollars and donated everything to his own museum."

Addie snorted and rapped her fingers on the steering wheel. "The tax break had to be sweet. How did all of these acquisitions go over in the antiquities world?"

"A lot of people complained. They said Kelley was careless with how his foundation sourced the artifacts it bought, purchasing forgeries and stolen goods in equal measure. And they weren't wrong—the foundation is in the process of returning a fair amount of what it bought to the rightful owners and discarding known forgeries. There have been a couple of scandals, including the arrest of a renowned scholar who was caught filching from the library of his own institute and selling the goods to Kelley. The scholar was arrested."

Addie's fingers slowed. "Were charges brought against Kelley?"

"No. In a statement, the foundation said it had regretfully trusted the scholar and claimed ignorance of the source of the artifacts. But after that, some of the academics originally hired by the foundation fled."

"Rats from a sinking ship."

"Except the ship is nowhere near sinking."

Addie pulled the key from the ignition and dropped it in her purse. "Still, when Elizabeth agreed to do some work for the foundation— per those conveniently missing invoices—she stepped into a hornet's nest. I'm guessing Veritas wanted to benefit from her reputation. But wouldn't she be risking that very reputation by associating herself with them?"

"Money is a powerful lure. She probably needed funding for her institute. And quite possibly she wanted money for cancer treatments." He looked out the window at the looming structure. Sun glinted off glass and steel. Radio antenna towers rose into the sky. It was impossible not to contrast the megastructure with Elizabeth's converted home on Woodlawn. If he was looking for a metaphor of David and Goliath, it was staring him in the face.

Addie said, "Maybe Elizabeth believed that sometimes you have to sleep with the devil."

~~~~~

A young woman in a pencil skirt and a pale-blue cashmere sweater set greeted them in the lobby. She looked askance at Perro.

"He's a disability dog," Evan explained with a straight face.

She looked again at Evan and flushed. "Of course. I'm Valerie Pellow." She offered her hand to first Addie and then Evan.

She had the fresh-scrubbed, wholesome look that only youth and unbridled optimism could provide. When she smiled—which, Evan would learn, was often—her teeth were perfect pearls set in a pink-lip-sticked mouth. He thought of the goths, hipsters, and punks in his classes and wondered what kind of institution had provided this woman's education.

"Mr. Kelley is on a conference call at the moment," she said. "He has asked me to escort you to his outer office. This way, please."

They trailed after her bouncing ponytail as she led the way through an elegant lobby filled with biblically themed works of art, past a receptionist's desk where Valerie's wholesome male equivalent minded the phones, and into a glass-and-chrome elevator.

"How long have you been with Veritas?" Addie asked as the elevator doors closed.

"Years and years," Valerie said. "Since Mr. Kelley started the foundation six years ago."

Addie's expression turned skeptical. "You would have been, what, fifteen?"

"Fourteen." Her smile deepened, revealing dimples. "My dad and Mr. Kelley are good friends. I did some secretarial work for him. Typing, filing, stuffing envelopes. It was a way for me to make a little money and help the cause."

The elevator came to a smooth stop, and the doors slid open, revealing a long hallway of thick burgundy carpet and paneled walls. Given the thickness of the carpet, Evan kept a careful eye on Perro, who strolled jauntily ahead of him. He should have had him water the bushes outside.

"The cause?" Addie asked. "You mean the foundation?"

"In a way," Valerie said as she led them down the hall. "But the foundation is more than just a business. It's a way of spreading God's word to the world."

She stopped in front of a pair of immense double doors, which she opened and then stepped aside as she waved them through. She gestured for them to have a seat in one of the accent chairs near a mahogany coffee table. The surface of the table held a tidy arrangement of back issues of *Biblical Archaeological Review*, *Biblical World*, and *Dead Sea Discoveries*. A desk guarded another door, beyond which, presumably, sat the man himself. The walls held bookshelves alternating with maps that depicted the world during biblical times. Potted plants added texture.

"Coffee or tea?" Valerie asked. "Sparkling water?"

"Nothing, thank you," Addie said for them both.

"Perfect." Valerie took a seat at the desk outside the double doors and turned her attention to the computer.

"Religion must pay really well," Addie said in a low voice.

"It always has," Evan answered. "There's also the food-and-beverage conglomerate."

"All of humanity's basic needs."

"Together under one roof."

A few minutes later, Valerie stopped typing and stood. "He's ready for you now. Would you like me to puppysit for you?"

"If you wouldn't mind. His name is Perro."

She laughed. "Spanish for *dog*?"

"It seemed appropriate."

She patted Perro's head, and the corgi panted. A blatant Casanova. Valerie straightened and opened the door.

With a backward glance toward Perro, who was making himself comfortable by Valerie's desk, Evan followed Addie inside. Valerie pulled the door closed.

If he'd been impressed with the outer office, he was stunned by the interior. Gone were all the baroque touches from the lobby downstairs and the outer office. The room was clean and airy, decorated in linen whites and browns a designer would likely call desert sand and raw umber. Glass cases, each internally lit, held artifacts that looked rare and expensive and were no doubt thousands of years old. Ceramic urns, floating papyri, a medieval Bible with astonishing gold leaf. An immense map dominated one wall, while a row of windows on the other side revealed a landscape of trees.

At the far end of the rectangular room, a man sat at a desk almost as large as the double doors that guarded the outer entrance. He was large and gangly, the kind of man who would have played center on his high school basketball team. In his midfifties, he had thick silver hair, a healthy-looking tan, and gray eyes. He wore charcoal slacks and a pressed white shirt, the cuffs turned back twice to reveal sinewy forearms and a black-and-silver Cartier watch.

He stood with a smile—more perfect teeth—and walked around the desk, his hand outstretched.

"Good afternoon!" he said in a booming voice that threatened to shake the windows. "I'm Bill."

"It's good of you to make time for us, Mr. Kelley," Addie said, shaking his hand, then showing her badge. "I'm Detective Bissett. And this is Dr. Wilding, an expert witness for Chicago PD."

"Please, call me Bill," Kelley said.

When he took Evan's hand, it was like being gripped by a friendly python—firm and unflinching but with an underlay of coiled power. Evan knew immediately that a smart person would never wish to be on

Kelley's bad side. Which, perversely, made him decide to be as offensive as possible.

"Nice little timepiece you have, Bill," he said.

Kelley glanced at the watch as if he'd forgotten it was there. "A bit fancy for me. But it was a gift from a benefactor."

"It fits well inside this building," Addie said. "Like the moneylenders in the temple."

She'd clearly decided to sidestep tact as well. But Kelley gave a loud laugh.

"It's all about image," he said. "My passion is for God's work, but I'm enough of a businessman to know that appearances are important. If people look at me and believe I have been blessed by God, maybe it will convince them that being close to God is a good thing." He winked, as if they were all in on the joke.

"You're a devotee of the prosperity doctrine?" Evan asked. The "gospel of success" taught that if one was devout and humble before God and did good works in God's name, God would return the favor by bestowing material wealth. It was a uniquely American approach to Christianity. "Didn't Jesus say you cannot serve both God and money?"

Kelley gave him an appraising look. "You're a biblical scholar."

"I have studied the Bible with a more than passing interest."

"Then I commend you. You're absolutely right. No one should serve money. But that doesn't mean a man shouldn't use what money he has to raise up God."

Kelley gave the watch a quick glance, then gestured them toward the saddle-colored leather sofa and chairs beneath the map. "What can I do for you?"

"You're acquainted with Elizabeth Lawrence and the Institute of Middle Eastern Antiquities," Addie said.

A cloud passed over Kelley's face, dimming his iron-gray eyes. "Dear Elizabeth," he murmured. "Valerie heard the news and informed me not even an hour ago. Such a senseless tragedy."

There it was again. *Dear* Elizabeth. Just like Avraham. Evan shifted in his seat. Had there been a side to his friend that every man in her life knew about but him? Or was it condescension for a woman making her way in a man's world?

"I understand she was doing some work for you," Addie continued.

Kelley leaned forward and planted his elbows on his knees. The watch caught the reflection from the lighted display cases and seemed to wink at all of them.

"She did a couple of jobs for us, and we were hoping to bring her on full-time," he said. "A woman of her talents would go far in helping us with our message."

"What do you mean?"

Another glance at his watch. "It isn't enough for me to create this museum and open the doors to people curious about the Bible. Any fool can slap a label on something they believe in and demand that other people believe it as well. We need more than that. We must provide tangible proof for people to hold and study. More, to hold and study with a skeptic's eye. The so-called proof we provide must be honest and valid. My aim is to bring in world-class academics and scholars to study the artifacts acquired by our foundation. Elizabeth was going to be an integral part of that."

Addie typed a quick note on her phone. "She believed in your mission?"

Kelley gave a rueful shake of his head. "Elizabeth was a skeptic's skeptic. She promised to be hard on us. Which is precisely what I wanted."

"And she would do what for you, exactly?"

"You may not be aware, but the foundation has been burned a few times. In our naivete and eagerness, we have occasionally trafficked with the wrong people. We are determined not to make that mistake again. Elizabeth agreed to verify items we are considering purchasing."

"Wouldn't that run counter to her interest in acquiring artifacts for her own institute?" Addie asked.

"Forgive me for saying so, but Elizabeth simply wasn't in our league. She couldn't compete with us in that regard. But to convince her to work with us, we also had an agreement that if we acquired an artifact that didn't serve our story, say an apocryphal text, we'd donate it to her institute."

Evan shifted. "You didn't worry about people seeing artifacts at the institute that didn't support your story of the Bible? Wouldn't that undermine your work?"

"Elizabeth's institute is scholarly. It isn't—or perhaps now *wasn't*—designed to appeal to the masses."

"Meaning you expect many more visitors to your museum," Addie said.

"I do." Kelley adjusted a cuff. "People need tangibles. It's a human weakness. We have the Bible, the very word of God. But for someone to be able to gaze down upon one of the Dead Sea Scrolls, to see with their own eyes a bit of parchment that was perhaps held by someone named in the Bible . . ." His gaze turned inward, reflective. "That is what will help lead people to God."

A deep hush descended. No sounds filtered in from either the rest of the building or the outside world. The relics in the room glowed in the soft lighting, gleaming with the promise to share their stories, reveal their history. To offer a little of the holiness that imbued them.

This space wasn't merely Kelley's office, Evan realized. It was his sanctuary.

Addie had stopped taking notes, but now she picked up her phone again. "What projects did Dr. Lawrence do for the foundation?"

"Three that I recall, although we were going to ask her to handle additional work." Kelley steepled his fingers and tapped them against his lips, thinking. "She verified the provenance on our purchase of four Greek gospels from eleventh-century Constantinople. It was a laborious, painstaking, and expensive process. The other two items were papyri from Egypt. The name of the source eludes me, I'm embarrassed to admit."

At the mention of papyri, Addie looked up from her note-taking.

"Oxyrhynchus," Evan offered.

"That's right." Kelley's gaze settled on Evan. "You're familiar with the collection?"

Evan nodded. Oxyrhynchus was the largest repository of papyri ever discovered. Five thousand documents tallied so far. At least half a million to go. The research on papyri from Oxyrhynchus was what had brought him and Elizabeth together in the first place.

"I did some research back in the day," he said.

Kelley looked interested. "What kind of an expert witness are you? Wait!" He snapped his fingers. "You're the one they call the Sparrow!"

"What about me was your first clue?" Evan asked dryly.

But Kelley said, "Your intelligence."

Evan felt an unexpected rush of warmth for the man.

"I've read about your work at the U of C," Kelley said. "And you helped with the Viking Poet case. *And* the Copper Hills Killer. Wow, wait until I tell my wife. The Sparrow sitting in my office."

Evan flushed as Addie nudged his instep with her shoe, reminding him to stay on topic.

"These papyri that Elizabeth was working on, do they have a name?" Addie asked. "A designation?"

"I'm certain they do." Kelley turned the watch on his wrist, watching as the light bounced off the crystal face. By contrast, the wedding band on his left hand was of plain gold, simple and a bit worn. "Why don't I turn you over to our head of acquisitions, Timothée Chablain? He'll be able to provide more information. And give you a tour of our facilities. Most of our acquisitions are in storage until the museum opens, but we have a small display open to visitors."

"Do you have a catalog of your purchases?" Evan asked.

"Nothing that's currently available to the public. We're still getting organized."

Evan thought of the empty space on Elizabeth's desk. The repair tools nearby. "Would Elizabeth have been meeting someone to take possession of these papyri?"

"Absolutely not. Our artifacts never go off-site."

Addie tapped an additional note into her phone. "Just two more questions, Mr. Kelley. Were any of the pieces Lawrence worked on controversial in any way? Perhaps a concern over the provenance?"

He smiled. "As I said, we've been burned a few times. We're working hard to rectify past mistakes. But although we hoped to bring Elizabeth on board to verify potentially risky purchases, she hadn't yet worked on anything questionable or scandalous. Or even, frankly, significant."

Addie stopped with her fingers poised over her phone, her attitude casual. "Have you heard of the Moses papyri?"

Kelley looked toward the ceiling as if seeking an answer in the recessed lighting, then returned his gaze to Addie. "I don't recall anything specifically labeled 'Moses papyri.' Why?"

The executive looked mildly curious, yet beneath his calm demeanor Evan sensed something more. A faint thrumming under the man's skin. Kelley kept his gaze riveted on Addie as he—ever so slightly—leaned in.

Addie glanced at Evan, perhaps wondering whether to push. Evan dipped his chin.

Addie turned back to Kelley. "You're very sure? Perhaps something mentioned in conversation or captured in a photo somewhere?"

"Hmm." Kelley glanced at his watch. "What are these papyri?"

Addie's face remained blank. "Nothing is coming to mind?"

"I'm afraid not."

Addie tucked away her phone. "If you do recall anything, please give me a call."

"Of course." Kelley stood. The faint humming vanished. If it had been there at all.

Addie and Evan rose as well.

"If we're all done here," Kelley said, "I'll walk you up to Tim's office."

Chapter 15

Evan retrieved Perro from Valerie, who smiled at her boss and Evan and Addie as if she'd cornered the market on sunshine. She offered to escort their visitors upstairs, but Kelley waved her off.

"I'll take them. I need to stretch my legs."

As they headed toward the elevator, Kelley explained that the offices of the employees who worked in acquisitions and collections were, for now, located one floor up from the administrative offices.

"They'll move to the museum once it's built," he said.

"And when is that?" Addie asked.

"We're still working out the details." He gave them a sheepish smile. "At the moment, we don't even know where we're going to end up."

Evan made a leap. "Perhaps in Alderman Bakker's ward?"

"We're hopeful." Kelley's smile held. "Tear down a couple of old buildings, and that mostly empty lot near the Blue Line has a lot of advantages. Progress is progress, although it's a shame to lose those murals."

Addie's expression had darkened. "Not to mention the drawback that Elizabeth was found dead there."

Kelley stopped short. "In David's ward? I hadn't made the connection." His brow creased. "What was she doing there?"

"Do you have any ideas about that?"

"None at all. Did she live near there? You're saying she *died* there?"

"Does that alarm you?" Addie asked.

"It saddens me. It must be a rougher neighborhood than I realized." He bowed his head for a moment. "We'll place a memorial for her in the museum's garden."

Evan couldn't imagine anything Elizabeth would like less. A reminder of her death emblazoned in bronze next to a bed of daffodils.

They continued toward the elevator. But Evan wondered if the Moses Museum's potential future location had any significance for a killer. His mind touched on the idea of a blood offering, then turned away. It was too much of a reach—certainly at this point in the investigation.

On the next floor, they walked past a series of closed doors—storage rooms and a state-of-the-art research and restoration laboratory, Kelley explained before they arrived at the end of the hall, which opened into a large area crowded with cubicles. He paused just inside the room and called out for Chablain. When that yielded no more response than a few heads popping over the cubicle walls and some friendly waves, Kelley switched tactics.

"Mark!" he called. "You around?"

Almost immediately a figure emerged from the maze and offered a mock bow. "Here I am."

"Glad to see someone's at work," Kelley said with a trace of irritation. "This is Detective Bissett and the famous Dr. Wilding. I was going to have Tim show them around. Do you know where our Indiana Jones is?"

Mark was tall and stocky, midthirties, dressed in the universal corporate uniform of khakis and polo shirt. In defiance of his stooped posture and casual garb, the gaze behind his tortoiseshell frames was strikingly intense.

"Nice to meet you," he said. If he was surprised to have a police detective and a dwarf in the building, he didn't show it. "Tim's with his wife at her doctor's appointment."

A shadow crossed Kelley's face. "Poor Angela." He turned to Addie—"Leukemia"—then back to Mark. "Would you mind showing them around?"

"Happy to," Mark said, with the same enthusiasm one would use to schedule a root canal.

"Mark Dawson is our curator of Jewish texts and Tim's right-hand man. He'll do you right."

Kelley clapped the younger man on the shoulder with his thanks, shook hands with Addie and Evan, gave Perro an indulgent smile, and vanished the way they'd come. The room felt de-energized when he left.

Dawson's smile was pained as he watched his boss depart. He appeared to be holding back a sigh. "Anything in particular you want to look at?"

"Whatever you can show us," Addie said. "We're trying to get a feel for the place. Maybe start with your lab?"

"That's off-limits for visitors at the moment. But I can give you a tour of our David Museum, which is usually what we show people who drop by. We call it David because the Moses Museum is going to be our Goliath."

"Sounds great."

"Let me just swing by my office for my phone."

Dawson's cubicle was cluttered with stacks of paperwork, the space impersonal save for two photos. One of Dawson accepting his diploma, the letters *TCU* in the background. And a second photo of him with a woman, presumably a girlfriend or wife, standing near the shore of what looked to be Lake Michigan. The wind had whipped the woman's wavy hair like a veil around them both so that only their sunglasses and radiant smiles were visible—to charming effect.

"Lucky man," Evan said, nodding toward the photograph. His eyes moved to a framed saying that hung from a thumbtack pressed into the soft-sided wall—the only other personal item.

Remember, God blasts those trees which try to touch the skies.

He pointed. "I've seen that before."

Dawson's upper lip curled. "Gift from the boss. Mr. Kelley, I mean, not Tim. Mr. Kelley gives them to everyone on their hiring day. He likes to remind us that we shouldn't overreach. It's easy to do in this field."

Evan wondered if Elizabeth's version of the quote had come from Kelley. If so, why had she merited only an index card instead of a frame?

"Did you know Elizabeth Lawrence?" Addie asked Dawson.

"*Did?*" Dawson gave a startled little jump. "What do you mean?"

Addie and Evan exchanged glances. "I'm sorry, Mr. Dawson. Elizabeth Lawrence died a few days ago."

Dawson sank onto a chair, unmindful of the papers teetering nearby, some of which scattered to the floor. "I knew she had cancer. But I didn't think it was imminent . . . I thought she had months. A year."

"You knew her well?"

"I wouldn't say well. Tim was supposed to be her primary point of contact. But Tim's very busy." This last came out with a flash of anger. "When Dr. Lawrence came by, it was usually me who handled the paperwork. She processed some eleventh-century Greek gospels for us. And two fragments of papyri. My wife was one of her postdocs when Dr. Lawrence was at Harvard Divinity. We'd been meaning to have her over for dinner." His face was pale. "I'm sorry. Can you give me a moment?"

"Of course."

Addie and Evan retreated from his office. Directly across the aisle, a larger cubicle bore the nameplate Tɪᴍᴏᴛʜᴇ́ᴇ Cʜᴀʙʟᴀɪɴ. Unlike Dawson's office, Chablain's held no visible paperwork. Instead, it was crowded with artifacts, presumably replicas, and auction-house catalogs. Like Dawson, he had a photo showing his graduation, his from the famed Université Paris 1 Panthéon-Sorbonne. A framed movie still on the far wall was straight out of *Raiders of the Lost Ark*. Indiana Jones flat on his stomach, staring with an alarmed expression at a rearing cobra.

The snake made Evan's stomach burn.

Behind them, Dawson reemerged. He seemed to have recovered his composure. "Sorry."

"We regret having to bring you bad news," Addie said. "You mentioned you and Elizabeth worked together on some papyri."

A nod. "One was a recipe to treat hangovers. Just shows people never change. But the other fragment was from the Book of Revelation."

Evan was immediately intrigued, not least because this ran counter to what Kelley had told them—that Elizabeth hadn't worked on anything significant. "Papyri from Revelation are quite rare."

"We were fortunate."

"How did you find it?"

Dawson's cheeks turned pink. He looked down, scuffing his shoe along a slight tear in the carpet. "You'd have to ask Tim. It's his baby."

"What about anything labeled the Moses papyri?" Addie asked.

Dawson visibly straightened. "Is it a new discovery?"

"You haven't heard of it?"

He shook his head, already losing interest. "Might be something Tim's working on. You ready to see the David?"

The David Museum occupied the room across the hall—a space that had probably been intended by the architects to serve as another open office area. Subdued lighting—the windows were covered with blackout shades—lent the space a somber cast while thick carpeting absorbed all sound. Glass cases held artifacts arranged chronologically starting in the fifth century anno Domini and working backward to God's call to the seventy-five-year-old Abraham to leave his home and family in modern-day Iraq and venture toward a new land, which God would give him. There were clay vessels from the First Temple period, when King David united and then ruled over the land of Israel. Coins with the image of Caesar Augustus. Bronze daggers from Jerusalem. New Testament papyri. Roman-era perfume bottles and inkwells and a delicate blue vessel labeled TEAR CATCHER. Fifth-century biblical manuscripts.

"It's impressive," Addie said in a subdued voice as they worked their way around the room.

"It's meant to be." Dawson's voice held a note of reluctant pride. "But this is nothing compared to what we'll have on display when the Moses Museum opens."

Evan marveled at what the ability to throw around millions of dollars could do when it came to acquisitions. No wonder Elizabeth had been tempted by Kelley's offer to work for him. It would give her access to treasures she could otherwise only dream of holding.

He paused in front of a three-by-eight-foot display case containing examples of ninth-century BCE Moabite pottery. He jumped when off to his right the door banged open, and a man in khaki pants and shirt barged in on a tide of energy and irritation, his thick hair standing up around his broad, tanned face, his brown eyes flashing sparks.

"Dawson!" he bellowed, then pulled up short when he caught sight of Evan and Addie. "Well, *bonjour!* I'm Timothée Chablain, the head of this collection. And you're . . . ?"

"I'm Detective Bisset with Chicago PD," Addie called as she approached, threading her way through the display cases. "And this is Dr. Wilding from the University of Chicago."

"Ah. Delighted." Chablain strode into the room, trailed by a thirtysomething woman who was dressed more conventionally in a tailored navy suit. Chablain blinked at Evan as if unsure whether to offer his hand, then grasped Addie's as soon as she drew near enough. "Confused . . . but delighted."

"Mr. Dawson was just giving us a tour," Addie said. "Quite impressive."

He beamed. "Isn't it? Wait until you see what we have for our actual museum. *Magnifique!*" Chablain finally decided it was safe to shake

Evan's hand, his large palm swallowing Evan's and pumping with vigor. "University of Chicago? Fabulous. But this Moabite pottery you're looking at? It's a bunch of fakes. A bad purchase from a trusted source. Two weeks after our purchase, I spotted the same damn vessels in an auction catalog. And *those*, I suspect, are the real thing. Damned cheeky."

"And your source?" Evan asked.

"That scoundrel, Chuma Hassan, aka the Egyptian. I'm sure he takes pride in having bamboozled poor Mr. Dawson. Isn't that right, Mark?"

Dawson had joined Addie. His cheeks turned scarlet, but Chablain leaned over to bump a fist lightly into his shoulder. "It happens. You'll improve. Maybe just don't be so eager to take my place. Now, what can I do for you, Detective Bisset and Dr. Wilding?"

The woman standing behind Chablain cleared her throat. "Dr. Chablain, you have a meeting in twenty minutes. And Dr. Felding from Baylor University is on the line."

"Right, right," Chablain said without looking around.

Addie turned to the woman. "And you are?"

Chablain answered. "Sorry. This is Miriam Fuller. My right-hand man. Woman. What's the polite thing to say these days? Right-hand pit bull? It's her job to keep me both honest and on time. And to provide security, should the need arise."

Dawson snorted. Chablain looked wounded.

Fuller tossed a contemptuous expression at Dawson—who tossed it right back—then tipped her chin at Evan and Addie but didn't offer to shake hands. Her smile was utterly without warmth. Evan noticed the white skin around her ring finger. She was newly divorced or had perhaps broken off a long engagement, which could explain the crankiness. She struck Evan as having about her the air of a soldier, one who'd swapped fatigues for a suit but who still carried on the battle.

She said, "Dr. Chablain, you really must—"

"Yes, yes." He'd kept his eyes on Addie while he spoke. His accent was Midwest American other than the occasional word in Parisian-inflected French. "To what do we owe this honor?"

"We're investigating the death of Dr. Elizabeth Lawrence."

For the first time since he'd entered the room, Chablain became perfectly still. "Excuse me?"

"Dr. Lawrence. She was found dead yesterday. We know she did some work for the Veritas Foundation, and we want to see what that involved."

"I see." He swallowed. "This is rather a shock. Was it . . . It must have been the cancer?"

"I'm sorry to be the bearer of bad news, Mr. Chablain. If you can just answer a few questions for us, we'll let you get on with your day."

Dawson interjected. "They want to know about some Moses papyri. And your Revelation text."

"Thank you, Mr. Dawson," Addie said. "We'll lead the discussion."

Chablain blinked rapidly. "Moses papyri? What? I don't know any Moses papyri. Never heard of them."

"And the fragment from the Book of Revelation?" she asked.

Now he smiled, a look that faded when he realized it was inappropriate. "It's a complete text of a third-century Greek copy of Revelation 16:8. About the fourth angel pouring out his bowl and scorching the people."

"Where did you make such an incredible find?" Evan asked.

"All will be revealed when the museum opens. But it's legit, purchased fair and square. All t's crossed and i's dotted, as Bill likes to say."

"And was Elizabeth part of that find?" he pressed.

"Elizabeth? Not at all. She had nothing to do with our discoveries. Her work for us was along administrative lines."

"Then why," Addie interjected, "have her sign a nondisclosure agreement?"

Chablain flapped a hand as if shooing flies. "Standard practice."

"But it isn't," Evan said. "It's extraordinary to ask a scholar to refrain from publishing their work on an artifact. Or even to avoid discussing it."

More shooing of flies. "No, no, no, no. It's merely a formality until the museum opens next year. All our scholars do the same."

Evan pivoted. "Have you ever purchased Cambodian artifacts?"

Chablain stopped waving his hand and peered at Evan. "Why would I do that?"

"Dr. Chablain," Fuller interjected again. If the news of Elizabeth's death affected her, she kept it to herself.

"Yes, yes." Chablain whipped out business cards and handed one each to Addie and Evan. "I really have to go. Call anytime. Poor Elizabeth. Terrible news."

He bustled out, trailed by Miriam Fuller, who gave them a final indecipherable look over her shoulder before disappearing through the door after her boss.

~

Dawson showed them out.

"Did you sign a nondisclosure, Mr. Dawson?" Addie asked as they boarded the elevator.

"We all did."

"And you aren't uncomfortable with that?"

Dawson punched a button for the lobby. "Maybe a little. But I wholeheartedly support Mr. Kelley's dream for his museum—I wouldn't share what I'm learning even if I hadn't signed an NDA. It's better that all of our finds get announced together."

In the ground-floor lobby, among insignias for the building's other occupants, a display case with the Veritas logo caught Evan's attention. This case held a basket of overturned apples. Coiled among the faux fruit was a taxidermized cobra, its hood flared, its tongue caught in midflick. A sign indicated it was a spectacled cobra from India.

"An odd way to advertise the Veritas Foundation," Evan said.

"It's not as if we can put something valuable here in the lobby," Dawson answered. "But this was Tim's idea. It's supposed to be like the original serpent in the garden. It does catch people's attention."

"Chablain doesn't share Indiana Jones's fear of snakes?"

"He says he does. But I think it's just part of his image. Mr. Kelley thought it was a brilliant concept, so here it is."

Dawson leaned in until his forehead almost touched the glass. Man and snake seemed to regard each other for a moment before Dawson stepped away.

"I take it you're not bothered by snakes," Addie said.

"Bothered? No." He shook his head. "I'm not overly afraid of them. But I do detest them. I grew up in the Smoky Mountains of Tennessee, and my parents were Pentecostals. It created a rift between us when I refused, unlike my siblings, to handle rattlers. I know Mark 16:18 says, 'They will take up serpents; and if they drink any deadly thing, it will in no way hurt them.' But I did it once, and that was more than enough."

They walked to the front doors. Sunlight streamed through the glass. Dawson paused in the warmth, lifting his palms as if he were going to photosynthesize.

Addie tipped back her head to study him. "Your Mr. Chablain seems fond of theatrics."

Dawson lowered his hands. "He's flashy, especially with the way he waves around money." Irritation edged his voice. "The work we do here is serious, and it requires serious scholarship. Sometimes that means sacrificing personal ambition for the greater good. It doesn't mean a half-assed effort led by some second-rate movie-star wannabe."

"You believe you'd do a better job as head of acquisitions?"

"On my worst day I'd do a better job than 'Indiana' Chablain."

~~~

As Addie and Evan headed toward her Jeep in the gusting spring wind, Evan spotted a figure made familiar from one of the articles in Elizabeth's vehicle. He nudged Addie.

"David Bakker," he said. "The alderman."

They turned and watched as Bakker—dressed in jeans and sporting a Chicago Cubs baseball cap—disappeared into the building.

"Must be time to hit up the donors." Addie unlocked her SUV, then waited until they were both seated. "You still think there might be a connection between Elizabeth and Bakker?"

"Maybe between Bakker and Kelley. It could be something as simple as a swap—I'll let you build in my ward if you help fund my senate campaign."

"Happens all the time," Addie said. "It's called politics. What's your take on Chablain and Dawson?"

"They might not be mortal enemies, but Chablain is arrogant and overbearing, and Dawson is quiet but proud. He wants Chablain's job."

"What about their relationship with Lawrence?"

"Chablain certainly wasn't torn up by her death. Dawson's relationship with her struck me as more personal."

"And Kelley?"

"Oddly cold," Evan said, thinking of the man's mention of a memorial. "He didn't ask for any details about Elizabeth's death."

Addie pulled out of the parking lot and joined the stream of traffic. "Dawson's wife was her postdoc at Harvard Divinity. And Dawson mentioned they'd wanted to have her join them for dinner."

"Could be he was positioning himself for a job at her institute if it survived its first year."

"Better a big fish in a little pond?"

"No one remembers Indiana Jones's sidekick."

CHAPTER 16

After Addie dropped Evan back at his car and headed out to tackle her investigative to-do list—most especially what she could learn about Samad Rasheed—Evan drove toward the university with the plan to leave Elizabeth's leather fragment at the lab, then try to track down anything that might be labeled "Moses papyri." He found himself checking the rearview mirror, but no black SUVs appeared. Not that he'd be able pick out a tail with the amount of traffic crowding the streets. Babe the Blue Ox could be following him, and he'd never know.

"You ever think of training as a guard dog?" he asked Perro.

The corgi, sprawled in the back seat with his Kong, growled softly.

"Save it for when there's an actual threat," Evan said.

At the university Evan parked, and he and Perro headed into UChicago's Oriental Institute and upstairs to the second floor, where the new wing—*new* being relative, as the addition had been built in the late 1990s—harbored the conservation laboratory. Allen Finch, the lab's manager, was what Evan imagined you would get if you crossed a brilliant scientist with a tank. Finch was built like a Bears linebacker—shoulders broad enough that he practically had to turn sideways to fit through a door. His large head was made even bigger by the shoulder-length locks he wore. His gaze was as penetrating as the business end of the aforementioned tank, while rimless spectacles—which should have softened his expression—only accentuated his intensity.

He'd once said with a rueful laugh that he carried himself like the kind of Black man who made a certain kind of white person cross the street.

As Evan approached the door that led to the warren of labs and offices, a prickling sensation shivered between his shoulder blades, as if he were being watched. He paused and glanced over his shoulder. The hallway held only a few students, all of whom were studying their phones. He watched for another minute, and when none of them spared him so much as a glance, he turned and punched in the access code.

He found Finch in the lab's office, sitting at a desk mounded with paperwork. Evan rapped on the partially opened door and saw a flash of irritation light up the man's eyes before Finch turned and spotted him.

"Sparrow!" he cried, moving to his feet with a grace that belied his bulk. He pumped Evan's hand. "Good to see you, my man. Where are you hiding out these days? It's been weeks. No, months. You haven't visited since you went to see your brother in Turkey. How is River?"

"He's doing well," Evan managed while carefully extracting his fingers from the vise of Finch's grip. The scientist was right—it had been months since Evan had dropped by. And it was a shame. Finch was a great conversationalist. His bull-in-a-china-shop immensity made Evan feel like a graceful whippet in comparison. And the man, an expat like himself, brewed a brilliant pot of tea.

"Good, good," Finch boomed. "Tell River to visit once in a while."

"I do. He never listens to me."

"You're the big brother. You must be firm, Sparrow. Tell him to get his ass to Chicago."

"He swears it's on his list. He just won't tell me how far down it is." He waited while Finch scooped papers off a chair and gestured for him to sit. "How have you been?"

"Busy, as you can see." Finch nodded toward the stacks of papers and the unopened boxes labeled **FRAGILE** and **HANDLE WITH CARE**. He looked around for a place to put the papers and finally set them on the floor behind his desk. "Ever since the powers that be decided it would make us look good to offer our help with the Dead Sea Scrolls, we've been so far behind we can see ourselves coming."

Evan took the newly cleared seat, his heart jumping at Finch's mention of the scrolls. "I hadn't heard about that."

"You shitting me? Like I said, where you been? I figured you'd had a hand in it. I might have used your name in vain a few times."

"The same way I often use yours."

Finch erupted in ringing laughter. "Aren't we a pair of Limeys?"

Evan smiled, enjoying the kinship. "But tell me. Does this project involve Elizabeth Lawrence?"

"Dr. El? Nah. Not that I heard of."

"You're sure?"

Finch narrowed his eyes. "It's my lab. If Dr. El had been working the Dead Sea papyri, I'm pretty sure somebody would have let me in on it."

"Sorry. I'm just . . . at a loss."

The director's gaze turned somber. "I saw Dr. El's name in the paper. Is it true? Is she dead?"

"Three days ago."

Finch's shoulders dropped. "Shame. A good human. A bitch to work with, but still. A great scholar. And a big heart under that stiff upper lip. Heard she was having some financial difficulties."

At least he hadn't called her *dear* Elizabeth. "What did you hear?"

"Oh"—Finch leaned back in his chair, which groaned dangerously—"nothing official. You know the university grapevine. Could have been jealousy for all I know."

"Who brought up Elizabeth's finances with you?"

"Honestly?" He scrubbed his chin with fingers the size of sausages. "Can't remember. So many people in and out of here. Any idea what happened to her?"

"I've been called in by the police. That's as much as I can say."

"She was murdered?" Finch's eyes opened wide behind the flash of his spectacles.

"You ever hear of any work she was involved in that might have attracted the wrong kind of attention?"

"Nah." Finch waved a hand, generating a hurricane-force wind in the office. "It was small stuff, at least what I knew about. She brought in a few items for me to test. Coins. Some medieval parchment."

Evan nodded with satisfaction—if Elizabeth was bringing artifacts for Finch to test, that was a good sign. You didn't take looted items to a world-class lab and expect no one to notice.

Finch seemed to be considering something. "There was one thing, though. And it makes her dying even more of a damn shame."

Evan drew a breath.

"A few weeks back she told me she was getting close to something she was pretty excited about. Excited for Dr. El, I mean. I think she might have even used the word *treasure*. I about had a heart attack—never seen her so wound up. She expected to bring it to me soon."

He released his held breath. "Did this treasure have a name?"

"Not that she shared. Her words, and I remember them clearly, were 'If, after I give it to you, you tell me what I want to hear, then I'll share the rest.'"

"Meaning if you gave her the answers she hoped for, she'd be ready to talk?"

"How I took it."

"She ever mention any Moses papyri?"

Finch pinched the bridge of his nose, then shook his head. "Don't think so. She did say she was considering doing some work for the Veritas Foundation, which surprised me. You've heard of them?"

He nodded. "The Moses Museum."

"That's right. Bunch of bullshit, you ask me. Never expected Elizabeth to be caught up in something like that."

"Do you know what kind of work Elizabeth was doing for them?" Evan asked, figuring it was better to hear the story from multiple sources.

But Finch said, "I don't know that she was. She just mentioned it as a possibility. Desperation makes strange bedfellows, right? So maybe the financial rumors are true. I do know this—she didn't trust their acquisitions guy, bloke by the name of Timothée Chablain."

"How did she know him?"

A shrug, like a whale breeching. "Out of my wheelhouse. They crossed paths somewhere, which isn't surprising. Chablain thinks he's some sort of archaeologist for Jesus. Now me, I'm a believer, don't get me wrong. I was raised in my mum's church. But you've got to keep your personal feelings out of your work if you're going to be a good scholar. Dr. El once told me if you know what you expect to find, then you'll find a way there, whether it's real or not."

Evan nodded. That certainly sounded like the Elizabeth he knew.

"Moving on," he said, "I'm afraid I've brought you more work."

Finch scowled, but Evan could tell that behind the scowl, the man was interested. "Something to do with Dr. El? No, I know. Can't talk. So what have you got?"

Evan extracted the sealed plastic bag and found a place on Finch's desk to set it.

"Okay," Finch said, peering at Addie's scrawled notation.

"The plastic bag is courtesy of Chicago PD. We have to follow chain of custody. Once I sign this over to you, it's either in your possession or it's locked away. And you must be gloved and masked every time you handle it."

"Okay," Finch said again. "Believe it or not, I've actually done this drill before. What's in the manila envelope?"

"A square of leather, possibly very old. And very blackened. It's presumably cut from a larger piece."

Finch picked up the plastic bag. He stared for a moment at the manila envelope inside, grunted, gently squeezed the bit of leather through the packaging, then replaced the bag on his desk. His curious gaze landed on Evan.

"I know Dr. El's handwriting," he said. "She wanted this to come to me. Is this what had her so psyched?"

Evan remained silent and Finch sighed.

"Be that way. You want the usual? Carbon 14 dating? Anything else? Should I analyze stains? You want me to clean off any mold or salts or other gunk?"

"If cleaning will help with your examination, please proceed. Stain analysis would also be appreciated. And an approximate date for the leather would be most helpful. I'd love it if you'd also look for any indications of writing. If there *is* writing, I'll need chemical analysis of the ink."

Finch scratched his chin. "If this piece has turned as black with age as you say, then pulling out any writing will take some real work. But if you want it, you got it. I'll tell you straightaway that if this is part of a scroll, it's a lot thicker than what we usually see. I can tell that by feel."

Evan nodded. He'd noted that as well.

"Okay, then." Finch placed a hand on Evan's shoulder. "Before we both get on to business, can I get you some tea so we can catch up for a few minutes?"

Reluctantly, Evan shook his head. "I've got a full docket today. When do you think you can squeeze this into your schedule?"

"If it's for Dr. El, then I'll jump on it right away. All the prima donnas can wait. It'll be good for them and their Jupiter-size egos. So, let me see. I need time to prep the specimen, and then a few hours to run the C14. Give me a day?"

"It is yours."

Perro began a chorus of barking as soon as he and Evan exited the elevator near Evan's office in the Harper Memorial Library. The corgi almost tripped over his own feet running down the hall. A second later, the door to Evan's office flew open, and a goddess appeared.

Or rather, not a goddess, per se, but Diana Alanis, a mortal woman who closely resembled a deity. Diana was tall and strongly built with brilliant-green eyes, copper-colored hair that fell in torrents to her waist, and a fine and curious mind.

"Diana!" Evan cried, as happy as Perro to see his postdoc. "You're home early."

She grinned at him as she backed out of the doorway and waved him into his own office. "I heard you couldn't manage without me."

"I'm perfectly capable—"

"And Perro!" She dropped to her knees to hug the corgi, who was leaping about in a golden, wriggling blur, his tail generating enough wind for a turbine. "Have you been a good boy? Mama's little angel?"

"He peed on my Berber—"

"It had to be something you did." She stood, the wriggling corgi in her arms. She tucked Perro under her arm as if he were a football. "I know you won't mind keeping him for a few more days. You just have to give him plenty of outside time. And his toys."

"I most certainly do mind . . . ," Evan started. But his voice trailed off as he realized that, despite the rug and the student papers, he'd become slightly—very slightly—fond of the beast.

"It's settled, then." Diana beamed. "I'm back early because my apartment flooded while I was gone. They've got to rip out the carpet and drywall. I'll probably need new furniture. Thank God I took my laptop with me and all my books were up on shelves. Anyway, I'm staying with a friend while the work is being done, and she's allergic to dogs."

"Well, I—"

"Wonderful. Now how can I repay you? Aside from my undying gratitude. You've said before that I make the perfect minion. So, order away."

It didn't take him long to put Diana to work. Since she also had a nondisclosure agreement on file with the Chicago PD, he caught her up on the case, then asked for her help in tracking down the mysterious pMoses I/II.

"We're looking for a possible link between the PEF, Lawrence of Arabia, and the Moses papyri," he said.

"Ah. Because T. E. Lawrence worked in the wilderness where Moses and the Israelites wandered for forty years."

"Right. And Elizabeth and Avraham worked in that same area fifteen years ago. When Avraham and I talked, he kept his cards close to his vest. Claimed he'd never heard of the Moses papyri. But Elizabeth was in and out of Israel. I can't help but wonder if they found something that she later returned for."

"And maybe now that Elizabeth is dead, he's trying to find it."

"Seems suspicious, doesn't it?"

Diana settled Perro in a patch of westering sunlight with one of his puzzles and settled herself with her laptop at her usual desk. She would start with an online search of the Palestine Exploration Fund. With luck, she'd find a digitized repository of their quarterly journals, maybe behind a paywall designed to keep out everyone but academics.

Evan decided to spend the next hour making phone calls, beginning with the thank-you card he'd found on Elizabeth's desk, the one offering hearty congratulations from the editor of the *Journal of Biblical Archaeology*. He wished now he'd read the entire note before it was stolen.

Joshua Holtz answered immediately. After explaining the purpose of his call and sharing the news of Elizabeth's death, Evan asked Holtz if he could tell him why he'd written a note of congratulations to Elizabeth. Holtz explained that Dr. Lawrence was working on two separate finds. Of the first, she would say only that it was currently in Israel and promised him more details soon.

The second discovery contained previously unknown Hebrew texts, which she believed were originally from the Dead Sea area of Jordan, and which were taken out of Jordan before the UNESCO laws went into effect. She said she'd found them in a private collection, and Holtz had leapt to the possibility that they were from the original sale in the 1950s of a few Dead Sea Scrolls, although Elizabeth hadn't specifically said this. She'd offered Holtz little more than a teaser to go with her request to hold a spot in each of his next two quarterly journals.

"How much of a teaser?" Evan asked.

"I hate making guesses," Holtz answered. "But I got the sense the second find might be biblical source texts from the Book of Deuteronomy."

"The fifth book of the Christian Old Testament," Evan murmured. "By source texts, do you mean an early version of the Deuteronomy?"

"Right. Much earlier than what appears in—say—the King James Version of the Bible. These texts are invaluable for the insight they provide on the religious and literary development of the Old Testament."

Evan thought of some of Elizabeth's earlier work on Deuteronomy and found himself nodding. If Elizabeth had, indeed, discovered biblical source texts, they would be worth millions. They would also be a treasure the Veritas Foundation would be eager to have, given that Deuteronomy was one of the five books of Moses.

They would also be a big enough discovery to kill for.

As Holtz continued talking, Evan scribbled *Deuteronomy* on a piece of paper and passed it to Diana. She nodded her understanding—in addition to references to T. E. Lawrence, look in the journals for anything about Deuteronomy.

Immediately after he and Holtz finished, Evan dialed an associate at Harvard. And then another at Princeton and a third at Colorado College. For the next half hour, he phoned colleagues, discreetly inquiring about Elizabeth's work. Whether she'd made any recent discoveries. Whether she had benefactors. It wasn't until the seventh call that he hit pay dirt.

Sara Kalanithi, a research fellow at Stanford's Hoover Institution who'd worked a couple of digs with Elizabeth, hadn't heard of the Moses papyri. But she knew about the money for Elizabeth's institute.

"Theodore Watts," she said. "Elizabeth was handling his entire collection."

"Watts? Why is that name familiar?"

"Theo Watts, the globe-trotting archaeologist? Made his mark in the 1980s and '90s as an artifact-hunting adventurer. He excavated in South America. India. Myanmar in the before-times when it was called Burma. A lot of his stuff landed in museums in the US and Europe. Back then, what he did was called acquisition work. These days we call it looting."

"How did Elizabeth connect with him?"

"She told me once that Theo's main interest was in relics from the Holy Lands. I think he funded some of her digs in Israel a while back. When she started her institute, the plan was for him to donate a large part of his private collection to her. He lives in Illinois somewhere. I think that's partly why she settled in Chicago."

Evan recalled the nearly empty shelves of the institute. "What happened to the plan?"

"A combination of things, from what I heard. Elizabeth got sick. And Theo's health was also failing. I mean, the guy was in his eighties when they connected. One thing I do know is that she was helping him itemize everything in the months before he passed away."

"What happened to the collection?"

"What usually happens in these cases. Theo's heir protested. The trust is hung up in probate."

"When did—?"

"Evan, can I call you right back? A student's been waiting to see me. Give me fifteen."

"Of course," Evan said, and disconnected.

He folded his arms and studied the ceiling.

Theo Watts. Evan pulled up a mental image he didn't even know he had—the man had made the cover of *Time* magazine decades ago. He'd been pictured standing in the rubble of a Khmer temple, holding aloft a broken sandstone bas-relief depicting the Khmer army.

He looked down at the notes he'd scribbled while Sara Kalanithi talked.

It now seemed possible that one of Elizabeth's finds—perhaps the Moses papyri mentioned in her calendar, perhaps something else—was from the Watts collection and that Elizabeth found the ancient texts while conducting an inventory. Her discovery would explain their sudden appearance and would mean that they might be legally available for purchase if they were acquired before the UNESCO decision.

On the other hand, it would be illegal for Elizabeth to take possession of an artifact tied up in litigation. Had she been desperate enough to do so? With the loss of her benefactor and the possible destruction of both their hopes for Theo's collection, was she still determined to have the papyri for her institute?

What if she wasn't *purchasing* the texts? Maybe she'd been meeting someone so she could *sell* the papyri after acquiring them from Theodore Watts before his death and before the heir tied up the rest of the collection in probate. The sale would be legal, and the millions generated by the sale could sustain the institute for a long time.

A great plan until the buyer, instead of handing over the money, killed her.

Evan's phone buzzed. Sara calling him back.

"I've heard some ugly rumors," she said. "About a month ago, not long after Theo died, someone with a connection to one of the big auction houses heard there was questionable stuff coming in. Artifacts of the 'too good to be true' variety. There's also been a few items that popped up online and vanished almost immediately."

"What's the rumor, exactly?"

Sara sighed. "You won't like it any more than I do, Evan. But what I've heard is that Theo's grandson is illegally selling items from the Watts collection to someone with deep pockets and a strong interest in biblical antiquities. And that Elizabeth is—or rather was—helping him so that she could offset expenses she'd incurred with her institute."

Evan closed his eyes. Why would Elizabeth help the heir rob her of what was rightfully hers before the courts had even decided? And to do so merely for a paltry commission?

Unless she thought she'd lose. The rumor, if true, could explain her association with the Moses papyri. She—and maybe Hassan—were the go-betweens, serving as middlemen for the grandson and any potential buyers.

"Where'd you hear the rumor?" he asked.

"Just departmental gossip. That could be all it is."

Unwillingly, Evan recalled the Veritas invoices in Elizabeth's office, where he'd noticed the word *provenance* several times. And, of course, the nondisclosure agreement forbidding Elizabeth from discussing the work she was doing for Veritas. Veritas and their millions to spend on artifacts, legal or not. Perhaps, out of a desperate hope that her institute would survive her death, Elizabeth *had* agreed to serve as broker between the heir and the Veritas foundation. Perhaps even to forge provenance for those artifacts that were acquired illegally by the adventuring Theodore Watts. Forged provenance would make them appear legal and thus more valuable. It meant she'd been working with the very man determined to rob her. But desperation drove people down strange alleys. And a healthy bank account would keep the institute alive.

Another alternative occurred to him. It was possible that someone else was selling artifacts on the heir's behalf and framing Elizabeth. Someone like Hassan, who had a large bank account and a known lack of scruples.

"Anything else you can tell me, Sara?"

"Just one last thing. Elizabeth mentioned something big and important coming from Jerusalem. But I have no idea what it was."

Just as the journal editor, Joshua Holtz, had said—that one of Elizabeth's two finds was in Israel.

Now that was interesting. Due to Israel's lax antiquities laws, Jerusalem was well known as the place where looters could bring their stolen treasures from Israel and neighboring countries to find a buyer.

Was Elizabeth involved in antiquity theft? And was the "big and important" artifact connected in any way to Lawrence of Arabia and the Palestine Exploration Fund?

Was Avraham in Chicago to get it back? One of the articles from the newspapers in Elizabeth's car had quoted the Israeli prime minister, who'd said that his own family had been victimized by art thieves.

After thanking Sara and hanging up, Evan shot off a text to Addie, telling her he had new information and asking if she was available to meet. While he waited for her response, he wandered over to Diana's desk where she had closed her laptop and was pulling on her coat.

"I have an early dinner engagement," she said. "But I'll get back to my research later tonight."

She knelt and hugged a forlorn-looking Perro, then vanished through the doorway, leaving the room empty and silent, the space haunted by what Evan had just learned about Elizabeth and her work.

Evan checked his phone—nothing from Addie. He texted Christina, who told him she was busy with party preparations, that he should invite Addie, and that she would see him in a few hours.

Perro looked up at Evan, his corgi smile gone.

"Why is Christina suggesting I bring Addie?" Evan asked him.

But Perro was silent on the matter.

"What we need, you little bratwurst, is a walk."

Evan grabbed Perro's leash. The dog sprang to life. As they headed for the door, Evan's phone chimed. Addie.

Lots on my end, too. Need a walk, then food. Meet at the pond behind the Lincoln Park Conservatory?

A dose of soothing nature to offset a bewildering day.

Perfect.

TWO—DISCOVERY

"Signs and Symbols in Literature, Culture, and Everyday Use"
Semiotics 300: Social Structures in Language
Dr. Evan Wilding, Professor of Semiotics, Linguistics, and Paleography
at the University of Chicago

Symbols are the shorthand by which humans communicate—across languages, across cultures, even across time and space. From the Paleolithic cave paintings of Lascaux to the extraterrestrial instructions encoded on the records launched into space aboard the Voyager spacecraft, certain forms speak to us. And speak as well, we hope, to lifeforms we can only guess at.

Carl Jung stated that symbols can appear as geometric forms, as animals and plants, or as humans and gods. He called these symbols archetypes, and believed they work by rising up from humanity's collective unconscious to find meaning in an individual's consciousness.

Take the cruciform, a simple figure of two crossed lines that, most commonly, run perpendicular to each other. Today, the cruciform known as the Latin cross is universally recognized as a symbol of Christianity and Christ. But the use of the cruciform dates to the Upper Paleolithic. The ancient Egyptians called it an ankh, and for them it symbolized life. Prehistoric farmers hung a man in effigy on a cross to protect their fields. Ancient Italians also saw the cross as a protector and placed it on their tombs.

In support of Jung's belief in archetypes, the cruciform—whether used by prehistoric humans or affixed to the side of one of today's mega churches—almost always carries a religious or cosmological meaning.

It is ironic that a symbol used to signify spiritual connection and even love also serves—in such physical manifestations known as crux simplex, crux commissa, crux decussata, and crux immissa—as an implement of torture and death.

Interlude

It surprised me to learn of my former beloved's fascination with the little book I'd found in Jerusalem.

This woman threw herself into the search for the "lost treasure of Jordan." She befriended people, whispered supposed secrets, and stirred resentment between those who'd long considered themselves friends and colleagues. She reasoned that if love no longer fortified our day-to-day interactions, then she and I could bond over the hunt. And, once successful, we would go our separate ways. After we split the glory and the cash.

People tend to think these false gods matter to me.

The scholar in me doubted that this so-called treasure had ever existed. But I remain vigilant. Heretical texts are everywhere; they pop up like mushrooms in the dark, dank mud of ignorance. They must be destroyed.

Thus, I did what I had to during my own careful search. Instructions came to me in dreams, and I arranged the necessary tools and artifices so that I could follow those directions. I used who I had to. And eliminated those whose actions had betrayed God.

Whatever the truth about the treasure, I couldn't shake the feeling I'd been guided to the book with its serpent cover. So I read the little volume—one might say—religiously. The author was given to rambling sentences and long-winded paragraphs that circled back on themselves without adding so much as a flicker of insight or tidbit of useful information. But I needed to understand the mind of the heretic who had created the ancient text. I needed to understand what drove men to commit sacrilege. And what sometimes urged them into acts of treachery.

I had been chosen to respond to these evils; ergo, I needed to understand them.

Night after night, sitting out on the deck or at my desk—a dead, dull-eyed toad my sole companion—I read, allowing myself only a few paragraphs.

Jerusalem, Christian Quarter, July 1878.

Sheik Mahmoud Erekat and his Arab entourage entered the tourist shop and strode past the wares—postcards, guidebooks, Bibles, assorted souvenirs of the Holy Land—and found the shopkeeper at his desk. The sheik, knowing the shopkeeper's interests, had come to tell him of some blackened leather strips that had come to his attention. Strips with undeciphered writing that had been found at Wadi Mujib near the Dead Sea.

The shopkeeper raised his head. "Yes," he said. "I am very interested in these strips."

Over the course of weeks, the shopkeeper—with the help of his friend the sheik—acquired fifteen of these leather strips before the sheik died suddenly and the shopkeeper lost contact with the Bedouin who had owned the strips.

Fifteen strips—fifteen small scrolls—were all he had,
and they would have to be enough.

I closed the book, the anger that had begun in Jerusalem sparking through my veins like lightning. Tonight, as on other nights, I heard my mother's voice, whispering in my ear as she had done when I was a child.

You're mad, she said. *Cracked, like a broken jar. They say it's only going to get worse.*

What would I say to her now? That the cracks let in the light.

CHAPTER 17

Evan found Addie standing at the edge of the quiet pond in Lincoln Park. Even from fifteen feet away he picked up her energy, the bulldog tenacity that hummed through her.

A detective on the hunt.

She looked up at the sound of Perro's dog tags, spotted Evan, glanced briefly past him, then dove right in.

"Was Lawrence doing something illegal?" she asked as he approached.

He stopped and considered his answer while Perro nosed about in the bushes.

"Maybe," he finally said.

She nodded as if he'd confirmed something. "Shall we walk?"

They strolled along the dirt path that circled the pond. The sun had just set. In the blue hush of twilight, the path shone palely in the dark gathering under the trees.

Addie switched on a headlamp, its band wrapped around her wrist, and told him about her day, ticking off items one by one.

Lawrence had, indeed, died from the bite of the cobra found in her car. They'd confirmed it was same cobra, thanks to Yaa Mensah's tests. The medical examiner could not yet rule whether the manner of death was suicide or homicide. They were still waiting on toxicology.

Evan processed the information. "Were there any surprises?"

"A few." Addie clicked the headlamp onto its brightest setting. Shadows jumped among the trees. "The ME confirmed the presence of puncture wounds from the bite. Which wasn't a surprise, of course. But she also detected a bruise on the back of her thigh."

"From being dragged into the driver's seat?"

"That's our current theory. The bruise on her thigh matches what we'd expect to see from her car's console. Additionally, there was a contusion on her scalp, which could have come from her thrashing about in the car, either to escape the cobra or her killer."

"No bruising that suggests she was restrained?"

"No. But based on what Yaa Mensah told us—that Elizabeth would have been quickly immobilized—it might not have been necessary. Especially if she believed her murderer was helping her."

So many unanswered and perhaps unanswerable questions. He wanted to close his eyes against the images playing like a movie in front of him—Elizabeth fighting for her life. And losing.

Addie went on with the details of her day.

Lawrence's phone records showed that other than a few take-out restaurants and her sister, she had called the following people: Evan; an antiquities dealer named Chuma Hassan; Samad Rasheed; and three numbers in Israel, two of which had been disconnected. The third Israeli number was to an antiquities dealer in Jerusalem, a man named Omar Rasheed—presumably the same man Evan had mentioned to Addie over breakfast. Rasheed hadn't returned her phone calls.

Samad—or Sam—remained elusive. He hadn't been in class all week, not since the night of Elizabeth's death. He didn't answer his phone or his door. Friends claimed to know nothing about where he might be. But her cop sense suggested that they weren't being entirely honest.

"We also dug into his social media activity," she said. "There's a photo of him standing outside Hassan's Galleries Extraordinaire. And a post in which he complains about having to work nights. I have an appointment with Mr. Hassan first thing tomorrow. In the meantime, we've issued an investigative alert for Sam. And we have someone checking his apartment periodically. His professors have agreed to contact us if he shows up."

She continued her summary. Lawrence's financial records suggested that she wasn't in debt—the building that held the institute was paid for, and money had been put aside in a separate account for taxes, insurance, and overhead. There was $5,000 and change in the institute's checking account, $7,000 in her personal accounts. Certainly, there didn't appear to be the kind of money required to pay for two-thousand-year-old texts, assuming that was what the Moses papyri were. And no recent large withdrawals or deposits.

"That's what we know about her finances at the moment," she said. "Our fraud people are digging deeper, looking for investments and pensions."

She went on to say they'd spoken with Ralph Raines, the attorney mentioned in Lawrence's note. It had come as a surprise to learn that Raines was no longer Lawrence's attorney. And no, he didn't know whom she'd transferred to beyond it being "some Asian chick." His secretary had handled the transfer. She and Patrick would learn the new attorney's name tomorrow.

"Another reason to believe that it wasn't Elizabeth who left the suicide note in her car," Evan said.

"Right," Addie agreed.

She continued. Theodore Watts was the name of Lawrence's benefactor—here, Evan nodded—and Raines was also Watts's attorney. Putting aside the fact that Lawrence had fired Raines, it wasn't an unexpected arrangement to have both parties to a trust share an attorney. Elizabeth had been Watts's power of attorney, and she and Raines had been directed by Watts to create a trust to hold his collection. Lawrence was the trustee; her institute was the beneficiary. According to Raines, the grandson was now contesting the trust based on Elizabeth having had undue influence over his grandfather.

As Addie spoke, Evan's gloom deepened. It wasn't unheard of for collectors—and antiquities collectors in particular—to secrete their ill-gotten goods inside trusts in the hopes that the Feds wouldn't sniff out any illegal assets.

Addie touched his hand. A familiar tingling started there, as it always did when her skin met his. Would he ever get over his crush on her?

"Is it worse for you, or better?" she asked. "About Lawrence."

"What do you mean?"

"That she was almost certainly murdered, rather than taking her own life."

Evan's breath escaped him in one deep sigh. The devil and the deep-blue sea. What could you possibly prefer for someone you cared about? That they lived their final moments in abject terror? Or in a blackness so profound that death felt like the only answer?

"I need to process it," he said.

She nodded her understanding. "Your turn to talk."

He told her what he'd learned that afternoon. About Elizabeth's plan to publish articles on two separate finds—one discovery currently in Israel, the other consisting of allegedly unknown texts from the Dead Sea area of Jordan. That he, too, had learned the name of her benefactor, Theodore Watts, and that the man's reputation wasn't entirely on the up-and-up. He also told her the rumor that Watts's grandson was selling off items that were supposedly being held in litigation.

"The buzz is that the buyer is someone with deep pockets and a great love of biblical antiquities," he said.

"Someone like the Veritas Foundation?"

"It's possible. We've heard Chablain isn't overly picky about his sources. But that description—wealthy, interested, and not overly concerned with provenance—could fit any number of collectors. And I suppose we also have to consider the possibility that Elizabeth was a player in those sales, maybe in conjunction with Hassan."

"Which puts us back to my original question. Do you think it's possible?"

"Based on what I know about Elizabeth, no. But people change. They especially change when death is imminent. She might have been motivated if she knew that the grandson was going to take what she thought of as rightfully hers."

"Do you have any thoughts about where the collection is?"

"As far as I know," Evan said, "as soon as the grandson contested the trust, the court would have issued an injunction that the items were to be held in a safe place under lock and key. But where that might be, I have no idea."

Addie stopped him with a hand on his arm. She flicked off her headlamp, pressed a finger to her lips, and pulled him off the trail. Evan dragged Perro into the bushes with them.

Addie leaned down to whisper in his ear. "I noticed a man walking behind you when you arrived. He saw me and veered away. But just now I heard footsteps."

Evan strained to listen. The only sound he caught was the breeze as it rattled the budding branches and murmured over the nearby grass. He hadn't realized how dark it had gotten.

Then Addie's grip tightened, and he heard what she must have.

A scuff of feet on the path.

Addie let go of him and called out, "Police! Show yourself."

Silence. Then the footsteps again, this time receding rapidly. Addie flicked on the light and told Evan to wait. Before he could protest, she'd started down the path at a run.

"Addie," he called after her, feeling helpless.

Within seconds, her footsteps faded. Evan strained to hear anything beyond the hum of far-off evening traffic. The breeze continued its clattering journey through the trees. A woman's laugh—faint and high—carried across the night from the opposite direction in which Addie had disappeared.

Evan jumped when Perro lifted his head from the tree trunk he'd been diligently watering. The corgi sniffed the air.

"What is it?" Evan whispered.

Somewhere, a scraping sound.

Perro offered a low growl. It occurred to Evan that whoever had been behind them on the path could have circled around. He cast about for a weapon, but the landscapers had been vigilant in their duty; not so much as a twig offered itself for his defense.

Perro barked, and Evan cried out as something small and fast hurtled from the trees and sped past. Perro lunged, nearly jerking his leash free from Evan's grasp.

The fleeing creature hit the path, and Evan made out the bushy tail of a squirrel.

"God's wounds, dog," Evan spat.

He yanked on Perro's leash, adrenaline making him pull hard enough to cause Perro to yelp in protest.

"We're hunting murderers," he whisper-shouted. "Not puffy-tailed tree rats."

Moments later, a car engine started. Tires squealed, and the headlights of a vehicle flashed through the trees and vanished as the car sped away.

Addie reappeared at his side, breathing hard.

"Missed him," she said. "But I spotted a black SUV peeling out. Couldn't catch the plate."

Evan shivered in the night's chill. The darkness suddenly felt very dark indeed.

"What do you say to bright lights and pizza?" he asked.

~~~

"He wasn't a big man," Addie said as they sat at a table with their slices of Chicago-style pepperoni and a pitcher of beer. "Under six feet, maybe a hundred and sixty. He had a thick beard."

"Not Polo Shirt, then. And not Ronen Avraham."

"You've heard nothing from your Israeli friend?"

"No. And when I call, all I get is a computer-generated voice mail. You know what I'd give my eyeteeth for?"

"The Moses papyri?"

"Those. But also an inventory of the Watts collection. If that's what Elizabeth was working on, then it must exist somewhere."

Addie's phone buzzed. She turned toward the wall, pressed the phone to her cheek, and stuck a finger in her other ear. Now she nodded a few times, murmured her thanks, and hung up.

"That was my financial-crimes guy," she said. "He tells me that a man named Gerrit Watts is Theodore Watts's grandson and that Gerrit has retained one of the attorneys in the same firm Ralph Raines belongs to. Looks a little suspicious, don't you think?"

"Not to mention unethical. Maybe that's why Elizabeth left." He plucked a slice of pepperoni off his pizza and passed it down to Perro.

Addie took the last bite of her slice, licked her fingers, then collapsed back in the chair. "Maybe we should go bother William Kelley again."

Evan glanced at his watch. "Not unless you want to face him down in his home."

"Don't tempt me. What about Hassan? His name keeps cropping up. He knew and maybe worked with Lawrence. Chablain claimed to have worked with him. Sam Rasheed photographed himself standing in front of Hassan's business. Maybe I shouldn't wait until tomorrow to talk to this guy."

"For what it's worth, I've heard Hassan keeps odd hours."

She'd been scrolling through her phone and now held the screen up for Evan to see. "Look at these baskets on Hassan's website. Round ones with conical lids. Just like the one in Lawrence's car."

Evan squinted at the screen. "I'm thinking we should get backup."

"I'll get patrol to meet us there." Her eyes had regained their sparkle. "Maybe we'll catch a break."

Lights shone through Hassan's office windows.

When the patrol car arrived, Addie asked the officers to wait just outside the doors unless they were needed. She didn't want to spook Hassan. Not yet.

The same luxurious lobby greeted their arrival. And the same receptionist—Rana—rose to greet them. She'd traded in the yellow headscarf for one in pale pink.

She smiled warmly at Evan. "You and Perro are back. And you brought a friend."

"Not your first time here?" Addie asked without looking at him.

He felt her anger, and his face turned hot. "Scouting mission," he murmured as he returned Rana's smile. "Is Mr. Hassan in? We have a matter to discuss with him."

"Mr. Hassan is here." Rana said. "But he has asked not to be disturbed unless the matter is urgent."

Addie held up her badge. "Consider it urgent."

Rana's eyes widened for the briefest of instants. "I'll tell Mr. Hassan you're here." She reached for the phone on her desk, but Addie stopped her.

"Please just show us to wherever he is."

Rana frowned but said, "Follow me."

At the door to Hassan's office, Rana rapped gently. When that got no response, she knocked more loudly. "Mr. Hassan!" she called through the door. "Sir!"

A loud growl started deep in Perro's chest. Evan glanced down at the corgi, who ended his growl with a single sharp bark.

"Let's go on in," Addie said.

Rana twisted the knob, but it was locked. She removed a small set of keys from her pocket and opened the door. She walked in, gave a cry, and fell back against the door.

Addie stepped around her, Evan and Perro following.

Chuma Hassan lay sprawled on the floor, his arms flung out as if he longed for an embrace. His open eyes studied the ceiling, and for the briefest of moments Evan thought the Egyptian was practicing a Middle Eastern form of meditation. Then he saw the blood pooling on the carpet beneath Hassan's bald scalp. And the apparent murder weapon on the floor next to him—a bronze statue of the Egyptian god, Aten, which Evan remembered seeing on his previous visit.

Balanced precariously on Hassan's generous stomach was a scrap of paper. Someone had scrawled **P119158** on it in black ink.

"Damn it," Addie said, dispensing one of her few curses.

Perro barked again, and an unfamiliar voice rose behind them. "The hell is going on?"

Evan turned and was greeted with the furious face of the woman he had spotted twice before. Once, when she'd been sitting at the bar at Boonoon's, taking notes on a legal pad. The second time when she'd walked past him and Addie at the Wildberry Café. She still wore the white earbuds.

"Who are you?" Addie demanded.

The woman held up a badge. "Homeland Security Investigations Special Agent Clarise Holliday. I'm with the Cultural Property, Arts, and Antiquities Unit." Her hard stare took in the Egyptian's corpse and rose to meet Addie's own glare.

Probably not earbuds, Evan realized in a detached part of his mind. Encrypted earpieces designed to look that way.

"What are you doing here?" Addie asked.

The woman gestured for Rana to leave the room. When the sobbing receptionist complied, pulling the door closed behind her, Holliday turned on Addie.

"I'm trying to capture the bad guys, Detective Bisset. But you have ruined months of my work and that of the Manhattan district attorney's antiquities trafficking unit. Not to mention what you've done to poor Mr. Hassan."

"We're hardly guilty of murder," Evan said.

Holliday whirled on him. "You have come dangerously close to destroying everything. And you should know that your sanctimonious Elizabeth Lawrence was the real criminal in all this. No better than the looters. Worse, actually. At least she had a choice."

"I don't believe you."

"I don't care what you believe, Dr. Wilding. Stay away from this investigation. Stop asking questions and keep your nose clean. It's vitally important. Do you understand?"

Her gaze locked on his, and Evan struggled to read the agent's expression. Beneath the clear anger he sensed another message. But he couldn't tell what it was or even if it was intended for him.

"Now"—Holliday tipped her head toward the door—"go."

"Wait," Addie snapped at Evan before spinning back to Holliday. "You have no authority to order him out. He's employed by Chicago PD."

"I don't care if the sainted Mother Mary brought him in. He's a civilian. A civilian who had a relationship with both victims. He does not get to stay at the crime scene."

Evan raised a hand. "It might be helpful if—"

Holliday raised a hand of her own. "Out."

With an apologetic look at Addie, Evan retreated. As he opened the door and slipped out, he heard Holliday's voice raised once again and Addie's words lifted in argument. But by then he was out in the hall and standing next to the weeping Rana. He took her back to her desk, fetched her some water, let her pet Perro for a few minutes, then left her in the capable hands of the female patrol officer who had come as backup.

~~~

Outside, the night had turned bitter. Evan stood to the side of the office building's main doors with Perro and watched as emergency vehicles arrived and the "three-ring circus in blue"—Addie's term—kicked into gear. After a time, he clicked his tongue at Perro, and they moved down the street until he found another set of stairs with far less activity. He settled himself on the broad granite steps and huddled into his coat while Perro snuggled next to him. Soft light from the building pooled around them.

Two people dead—one by cobra bite, the other by the bronze statue of a long-vanquished Egyptian sun god, Aten, who had briefly held sway over the Egyptians.

Compartmentalize, Evan told himself. He turned away from the image of Hassan's broken skull and focused on the killer's choice of weapon. He might believe the choice was mere expediency, except that he'd noted the statue when he'd been in Hassan's office the day before; then, the bronze Aten had been located high on a shelf and far from where Hassan's corpse now lay.

It hadn't been a weapon of convenience.

Many, perhaps most, Egyptians had refused to accept the sun god Aten as their supreme deity when instructed to do so during the reign of Pharaoh Akhenaten more than thirteen hundred years before Christ. After the pharaoh's death, Aten had been dethroned. Some among the Egyptian elite considered the pharaoh a traitor for daring to raise his own god above all others.

Evan tipped his head back to gaze at a cloudy sky transformed into a reflective pink by the city lights.

And what of the scrawled alphanumerics written on a piece of paper and left on Hassan's body? P119158. Presumably another Bible verse. There were seven books in the Bible that began with the letter *P,* but after a quick search on his phone, Evan suspected the killer referred to Psalm 119158 in the Hebrew Bible.

"I look at the faithless with loathing, because they don't observe your word."

Hassan had betrayed someone. Perhaps, in the killer's mind, Elizabeth had as well. The serpent, after all, was the representation of treachery in Christianity.

He fired off a text to Addie with his thoughts but received no reply. She had a murder investigation to run and now a federal agent to manage.

The stone steps seeped cold through his jeans. His white trainers glowed like phosphorescence in the soft light. The only warm part of him was where Perro lay pressed against his thigh.

Down the street, away from Hassan's office, a group of drunken men lurched along the sidewalk. One of them spotted Evan and pointed. The entire group swung around to view the spectacle of a dwarf sitting in solitary gloom. One of the men headed toward him, and Perro jumped up with a growl.

But the man's friends pulled him back. *What sport in menacing a dwarf?* he imagined them saying. After a brief argument, they continued their weaving way toward another tavern.

Evan watched them vanish down the street with an odd detachment from the world and his own safety. When a form separated itself from the shadows and glided in, he barely stirred himself. Perro didn't react at all.

"Evening," said Ronen Avraham.

Evan didn't bother responding.

"Hassan is dead?" Avraham asked.

Now Evan turned to look at the Israeli. Avraham's face was drawn, his eyes shadowed. In deference to the chill, he'd traded the suit coat for a leather jacket.

"Was it you who made him that way?" Evan asked.

Avraham reached into his jacket and pulled out a pack of Marlboros. He tapped one out, then offered the pack to Evan. Cigarettes had never caught on with Evan the way they had with his classmates at Oxford. But tonight, it seemed like a damn good idea.

Avraham lit Evan's cigarette, then his own. For a few minutes, they smoked silently, the air swirling the burned aroma around their heads.

Finally, Avraham said, "Hassan was as crooked as they come, despite what you might hear in the coming days from Homeland Security agents. He played both ends against the middle every chance he got, robbing the other thieves and fleecing ignorant buyers."

"One of whom, presumably, figured this out."

Avraham didn't take the bait. He said, "I can't agree that being a thief deserves a death sentence. Especially given that most of his victims were guilty of the same charge. And probably worse things. But in the antiquities business, the most horrific violence is usually confined to the lower levels. By the time a deal rises to Hassan's level, it has turned into white-collar crime. Laundering, lying, forging provenance. Hassan's death—and Elizabeth's—they don't fit the pattern."

"Where *is* Elizabeth in all of this? Did she steal the Moses papyri? Was she forging provenance for them? And don't tell me you haven't heard of them. When I asked before, your answer should have made your nose lengthen like Pinocchio's."

Avraham gave a dry chuckle. "I'm losing my touch. You're right. I do know about the Moses papyri."

"And?"

"They're fakes, Dr. Wilding."

"Say what?"

"They're brilliant forgeries. Modeled on Hebrew texts Elizabeth and I first spotted years ago in the Jordanian desert, and expertly copied from looted papyri that recently arrived at the offices of the Israel Antiquities Authority."

"If they're fakes, then what was Elizabeth—?"

"It was a sting."

Evan sat up straight, the cigarette smoldering between his fingers. "Come again?"

"It was Elizabeth's idea. She was tired of the greed and theft, the plundering and destruction. Antiquities theft is as old as civilization. But the way it funds terrorism and violent racketeering has reached catastrophic levels. So when Elizabeth learned from Omar Rasheed that a pair of exceedingly rare and unprovenanced texts had appeared in the underground antiquities market in Jerusalem, ancient texts from Jordan, she decided she'd had enough. As soon as we learned the thieves had been in touch with Hassan, we intercepted the texts, made duplicates of them, then slipped them back on the market."

"How did you manage to intercept them without tipping your hand?"

"We have secret sources and hidden ways. The originals are now safely stored with the IAA. Elizabeth and I, along with a few others, were determined to shine a light on a criminal network responsible for tens of millions in artifact thefts. The network's supply line ran from the looters in Israel and Jordan to dealers like Hassan, and end buyers in New York, Chicago, and elsewhere. We wanted to expose all of them."

Evan thought of Mossad's former motto: "By way of deception, thou shalt make war." He said, "You'd nail everyone by tempting them with a two-thousand-year-old biblical text. Who would say no?"

Avraham lit a second cigarette from his first and pocketed the stub. "We allowed the forged papyri to appear on the market in Jerusalem, then sent them here, to Chicago. The scrolls passed through the hands of several of Hassan's associates, who are part of a damn impressive criminal network, then ultimately to him. The plan was for Elizabeth to launder the papyri by pretending to authenticate them, then create a provenance so that Hassan could sell the artifacts to gullible—or willfully ignorant—buyers like Veritas. Once the sale went through, we'd step in, nabbing everyone who handled the papyri, from the first dealers, through Hassan, and on to the buyer."

"You said these texts resembled ones you'd seen."

"On our first trip together in the Negev. We crossed into Jordan."

"Illegally."

Avraham took a long drag. "The past, Elizabeth told me, has no borders. She had a theory about what we might find near Wadi Mujib."

"Not that you were overly concerned, I suspect, with legalities. Starting with the fact you have no right to run an operation on American soil."

"I'm not. I never was. I'm here merely as an archaeologist temporarily working for the IAA. It was all Elizabeth. We didn't have time to arrange for more or to pull in anyone else. Once the papyri appeared on the market and the looter contacted Hassan's associates, we had to move fast to insert Elizabeth into the plan. We planned to come clean to the authorities once we had our buyer. Or buyers, plural. Then Homeland Security's antiquities agents could swoop in and make the arrests. Our actions would force the US Feds to acknowledge what Hassan and Veritas are up to. And expose others in Hassan's network who have been operating without restraint."

Which meant that, in her own way, Elizabeth *had* been a spy. Just like her hero.

"Why would Hassan believe Elizabeth?" he asked. "She always spoke out against the illicit trade."

"We spread the rumor that she was having financial difficulties. After Theodore Watts's heir contested the trust his grandfather created, it was no longer a lie."

Evan remembered what Finch had said. And Sara Kalanithi. The gossip about Elizabeth's finances. It hadn't taken long for the story to circulate.

He ground the remnants of his own cigarette under his shoe. "What went wrong?"

"The sale was supposed to happen after I'd arrived in the States. But Hassan grew anxious. Maybe he heard something on the grapevine. He pressured Elizabeth into taking possession of the papyri immediately so she could begin her work. I can only guess that she, too, wanted the deed done. None of us anticipated physical danger. And the fact that Sam Rasheed would do the delivery no doubt reassured her that all was well."

"But Rasheed delivered a cobra along with the papyri."

"I don't know how the cobra got into her car. But Sam isn't a killer. He's an innocent go-between who has gone into hiding." Avraham's expression turned bleak. "Palestinians and Arab Israelis have learned not to trust authority. Now with Elizabeth dead, I'm sure he's afraid for his own safety."

"Why would an innocent young man work for someone like Hassan?"

"To learn the illicit business from the inside out," Avraham said. "After his apprenticeship with Hassan, Sam wants to work for the Antiquities Coalition or a similar organization, fighting the good fight. Like his grandfather, Omar, he is angry at how the Middle East has been plundered."

"You must have some idea where he is?"

"None at all."

"When we last spoke, you didn't tell me Sam lives in Chicago."

"I was trying to protect him."

"And the fake papyri? Where they are now?"

"I don't know that, either."

"And Hassan's killer?"

"We don't even know it's related."

"Thanks," Evan snapped. "You've been very helpful."

Avraham stuck his cigarette in his mouth and spread his hands in a "sorry" gesture.

"And the real Moses papyri, the ones with the IAA back in Jerusalem?"

"Elizabeth was supposed to be one of the scholars who published them. Now others will have to take her place."

"Why tell me all of this now?" Evan asked. "Why not that morning in my office or at Simon's?"

"You yourself know how risky it is to share. But the cat is at least partially out of the bag now. And you've proven yourself."

Evan sighed and considered asking for another cigarette but contented himself with the whiff of tobacco. "Just tell me one more thing. Why is Mossad involved?"

Avraham laughed. "Your sources are a little out of date."

"Enlighten me."

But the Israeli shook his head. "'There is nothing covered up that will not be revealed, nor hidden that will not be known.' Luke 12:2."

"Forgive me if I remain a skeptic."

They fell silent. Avraham produced a silver flask, which he uncorked, drank from, then passed to Evan.

"It's poison, right?" Evan said. "And you've taken the antidote."

"Classic Mossad."

Evan drank and returned the flask. "Passable."

Avraham grinned. "You bastard. That's Johnnie Walker Black." He took a long swallow. "I'd give a lot to know what Elizabeth was searching for that she was so eager to find."

"That part of your story is true?"

Avraham passed the flask. "One hundred percent."

"Maybe something she found in Theodore Watts's collection," Evan suggested.

"That makes sense. But *what* did she find? And what has happened to it?"

"Two very important questions."

They continued to hand the flask back and forth. Avraham stood and stretched, then resumed his seat. It crossed Evan's mind to wonder if it was a signal to someone. If so, there was nothing he could do about it.

The Israeli pulled out his cigarettes again, but he didn't light up. "How long have you been in love with Detective Bisset?"

Evan's face flushed with heat. How in deuces had Avraham figured that out? Was Evan so obvious that even a stranger could pick up his feelings?

"Since time immemorial," he said. "Not that it matters. But since we're sharing a smoke and a drink like mates, let me ask you something else. Why did you threaten my brother?"

"In case I needed leverage." Avraham shrugged. "I had no intention of hurting River. But I know you're a family man."

Family. So important. And often irritating. All he had to do was think about his long-gone father and his self-absorbed mother to darken an already bad mood. A lot of the time, you were better off with the family you made.

With that, he remembered Christina and the party. He rubbed Perro behind the ears for a moment, then stood and looked down at Avraham. The Israeli peered up at him, bemused. The sadness in his eyes no doubt reflected Evan's own.

What the hell, he thought. "Want to go to a party?"

CHAPTER 18

Christina lived in a two-story condominium in a leafy neighborhood in Near South Side. When Evan and Avraham arrived, the laughter and lively banter spilling through the open windows revealed a party in midswing.

At the door, Evan paused. Perro cocked his head and peered up at Evan, wondering what the delay was about.

"Once more into the breach?" Avraham asked, correctly guessing the source of Evan's hesitation.

"It's always awkward when the hostess springs a dwarf on the guests. Especially for the dwarf."

"We could go to a bar instead."

"Tempting. But only if I want to end the relationship."

"Do you?"

"You'll know the answer to that as soon as you meet Christina."

"Then," Avraham said as he reached for the doorknob, "let's beard the lion in the den."

The door opened onto a living room packed with thirty- and forty-something professionals, all fashionably dressed, all engaged in conversation, all holding drinks. Evan freed Perro from his leash and hung it on a hook. He paused again, tucking in his shirt, and wondering when he'd last combed his hair.

Avraham watched him with amusement until, shirt retucked, Perro free to roam, Evan said, "I'm heading for the bar."

"Right behind you."

As Evan forged into the crowd, Avraham and Perro in his wake, the conversation stuttered and, in places, fell silent. He proceeded with grim determination, hoping the kitchen held a smaller crowd. And Christina.

She spotted him as soon as he squeezed between a young professor he'd seen occasionally on campus, and a perfect stranger who appeared to need the refrigerator in order to remain upright.

"Evan!" Christina cried, opening her arms.

Grateful for her hug, he breathed in her perfume. She looked magnificent in a sapphire-blue cocktail dress. Her long earrings sparkled in the light, and she'd fluffed her short hair around a beaded headband.

After a moment, he pulled back to introduce Avraham. But the Israeli was already in process.

"Ronen," he said, offering his hand. "Archaeologist."

"Christina." She took his hand. "Historian."

For a moment, the air sparked with electricity as Christina's eyes met Avraham's. Really, what could go together better than an archaeologist and a historian? They were like peanut butter and chocolate. Or single malt and a crystal glass. For a moment, Evan looked back and forth between the two, suddenly feeling like the third wheel. Or perhaps the child at a party meant for grown-ups.

"I'll just find the whiskey," he said.

Christina shook herself. "I'm on it. Ronen, what's your poison?"

"Whatever Evan is having."

She looked back at Evan. "You didn't bring your brilliant detective friend?"

"She's busy being a brilliant detective."

~~~

An hour later and God alone knew how many drinks in, Evan found himself watching the party from the sidelines while Perro fraternized enough for both of them. People, he'd noticed at social occasions, generally fell into one of two types when it came to addressing his dwarfism. Either they ignored it—and him. Or they headed determinedly in his direction and made it their mission to reassure him that his dwarfism mattered not one whit. People in this latter camp often called him an inspiration and asked deeply personal questions under the theory it was best to not only address the elephant in the room but also dissect it, put sections under a microscope, then create a PowerPoint presentation to share with the world.

He was usually able to overcome people's initial discomfort and demonstrate that he could, conversationally speaking, hold his own. But tonight, his thoughts were with Elizabeth and Hassan and the fact that if Avraham was telling the truth—and he believed he was—then Elizabeth might well have died for a forgery. For nothing. All while her real work went unfinished.

The thought did not sit well.

When his phone buzzed and he saw that it was from Addie, he skirted the crowd and pushed his way up the stairs to Christina's bedroom, which was blessedly unoccupied. He closed the door and returned Addie's call.

"Thanks for your text about the crime scene," she said.

"You still on-site?"

"Playing step-and-fetch for Agent Holliday. What are you doing?"

"Hiding."

"From whom?"

"Social event. Unavoidable." He sat on Christina's bed, realizing he'd never seen it before. They'd always gone to his place.

"I'm sorry. Maybe you should just get drunk."

"I believe I've glided effortlessly past drunk and am now staggering straight into shit-faced. Can't wait to see how I feel in the morning."

"Call an Uber and go home. Why be miserable?"

Evan didn't mention that he'd be almost as miserable at home. But the Uber part sounded reasonable. If only it hadn't become so difficult to stand.

"I will," he said. "And . . . I'm sorry Holliday is treading on your toes." Or that was what he meant to say. Even to his own ears it sounded a bit fuzzy.

"Go home," she said. "And don't drive."

Back downstairs, Evan intended to find Christina and make his apologies. But the room had begun to spin, and he couldn't see past the torsos packing the small space. He stepped gracelessly up on a side table and saw Christina deep in conversation with Avraham. The Israeli noticed him and rose to his feet, but Evan waved him down, deciding farewells were unnecessary. When Perro trotted out of the crowd and perched at his feet, he snapped on the dog's leash and eased out the door.

On the front porch, he stopped long enough to arrange for a ride, then headed toward his car to wait. The air was heavy with moisture, and the faintest of cool breezes brushed his skin. Clouds hung low, and from somewhere nearby came the tantalizing aroma of steaks sizzling on a grill. Evan ambled, letting Perro sniff anything of interest along the way. As soon as he reached the Jag, he realized he should have stopped for a bathroom break on his way out. Fortunately, there was a nearby bush.

He was just zipping his pants when he heard the Uber driver pull up.

The snappily dressed driver was kind enough to open the back door for him. Evan scooped up Perro, tossed the corgi inside, used the door handle to haul himself onto the vehicle's side bar, then pitched forward into the back seat. The door closed behind him, and from somewhere nearby, a man said, "Dr. Wilding, I believe you are—as the Americans say—pickled."

"There's an understatement," he mumbled before he drifted away.

~~~

When he came to, he found himself sitting in a black Mercedes SUV next to a tall, bearded man who wore a neatly tailored black suit, a navy tie, and a gold-and-sapphire ring on his right hand. His haircut looked to be of the $500 quality. He smelled of cigarettes and cardamom and sat upright with the unmistakable bearing of a man on a mission.

Evan turned to stare out at the lights of downtown Chicago slipping past.

"Wrong vehicle," he said in a slurred voice. "Drop us off at the next corner, would be wonderful."

There was no response. The vehicle purred steadily ahead.

Evan turned around again to face his fellow passenger. The bearded man regarded him somberly, but there was also curiosity in his gaze. Perhaps he'd never seen a drunken dwarf.

"Mistake about your car," Evan muttered. "Sorry."

"It is not a problem," the man said, his accented English perfect. "I've been waiting for an opportunity to speak privately with you."

Evan recalled Addie's words—that she'd seen a black SUV speeding away at Lincoln Park.

"You've been following me," he said.

The man gave a faint nod. "I'm Yosef Khalil."

"Should that mean something to me?"

"Probably not. I am here as part of the Jordanian diplomatic presence in the US."

Evan took a minute to let that work its way through his sodden brain. "In Chicago? Not DC?"

"Sometimes my work requires that I travel. I am in Chicago because of Ronen Avraham."

"Good. Then you should go to the party. That's where he is. With my girlfriend."

"I believe it is better that you and I talk."

The gravity of the man's voice penetrated Evan's whiskey-induced fog, and he groped for sobriety like a drowning man splashing about for a hand to grasp. He pressed the button to roll down the window a few inches and was surprised when the window complied. Cold air rushed in.

"Go ahead, then," he managed. "Talk."

"I have known Ronen Avraham for a long time. Sometimes as an ally, sometimes as an enemy."

"I know the feeling."

Khalil smiled. "He is a complicated man, Ronen Avraham. We first crossed paths fifteen years ago, when he and Dr. Lawrence illegally traversed the border from Israel into Jordan. At that time, I was a member of the Royal Bedouin Police, and I personally chased the pair of them back across the border into Israel. We have had our differences, and the occasional understanding, ever since."

Evan felt the first tremors of a seismic headache behind his eyes. "If you're here about the papyri, there's no point."

"Ah, you refer to the Moses papyri. My driver heard Mr. Avraham tell you they are forgeries."

"And here I thought Ronen and I were having a private conversation."

"My driver is intimately familiar with the shadows."

"I see," Evan said. "Then I suppose I should commend him for his skill."

Khalil nodded gravely. "Regarding what Mr. Avraham said about the papyri being forgeries—I believe this to be true. Our sources suggest the real artifacts remain in Jerusalem. Which is good but also, for Jordan, a problem. Do you know what it means to a country to lose its heritage to thieves?"

Evan recalled sites River had discovered, only to find that thieves had been there first. Of his own experience with fragmented treasures, missing icons. "I have some idea."

He felt Khalil's eyes on him. "I suppose, because of your work, that you do understand. My driver also heard the Israeli tell you that Elizabeth was after something else."

"Your driver does get around. Was he the man trailing Detective Bisset and me at Lincoln Park?"

A faint smile. "Salah is proficient at his work."

"Just curious—does Agent Holliday know you're here?"

"We have worked together in the past."

Which wasn't an answer. Evan shrugged. "Anyway. Seems you're all up to date."

A smile flashed behind Khalil's beard. "Did Avraham tell you he is good friends with the prime minister of his country?"

Roberto's words floated through Evan's mind. *He's a friend to Israelis at the highest echelons. The very highest, if you get my drift.*

He said, "I heard a rumor."

"And that the prime minister is very interested in Elizabeth's work?"

Evan met Khalil's gaze. "Why is that?"

"Ah. He didn't tell you. I am not surprised. The Jews have survived through secrecy. But it is my understanding that the prime minister is curious about the Watts collection."

"Tell him welcome to the club."

"There's a story that something stolen from his family ended up belonging to Theodore Watts. And that Avraham's work here—while not sanctioned by your government—is sanctioned by his."

A jolt of surprise made its way through the alcoholic fog. If it were true, it would certainly explain Avraham's interest in Elizabeth's work. And his presence here, apart from the Moses papyri.

Khalil turned toward the window. The driver had ventured into Gage Park, and the Jordanian appeared engrossed by the run-down buildings, the cracked sidewalks, the empty window fronts. "A shame," he said after a time. "Such a rich country and still so much poverty."

"Lots of difference between the haves and have-nots. Even here."

"It is a disappointment."

"True. But you didn't kidnap me—or whatever you want to call it—to talk about social inequality. If you know Elizabeth was looking for something, *Sayyid* Khalil, maybe you have a guess as to what it was?"

"I am here partly in the hope that you can tell me."

"Not a clue."

"Another shame." Khalil turned back from the window. "We are in the middle of a race, Dr. Wilding. Many are searching for this wondrous enigmatic object. And it is clear from the murders of Dr. Lawrence and the dealer, Chuma Hassan, that for at least one person, it is a race to the death."

"You think Elizabeth died because of this mysterious artifact? What about the Moses papyri?"

He found himself waiting intently for Khalil's answer. If the mysterious artifact was the cause of her death, Elizabeth's loss might feel like less of a blow. Better to have died for something that was real. Something that existed beyond a forger's skill.

But Khalil only shrugged. "I suppose that is for you and the police and Agent Holliday to determine."

"Is it a race to the death for you?" Evan asked, more bravely than he felt. "Are you a killer hiding behind diplomatic plates?"

Khalil's laughter boomed around the car's interior. He reached into his jacket, and Evan braced himself, but his hand emerged holding nothing more threatening than a business card. "I am only a diplomat. But I suspect that there are items in the Watts collection that rightfully belong to the king of Jordan. To the people of Jordan. And I think this is also true for whatever Elizabeth was searching for."

When he didn't take the business card, Khalil reached over and slipped it into Evan's coat pocket. "If you find this treasure before anyone else, I trust that you will do the right thing and return it to its rightful place of origin."

They drove in silence for a time. The driver had merged onto the nearly empty highway and was headed north, presumably intending to take Evan home. Sure enough, in a short while they exited the freeway and entered Evan's neighborhood. The driver turned onto his street and stopped, unprompted, at Evan's gate.

"You were here last night," Evan said.

"We don't always operate in the shadows."

The driver slipped out from behind the wheel, walked around, and opened the door for Evan and Perro. Evan half stumbled out, while Perro followed with only a little more grace, Evan catching him middrop.

"Good night, Dr. Wilding," Khalil called before the driver closed the door.

"I still have to pay for the Uber, you know," Evan yelled.

He stood outside his gate and watched the retreating SUV, his mind all but sloshing with alcohol, his thoughts still addled by both Khalil's presence and his words. Half the world seemed interested in the actions of a murdered historian. He would need a playbill to sort out the actors.

After he punched in the gate code, Evan checked his recent calls. Nothing from Christina. Or Addie.

With a gentle tug on Perro's leash, he began the long trudge up the hill to his house, wondering what it would be like to have long legs.

Probably Perro wondered the same.

A spattering of rain struck.

His headache swelled.

Evan lowered his head and plowed into the rising storm.

CHAPTER 19

The sun was just rising over the distant trees, and birdsong filled the air as Evan drove his pickup truck through the gate of the forest preserve and parked.

His headache had faded somewhat with sleep, breakfast, and an extra-large cup of red-blooded American coffee, served black. From time to time, the remnants of a hangover knocked at his temples to remind him that, no matter how well you think you can handle drink, the drink always wins. He focused on the weight of the investigation and tried to erase his embarrassment over last night's drunkenness. Too, he felt a lingering concern over his late-night conversation with the Jordanian, Yosef Khalil.

To really gild the lily, he also carried an image of Christina laughing with Avraham.

Evan was mostly content with his life and proud of the place he'd made in it. But now and again he was reminded that—for some, perhaps for many—he would always be a man who came up short.

He slid out of the pickup and walked to the back to open the topper and ease Ginny out on her wheeled perch. The leather hood had kept her quiet during the drive, but now she smelled wild things all around, and she shook herself on his gloved fist in anticipation.

"You ready to fly, my beautiful girl?" he murmured as he laced her jesses between the fingers of his left hand. He'd inspected her feathers at home, but now he ran his fingers along her wings once more. All was as it should be. Her molt was almost complete.

The fields lay wet with the previous night's rain, and his pant legs turned dark with moisture as he tromped through the grass in his Wellies. All around, the cacophonous world fell silent as the small creatures—birds and rabbits and squirrels—sensed Ginny's presence. She smelled them, too, and stretched and fluttered her wings. When he removed her hood, she bobbed her head and looked about. Something caught her eye, and as he lifted his fist and loosened his fingers, she pushed off his glove and flew free.

He soon saw where she was headed. A flock of starlings had taken to the air. He'd watched Ginny hunt starlings before and was fascinated by the way the flock changed its formation as she approached; it was a common and ingenious way the birds strove to avoid predation. The birds flew up and up and up, seeking a height advantage as Ginny circled in preparation for her attack. As she darted forward, a wave rippled through the flock, and then the murmuration split into two and soared higher. Ginny dropped back before circling for a second attempt. This time, in response, the starlings swooped close together, creating a dense flock.

The shape-shifting flock put Evan in mind of the illicit antiquities business and the layers of complicity involved. Even as organizations like Avraham's IAA and Agent Holliday's antiquities unit designed strategies to foil the criminals, the bad guys—like the starlings—broke apart and re-formed elsewhere, always managing to stay a few steps ahead of the authorities.

Or almost always. Ginny at last snagged her prey, snatching it out of the air and plunging toward earth with the black-feathered bird fluttering in her talons.

If only Avraham and Holliday could be so lucky with their own starlings.

He ran to Ginny and reached down. With a quick twist of its neck, he put the starling out of its misery.

~~~

On the way back to his truck, Evan phoned Addie while Ginny sat heavy lidded on his fist. Addie had called him last night to make sure he was safely home, but she'd still been at the crime scene with no time to talk.

Now the exhaustion in her voice was clear when she answered.

"Are you out with Ginny?"

"Just heading back to the truck." He filled her in on his conversation with Avraham and the fact that—at least according to the Israeli—the Moses papyri were forgeries and part of a sting to entrap Hassan and whoever offered to buy the illicit fragments.

"Wait," Addie said. "The papyri are forgeries? And that's why Lawrence died? And why Holliday is riding us now?"

"I do believe they're forgeries, although Holliday may not yet be aware. They're based on real artifacts. But I'm not sure the papyri are why Elizabeth was murdered. And more players keep popping up." He went on to tell her about his joyride with Yosef Khalil and the diplomat's belief that there were items in Theodore Watts's collection that belonged to Jordan. Which—by the way—the king would very much like returned.

"We need that inventory to sort it all out," he said.

"If it exists. I spoke with Ralph Raines again. He says that with the grandson fighting the trust, everything is locked down tighter than my boss's wallet when it's time to buy a round."

"I'm surprised Raines doesn't have a copy. Did you ask?"

A sigh. "You know, how to ask basic questions was covered the first day of Detective School. I also asked if he'd checked with whoever in his office knows the name of Lawrence's new attorney. Negatory on that. Swears he'll take care of it today. As for the inventory, it's possible that Raines does have it and feels no need to hand it over to Chicago PD. He *says* he's cooperating with Agent Holliday, but my cop instincts tell me he's stonewalling her, too, while he waits to see how things shake out with the trust. Regardless, for the moment everything goes through Holliday, and Patrick and I are mostly out. I can't even get to Hassan's files or look at his computer yet. Holliday and her team took everything."

Evan slowed. "Is that legal?"

"Apparently, it doesn't matter," she fumed. "The lieutenant is squawking about it, but so far, the chief is unmoved."

"You're saying the brass will support the Feds over their own people?"

"Why do you sound surprised? It's political. I don't even want to guess who's pulling whose strings. But until the brass have convinced the Feds that we belong on the same team, Patrick and I get the distinct idea we're supposed to back away from Kelley and Veritas."

"They can't do that," Evan protested. "We're talking about two deaths."

"This *is* Chicago," Addie reminded him. "Corruption is practically mandated. Look, I have to run. Departmental meeting. Talk later?"

"Of course."

As he neared the truck, a second flock of starlings exploded into the air. Evan thought at first it was a response to Ginny's presence. But when he shielded his eyes against the sun, he saw a white Cadillac pull in behind his truck and park. A door opened, and a man emerged from the back seat.

Evan stopped. Ginny paused in her preening to squeak.

"It's déjà vu all over again, Ginny," Evan said. He was starting to feel like he stood at the center of a revolving door of suspicious characters.

This suspicious character turned out to be William Kelley. In his nylon pants and polar fleece, the executive looked dressed for a day in the damp fields. Evan stopped and waited for the Veritas founder to join him.

"I apologize if I'm disturbing you and your hawk," Kelley said. "One of your neighbors was out jogging and said I might find you here."

"Has something happened?"

"I heard about Hassan, the art dealer," Kelley said. Evan said nothing, and Kelley pressed on. "I wondered if you knew anything more than what was in the papers."

"You'll have to reach out to Agent Holliday."

Kelley gave a nod. Interestingly, he didn't ask who Agent Holliday was.

"You worked with Hassan," Evan said.

Kelley shook his head. "Not personally. Tim Chablain did."

"As the head of the Veritas Foundation, you weren't concerned about Hassan's reputation for dealing with illicit artifacts?"

"I trust the people I hire, Dr. Wilding. If Tim had found anything suspicious in our acquisitions, he wouldn't have gone through with them."

"Tell me about your responsibility in all of this, Mr. Kelley."

"What do you mean?"

"Have you considered that by pumping millions into the antiquities market, you're encouraging looting? Your money, rather than ensuring the legal acquisition and export of artifacts, promotes violence and criminality. You've seen, as a related example, what people do to elephants to acquire their tusks."

"And have you considered," Kelley said coolly, "that by removing these treasures from war-torn and impoverished countries, I'm saving them? I don't approve of illegal activity, of course. But neither can I turn a blind eye to the fate of these relics or the sites they come from. The palace of Nimrud, destroyed by ISIS. Artifacts wrecked in the Mosul Museum, again by ISIS."

"The destruction is horrific," Evan agreed. "But what about everything ISIS or its regional affiliates have stolen and then sold on the black market to men like you who are willing to pay? Books and papers dating back seven thousand years, stolen from the Central Library of Mosul, then sold on the black market. Likewise for treasures taken from the national museum of Iraq in Baghdad. Thousands of items looted from archaeological sites in Iraq and Syria."

Kelley flicked a dismissive hand. "There are dozens of laws in place to prevent smuggling. It's not my place to enforce—"

Evan's anger soared. "Those laws don't work. As long as there are buyers, there will be smugglers. Look at the drugs flowing in across our border. Demand enables supply. Only when collectors agree to purchase items with legal and definitive provenance and nothing else will the black market disappear."

Kelley stopped walking, bringing Evan up short. The businessman seemed, for a moment, to have gone far from the rain-sodden field. When he looked again at Evan, his entire being vibrated with surety. He moved closer, so that Evan had to crane his neck to look into the man's eyes.

"On the one hand, you're right," Kelley said. "It's a terrible thing. But I also know that I have a calling. And that is to get the story of the Old Testament in front of as many people as possible. Only if these artifacts are removed from the hands of terrorists and kept in a place of safety will we have full and unfettered access to our rightful and righteous history."

Evan was suddenly tired. He backed away from Kelley and braced the arm holding Ginny against his chest.

"And that's the other problem, Mr. Kelley. Any given artifact has two values. One is what it's worth on the commodities market. The other is what these items reveal of our past, our history. Even our humanity. And especially to the culture that created that artifact. Or their descendants. Imagine how important these treasures are to them."

"Which is why they must be saved. So that people can experience them. So that history becomes real for them."

"But when artifacts are ripped from the ground without regard to where they're from, the other items they were discovered with, we lose that connection to the past. An archaeological dig is like an epic saga. An *Iliad* or a *Beowulf*. But we can't piece the story together if it is strewn, page by page, around the globe. The pages—the artifacts—become mere commodities. There are other options."

"Like what?"

"A country that worries it can't adequately protect its treasures can loan an artifact to whomever they wish for as long as they wish. They can make it available for scholarly research. Send it on an international tour."

"As if they would." Kelley's look now could only be described as smug. "By now you might have guessed that Elizabeth had come to see things my way. She had agreed to help by assisting us in our search for artifacts. And by verifying provenance on those we've already acquired. Now that she's gone, we need someone to take her place."

"Isn't that Chablain's job as head of acquisitions?" Evan asked.

"Chablain, regretfully, has told us he's accepted an offer elsewhere."

"Elizabeth had said she would take his place?"

"She'd promised to give it careful consideration."

"What about Dawson?"

Something rippled across Kelley's face. "Here I am," he murmured so softly that Evan wasn't sure he heard him correctly. "Mark is sincere and earnest. But I fear he lacks the necessary passion for our work. He's a bit too rigid in his scholarship."

"What you mean is, everything you acquire must support your story," Evan said. "What happens when you find an artifact that doesn't? Doesn't your work—for it to be honest, for you to be honest—demand the very thing you condemn Dawson for? Rigid scholarship?"

"Ultimately, all our artifacts lead to the truth. One way or another." Kelley pointed at Ginny. "Your hawk doesn't worry about how the dove feels when she sinks her talons into its soft breast. The hawk must feed. It is a simple imperative."

"So now you're a hawk?"

Kelley pushed on. "I have been chosen to help lead people to God. Elizabeth saw the value of our work. She agreed to help." He peered down at Evan. "But now she is gone. Help me. Help us. Help all of us. I can make it worth your while."

Evan took a step back. "What?"

"Your presence would add immensely to our mission."

"Are you offering me a job?"

"To be our most esteemed scholar. Not to mention providing you unfettered access to our collection."

But Evan raised his free hand in protest. "I'm neither historian nor archaeologist. I'm hardly qualified."

"I'm told that your work as a paleographer is brilliant."

"My specialty is deciphering and dating manuscripts. Not analyzing their content."

Kelley leaned in. "Doesn't that give you the skills necessary to examine provenance for an artifact? And to approve purchases based on that analysis? Elizabeth was a papyrologist. Very similar."

"She was also a historian."

"Then there's your untouchable reputation, Dr. Wilding."

"Which you need."

Kelley gravely tipped his head. "Which we need."

Evan ran his hand down Ginny's back, and she piped her pleasure.

Kelley continued. "Elizabeth was onto something. Something big. She'd agreed to find this thing—whatever it is—and bring it to us. You were her friend. Maybe you can learn what it was. Maybe you already know."

He had no intention of accepting Kelley's offer. But what might he gain if he pretended to?

"I'll think about it," he said.

"Good. Good." Kelley clapped his gloved hands together. "I'll be waiting to hear from you."

Evan watched Kelley stride effortlessly across the field and return to his Cadillac. He noticed Kelley's driver for the first time, leaning against the front fender, smoking. It was Miriam Fuller, Timothée Chablain's assistant. Kelley must have co-opted her for this mission. Her cold gaze was fixed on Evan; whatever she might be looking for in him, he got the sense he came up short. In a manner of speaking.

He smiled and waved. She frowned, then tossed away her cigarette and climbed behind the wheel.

Overhead, the restless starlings flew toward the glow in the east, filling the sky with darkness.

~~~

After returning home and placing Ginny in her mews, Evan took a quick shower, retrieved Perro, then took an Uber to Christina's to pick up his car where he'd left it the night before. Once he and Perro were comfortably settled in the Jaguar, he headed toward the University of Chicago.

As he neared the campus, first an ambulance and then a police car passed him and turned through the gates onto university grounds. The campus held more than thirty thousand students, faculty, and staff, but sudden worry flooded Evan. Hurriedly he parked, clipped on Perro's leash, then walked toward the quad, where the emergency vehicles had been headed.

Both the ambulance and the cruiser were parked in front of the Oriental Institute. And Finch's lab.

A small crowd had collected near the front door, where a campus security officer had arrived to keep order. He recognized Evan and waved him through. Evan's hand was shaking as he punched the elevator button. When he reached the floor of the lab, he hurriedly exited the elevator and jogged down the hall.

He found Finch in the lab, sitting on the floor, being tended by a paramedic, and talking to a cop.

"Never saw him," Finch was saying. "The guy walloped me from behind, and I must have hit my head when I fell." He looked up and saw Evan. "Bastard took the piece of leather you left with me."

"Never mind that," Evan said, even as disappointment fisted in his stomach. "Are you going to be all right?"

Finch chuckled. "Not entirely sure I was all right before I was hit."

"He'll live," said the paramedic as he reached to tape a gauze bandage onto Finch's broad forehead.

"Wait." Finch waved him away. "Do you have that in my color? What would you call me, Evan? Creamy mocha? Cuddly caramel?"

"Daft is what I'd call you."

Finch laughed.

"Looks like you'll have to live with lily white," the paramedic said.

Evan frowned down at his friend. A strike from behind, followed by a theft. It was the same MO as Polo Shirt's actions with Simon outside the bookstore. "There are cameras here, right?"

Both Finch and the cop, whose name tag read **HERNANDEZ**, nodded.

"Hold still," the paramedic said to Finch.

"We'll take a look," said Hernandez.

Evan told the officer about Simon's assault, and that Chicago PD had responded to that incident as well.

Hernandez scowled. "We'll get him. The guy's got to be on camera."

"I'm sorry, my friend," Finch said to Evan as the paramedic finished and began cleaning up.

"It's not your fault. I should have warned you."

"It's not a total loss," Finch said. "I was able to run some tests before that asshole got here. I was standing at my desk getting ready to write it up. You're looking at some old shit, Evan. Older than God. Or at least in the general vicinity."

Finch sounded like himself. Evan started breathing normally again.

Finch said, "Carbon 14 suggests that the piece dates from the eighth century BCE."

"That's hundreds of years older than the Dead Sea Scrolls. Are you sure?"

"I really hate it when people ask if I'm sure. Unless I'm buying an ugly Christmas sweater. Or if I want to wear my Speedo at the beach."

"I'll try to remember that the next time I ask a professional for his professional opinion."

"As for the age, papyri from some of the associated Jordanian caves are that old," Finch reminded Evan.

Evan recalled Khalil's words. *I suspect that there are items in the Watts collection that rightfully belong to the king of Jordan. To the people of Jordan. And I think this is also true for whatever Elizabeth was searching for.*

"Did you detect any ink?" Evan asked.

"It was a *mother* to pull out. But yes, I detected traces of ink in what might be partial letters. A water test confirmed carbon black."

"Used by the folks who wrote the Dead Sea Scrolls. But . . ." Evan held his excitement in firm check. "Could it be a modern re-creation of the ink?"

"Can't help you with that. Even if it was still in my possession, there isn't enough ink on that scrap to fit on the head of the pin. No way can I date the stuff."

"All right, buddy," the paramedic said, done packing up and now checking his handiwork. "I recommend you go to the hospital for observation. You've got a mild concussion. Any minute now you're probably going to get woozy and start throwing up."

"Like the Friday nights of my youth," Finch said. "I'll be fine."

The paramedic closed his bag. "Why don't I rephrase? I insist you go to the hospital for observation. I don't want to get another call back here because you've toppled like a sequoia. Again."

~~~

Addie was sitting at the top of the steps outside his office when Evan and Perro arrived. Perro, recognizing the detective, wagged his tail with a level of enthusiasm that shook his entire body. She reached over and scooped him into her lap and was rewarded with a wet kiss.

Evan took the stair next to her. "You look like you lost your last friend."

"Well, you're here, so that clearly isn't the case. But . . ." She sighed as she pushed Perro gently from her lap and stood. "Patrick and I are stuck. Sam Rasheed's car appeared on cameras near the church around the same time Elizabeth was there—we found her car on camera as well, and we'll run down all the other vehicles in the vicinity. Outside of that, Sam remains a ghost. One of the few things we've managed to learn about him is that he has large student debts, which could go toward motive. And if Sam is a ghost, Polo Shirt is a friggin' cipher wrapped in a mystery and bow-tied with an enigma."

"To badly paraphrase Winston Churchill."

Addie glared. "On top of that, Agent Holliday thinks she owns Chi-Town. Patrick and I are lowly foot soldiers. I absolutely hate the brass. And—"

She looked down at Perro.

"And?"

She pinched the bridge of her nose. "And Jeff told me he's tired of competing with every criminal in Chicago for my attention. After I canceled late-night drinks because there was a *murder*, he broke it off."

Evan pushed up from the stairs and regarded Addie's melancholy expression. "Why don't I make tea? Tea always helps."

"You're such a Brit," she groused. But she followed him into the office.

While Evan turned on the electric kettle and dug around for a box of cookies, he spent a few minutes listing for her all the reasons why Jeff Minzer was the wrong guy. Starting with the fact that anytime a man told a woman she needed to laugh more, he was clearly a schmuck.

"How's Christina?" Addie asked, seating herself at Evan's desk and sliding a chocolate digestive out of the package while he finished the tea.

"Probably livid that I walked out of the party drunk and without even saying goodbye. Not my best moment." He didn't add how it made him feel to see Christina and Avraham together. How could he compete with Mr. Tall, Dark, Handsome, *and* Mysterious?

While they drank—tea really was a restorative—he filled her in on his early-morning job offer from Kelley, then brought up Finch's assault. "Same MO as Polo Shirt. Finch's attacker slipped up from behind, hit him hard enough to make him fall, then made off with Elizabeth's parchment."

"Finch wasn't badly hurt?"

"He has a head like a rock. Probably did more damage to the floor tiles."

She finished her cookie and reached for another. "I imagine there are cameras."

"There are. And Finch was able to run the tests before the theft. The leather is ancient. As in Dead Sea Scrolls ancient. There's also ink, which is intriguing. But not enough for Finch to age-test."

Addie planted her elbows on his desk. "I should feel excited, I guess. It's cool to hold something that old. But . . ." She popped a piece of cookie in her mouth and chewed. "Do you really think that bit of leather is Elizabeth's great treasure?"

He shook his head. It seemed unlikely. A scrap of unprovenanced leather with a tiny amount of untestable ink hardly seemed something to get worked up about. Even for scholars, who had notoriously low bars when it came to getting excited about old things.

"It's *possible* Elizabeth cut a strip from a larger piece," he said. "But she would have done so in a carefully controlled environment. And she definitely wouldn't have just dropped the piece in an old envelope and then into a newer envelope and stuffed it in her pocket."

"Then what was it doing there?"

"It must have come to her that way."

"Come from where?"

"Maybe the Watts collection? Although why a man with a fondness for showy pieces like Cambodian bronzes would have a scrap of leather is difficult to fathom." He finished his tea and rose to clear their cups. "It's a mystery."

"Oh, good," she said. "Because we need more of those. Why do you think Kelley offered you a job?"

"Because I'm brilliant and imminently qualified?"

"Uh-huh."

"Ouch. Honestly? No idea. Has Agent Holliday shared anything?"

Addie's sigh seemed to come all the way from her feet.

"Elizabeth's death appears to be wrapped up in a long-term surveillance operation being run by Homeland Security's Arts and Antiquities Unit. How, exactly, Holliday won't say. The operation started with dealers in New York and spread from there to include Chuma Hassan and other Chicago-based parties that Holliday refuses to name. She is trying to maintain the operation even though Patrick and I barged in like gate-crashers, trampling on the party favors and spitting in the punch bowl."

Evan stopped, still holding the mugs. "Elizabeth was caught up in their surveillance?"

Addie nodded. "Holliday won't elaborate on what she said last night—that Lawrence was the real criminal. But don't panic. There's more to the story, and I think she's hanging Lawrence out to dry in order to maintain cover. I'm sure that when everything is revealed, Lawrence will have proved to be true to herself and to the law. Because I know you trusted her. And you're a good judge of character." She lifted her chin. "Right?"

Evan released the breath he'd been holding. "Right."

She reached back and loosened her ponytail. "Talk to me about snakes."

He tried not to admire the fall of her hair. "Have we returned to Jeff Minzer?"

She rolled her eyes at him. "Show off your semiotics, Dr. Wilding. Give me some subtext. Tell me what you noticed about the two crime scenes. And especially the murder weapons."

He set the mugs near the electric kettle and returned to his desk. He riffled through his unsorted mail until he found the catalog he'd spotted previously for an antiquities gallery—perhaps the gallery owner thought Evan had the power to sway the money people at the university.

He handed the catalog over to Addie and revisited what Avraham had said the night before. "Crime in the antiquities business—once you move up the ladder from armed groups of looters and terrorists—is usually of the transnational white-collar kind—crimes among the elite based on deceit and fraud rather than violence. It's an unfortunate side effect anytime someone has millions to throw around and a burning passion for something they have no business owning. In the antiquities world, almost no one is immune. Reputable dealers, businesspeople, and even the biggest auction houses have been caught with their hands in the—if you'll pardon the expression—twenty-six-hundred-year-old Greek cookie jar."

"You're saying we follow the money?"

"Normally, that would be the case. But in our investigation, the money is interesting but perhaps not definitive."

"Because of other aspects of the case? Other signs."

"Exactly." He leaned against the armrest of his chair and folded his hands in his lap. "Our unusual murder weapons suggest something different from ambition or greed. Indeed, I suspect both the cobra and the statue are very specific messages."

"For the police," Addie stated.

"I don't think so. The statue of Aten and the serpent are religious messages. When we add in the biblical references found on the notes with the bodies, then what we are looking at is quite striking. We have a deeply religious person who has chosen to defy God. After all, the very first commandment in the Bible is 'Thou shall not kill.' In the Christian context, murder is as much a moral failing as a crime. It's a sin, not a legal matter."

"Maybe the killer wants to make the murders look as if there's a moral angle," Addie said. "To frame someone. It could still be about money."

"Perhaps. Although given the level of complexity involved in Elizabeth's death, it becomes less likely. The killer not only had to find the cobra and get it into Elizabeth's car, he also had to keep her from calling for help after she'd been struck. Whilst simultaneously subduing the snake."

"And the killer used a different weapon with Hassan because he had to act without premeditation?"

"Or because he was fresh out of cobras. Even if he acted in haste, I suspect he chose his weapon with at least some forethought."

Addie picked up the same bit of pottery that Avraham had toyed with only a few days earlier. She began turning it over in her hands. "The fact that he had time to fetch the statue down from the shelf suggests that Hassan was comfortable in his presence. Someone known to him, or at least not suspicious."

"Agreed."

"And maybe he knew he didn't have to bring his own weapon. Which would suggest he'd been in Hassan's office before. According to his receptionist, Hassan didn't have any appointments scheduled for last night, although—as she told us—he'd asked not to be disturbed. He often worked late, and she usually stayed until at least eight o'clock. She didn't see anyone enter the office area after Hassan's four-o'clock appointment with his attorney. She stepped out briefly at five thirty to grab a bite to eat. She didn't check back in with him when she returned."

"Cameras?"

"Mr. Hassan was camera shy," Addie said. "I suspect his clientele was, too."

"It's common in this business."

"So what message was the killer sending? And to whom?"

"The question might more correctly be viewed as one of how the killer sees himself. Does he consider himself a killer and thus a sinner? Or is he merely a messenger?"

"Can't he be both?"

"Maybe." Gently, Evan rescued the bit of pottery from Addie and replaced it on his desk. "According to the biblical verses on Elizabeth's note, which focus on God's punishment of the Israelites, the choice of serpent suggests she got out of line. That she changed the playbook in some way."

"In a way that God wouldn't approve of." Addie selected a pencil from a cup on the desk and tapped it lightly against her chin. "The Israelites got in trouble with God when they doubted Him and turned to other gods. A betrayal."

"The choice of the statue of Aten also suggests treachery. By raising Aten up as a supreme god, Pharaoh Akhenaten was betraying the other gods. And his own people."

"Speaking of betraying your people, there's something I haven't told you." Addie turned the pencil toward the desk, tapping out a rhythm. "The dirt lot where Elizabeth was found was earmarked for affordable housing. But Bakker exercised what's known as 'aldermanic prerogative' and stopped the development."

"He can do that?"

"With a little help from his friends on the city council zoning committee. He has de facto veto power over most development plans in his ward."

"Which suggests he's paving the way for Kelley's museum. And that could mean the killer was leaving another message."

A crease appeared between Addie's eyes. "What kind of message?"

Evan returned to the thought he'd had outside Kelley's office at Veritas. "Blood sacrifice."

She shivered. "That went out with the Old Testament."

"Still." Evan's voice dropped. "The blood sacrifice of animals was intended to give Adam and Eve and their descendants a way of partially atoning for their fall from grace. A fall brought about because of treachery, I might point out. The sacrifice of animals continued throughout the Old Testament."

"Until Jesus's death made it unnecessary." Addie's expression was pensive. "Except that Elizabeth was neither lamb nor goat."

"No," Evan agreed. "She was very human."

"For grins and laughs I checked out the alderman's schedule for the time when Elizabeth was murdered."

"And?"

"Bakker spent the day at a fundraising picnic and the evening huddled over spreadsheets with his campaign team. They didn't break until well after midnight." Addie checked the time on her phone, then replaced the pencil and stood. "I have to get rolling. We're talking to Leah Zielinski again as well as reaching out to Hassan's known associates. I'll keep you posted."

After Addie left and Perro dug out a toy from the cloth sack where Evan kept them, Evan stared at the ceiling, putting aside blood sacrifice for the moment to ponder the letter from Cambodia that he'd seen in Elizabeth's office.

Why did Elizabeth, a specialist in Middle Eastern artifacts, have a letter from the Cambodian Minister of Culture and Fine Arts? The only logical answer was that Theodore Watts, the adventuring archaeologist, had Cambodian artifacts in his collection. After the fall of the Khmer Rouge in 1979, Cambodia had opened to the West. And to Western archaeologists. And to Western buyers with lots of Western money.

More recently, countries like Cambodia had begun a concerted effort to repatriate stolen artifacts. Maybe the Cambodian minister had learned that Theodore Watts possessed looted Khmer Empire relics from Cambodian temples.

Or . . . Evan rose and went to the window to stare down at the quad, at the students lingering in the warm spring air while they checked their phones.

He watched one student charge across the squad, then slide to a stop. The young man paused in apparent deep thought, then spun around and charged off in the direction he'd come from. Evan laughed. Just when you think things were going one way, well, sometimes they surprised you and swung the opposite way.

He smoothed his beard. Maybe it was the other way around with Elizabeth, too. Maybe Theodore Watts and Elizabeth had been attempting to *return* items before the collection converted over to Elizabeth's institute.

He called a friend, a professor of Asian art history, who offered to reach out to a Cambodian associate. Half an hour later, she called him back. She told him that Elizabeth had indeed contacted the Cambodian ministry about returning several bronze antiquities. They were already making arrangements.

A slow drip of relief trickled into Evan's veins, warm and welcome. Elizabeth had been doing the right thing. So had her benefactor. The fact that they were being so scrupulous with items in the collection suggested they'd made a catalog of its contents—it was what a reputable owner would do. It was what Elizabeth would do. She'd probably taken photos of everything and sent relevant ones to the Cambodian minister.

So where were these photos? On her stolen computer? Her inaccessible phone? Printed out and bound and sitting in the hands of Theodore Watts's grandson?

The thought of photos gave him an idea. He returned to his desk and his computer and searched online to see if Theodore Watts had ever allowed a journalist or photographer to view his collection. Within minutes, he found a five-year-old write-up in *Architectural Digest* showcasing Watts's home and part of his collection.

Evan sank into his chair and scrolled through the piece. What he could see of Watts's collection was magnificent. A seated bronze Buddha. A sandstone statue of Ganesh, the Hindu elephant god. There were cuneiform tablets, death masks and, under glass, illuminated manuscripts.

Evan dialed Simon.

"I'm feeling fine," Simon told him. "Just angry. I'm having cameras mounted over the door to the alley as we speak."

"I'm glad it wasn't worse."

"As am I. How goes your investigation? Are the police about to arrest my assailant?"

"Not yet. Didn't you mention that you purchased those PEF journals from an estate?"

"That's correct. The estate of Theodore Watts. The sale included only the contents of the library, which had been moved out to the six-car garage. Can't have the riffraff traipsing through the main house."

"Did you purchase anything else from him?"

"A few books on Palestine. I thought anyone interested in the journals might want other titles from that period."

"Were there a lot of buyers present?"

"Just me. The deceased's grandson, Gerrit, had reached out to me, presumably since he knows estate sales are a specialty of mine. He was disappointed that I wanted so little, but there wasn't much of value. Lots of adventure novels and decades-old art catalogs. I heard the sale opened to the public later that day."

"Simon, would you hold on to the other books you bought from the estate? I'd like to see them."

"They don't look like much." He rattled off the titles, all of which had to do with nineteenth-century Jerusalem. Much like the books that had once been in Elizabeth's office before someone—presumably her killer—carted them off.

"They might be relevant," Evan said.

"Then I'll do better than that and have the books couriered over."

After Evan hung up, he resumed his stance at the window and watched a group of students toss a football; their shouts penetrated the glass and made him long for his Oxford days.

Serpents, treacherous Israelis—which brought Avraham and then Christina to mind—archaeological spies, Jordanian diplomats. Where was the keystone that would lock all of these elements in place and offer a complete picture?

He returned to the electric kettle and added water, then selected Ahmad tea from his well-stocked supply. With a hot mug, he returned to his computer and the pictures of Watts's home.

Surely, he and Addie and Patrick were teetering on the edge of understanding.

Hopefully the entire cliff wouldn't give way beneath their feet before they found their man.

Chapter 20

Evan had lost track of how many cups of tea he'd consumed when Diana arrived at the office.

She breezed in, her face flushed with the chill of the morning, her eyes sparkling with whatever made a woman's eyes sparkle.

Evan put more water in the kettle and tried to match her enthusiasm while she told him about her dinner engagement with the fascinating young man from Brazil whom she'd met on her travels; Diego was in Chicago on business and seemed likely to stay around for at least a few weeks.

"He wants to learn how to throw an axe," she said, beaming. "And start training with me for an Ironman. He'll be incredible. Great stamina. And he's . . . Diego is . . ." She sighed. "Delectable."

Evan interrupted before she could launch into a detailed description of Diego's delectability. "Did you find anything about T. E. Lawrence in the PEF quarterlies?"

Diana scooped the overexcited Perro onto her lap and settled in behind her desk. "Plenty. There's his work in the Wilderness of Zion, an account of which was first published in the PEF journals. You see these circles under my eyes? I stayed up all night reading the text on Google Books."

Given the delectable Diego's presence in town, Evan doubted that was the only thing that had kept her busy. But he let it pass.

"If there is a hint of a great treasure somewhere in his report," Diana went on, "it's too subtle for me to find. It's true that T. E. Lawrence was an archaeologist, but it's also true that he was a spy. He was far more interested in the Germans and their railroad than archaeological finds."

One more possible thread clipped, it seemed. "And Deuteronomy?" he asked.

She pressed the back of her hand to her forehead to mime swooning. "*Tons* of information on that. There are clearly people who spend their entire lives devoted to this one book of the Bible."

"Says the woman who's laser focused on Incan accounting knots."

She snorted and waved him over to her laptop. Evan grabbed a folding chair and sat next to her.

She opened tabs. "There were some thirty copies of Deuteronomy found among the Dead Sea Scrolls. But the authors of the early articles in the PEF journals were more concerned with the archaeology of the caves where the scrolls were discovered. They didn't say much about the content of the caves' Deuteronomic texts."

Evan skimmed along as Diana opened the articles.

"Later articles on Deuteronomy mostly parse examples of the text as they appear in the Dead Sea Scrolls. And there's a lot on the specific process of dating the texts. I did find one unusual item that was mildly interesting." Diana opened another tab. "It's a reference to a find known as the Shapira Scrolls, which was a forged Deuteronomy text. An antiquities dealer named Moses Wilhelm Shapira—"

Evan leaned in. "MS," he murmured. The notation on the envelope holding the leather scrap.

Perro opened one eye, yawned in Evan's direction.

"That means something to you?" Diana asked.

"Probably not." Evan refused to get excited. "Go on."

"Shapira claimed to have discovered a millennia-old text of Deuteronomy. The entire world was abuzz over the find, in part because it didn't entirely match accepted versions of the biblical book. But it was soon judged a forgery."

Evan's brief flair of interest died with the surety of a match thrust in a pail of water.

"After the forgery was exposed," Diana went on, scrolling through a website, "Shapira committed suicide. Tough business, the antiquities world. The entire sorry tale was covered extensively by the PEF in their quarterlies."

"Wait!" Evan cried as a drawing flashed by on the website. "Go back."

Diana scrolled back up, and Evan leaned in for a closer look.

"There," he said. "Stop."

The computer screen showed an ink sketch of some sample Hebrew texts along with the drawing of a *wadi*—a valley or ravine—and some tumbled stone. "What is that?"

"I noticed it last night when I was reading about Shapira," Diana answered. "The drawing appeared in the 1883 issue of *Scientific American*. It shows Wadi Mujib in modern-day Jordan—the *wadi* leads from the surrounding hills down to the Dead Sea. The sketch in the upper right is of one of Shapira's leather scrolls. Even before the scrolls were ruled a fraud, Europeans considered them scandalous when Shapira first brought them from the Holy Land."

"Why was that?"

Still holding Perro, she tipped back in her chair. "The writing on the scrolls contradicted the Bible in several ways. Most strikingly, the scrolls offer a different version of the Ten Commandments—different from what is now conventionally accepted, anyway. The first two commandants are combined into one. And a new commandment is given." She lowered her chair. "'Thou shalt not hate thy brother in thy heart.'"

Evan closed his eyes to eliminate all distraction. "Would you mind reading aloud a description of the scrolls?"

"Whatever the professor wants, the professor gets." There came a pause, presumably while she searched for what she wanted. Then she said, "The scrolls consisted of fifteen darkened leather strips, each about three-and-a-half inches wide and ranging in length, although typically around seven inches long. The strips were folded rather than rolled, and each strip carried roughly ten lines of text. Some were so blackened as to be almost illegible."

Evan recalled Finch's words. *It was a* mother *to pull out. But yes, I detected traces of ink in what might be partial letters.*

Evan's blood flurried with an excitement he could no longer hold. "Anything else about these scrolls?"

"Just that they were described as smelling of funeral spices."

Evan opened his eyes with a grin. "The scrolls smelled like mummies. Just like those from the Dead Sea." He directed her to the link to Theodore Watts in *Architectural Digest* and asked her to scroll down to one of the photos. "There, see the corner of that framed sketch? The one above the console table?"

Diana enlarged the picture on her screen. "It's the same drawing as the one that appeared in *Scientific American*."

"Which means Theodore Watts was at least somewhat interested in the Shapira Scrolls."

"Maybe as a reminder to be leery of forgeries?" Diana guessed. "The text under the photo says the picture was snapped in the master suite. Maybe a humbling bedtime thought for a billionaire collector."

"Maybe," Evan murmured. "Then again—"

He grabbed his laptop and opened it on the desk next to Diana's.

"Elizabeth might have had a reason to believe the scrolls were real, despite what nineteenth-century scholars thought. Look at this." He turned the computer so that she could see the screen. "If so, she had company. Several modern scholars believe the scrolls weren't forgeries at all. That they were, in fact, the first Dead Sea Scrolls, the rest of which wouldn't be discovered until sixty-five years after Shapira's death.

Indeed, at least one scholar says the scrolls date all the way back to the time of the first temple in Jerusalem. Maybe as early as 957 BCE." He drew in a breath, trying to contain his excitement. "That's within shouting distance of the date Finch gave the scrap of leather in Elizabeth's coat pocket. The one labeled *MS*. What if *MS* doesn't mean *manuscript*? What if it stands for Moses Shapira?"

Diana's face shone in the glow from the computer screen. Her voice rose to match Evan's. "Wouldn't that make the Shapira Scrolls the oldest known biblical artifacts ever found?"

"It would, indeed."

"But the scrolls disappeared. Listen to this." She nodded toward her screen. "They were sold off by the British Museum as a curiosity and traded hands several times. The scrolls were last displayed in 1889, after being purchased by a doctor and amateur naturalist, Dr. Philip Brookes Mason. They vanished after his death, presumably sold off with the rest of his collection, never to resurface."

Evan clapped his hands, his excitement growing. "The last time I saw Elizabeth, she told me that before she died she was determined to vindicate someone. I'll bet you all of your Incan accounting knots that it was Moses Wilhelm Shapira. A man who was hounded into suicide merely because he found an artifact that scholars couldn't or wouldn't accept as real. Not until decades later, when the Dead Sea Scrolls proved wrong their theories about what could survive in the caves for all those years."

But Diana frowned. "Dozens, if not hundreds, of people have tried to find the scrolls. What would make Elizabeth think she could find them when no one else has?"

"Maybe she knew something no one else did."

Diana's eyes widened. "The Watts collection."

"Presumably whoever went through Elizabeth's office and home was looking for the scrolls. Or evidence that she'd found them. Polo Shirt must have thought there was a clue to their location in the PEF journals. What I don't understand is why Elizabeth would have been walking around with a piece of the scrolls. She'd never take a razor to them."

"I'll bet I know what Elizabeth's scrap is. Shapira's wife, Rosette, had two small pieces of the scrolls, which she took to Europe after her husband's death. The scraps, like the scrolls, disappeared. But maybe a collector—someone who was interested in the Shapira story—put the pieces together sometime after the naturalist Phillip Mason died. Or it could have been Mason himself who brought the pieces together. If Elizabeth found the scrap in the Watts collection, she'd have reason to hope the actual scrolls might also be there."

"But why would she be so careless with it?"

"It makes sense to me. If someone had already been offhand enough to stuff the piece into a manila envelope, then of course Elizabeth would leave it intact until she could get the whole thing to Finch."

"The Dead Sea Scrolls," he said, typing on his laptop. "They were kept in manila envelopes for a few years in the 1950s until archaeologists realized the glue and paper was destroying the papyri."

"When were manila envelopes invented?"

He pointed at the screen. "In the 1830s. Decades before Shapira found his famous scrolls."

"There you go."

"She wouldn't be so careless."

"She would if someone was breathing down her neck."

Someone hell-bent on acquisition. Someone like Timothée Chablain.

Evan felt as though his blood was singing. He stood, unable to continue sitting. He imagined Elizabeth's joy when she discovered what so many others had only dreamed of finding—or at least discovered a clue to their location. It would also explain the unease Avraham had mentioned she confessed to feeling; if anyone knew she had a lead on the Shapira Scrolls, she'd be worried that someone would make the connection between her and the Watts collection.

Perhaps someone who themselves had access. Like Watts's grandson.

He turned back to Diana. "What if the bad guys weren't the only ones morphing to protect themselves? What if Elizabeth was, too?"

"Explain."

"We've been trying to link Elizabeth's treasure to T. E. Lawrence. But maybe Lawrence of Arabia was merely a cover to disguise her interest in the PEF. It was *Shapira* she was looking for. Lawrence of Arabia was a trick to mislead those who were watching her. A spy's simplest sleight of hand."

"And it fooled Polo Shirt," Diana said. "Driving him to steal the PEF journals."

"Right. Then, when he didn't find what he was looking for in the quarterlies, he went after Finch at the lab."

"Which means he has Rosette's fragment of her husband's scrolls. If that's what it is."

"True. But he may have just played into our hands."

"What do you mean?"

"A lot of treasure hunters like to document the hunt. So maybe he kept a record of his search online. A website. A blog. Maybe just comments or questions on someone else's blog. Treasure hunters rarely work in the shadows. They need too much information."

Simultaneously, they turned back to their laptops, scrolling through the numerous sites that mentioned the Shapira Scrolls.

Twenty minutes later, Diana said, "It's too bad we can't enter *Polo Shirt* in the search engine."

"Or *thief*."

A few minutes after that, Diana tapped his arm. "What about this? It's a website created by a man named Kevin Grady. He's been blogging about his search for the Shapira Scrolls for more than five years, including details about all the avenues he tried, all the places he visited. His last visit was to the archives of the PEF in London. He stopped posting after that, about six weeks ago. Look."

Evan leaned over and came face-to-face with a photo of Simon's assailant.

"That's him. That's Polo Shirt."

He read the man's bio. Kevin Grady. Software engineer by day. Treasure hunter by night. "No wonder he wanted those journals— he must have known they came from the Watts's estate. Maybe he thought Watts had written clues in the margins on the articles about Shapira during his own search for the scrolls. Reason enough in his mind to commit a felony assault to get his hands on those particular copies."

"How did he know he and Elizabeth were both hunting for the scrolls?"

Evan snapped his fingers. "London. That was Elizabeth's last trip. A research trip, according to her assistant. If she was pulling archives, she would have had to sign for them. Grady must have seen her name and later learned of her connection to the Watts estate. Your brilliance shines again, Diana. Excellent work."

"That's how I earn my miserly salary," she said. She closed her laptop, then gently woke the sleeping Perro and eased him to the floor. She stood and collected her coat. "If there might be clues hidden in Theodore Watts's copies of the quarterlies, why didn't Elizabeth take them?"

"Maybe she already knew what was in them."

While Diana went out to get lunch and Perro sat forlornly at the door after she left, Evan called Addie with the news about Polo Shirt.

"Kevin Grady," she said. "Got it. We'll jump on this. You're brilliant."

"It was Diana."

"That explains it. Diana is *truly* brilliant. I'm going to buy that woman dinner."

"Actually . . . it was more mutual."

Addie laughed. "Okay, Sherlock. Dinner for both of you. Now fill me in. How did you figure it out?"

"Are you near your computer? This is better with a big screen."

"I'm ready."

"Start by entering *lost scrolls of Deuteronomy*."

A few seconds later she said, "Top of the search is an article from the *New York Times*. Should I click on it?"

"Hold off on that one for the moment. Scroll down until you see an article about a lost biblical scroll."

"Got it. Give me a minute to read."

When she spoke again, her voice trilled with excitement. "You think these Shapira Scrolls are what Elizabeth was after?"

"I do. And they are also what Kevin Grady wants. He picked up her trail in London."

"This is good, Evan. Really, really good. You've brought us this far. We'll find him."

Reassured, Evan took a deep breath in a futile effort to calm himself. "Do you have any news?"

"Just this. Hassan's receptionist shared her boss's calendar with Holliday, who deigned to share it with us. He had only two appointments the day he died. One was with a representative from an auction house. Agent Holliday is investigating that angle."

"Of course."

"The other appointment was with his attorney, who says all the pair discussed was Hassan's desire to purchase a life insurance policy for his wife."

"Interesting, given he was the one who died a few hours later."

"Right. Except that the beneficiaries of the policy were their children, not Hassan. When we talked with his wife, she explained that her husband was expanding her policy at her request. Hassan wouldn't be the first dealer to have to close shop due to improprieties."

"And lose his income. What about appointments earlier in the week?"

"It was a quiet week, apparently, although the receptionist said that sometimes clients' names were deliberately kept off any written record. She's putting together a list, according to Holliday. One name I do know. Miriam Fuller."

"Chablain's pit bull, as he unkindly called her. I saw her this morning, driving Kelley around."

"The receptionist says she and Hassan met briefly. About twenty minutes. This was a regular meeting for the last couple of months. Once every couple of weeks for twenty or thirty minutes, always behind a closed door."

"I could read all kinds of things into that."

"No kidding, although the receptionist said that was typical for Hassan. Regular, brief meetings with potential buyers. It gets more interesting. According to his wife, Hassan had scheduled an off-the-books meeting with a man named Gerrit Watts."

"The grandson."

"Right," Addie says. "Mrs. Hassan doesn't know the reason for the meeting. But her husband told her that Watts canceled a couple of hours before the meeting, claiming that his flight out of LAX was delayed."

"The story checks?"

"It does. We'd love to talk to Gerrit, but thanks to Agent Holliday, we're not allowed anywhere near him. He's a person of interest in her investigation, and Patrick and I aren't invited to the party. You ready for the cherry on the ice cream sundae?"

"I'm lactose intolerant. And on a diet."

Another dismissive sputter. "Ha! Mrs. Hassan heard her husband on the phone a couple of nights ago. She got the sense that Timothée Chablain was also supposed to be part of the meeting."

"What does Chablain say?"

"According to a coworker, he's with his wife at the hospital and out of pocket. Hospital staff confirmed that Angela Chablain checked in yesterday afternoon. Fever and cough. Routine bloodwork showed her counts were low, so they're doing a bone-marrow biopsy."

"I hope she's all right," Evan murmured. But he thought back to his conversation with Kelley earlier. "I have an idea."

CHAPTER 21

As Evan had hoped, Gerrit Watts was more than happy to talk to Elizabeth's old friend. Especially a friend who had just been offered a job by William Kelley. So eager, in fact, that Gerrit invited Evan to cocktails at his penthouse apartment in the Near North Side that evening. On the one hand, Evan was always happy to be offered cocktails. But he was disappointed that they weren't meeting at Theodore Watts's palatial estate in the suburb of Glencoe—the home where the *Architectural Digest* photos were taken.

For the rest of the day, Evan alternated between teaching his Friday class, meeting with students, and continuing his research on Shapira. Simon's courier arrived with the requested books: *The Little Daughter of Jerusalem*; *The Rediscovery of the Holy Land in the Nineteenth Century*; and *Jerusalem in the Nineteenth Century—The Old City*. Immediately he began to read *The Little Daughter of Jerusalem*, which was described as a fictionalized account of the Shapira family leading up to Moses Shapira's discovery of the leather scrolls and his disappearance after the scrolls were declared fakes. It was written by Shapira's oldest daughter, who used the pen name Myriam Harry. She was a lively and entertaining narrator.

Addie called to say they'd traced Kevin Grady to a Best Western near O'Hare Airport and brought him in for questioning. Agent Holliday—who was already aware of Grady's treasure hunt—had been present. Grady admitted he was searching for the Shapira Scrolls, broke down in tears when asked about Lawrence and Hassan's deaths, and finally confessed to assaulting Simon and Allen Finch. Holliday—having no use for what she dismissively called a Shapirologist—had departed after an hour. Addie and Patrick arrested Grady for the assaults, but he had an alibi for the night of Lawrence's death—he'd been home in Colorado with his brother and nephews. As for Hassan's murder, Grady had spent much of the evening at a diner. A patrol officer had confirmed the story.

No scrap of leather had been found in his belongings, and he denied taking it from Finch's lab. They'd keep on him.

At four in the afternoon, Addie came by Evan's office to give him a small recorder. She also handed over an elegant wristwatch. When he gave her a questioning look as he strapped on the watch, she offered a faint smile in return.

"It's a camera."

"In case I happen to stumble upon an inventory of the Watts collection."

"Or anything that you suspect might have been illegally removed to Gerrit's apartment from the Watts estate. Not for the court, of course. Just to give us some idea of what's going on."

"Can't I just use my phone?"

"Pulling out a phone to take a photo is rather obvious, isn't it? Okay, smile on three, you art thief. One more thing you should know—Gerrit Watts's finances are a mess. He's a self-proclaimed gambler who hasn't gambled well. Creditors are knocking on his door. His wife has sued for divorce and is probably hoping to keep what's left. He has good reason to want to hold on to his grandfather's estate."

She gave him a rundown on how to use the voice-activated recorder and the watch. When he'd demonstrated his proficiency to her satisfaction, she leaned back in her chair and crossed her arms.

"Maybe I should go with you, and never mind the Feds. If it turns out Gerrit Watts murdered Elizabeth and Hassan to gain control of his grandfather's collection, things could get dangerous."

A small warmth settled in Evan's heart. But he laughed. "Having a cop there will definitely convince Gerrit that he should be open and honest. Look at me, Addie. The advantage I have is that I'm utterly unthreatening. That, and the fact that William Kelley really did offer me a job."

Reluctantly, she nodded. "Just don't take any unnecessary risks."

He looked at the watch, then the recorder. "How do you define *unnecessary?*"

She eyeballed him for a moment, then said, "I couldn't get a transmitter from the department. But Patrick and I—off duty—will be parked close by. If you feel threatened, just dial me. The phone rings, Patrick and I will move in."

"What would Agent Holliday and the people of Chicago think about two detectives cooling their heels while a dwarf has drinks with a gambler? Shouldn't you be doing cop things?"

"We *are* doing cop things. This is *our* case. If the good people of Chicagoland knew what we were doing, they'd cheer. As for Agent Holliday," she added darkly, "what's to know? Two people interested in antiquities are having drinks together."

~~~

At five o'clock, Evan left Perro with Diana and headed toward the Near North Side and Gerrit's penthouse suite. He briefly considered taking Perro with him—surely it would be harder to murder a man when he'd brought along man's best friend. But he didn't want to endanger Diana's walking ottoman.

As he drove, he mulled over possible motivations for Gerrit to murder Elizabeth and then Hassan. Certainly, if Theodore Watts had intended his collection to go to Elizabeth's institute, Gerrit could very well consider his grandfather's actions treacherous and Elizabeth the instrument of that betrayal. Or perhaps Gerrit knew or believed that Elizabeth had taken artifacts from Theodore's collection that Gerrit felt were rightfully his. Then, too, it was possible that Gerrit was operating under the mistaken belief that if Elizabeth were dead, the collection would revert to him.

Of course, maybe Gerrit would try to convince him he was as pure as the driven snow.

Evan hated snow.

He turned on to North Wells Street.

What of Chuma Hassan? Perhaps the Egyptian had gotten in the middle somehow, brokering artifacts from Theodore Watts's collection. Or threatening to expose Gerrit. That, too, could be considered treachery.

Evan arrived at the Old Town Park development and followed Gerrit's instructions for the underground garage parking. After the concierge made a call upstairs to confirm that Gerrit was expecting Evan, the doorman ushered Evan into a swank elevator. The man wished him a good evening, then leaned in to push the button for the thirty-second floor. As the doors closed, Evan found himself wishing he'd come armed with more than a voice recorder, a camera, and his wits.

He double-checked that the recorder was still in his pocket and glanced at the time on the camera watch. Within seconds, the elevator opened directly onto Gerrit's penthouse apartment.

A softly lit, gray-walled antechamber with a pair of chairs and a console table bearing a tasteful scattering of silver-tinted accent pieces led to a living room with vaulted ceilings, marble floors, and impeccable modern decor in blues and grays. A curving staircase—also marble—led to the second floor, where a long hallway, lit by sconces, disappeared around a bend.

The place screamed money and modernity. There wasn't an antiquity in sight.

Evan edged into the room. "Mr. Watts?"

A voice answered from somewhere in the bowels of the penthouse. "Making drinks on the deck! Come on back!"

Evan walked through the living room, down a hallway and into a kitchen that boasted a subzero freezer and a gas stove fit to service a busy restaurant. He figured the place cost more per month than he made in a year.

No wonder Gerrit's finances were a mess.

Glass doors lay open to the evening, and Evan spotted a man standing at the railing, his back turned as he gazed at the majestic view of Chicago's skyline. Gerrit Watts, presumably. The glass-and-iron railing where he stood was only a few feet high—and the only thing between a drunken guest and a thirty-two-floor drop. Evan wondered if the potential for danger suited a man who thrived on risk.

Perhaps sensing Evan's presence, Gerrit turned.

He was a handsome man in his early thirties with blond hair worn in a low ponytail and a neatly trimmed beard. He wore dove-gray slacks and a cashmere sweater. A Rolex gleamed on his left wrist as he came forward to shake Evan's hand. The tilt of his smile suggested cynicism.

"I appreciate your call," he said. "I hope you like vermouth. I mixed us a batch of aperitifs."

"Sounds perfect," Evan managed.

Gerrit waved Evan to a chair near the small pool and hot tub, then took a seat on the other side of a coffee table, choosing the side with the view. Nearby, outdoor heaters turned the chilly spring night into sweater weather. Gerrit poured drinks for them both, raised his glass and clinked it against Evan's, then took a healthy swallow.

He gave a satisfied sigh. "Perfect finish to the day."

"This is very good," Evan agreed as he tried to find a comfortable way to sit in the deep chair. "Do I detect a hint of . . . is it mugwort?"

"A connoisseur, I see. Yes, the vermouth is from a wine fortified with mugwort. According to the vintner, mugwort is easier to find than wormwood, but just as good for the digestion. I first learned about the medicinal benefits of wormwood on a trip with my grandfather."

Evan braced himself on the armrest. "Did you travel a lot with him?"

"When I was in high school. And sometimes during my college years. My parents died when I was sixteen, and Theo felt sorry for me. He was my only living relative, so I guess he thought he had to step up."

Evan finally perched on the edge of the chair so that his feet were firmly on the ground. "Why did you stop traveling together?"

"It was Theo's call. He was nearly seventy when he adopted me, and it got difficult for him. The long plane rides, sleeping on cots or on the ground. But he was a real adventurer when he was young."

"You must have enjoyed your time together."

Gerrit tipped his hand in a back-and-forth gesture. "Not really my thing, archaeological digs. Jungles. Bugs. Call me a hothouse orchid, but I preferred the comforts of urbanity to nights under the stars."

"Yet you're interested in Theo's collection."

Gerrit tossed back his drink and poured another, topping off Evan's. "Ah, the collection. With everyone, it's always Theo's collection." He grabbed a remote from the table and pressed a button, igniting a gas firepit Evan hadn't noticed before. A wall of warmth enveloped them even as the potted shrubberies shivered in the breeze.

"Rumor has it, it's a good collection," Evan said.

"And you'd like to lay your hands on it."

"Not at all," Evan said easily. "Although I admit a certain curiosity as to its contents."

Gerrit's gaze narrowed, giving him the look of an inquisitive weasel. "Why is Kelley offering you a job? You're the famous Sparrow. World-renowned forensic semiotician. Aren't you helping the police with Dr. Lawrence's murder?"

"I'm operating at a distance from the investigation."

But Gerrit leaned back in his chair. "Are you here because I'm a suspect?"

Evan sensed the glittering skyline that lay close behind him. The long, long drop to the street. He forced a laugh. "Would I be sharing cocktails with you three hundred feet above the pavement if I had any thought that you were a killer?"

Gerrit laughed, too, but there was an odd look in his eye. He poured the third round of drinks, then lifted a bent leg and crossed it over the other, his ankle atop his knee.

"I know I'm a suspect," he said. "With Elizabeth out of the way, there is little standing between me and Theo's collection. Hell, *I'd* look at me."

He took a large swallow of his aperitif. Evan could almost see the cogs whirling behind the man's pale-blue eyes.

"Do you have any theories as to Elizabeth's killer?" Evan asked.

"You're the profiler, right? How do you read the signs?"

"I'm not at liberty to expound on my thoughts."

Gerrit grunted. His restless gaze roamed the rooftop ornaments and the skyline. Evan imagined he was thinking of all he could lose if things went badly for him. A minute or two ticked by before he nodded as if to himself and his eyes returned to Evan.

"I assume you and the cops are looking at Timothée Chablain," he said.

"Why him?"

"Oh, let me count the ways, as Theo used to say. It all has to do with desperation. Isn't that what drives so many murderers?"

"Why is Chablain desperate? He seems to be in a good position."

"He'd want you to think that, the arrogant prick. But his job at Veritas is hanging by a thread. Which is probably why Kelley came to you."

Evan made a noncommittal sound, but he found the tidbit—true or not—interesting. Kelley had implied that Chablain was leaving of his own choice.

"Then there's the fact of his home life," Gerrit continued. "He's been unhappily married for years. His wife is the daughter of a Texas pastor, and she's the one who introduced Chablain to Kelley. She got him the job, then started riding his back about all the travel he was doing. You should be home. You have kids. Blah, blah, blah."

"Home and hearth aren't your scene, I take it," Evan said dryly.

"I gave it a try. Turns out I'm not cut out for family life. My marriage was a mistake and will soon be buried in the past." He raised his glass in mock salute. "I like my freedom. Chablain does, too. No wonder he found something on the side to amuse him. He was getting ready to jump ship, is what I heard. Tell the wife to take the kids and go back to Texas and let him do his work in peace. But guess what happened?"

"Mrs. Chablain got sick."

"Hand of Murphy. That's right. She got cancer. Not long to live. Terrible tragedy. And now he's saddled with her until the bitter end."

Evan decided that it wasn't only Gerrit's expression that put him in mind of a weasel.

"What of the other woman?" he asked. "I assume that's what you mean by something on the side."

Gerrit's smile was sly. "What would you do if your bitch of a wife wouldn't even let you in her bed anymore? A man's gotta sleep somewhere. With someone."

Evan kept his expression neutral. "You seem to know a lot about Chablain."

"You think?" He gave another of his hiccupping laughs. "We've shared a few drinks together, talking shop. And other things."

"Shop meaning antiquities."

"More about travel. And what it's like to have nice things, to be a little up in the world. Chablain and I met at an auction at Christie's, and we hit it off."

"None of this makes him sound like a killer."

"None of it would unless he got tempted to put a pillow on his wife's face and put them both out of their misery. But here's my theory: every human is just one good reason away from committing murder. All it takes is the right push. And in my humble opinion, it was Elizabeth's own actions that drove Chablain to kill her."

Sudden anger popped and fizzed in Evan's blood. Casually, he reached for his drink. "What did she do to earn her own death?"

"I'm not saying she *earned* it. Just that she provoked Chablain. You know Elizabeth agreed to do some work for Veritas, right? With Theo's collection tied up in litigation, she was out of a job, and I think she was getting desperate. Had to be rough, you follow?"

Evan was struck by the disconnect between Gerrit's apparent compassion for Elizabeth's loss of work and the fact that he was solely responsible for it. He wondered what—if anything—Theo had left in his will for his grandson. This penthouse? The estate in Glencoe? Both of which required upkeep and tax payments.

Speaking of Timothée Chablain's desperation, just how desperate was Gerrit Watts?

Evan said, "I heard she'd done a few things for Veritas, yes."

"Apparently, she did more than a 'few things.' She was Kelley's new darling. A scholar with an unimpeachable rep. But she also complained to Kelley about Chablain's shady ways, told him it was hurting Veritas's reputation. Kelley must have listened because he had a long talk with Chablain. Told him to start looking for other opportunities. Now Chablain is going to lose the cash cow that let him live out his Indiana Jones fantasy, and ain't that a kick in the nuts? He's also going to lose access to the treasures owned by the Veritas Foundation."

"Access—you mean for scholarly purposes?" Evan was thinking of the nondisclosures Kelley required and that kept his scholars from publishing.

"Scholarly purposes? Right!" Gerrit snickered. "I liked Chablain before I figured out that he must have killed Elizabeth. But I'm also an honest man, so I'm going to tell you the truth. Feel free to pass it along to your cop friends."

Evan took a sip of his drink, said nothing.

"Veritas has purchased a bunch of stuff that they're never going to put on display. Some because it doesn't add anything to the story they're going to push in their museum. Some because"—here he glanced around as if expecting Kelley to materialize from behind the potted plants—"not everything they have is legit."

"Meaning what, exactly?" Evan asked, thinking of the recorder humming quietly in his pocket.

"Let's just say Chablain was more interested in acquiring goodies than checking out the paperwork." Gerrit's voice had taken on a slight slur from the cocktails. "I'd bet you anything Chablain is stealing the stuff Veritas has socked away, taking it right out from under Kelley and Dawson's noses and squirreling it somewhere. Waiting for the right chance to sell it to a private collector. Or to sell it back to some bumfuck museum in some bumfuck, backwater, war-torn country. And he walks away with a pocketful."

"You sound angry."

Gerrit tossed back the rest of his drink and drew in a deep breath. "The motherfucker had the balls to ask *me* for a job handling Theo's collection. *Me!* When he knows perfectly well the collection can't be touched until the judge unfreezes the assets. He was asking me to break the law. Wouldn't surprise me if he'd already managed to get his hands on some of Theo's things."

"How would he do that?"

"He did a walk-through a long time ago. Back before Theo hired Elizabeth."

Evan wondered if Gerrit wasn't telling him a story that was bass-ackward. It seemed equally possible that Gerrit had gone to Chablain and asked for his help pilfering artifacts from Theo's collection to sell them on the black market. Chablain—if he was smart—almost certainly would have turned down Gerrit's offer as too risky. Which could explain Gerrit's decision to smear Chablain. The dirt had to end up somewhere.

"Why haven't you taken your theory to the police?"

"I'm still thinking things through. Lots of things."

A distinct chill brushed Evan's back, despite the heat rising from the firepit. He wondered why Gerrit had so readily invited him over for drinks. If it was to paint Chablain as a murderer, it would have been far simpler to make a statement to the police.

Gerrit pushed up the sleeves of his cashmere sweater, revealing heavily muscled forearms. Time in a gym or a lot of golf, Evan figured. Either way, the man's agitation was alarming. He decided to change gears.

"How well did you know Elizabeth?"

"Well enough. She was in and out of my grandfather's home in Glencoe for the last year. Digging through all the crap he'd bought over the decades. They were a pair, those two. Knee deep in old things, digging through boxes, laying out old bits and fragments, piecing pottery and broken figurines back together. Elizabeth taking hundreds of notes and photos, making sketches." Gerrit rolled his eyes. "Unbelievably boring. My grandfather was so interested in the past he hardly cared about what was going on here and now."

Evan heard a plaintive note in Gerrit's voice. Had the grandson felt like he came in second, behind his grandfather's love of antiquities? It wouldn't be the first time.

"Elizabeth was making an inventory?" Evan asked.

"Like I said. And before you bother, I don't have it."

With this last statement, Gerrit gave off multiple tells of a liar—smoothing his hair, offering a bored expression, fidgeting. But Evan understood why he would lie. It could be damaging for Gerrit's lawsuit if the contents of his grandfather's collection were to become public. Especially if the collection contained looted or stolen items, which it almost certainly did.

"And your relationship with Hassan?" Evan asked. "His receptionist mentioned you canceled an appointment with him."

Gerrit looked alarmed. "Is it the police who've been tracking me? Or is it you?"

Evan sidestepped the question. "My interest is with Hassan. I thought he might have had a relationship with Elizabeth."

Gerrit settled back in his seat. "With Elizabeth gone, I wanted to know if the Egyptian would be willing to do an appraisal of Theo's collection. And if you're looking at me as Hassan's killer, I'm sure the cops already checked my alibi. I was in LA and had to cancel our meeting. Now with him dead, too, maybe I should be alarmed. What if I'd been there last night?"

"Perhaps you would have stopped a murder."

Gerrit's eyes widened. "You think?"

"Impossible to know." Evan set his empty glass on the table and waved off Gerrit's offer of more. "Would you mind if I ask you one thing about your grandfather's collection?"

Gerrit patted his pockets as if looking for cigarettes. "You ask a lot of questions. I invited you here tonight to size you up, figure out why Kelley wants you to take Chablain's place. And why you might be interested. I thought I'd also share my suspicions about Chablain and get that off my chest. But it seems like you're the one asking all the questions."

"I appreciate your thoughts about Chablain," Evan said. "As for why Kelley offered his job to me, I can only guess that he sees me as an adequate substitute for Elizabeth."

"Two unimpeachable academics, huh?" Gerrit narrowed his eyes. "Go on, then. What do you want to know about Theo's goodies?"

Evan slid his phone from his pocket and pulled up a photo from *Architectural Digest*, the one with the framed sketch showing a fragment of the Shapira Scrolls. He zoomed in, then held up his phone for Gerrit to see.

"Do you know what your grandfather's interest was in this drawing?"

Gerrit took the phone and zoomed in farther. "What is it?"

"It's a replica of a drawing that appeared in a science magazine in 1883."

"I do kind of remember that picture. Theo hung it in his bedroom years ago. It doesn't look like much." A hitch entered his voice. "Is it worth something?"

Leery of tipping his hand even more but wanting to see Gerrit's reaction, Evan said, "Did your grandfather ever mention the Shapira Scrolls?"

Slowly, Gerrit lowered his crossed leg. Some unspoken thought moved across his face. "I think so. Something about how even the best can be fooled. Does that sound right?"

"Probably. They were a nineteenth-century forgery. Worth more as a curiosity than for any intrinsic value."

Gerrit scratched the side of his face. Tugged on his beard. "I might have heard something about them being real. Not fakes at all. What do they look like?"

"Thick leather scrolls, folded. Roughly three or four inches wide and variable in length."

Gerrit knotted his hands together, cracked his knuckles.

"People dream, Mr. Watts," Evan said, watching Gerrit carefully. "They dream big."

"Real big, right?" A flush brightened his cheeks. Gerrit pushed himself out of the chair and yanked his phone out of his pocket. The screen was dark.

"I have to take this," he said, waving the phone.

"Of course. If you'll excuse me, I need to make use of your facilities."

"Bathroom is on the other side of the stairs."

Gerrit's voice rose behind him as Evan stepped between the glass sliders and into the apartment.

He bypassed the half bath on the main floor and hurried up the stairs. If Gerrit caught him roaming the second floor, he could pretend he'd somehow missed the downstairs bath. At the top of the stairs, he noted a console table holding family photos and an heirloom Bible. He spared a glance for the Bible, then turned right. This side of the hall held a guest bedroom, the master suite, and a small game room. He returned to the stairs, listened for Gerrit's voice on the phone, then race-walked to the other side. Only one room occupied this side of the stairs.

The door was locked, but Evan had come prepared. Lockpicking was yet another skill his brother had taught him. River was nothing if not resourceful.

Within a few moments, he was inside the room, which proved to be Gerrit's office.

He started with the two-drawer filing cabinet, thumbing rapidly through the contents. He bypassed a great many folders with labels suggesting that Gerrit was not only a casino gambler but a man who had wagered in other ways—stock options, IPOs, hedge funds, high-yield bonds, and investments in everything from cryptocurrency to orange juice. Evan snapped a few pictures, then quickly moved on—while it might be desirable to paint Gerrit as a murderer desperate for money, any photo he took under these circumstances would be tossed out in court. This was purely a fishing expedition.

What he wanted was an inventory of the Watts collection. Or evidence that the Shapira Scrolls might have once resided there. Or perhaps still did.

The contents of the desk were equally unhelpful. Papers consisted of more mundane matters such as routine bills and invoices for mechanical work on his Land Rover SUV. Evan touched a wireless mouse, and the laptop blinked on. Password protected, so no help there.

He skimmed through the scattering of file folders on top of the desk; a single slim folder caught his eye. Labeled **T. W.**, the folder held eight invoices. Three bore Hassan's name and signature. The other five were labeled **VERITAS FOUNDATION** and were signed **T. CHABLAIN**.

Evan took photos in rapid succession, scarcely noting the objects listed. Time for that later. He replaced the papers and the folder, slid his phone back into his pocket, then hurried back out to the hallway where he relocked and closed the door.

Silence greeted him. He strained to hear and was relieved when Gerrit's voice floated in from outside.

He sped back toward the stairs, pausing at the table he'd noticed earlier. The photos were of family—a young Gerrit with his parents before their deaths. A few more of him with his grandfather. None of his wife.

It was the Bible on its elegantly carved book stand that most caught Evan's attention. The book was the only thing in the apartment that looked old and worn. It lay open to the Gospel According to Matthew, but he gently turned the pages, wanting to see if the Bible passages left near the bodies of Elizabeth and Hassan were marked in Gerrit's Bible.

From the deck came a shout. Gerrit, calling his name.

"Be right down!" Evan called back.

There! First Corinthians 10:9 had been underlined in pencil. "Neither let us test the lord, as some of them tested, and perished by the serpents."

He raised his hand with the watch Addie had given him.

Starting up the stairs, Gerrit said, "What are you doing?"

A quick click, then Evan flipped back to the Gospel According to Matthew and straightened before he turned around. "I'm so sorry," he said, pressing a hand to his stomach. "Something in my lunch must have disagreed with me. I thought a bathroom upstairs would be better, if you catch my drift. I was on my way downstairs when I noticed your Bible. Early twentieth century, isn't it?"

Gerrit gave him a searching gaze, looking for the lie. His eyes flicked toward the closed door of his study then back to the Bible.

"Why don't we head back outside?" he said. "I don't think we finished our conversation."

Thinking of the three-hundred-foot drop, Evan pressed a hand to his stomach. "I think it's best I get home. I'm not well."

Gerrit dogged his steps as they returned to the main level. At the bottom of the staircase, he slid around Evan, then turned to face him. His expression was contorted with the rage he'd held close all evening.

"That collection belongs to me!" he cried. "I'm the grandson! Theo had no right to offer it to Elizabeth."

At the mention of Elizabeth's name, Evan's own anger surged. "She would have made it possible for scholars to study his collection. For art lovers to go to her institute and take in the beauty of another culture."

"It wasn't hers! Theo was losing his mind. That's the only reason he would give her what is rightfully mine."

Evan swept his arms open, encompassing the room with its luxurious furnishings, the dazzling skyline visible through the windows. "So that you could use it for this? That's what you're doing, isn't it, Gerrit? Selling off your grandfather's collection to support yourself. To support this lifestyle. And Chablain is helping you. Did he help you murder Elizabeth, too?"

Gerrit's eyes grew wide, and he sagged to the stairs, all fight gone out of him.

Evan stayed clear, not trusting this new Gerrit. "But Chablain did something to anger you, didn't he? Maybe he lied about how much money an artifact brought, then pocketed the difference. Or maybe he told you he would no longer sell Theo's artifacts."

Gerrit sank his face into his hands.

Evan, mindful of the recorder in his pocket, continued. "You killed Hassan because he got wind of what you and Chablain were doing and wanted a piece of the action. Or maybe he'd been helping all along and simply wanted a bigger piece. So you killed him, then somehow created your alibi. Or do you have a partner?"

"I'm not a killer," Gerrit said.

"Then talk to me," Evan said. "Talk to the police. You'll never get your grandfather's collection if you're in prison."

Gerrit kept his face in his hands.

At a sound, Evan whirled around. The elevators doors opened. Miriam Fuller, Chablain's so-called pit bull, stepped into the atrium. Her eyes stared daggers at Evan.

CHAPTER 22

Miriam strode past Evan and went to Gerrit. She sat next to him on the stairs and took one of his hands between both of hers.

"Get out," she snarled at Evan. "Little man."

He didn't need a second invitation. He walked hurriedly toward the still-gaping doors of the elevator. Once inside, he turned back.

Gerrit still sat, his head against Miriam's shoulder. She had closed her eyes and was patting Gerrit's hand.

The doors whisked shut.

~~~~~

A short time later, Evan pulled in behind Addie's Jeep Cherokee. Addie hopped out and opened the back door for him.

"Are you okay?" she asked. He must have looked as shaky as he felt.

"Now I know how spies feel."

He climbed into the Jeep and took a few deep breaths while Addie slid behind the wheel. She and Patrick swiveled around to look at him. Silently, he removed the voice recorder from his pocket and set it on the console. Addie pressed "Play."

The two detectives listened in silence. Then they listened again.

"Who is that at the end?" Addie asked after their second listen.

"Miriam Fuller. Chablain's assistant. We met her at the Veritas headquarters."

"Was she there on Chablain's behalf?"

"Impossible to know."

Evan filled them in on what wasn't on the recording because he'd been alone—the underlined passage in the Bible on Gerrit's table and the documents he'd seen on Gerrit's desk. Then he handed over his phone and stared outside at the passing traffic while Addie and Patrick skimmed through what he'd photographed. His itch—or rather, his burning desire—to study the sales invoices would have to wait a little longer.

Finally, Addie and Patrick looked up. Patrick ran a hand over his scalp and gave a long whistle.

"I'd hate to have this guy's financial problems," he said.

Addie looked down at the phone again. "These invoices suggest that Chablain is helping Gerrit sell off items from the Watts collection. But there's no indication who the end buyer is."

"What did he sell?" Evan asked, unable to wait a second longer.

She handed his phone back to him. "You're a better judge than I am."

Evan studied the invoices he'd photographed. A cuneiform tablet. A sandstone bas-relief. A bronze bell. Several Greek papyri. There were no details offered in the invoices, and no way to confirm that what was listed on the form was what Gerrit had actually sold. Those in the business knew: if you want to launder an artifact, simply change the description.

Only one listing stood out by its very innocuousness. *Blackened leather scroll, 7x9, Hebrew writing.*

He raised the phone. "This entry could be for one of the Shapira Scrolls."

Addie looked at the invoice again. "If so, wouldn't that suggest Lawrence's death wasn't linked to them?"

"This invoice mentions only one scroll. But there's a total of fifteen, assuming Watts found them all. Maybe she had the rest."

"Hate to state the obvious here," Patrick said, "but if Gerrit is selling off artifacts to Chablain, why would he point us right toward him?"

Addie took a swig from her water bottle. "For all we know, the items listed here weren't in the collection. They could be privately held and part of Gerrit's inheritance. Which would make their sale legal." She glanced back at Evan. "Beg to differ?"

"As long as they're not looted or listed as part of the collection being held in trust, then I would assume Gerrit can do whatever he wants with them."

"Both of which are easy to claim since Lawrence is dead and we don't have an inventory. Sounds like it's time for us to have a sit-down with Mr. Watts."

Patrick looked glum. "As long as we can get a papal dispensation from her holiness Agent Holliday."

～～～

Evan left the detectives as they planned their next move and returned to his car. Christina called just as he started the engine. His heart lifted.

He answered the phone with, "I'm sorry."

"It was rather unkind," she said. "Even for an absentminded professor."

"I can only plead that it was a bad day. I throw myself on your mercy."

Her voice lightened. "I'll ponder your punishment."

"Maybe you should come to the house and mete it out," he said. "Whatever it is."

She laughed, and his heart lifted further. But then she said, "I called because a few of us are heading out for a late dinner at Chant for a little inspired global cuisine. I was hoping you could meet us there."

Evan considered it. Checked the time. He wasn't that far away. And he missed Christina.

Christina mistook his hesitation for uncertainty. "Your friend Avraham is coming, too, if that helps persuade you. He's the one who suggested the place."

Evan's chest suddenly hurt. He pictured the pair of them together, both tall, both devastatingly attractive. Smart. Gainfully employed. Unquestionably suitable—for a fling if not for something more. Ah, the trampled male ego. He held his sigh and cleared his throat. "Thanks for the invite. But it's been a long day, and I seem to have eaten something that disagrees with me." A good liar knows to stick with his story.

"Oh," she said.

"I'll call you tomorrow."

"You sure you don't need company? I mean, if you aren't feeling well . . ."

"I'll take some antacids and get a good night's sleep."

Now *that* would have her swooning over him. Pragmatic, practical Evan.

"Sleep well, then," she said. "Call me if you need me."

I need you echoed through his mind as the line went dead.

Traffic was blessedly light, for which Evan was grateful. He figured he'd used up all his goodwill and patience during the day. He swung by Diana's friend's house to pick up Perro—the allergic friend was sneezing, but at least the dog was happy to see him—and drove home. He fed Ginny, took Perro out for a final tour of the bushes, turned his phone on "Do Not Disturb," and silenced the ringer. In case of an emergency, only three people would be able to reach him—his mother, River, and Addie.

But when he finally got into bed, he tossed and turned, staring into the dark while his mind made a list. Finch's injury and Kevin Grady, aka Polo Shirt. Gerrit's lies. The unexplained presence of Miriam Fuller. Christina's phone call. And, more than anything, the tantalizing, mysterious, and very missing Shapira Scrolls, which—even as he struggled for sleep—might be making their way to the four corners of the earth.

Did Gerrit know that he'd likely sold Chablain and/or Veritas one of the Shapira Scrolls? Did he have more of them? Had he planned to meet with Hassan to discuss a sale? Perhaps, when Gerrit had to reschedule and Hassan couldn't take possession, the intended buyer had struck the Egyptian down in fury. It fit Kevin Grady's pattern.

Except Grady had an alibi for both Elizabeth's death and Hassan's.

What if Hassan had promised the scrolls to someone else, and when he couldn't deliver, the killer accused him of treachery by bashing him with the statue of Aten?

None of this lined up with the blackhearted but lily-handed people who lived at the top of the antiquities food chain.

No. A sense of brutality hovered over this.

Evan closed his eyes. Opened them. Closed them again.

One image kept recurring in the darkness.

Elizabeth's upright body, trapped in her car with a cobra.

Evan tried—and failed—to imagine Gerrit Watts wielding a cobra. What of Chablain, who claimed to hate snakes? And Dawson, who also loathed them but admitted to some experience?

Then there was the mysterious Miriam Fuller, who clearly had a personal relationship with Gerrit, despite working for the man whom Gerrit had accused of murder.

~~~

Sleep finally came for him around 4:00 a.m. Perro came for him at five thirty. With a groan, Evan dragged himself out of bed, fed and watered both the dog and the hawk, then cooked up eggs and ham for himself. He ate in the kitchen, staring out at a garden that was slowly recovering from the ravages of winter.

Only after breakfast did he pick up his phone. There were two calls and two messages, all from numbers he didn't recognize.

Nothing from Christina. Or Avraham.

He went to his voice mail and pressed the speaker icon.

The first message was from a woman, Sandra Yee. She identified herself as Elizabeth's attorney, apologized for not phoning sooner, and asked him to call back immediately.

Evan blinked stupidly at the phone. He was sleep deprived. It was 7:00 a.m. on a Saturday, but he dialed Yee, left a message, and prepared a large pot of coffee while he waited for a callback. Over his first cup of coffee, he conducted an online search of the attorney. Her name popped right up. Sandra Yee, attorney-at-law specializing in trusts and estate planning. He scrolled through her website and looked at reviews. She appeared legit.

He was on his second cup of coffee when Yee returned his call.

"I have a few things for you from Elizabeth," she said in a crisp voice. "And some paperwork for you to review and sign. Again, I apologize for not reaching out sooner. I was out of town and didn't learn of Elizabeth's passing until I returned to Chicago late yesterday. But I'm in the office today."

"Pardon my confusion, Ms. Yee. But until recently, Elizabeth's attorney was Ralph Raines. Did Elizabeth tell you why she made the change?"

"Elizabeth mentioned a potential conflict of interest. Another attorney in the same firm is handling Gerrit Watts's case—the younger Mr. Watts is contesting his grandfather's trust, as you might have heard. Elizabeth didn't feel comfortable with the same firm handling both her estate and Gerrit Watts's case. Especially given that she wasn't informed of the conflict or given a waiver to sign agreeing to this. Attorneys will debate whether Mr. Raines's actions and those of the other attorney are technically illegal. But it is most certainly unethical. Now, do you have time later this morning to come in? I'm free after nine thirty."

He looked at the address on her website. "I can be there by ten."

"Good. Brace yourself, Dr. Wilding. Your life is about to change."

"What do you mean?"

"For one thing, Elizabeth gave you power of attorney over the trust she inherited from Theodore Watts. She also named you heir of that trust and, in her will, gave you ownership of her institute."

"She—I—"

"I'll explain more in person," Yee said and disconnected.

Evan stared through the window at the crocuses pushing their way up through the rich garden soil. Power of attorney? He was in charge of the institute? He was going to *inherit* the institute?

Even a third cup of coffee didn't give him enough brain power to process the news. He listened to the second voice mail.

It was from Omar Rasheed, the antiquities dealer in Jerusalem, returning Evan's own call. Evan dialed immediately.

Rasheed picked up on the third ring. "Dr. Wilding? How can I help you?" His English was very good.

"I'm hoping you can help me reach your grandson, Samad. I need to speak with him."

"I wish I could help you," Rasheed said. "But Sam has gone into hiding."

"Do you know why?"

"I do. And I assume you do as well since you knew enough to reach out to me. Sam and I are very close, but even I do not know where he is."

Evan stood and poured a final cup of coffee. "If he contacts you, please tell him I'm a good friend of Elizabeth's. And that I don't believe he had anything to do with her death. But he might have important information that could help us find the killer. It's possible he saw something. Or heard something."

The silence lasted along enough that Evan looked at his phone to see if they were still connected.

Then Omar said, "Elizabeth trusted you. This much I know. If Sam calls me, I will let him know that you wish to speak with him."

He hung up before Evan could thank him.

~~~

"She said nothing to you about this?" Yee asked him.

Evan sat in the sun-filled office of Sandra Yee and stared in disbelief at the paperwork spread across her desk. And at the nine-by-twelve metal box to which he now possessed the key.

"She didn't say a word," he finally managed.

"Well, congratulations."

He fell back in his seat, unsure what to think or do. He looked down, half expecting to see Perro sitting at his feet. But he'd left the dog to fend for himself at the house. No doubt the corgi would make short work of the carpets. Or maybe a stack of books.

"I could get you some water," Yee said. "Or would you like something stronger?"

He looked up and she smiled. She removed a small bottle of Islay scotch and two glasses from a desk drawer and poured a finger of amber liquid into each glass. "It's five o'clock somewhere," she said.

Evan accepted the whisky gratefully, and after clinking his glass to Yee's, he tossed back the drink. "This happens often?"

"Often enough." She sipped her scotch and set the glass aside. "Are you ready to sign?"

"May I ask a few questions first?"

"Ask as many as you wish."

"Do you know where Theodore Watts's collection is being held?"

"Before his death, Mr. Watts had most of his collection moved to a secure storage location in Glencoe. A place that puts Fort Knox to shame. Yes, I have the key. And no, I can't give it to you until the court makes a ruling either for or against Gerrit Watts's case. The court has issued an injunction that the collection isn't to be moved until they reach a decision. In light of Elizabeth's death, I am now the trustee until the case is decided. These are the terms that were dictated by Elizabeth herself—she must have anticipated both Gerrit Watts's case and that you might not be immediately ready to step in as trustee."

Evan forced his stunned brain to stay in step. "Why wasn't the collection transferred to the institute before Mr. Watts's death?"

"Mr. Watts did originally intend to move the collection to Elizabeth's institute on Woodlawn Avenue. But there were several concerns. One is that there are likely illicit items in the collection, and Mr. Watts wanted these issues resolved before Elizabeth's institute took possession. This was to avoid any possible taint on her business. He also knew that his grandson was likely to contest the trust, and both he and Dr. Lawrence were concerned with any appearance of fraud or impropriety. Elizabeth was worried that if the trust was frozen, she ran the risk of being accused of editing the inventory and selling off any items in her possession for her personal benefit."

"Meaning, there is an inventory?"

"I suspect it's in that metal case, although Elizabeth didn't make me privy to its contents." She tapped her palm on the box. "I also have in my possession a self-published book that Mr. Watts put together years ago with the help of a scholar from the Art Institute of Chicago. I can't say how the photos match up with the inventory."

"I take it the book isn't tied up by the lawsuit?"

She smiled again. Her glossy black bob swung as she shook her head. "It's in the manila envelope next to the box. What other questions do you have?"

"Does the fact that the trust is being contested prevent federal authorities from confiscating and returning artifacts to their country of origin?" Evan was thinking of Agent Holliday.

Yee folded her hands in front of her on the desk. "There are two separate issues here—the civil law that covers the trust. And the criminality of possible fraud. The probate case is immaterial to the Feds since they aren't concerned with who owns an artifact. They care only whether an item was legally acquired."

"Meaning the answer is no—the probate case won't prevent the Feds from confiscating items."

"Correct. If investigators from the FBI or Homeland Security know or have reason to suspect there are illicit items in Mr. Watts's collection, they can make a move at any time. And I want to be clear. Mr. Watts didn't create a trust to protect assets that didn't rightfully belong to him. Quite the opposite. He and Elizabeth were in the process of researching questionable items in his collection and returning them to their rightful owners. On the one hand, I believe he wanted credit for doing the right thing. But on the other, he won't turn over in his grave if federal agents learn what's in the collection and take possession on their own."

The sudden lightness in Evan's chest made him realize the load he'd been carrying—his fear that Holliday had been right, that his friend had gone to the dark side.

He forced himself to focus. "Putting aside the contents of the collection, what happens if Gerrit Watts's lawsuit succeeds and the judge rules in his favor?"

She arched a slender brow. "Then I will appeal the case to the appellate court. Now, if you have no further questions, we should move on. There are conditions to your acceptance of the inheritance."

"Does that explain all this paperwork?"

"It does. Elizabeth wanted to ensure you would continue the work of repatriating illegally obtained artifacts either with or without the help of federal agencies. And to continue her work repairing and restoring the remaining artifacts in the Watts collection, making them available to both scholars and the public."

Evan opened his mouth to speak, but Yee held up a hand.

"I know this is a shock for you, Dr. Wilding. Elizabeth expected you to have concerns. She said that since you are neither a historian nor an archaeologist, her hope was that you would oversee the institute in a managerial sense and hire someone from your vast network to handle the day-to-day. And to expand the scope of the institute if you wished. If it helps, Dr. Lawrence was very much aware of the many demands on your time. Thus, she also left instructions for the sale of her institute and the Watts collection, should that be what you decide to do." She moved her hands to her lap. "I can see that you have more questions."

Overwhelmed by Yee's news that he might become the owner of the Chicago Institute of Middle Eastern Antiquities, Evan found himself focusing on the box. On its possible contents. On the tantalizing fragment of leather the detectives had found in Elizabeth's pocket—a fragment that she'd been unable to deliver to Finch and his laboratory.

"Did Elizabeth ever mention the Shapira Scrolls?"

Yee thought for a moment, then shook her head. "Not that I recall. The only artifacts she talked about in specific terms were two items she was in the process of returning to Cambodia. Are these scrolls something you believe are in the Watts collection?"

"They might be."

She nodded as if that was sufficient. "There are two other things Dr. Lawrence wanted you to know. The first is that Kelley and his employees will assure you that any mistakes they have made during their acquisition of artifacts—and here I'm referring to their purchases of looted antiquities—was due to their inexperience and naivete. However, employees of the Veritas Foundation were made aware of the risks and how to avoid them more than two years ago by an expert in cultural property law. An attorney by the name of Mr. Charles Weyden presented to Mr. Kelley, his wife, and their employees detailed guidelines to follow whenever they were considering a purchase. Most specifically, how to check on the history of ownership of an artifact—that is, its provenance. According to Dr. Lawrence, Timothée Chablain and others at the foundation were aware of these guidelines and frequently chose to ignore them."

Evan was unsurprised by the news. Dawson had called Chablain flashy, a movie-star wannabe. Maybe he wasn't the only bad actor Kelley had employed.

Yee pulled a ring binder out from one of the piles of paperwork and placed it on top of the stack. "This is a copy of Mr. Weyden's report. Elizabeth wanted you to have it. There is no indication of how many employees attended Mr. Weyden's talk or were made aware of his report. And you should know that Weyden wasn't engaged as an attorney for the Kelleys or their foundation. Rather, he acted as an expert consultant."

"Got it. You said there were two things?"

"Dr. Lawrence thought it likely that William Kelley would learn of your upcoming inheritance and offer you a job in order to gain access to the Watts collection. He would present his offer as a way to offer you financial help until the institute is up and running."

"How would Kelley know Elizabeth wanted me to have the institute?"

"This might come as a shock," Yee said, her voice dripping with sarcasm, "but not all attorneys are ethical. Within the same firm we have attorneys representing Theodore Watts, Gerrit Watts, and the Kelley family. Originally, Elizabeth accepted Kelley's recommendation that she hire Ralph Raines to help her with her estate. At the time, it seemed like an innocent suggestion."

"It wasn't?"

"Not at all." Yee set down her pen and picked up her scotch. "It turned out there exists a covetous nest of people eager to get their hands on Theodore Watts's collection. By hook or by crook."

CHAPTER 23

Attorney Sandra Yee offered Evan the privacy of a conference room in which to review the paperwork and to study the contents of the lockbox. But Evan asked if he could save the paperwork for later and take the box with him.

"I need time and privacy to process this," he said. "Whatever it is."

"I understand. Give me a call when you've thought things through so we can take the next steps. As I said, you aren't obliged to accept ownership of the institute or Mr. Watts's collection."

"What happens if I refuse?"

"Then I'll handle the sale of Dr. Lawrence's estate and appoint someone to care for the collection. Likely, most artifacts will be donated to museums. Any questionable items will be turned over to the appropriate federal agency."

Evan nodded. Yee walked him out of the office, stopping in the doorway.

"I know what Dr. Lawrence asks of you is a lot," she said. "But I hope you'll give it serious consideration. From what I know of you, you and the institute would be a good fit for each other."

~~~

The urge to open Elizabeth's box was almost overpowering. But it felt important to do things the right way. He drove around for a time, contemplating the divergent paths of his future, then stopped for lunch at a food truck. Eventually, he made it to the institute, parked, and carried the box with him up the path to the door. He used his key to let himself in, then climbed the stairs to Elizabeth's office, pausing for a moment to gaze upon Cleopatra's serene face.

Decision brought serenity. But the work that led to that moment consisted of storm and chaos.

In Elizabeth's office, the crime-scene techs had come and gone. The items that remained—the photos, some books, the sinister toad—were slightly out of place. Tracings of fingerprint powder lingered on door-knobs and desk pulls.

He placed the box on the desk, then reluctantly sat in Elizabeth's chair. It was much too big for him—Elizabeth had been a tall and large-boned woman. He wondered if he should read something into his inability to rest comfortably at her desk. If he should consider it a sign that he could never take her place. That he shouldn't even consider it.

How could he possibly continue her work?

"You know how to humble a man," he said to the quiet air in her office.

The toad's baleful glare suggested it agreed.

He stared at the box. He hoped against hope that it held an inventory for the Watts's Collection. He hoped even more that it contained a hint to the location of the Shapira Scrolls. Or perhaps one or more of the scrolls themselves. He was glad to see that when he examined his heart, his hope was for Elizabeth and her legacy. Not for himself.

His mind cycled through the agonizing questions. Why had Elizabeth died? What treasure had she held that someone believed she must die to relinquish? Why had the killer thought it necessary for Hassan to follow Elizabeth in death?

Serpents and treachery. The serpent as the great betrayer.

Perhaps Evan was giving the killer too much credit for being rational. Maybe there was no logic behind his or her actions—at least not the kind of logic that would appear reasonable to most. He'd entered the minds of enough murderers to know that while they created a coherent world within their own minds, their thoughts proved a dark, impenetrable forest to most.

Certainly, one could argue that murder was the most illogical of acts, the lashing out of the primitive brain. All too often, Evan had seen murder and darkness tip the scales on one side, while the virtues of literature, music, and art struggled for balance on the other. These opposing forces were frequently compelled to reside in a single body. Unlike Janus, the two-faced god who could look forward and back in time simultaneously, humans had to choose which way to turn their gaze.

You could also argue that murder was sometimes the most *rational* of acts. For some, murder was the only answer to betrayal, fear, or ambition. It was about survival—either of the physical self or the ego.

Evan heard Elizabeth's voice in his mind: *Stop stalling, and put a shoulder into it, boy.*

He pulled the box toward him, inserted the key, and raised the lid.

Only one thing lay inside the box. A folded leather scroll.

Hope wormed its way into his stomach even as cold breathed down his back.

He pulled a pair of disposable gloves from the cardboard box that still sat on Elizabeth's desk. He took out a fresh linen cloth from a drawer and unfurled the cloth across the wooden expanse. Finally, he placed the scroll on top and gently unfolded it.

The leather didn't creak or protest. It yielded itself willingly as he laid it open on the cloth, presenting its heavily inscribed words to his gaze.

Evan stared. Then recoiled. The words written on the leather seemed to hang in the air in front of him, as if the soul of the killer glared back at his bewildered gaze.

Written over and over on the leather, covering it entirely, were the words, *God blasts those trees which try to touch the skies.*

~~~

The first thing he did was call the attorney, Sandra Yee, to ask her who else might have had access to Elizabeth's belongings while they were in Yee's office.

"No one," Yee said. "Elizabeth had the box delivered to us a few days before her death, along with the other items I gave you. It was all locked away until this morning. Why do you ask?"

"I believe someone took whatever Elizabeth had placed in the box and substituted another item." He found himself thinking of Leah Zielinski, who might have had access to the box before it was delivered to Yee.

Yee said, "I don't—I don't know what could have happened. I'll speak with my paralegal. He covered for me while I was out of town. What *is* in the box?"

"It has to do with the investigation into Elizabeth's death."

"I—" There came a long silence. "I'm sorry, Dr. Wilding. I don't understand. Would you like me to put a call in to the police?"

"Not yet. Most likely, the switch happened before the box was in your charge. I'll get back to you."

After they hung up, Evan returned the scroll to the box.

He was certain the killer had placed it there. And that it was a message. More specifically, it was a threat.

Because to think otherwise was to believe that Elizabeth's impending death had driven her to madness. Better that the scroll was evidence of the broken mind of a killer than his friend's despair.

God blasts those trees which try to touch the skies. Was the killer referring to Elizabeth's ambition? Or to his own perhaps thwarted desire for the Shapira Scrolls? Maybe he was warning Evan away from the institute.

Perhaps all of the above.

He stared at Elizabeth's own version of the quote, written on an index card, and now lying flat on the desk after the theft of the books she'd propped it against. The quote had appeared again in her suicide note, which he was now sure the killer had edited on her computer.

He dialed Diana, explained what he was looking for. She promised to call him back shortly.

He'd also seen the quote in Mark Dawson's cubicle at the Veritas Foundation. *Gift from the boss,* Dawson had said. *Mr. Kelley gives them to everyone on their hiring day. He likes to remind us that we shouldn't overreach. It's easy to do in this field.*

After a moment of silent pondering, Evan opened the book Yee had given him from Elizabeth. The one Theodore Watts had written and self-published. The date was twenty years back, long before Theo had met Elizabeth and decided to support her institute. It was a photographic record of his many acquisitions during his years of travel. Page after page of statuary, bronze bells, limestone reliefs, mosaics from a ship in Caligula's fleet, jade figurines. A treasure trove collected by a man with a curious mind who appeared unwilling to narrow his passion to a particular culture or geography.

Evan could relate.

He went through the book twice, looking for any reference to Shapira or his scrolls. The only thing of interest was a small collection of Anglo-Saxon coins. A spectacular find in and of itself. But what caught Evan's attention were the framed butterflies next to the Viking artifacts. And the photo's caption, which indicated the items were from a larger collection Watts had bought off the descendants of a woman who had inherited the collection from her uncle, who had purchased them long ago from the widow of a naturalist in the English town of Burton-on-Trent.

Evan recalled what Diana had told him about the naturalist, Philip Mason, then looked up additional details for himself.

Burton-on-Trent was the last known location of the Shapira Scrolls. On the night of March 8, 1889, Philip Brookes Mason had presented a paper called "The Forgery of Shapira" at a meeting of the Burton-on-Trent Natural History and Archaeological Society.

After that rainy night, the scrolls disappeared. All attempts to track them had failed.

Until now.

Maybe until now.

Theodore Watts might have purchased them, along with the butterflies and coins, without knowing what they were. Elizabeth, beginning the laborious process of cataloging Watts's collection, had likely carried some suspicion of what that random purchase might contain. From there—somehow—the killer had learned what Elizabeth sought.

And if the scrolls had been in the security box, they were now in the hands of the killer.

He recalled the invoice he'd found on Gerrit's desk. *Blackened leather scroll, 7x9, Hebrew writing.* Which suggested at least one of the Shapira Scrolls had passed through Gerrit's hands and presumably into Chablain's. Maybe he'd sold the others before realizing what they were worth.

He called Addie, and when she didn't answer, he left a message with his suspicion that someone had switched out the contents of Elizabeth's box.

His phone buzzed. Diana.

"I found the quote you're looking for," she said. "You were right about it being associated with Shapira. It's from a 1919 book called *The Little Daughter of Jerusalem*, written by Shapira's daughter. His wife used to say it to him whenever she felt he was trying to rise above his station."

"Fascinating," he said aloud after they'd hung up. He dialed the Veritas Foundation. Kelley's receptionist informed him that her boss was at an off-site meeting, but she would make sure he got the message to call Evan.

"Maybe I don't need to talk to him," Evan said. "Does Mr. Kelley give every employee a gift when they join the foundation?"

"A gift? Like what?"

"A framed quote. Or maybe a book."

"Not that I've heard," she said. "But I'll double-check with Mr. Kelley."

Evan thanked her and disconnected.

Pieces of the puzzle came together and broke apart in his brain with astonishing speed as he searched for the most logical links, the likeliest relationships.

He picked up the framed photo of Lawrence of Arabia on Elizabeth's desk, studied it, then returned it to its place among the other photos. T. E. Lawrence stared back at him with the implacable confidence of a man certain he was doing the right thing.

Evan longed to share in that confidence. But he and the world at large had done nothing but let Elizabeth down. Her killer remained at large. The Watts collection, which she'd worked so hard on, was caught in a lawsuit that—he suspected—allowed Gerrit Watts to pilfer items and sell them off into private collections like that belonging to the Kelleys. What would be left by the time the judge ruled?

As for the institute—the very building where he now sat, the work Elizabeth had left unfinished—how would he get the kind of funding needed to continue her efforts? Especially if the court ruled in Gerrit's favor.

He rose and went to the window, raising the blinds. He thought about the promises Lawrence of Arabia had made to the Arabs to convince them to unite with the British against the Ottoman Empire. T. E. Lawrence had thought his promises were gold. He'd expected the British Empire to remain true to their word. And look at how that turned out. The Brits had broken their promise almost before the war was over. And because of that betrayal, the Middle East threatened to remain in turmoil forever.

He turned his mind to the way the starlings had grouped and regrouped in the skies above the field to avoid Ginny. Nature was full of feints and counter feints. Like the way orcas terrorized herring into a "bait ball" so that they could gulp down the smaller fish with ease.

Every predator had a plan. And all prey developed counterplans, or else died.

His mind did a roll call of all the players who had surrounded Elizabeth in her final days. William Kelley, head of the Veritas Foundation, who was determined to build a world-class collection for his Moses Museum. His man in charge of acquisitions, the free-wheeling, allegedly wife-hating Timothée Chablain. Chablain's assistant, Miriam Fuller, who had some kind of relationship with Gerrit Watts. Perhaps she was the one feeding Gerrit with information about Chablain, although Evan couldn't guess at her motive. There was Gerrit himself, the disinherited heir who was selling off his grandfather's treasures—legally or not. And what of Mark Dawson, the curator of Jewish texts? He loathed Chablain and wanted his job. And yet Kelley had offered the job to Evan to get access to the Watts collection. Was Dawson aware of that? Did he consider it a betrayal? If so, why not go after Kelley?

Why had Dawson lied about the Shapira quote? Or was it Kelley who had lied to Dawson—claiming he gave it to everyone? And if so, why?

There was Kevin Grady, who had proved himself willing to use violence to get the scrolls. Driven by desperation, he could have bribed a student for the access code to the lab.

Maybe his alibis wouldn't hold up.

And what of the still-missing Samad Rasheed? Sam had worked for the now-dead Hassan and had almost certainly met Elizabeth at St. Paul Coptic Orthodox Church the night of Elizabeth's death. Avraham and Sam's grandfather, Omar, could profess Sam's innocence all they wished. Until they found him—or until the DNA results came back on the bloodied glass—Addie and Patrick could neither prove nor disprove Sam's innocence or guilt.

Finally, there was Elizabeth's assistant, the beautiful and reticent Leah Zielinski.

As he continued to stare at the picture of Lawrence of Arabia, his mind returned to his meeting with Elizabeth's assistant. He remembered the only time Leah spoke freely—it was when she was discussing Elizabeth's interest in T. E. Lawrence.

Evan pondered the seemingly insurmountable odds that T. E. Lawrence had overcome to unite the warring Arab tribes. He had succeeded by becoming one of them. Dressing like them, riding like them, living in the desert in the manner they had used for centuries. In the same way, a murderer moved among the antiquities dealers. Perhaps he posed as a buyer or a seller or even a restorer. If your victim believed you to be trustworthy, you could get as close as you wished.

A killer, like insanity itself, could wear many masks.

He recalled how Leah had slipped her right hand behind her back when he asked about Elizabeth's most recent work. It had seemed like an odd gesture at the time. But what did a liar do to unjinx themselves from lying? They crossed their fingers.

Was that what Leah had been doing?

Then there was the ring on her finger. The way she'd blushed and looked down when he commented on it. Not exactly the action of a woman who was sharing her good news with the world. Gerrit had claimed Chablain had a lover. Someone he'd taken up with after his wife fell ill.

Maybe with someone who could offer him access to the very thing he desired. If you couldn't get something one way, you got it another.

By hook or by crook, as Yee had said.

Being Leah's lover would mean that Chablain could have had unfettered access to Elizabeth's institute. Perhaps to her lockbox before she gave it to her attorney. Even to her computer.

And from there, to her suicide note.

Whatever the truth, Evan was certain Leah had more information than what she'd shared with him or even with Addie and Patrick. In fact, she'd given Addie a big fat nothing.

She knew far more than she'd been willing to say. Time to reengage with Ms. Zielinski.

He grabbed his coat and headed downstairs. Then stopped just inside the front door. Something niggled at him.

He closed his eyes, picturing Dawson's and Chablain's offices. Their graduation photos, with each man pictured receiving his diploma. Chablain's from the Université Paris 1 Panthéon-Sorbonne. Dawson's from TCU—Texas Christian University.

Evan pulled out his phone. TCU's mascot was a horned lizard, more commonly referred to as a horny toad.

A memory of his long-ago copy of John Milton's *Paradise Lost* swam before his eyes.

It was a big leap from a college in Texas to one of the most famous poems ever written. But we carry our symbols with us as we go through life—altering them, reusing them, sometimes transferring their meaning from one object to another. Especially symbols that carry emotional weight for us. Like a college mascot.

He opened another tab on his phone, searched for *Paradise Lost toad*, and was rewarded with a quote: "Him there they found / Squat like a toad, close at the ear of Eve." Satan, in the world according to Milton, had first attempted to seduce Eve into eating the apple by appearing as a toad. The serpent came later.

As with Elizabeth. First, the warning shot of the toad.

Then the cobra.

It pained him that he hadn't made the connection earlier. But he wasn't exactly up to speed on seventeenth-century literature.

He leaned against the door while Perro regarded him with wagging tail and a furrowed brow.

Once again, he pulled up his memory of Dawson's office. The quote and the photo of him with a woman had been the only personal items. In the photo, wind whipping off the water had concealed everything about the woman save her hair, her sunglasses, and her smile.

Was that why Dawson had picked that picture to display?

She'd had long, wavy hair. Like Leah's, except it was brown, not auburn.

He recalled Leah's dark brows and lashes. Redheads normally had fair lashes. But of course, makeup could serve to darken.

The brilliant smile of the woman in the photo was also much like Leah's.

His thoughts turned to Dawson emerging from the warren of cubicles, bowing slightly as he said, *Here I am*. Evan had taken it as mockery. But now Kelley's voice rose in his head. *Here I am,* the executive had said at the forest preserve. At first, Evan hadn't been sure he'd heard him correctly. Out of context, the words made no sense.

But now he understood the framework.

Here I am. Abraham's answer when God called to him before asking him to sacrifice his son.

Dawson's choice of words—a choice that wouldn't go unmarked by a man with Kelley's knowledge—suggested that Dawson was willing to sacrifice himself for the cause. And, perhaps, anyone who got in the way of Kelley's mission.

Like Elizabeth. She had intended to betray Veritas. Hassan had, too, if Evan read the signs right.

It wasn't Chablain whom Leah was sleeping with. It was a man who had expressed his loyalty for Kelley right under Evan's nose.

And he'd missed it.

He headed out the door.

CHAPTER 24

Leah Zielinski lived in an upstairs apartment in a renovated redbrick home in West Woodlawn. On the way over, Evan stopped by his office and picked up his gun, which he put in his satchel. When he reached Leah's house, he surprised her as she was coming out of the building with a large potted plant in her arms. Her eyes were red, and her face was twisted into a scowl.

She nodded at his greeting and let him help her maneuver the plant into the back of her aging Honda van.

"If you want to talk, then you'll have to do it while I pack," she told him. She didn't ask why he was there.

"Are you relocating?"

"I'm leaving Chicago. I've had enough."

"Is anyone helping you?" he asked, looking toward the house.

"Other than you?"

He followed her up the stairs and into a studio apartment with a single small window and a kitchen the size of a closet. In fact, it had probably been a closet at some point. The space was cluttered with cardboard boxes. The mattress had been tipped to lean against the wall, and a metal bed frame lay folded nearby.

Leah knelt and tossed books into a box, sealed it shut with packing tape, then labeled it—helpfully—BOOKS.

Evan remained standing. "Are you leaving because of Elizabeth?"

Leah shook her head. Then nodded. "Partly."

"What about school? It's only halfway through the semester."

She sank from her knees to the floor and stared at him with stricken eyes. He noticed that the emerald ring was gone from her finger.

"Did he break up with you?" he asked, nodding toward her hand.

She stared at him miserably, then fished a tissue out of the pocket of her jeans and wiped her nose. "Elizabeth left the institute to you, didn't she?"

"Is that what she told you?"

"No, it was someone—no." She stared out the window.

"Why don't you tell me what's going on, Leah. I know you haven't been truthful with me or the police. Me, you can lie to as much as you like, although I can't say I appreciate it. But it's a different matter with the cops."

The scowl returned. "Why should I talk to you?"

"I can see that you're in a lot of pain. You need to talk to someone. You know something about Elizabeth's death. And Hassan's. And since I'm not a detective, I'm safe."

"You work for them."

"That's true. But I won't put you in cuffs and haul you down to the station. Plus, we have something besides the institute in common."

"What's that?"

"We both cared about Elizabeth."

She returned her gaze to him, then pushed herself up off the floor. "Coffee? Or would you prefer tea?"

While Leah plugged in an electric kettle and dug a package of cookies out from one of the boxes in the kitchen, Evan managed to seat himself on one of the only two chairs left—a rickety barstool. He waited while Leah poured hot water over tea bags and offered milk and sugar. She settled herself on the other barstool across the high round table and looked at him over her tea mug.

"I didn't have anything to do with Elizabeth's death," she said.

"Okay."

"You don't believe me?"

"I'm still sorting it out. Why don't you tell me about your relationship with Mark Dawson?"

She set down her mug. Hot tea splashed on her hand, and she gave a small cry. She grabbed a dish towel and wiped up the mess. She glared at him.

"How did you know?"

"A lot of clues. What happened?"

"He's a hypocrite. A *snake*."

Evan nodded. *Snake* was often used to refer to a treacherous man, especially in a romantic context. The question was, did it have a deeper meaning in this case?

Leah picked up her mug again. Tears ran unheeded down her face. "He called *me* a serpent. What the hell is that supposed to mean?"

"Was that after you broke up with him?"

She nodded.

"And when was that?"

She gaped at him. "What does that matter?"

"Because people whom Mark Dawson considers traitors don't seem to live very long."

Now she looked alarmed. "He wouldn't hurt me."

Evan said nothing.

"Wait. Are you saying Mark killed Elizabeth?" Her voice rose. "And Hassan?"

Evan waited her out. She slid off the barstool and disappeared into the bathroom, closing the door. Evan fired off a text to Addie, Look at Mark Dawson, and kept his satchel close. When Leah reemerged, she had a roll of toilet paper in her hand. She pulled off a strip and pressed it to her eyes.

"He's strange," she said quietly, retaking her seat across from Evan. "Mark is."

"What do you mean?"

"His childhood was totally messed up. He told me that when he was a teenager, he started acting out. Staying out late. Smoking. He refused to go to church. His parents put him in a group called Teen Confront."

"What is that?"

"A totally whacked-out place. It's a so-called Christian organization where they make rebellious teens live like they're in a cult. No talking. No games. No movies. No internet. It's just like a prison, and you can't get out. Your parents sign you in, and you're stuck until you're eighteen. Mark was there for four years. He said when he left, he had a better appreciation for hell."

"You think the experience at Teen Confront was what made him, as you say, strange?"

"That and having snake handlers for parents. His family was truly and totally nuts. Mark wasn't allowed to have friends outside his church or go to school events or play sports. Then, at Teen Confront, he wouldn't play along with their rules. They made him write his sins over and over. Things like, 'I will not talk to the others.' Or 'The devil is in me.' He said one time he wrote until the skin on his fingers split open."

A vision rose in Evan's mind of the leather scroll in Elizabeth's lockbox.

"I thought he overcame it," Leah said. "That it had made him compassionate. But he can be cruel." She winced at a memory. "He's honest. I'll give him that. But also . . . cruel."

"Yet you were having an affair with him," Evan gently pointed out.

She recoiled. "It wasn't like that. He told me he and his wife were divorcing. In God's eyes, he was free to be with me."

Evan didn't argue. "Was he interested in Elizabeth's work?"

"Sure. They're both biblical scholars."

"Did he ever mention the Shapira Scrolls?"

"He—" She seemed struck by a thought. "He did ask me if Elizabeth was looking for them."

"And what did you say?"

"That once she had me do some research on Shapira. But—but that was all. Why? That didn't have anything to do with Elizabeth's death, did it?"

"Was he ever alone at the institute?"

She shook her head. A curl stuck to her wet cheek. "Sometimes he was there with me, and he'd, like, roam around. But I was always close by, working."

"Do you recall seeing a metal lockbox on Elizabeth's desk?"

"The one she wanted her attorney to have? I delivered it to the attorney's office myself, along with the key. Dr. El wasn't feeling well that day."

"Did you deliver it before or after Dawson was in the institute?"

"After. I'm pretty sure." She picked worriedly at a cuticle. "Definitely after. Why?"

"What about computer passwords?"

"What about them?"

"Did Elizabeth write them down?"

"She had lately." Leah nodded slowly. "She said she was having trouble remembering things."

"Meaning Mark could have found them and accessed her computer files?"

Leah's face went scarlet, which was answer enough. Dawson had spent unsupervised time in Elizabeth's office.

"What about snakes?" Evan said. "Did Mark own a cobra?"

"That's a weird question."

Evan waited, and Leah shrugged and continued. "Okay, yeah. He used to. He bought it a year ago, but something happened to it. He said the snake was to remind him that—" Her eyes went wide, and her hand flew to her mouth. "Oh my God. Is that how she died?"

Evan nodded.

Leah shook her head furiously. "There's no way Mark would hurt Elizabeth. No way! I mean, first of all, he's not a killer. And second, he's a coward. Only a coward would do what he did to me."

"Which was?"

"Choose his career over me. As if it had to be one or the other. Plus, Mark is, like, OCD. He'd never get his hands dirty."

Except, perhaps, if he thought he was doing God's work.

After extracting a promise from Leah to stop packing for the moment and go stay with a friend—preferably one Dawson knew nothing about—Evan watched her leave, suitcase in hand, then returned to his car. He tossed his coat in the passenger seat and walked around to the driver's side. Dusk had colored the sky purple, and lights began to glimmer in the gloom.

Once behind the wheel, he called Addie.

"It's Mark Dawson," he said when she picked up.

"That's interesting," Addie answered. "We found the reptile dealer who sold him the cobra. A guy in Michigan. Given just that bit of news, I'll bet you're right. But tell me what you're thinking."

Evan listed his reasons, starting with the means and opportunity. He'd get to motivation.

Dawson had, as Addie just confirmed, owned a cobra. Because of his relationship with Leah, he'd been able to freely roam Elizabeth's institute, giving him access to her computer, her calendar, and the lockbox.

"I suspect Elizabeth wrote her meeting with Sam in her calendar as part of the paper trail she kept as she and Avraham worked their sting against Hassan with the Moses papyri. Before that night, Dawson had accessed her lockbox. So, either he already had the scrolls and was looking for an opportunity to murder her. Or, if he hadn't found the scrolls, he could have interpreted *pMoses* in her calendar as a reference to Moses Shapira's discovery, then gone to her that night to steal them."

"From pMoses to the Shapira Scrolls? That seems like a leap."

"Not at all. Sometimes the scrolls are referred to as the Moses scrolls or the Moses fragments. Leather, not papyrus, but maybe he thought she was being coy. Or that the *p* stood for *parchment*, a form of leather. That night he decided to kill two birds with one snake, if you'll forgive my putting it that way. Murder Elizabeth for her treachery against Veritas. And walk away with a great treasure. Or, in his mind, a blasphemous contradiction of his beliefs."

He went on to tell her about Dawson's unusual background—a childhood that might warp an already fragile mind. Severely strict parents. Being forced to handle poisonous snakes, which he'd already admitted to when they were at Veritas. His experience at Teen Confront, where writing a self-incriminating phrase over and over was standard punishment. An action Dawson had repeated with the lines he'd written on the leather in Elizabeth's lockbox.

"The words were a warning," Evan said. "He was reminding her to not overreach. Telling her that if she persisted in doing so, she would pay a price. She probably never even saw it. But in Dawson's mind, whether or not she actually *saw* the warning and had a chance to act on it didn't matter. His job was to give her the warning. It was God's choice whether or not she saw it."

"Meaning Dawson wouldn't be responsible for her death?"

"Exactly."

"I can tell by your voice there's something more."

"Dawson has an unusual relationship with William Kelley. Almost father and son, but in a deeply distorted way. By using a phrase that invokes the story in Genesis of God's order to Abraham to sacrifice his son, I think Kelley is playing upon Dawson's faith, warping it for his own ends."

"You think Kelley told him to commit murder?"

"I think Dawson is acting on his own, and if Kelley is suspicious, he has chosen to look the other way. And there's good reason for him to do so. By eliminating Elizabeth and Hassan, Dawson gave Veritas a shot at the collection. Gerrit was already selling items to Chablain. Maybe Dawson as well. If the collection legally becomes Gerrit's, and with Chablain moving on, then Dawson will take Chablain's place and purchase the entire collection for Veritas. He will become the favored son. If, on the other hand, the court rules in Elizabeth's favor, then offering me a job is their backup plan."

"I get why they want Watts's collection," Addie said. "But why are the Shapira Scrolls so important to them?"

"Dawson doesn't want the scrolls so that Veritas can display them. He wants to hide or destroy them before the world can learn they're real."

"What? But . . . why?"

"The scrolls reveal a different version—an earlier version—of Deuteronomy than what appears in the King James and other versions of the Bible. Dawson sees the very existence of the scrolls as heresy. They fly in the face of his belief that the Bible is the immutable word of God. That the words were written down and haven't changed in the millennia since Moses died at the edge of the Promised Land."

"And he killed Hassan because the Egyptian was also trying to purchase items from Gerrit?"

"Which made him a traitor to Veritas. Especially if he, too, was trying to obtain the scrolls."

"Smart work, Evan," Addie said. "And pretty damning, if you'll pardon my use of that term. But what we've got, even with the cobra, is still circumstantial until we find something that puts Dawson in Elizabeth's car that night. He could always claim that the killer stole his cobra. There were no fingerprints on the statue that was used to kill Hassan. Nothing concrete. If it turns out it's Elizabeth's blood on that glass, we'll need something more. Because right now, Samad Rasheed is still our top suspect. He ran. Dawson didn't."

"What are you going to do in the meantime?"

"We'll pay a visit to Mr. Dawson. Then—" She paused. "Can you hold on a sec?"

Evan had started to say "Sure" when his passenger door opened and a man dropped into his seat. Evan's eyes widened. The man pressed his finger to his lips and shook his head.

Addie came back on the line. "I just got word. Timothée Chablain is missing. I'll call you back when I know more."

She disconnected before Evan could say anything.

THREE—VERITAS

"The Architecture of Human Sacrifice" by Dr. Evan Wilding
Proceedings of the International Conference on Semiotics
Semiotician: Evan Wilding, PhD, SSA, IASS

My talk this morning concerns the relationship between architecture and human sacrifice. From the time when humans raised their first structures, societies around the world have employed human flesh and blood to ensure the longevity and sanctity of their buildings.

These so-called construction sacrifices, in which a man, woman, or child is slain and buried beneath the foundation or—more grue-somely—buried alive under the gate or cornerstones, have occurred in nearly all societies. The sacrifices generally served one of two functions. The first was appeasement, an example of which is the use of sacrificial blood as a form of rent—a payment to the spirits of the site. The second role was to provide protection, especially in buildings that served as a town's fortification. In those cases, sacrificed individuals were thought to act as guardian spirits.

The word for such sacrifice in China was hitobashira, a term meaning "human pillar." In Burma, victims were called myosade. We find mention of foundational sacrifice taking place in Europe, India, Japan, Indonesia, the Americas, and elsewhere. Construction sacrifices are mentioned in articles from the Palestine Exploration Fund regarding the sites of Gezer and Taanach.

Construction sacrifice is also mentioned in the Bible in I Kings 16:34 concerning the rebuilding of the walls and gates of Jericho: "In his days Hiel the Bethelite built Jericho. He laid its foundation with the loss of Abiram his firstborn, and set up its gates with the loss of his youngest son Segub, according to Yahweh's word, which he spoke by Joshua the son of Nun."

Among the most heartbreaking tales is that of a child who was set to play among the stones of Copenhagen. Townspeople seated the girl at a table filled with toys and sweets. While she played unaware, masons sealed her, alive, into the wall.

INTERLUDE

I want to point out that through it all, I stayed busy with the work I had been given. Not the labor I did to earn a paycheck, though there was also that. But rather the work that had come to me when I'd been guided into that bookstore in Jerusalem.

It was not gentle work, for death is a hard business. Nor did it fit with how I had imagined my life would be.

But a man does not shirk from his calling.

Every day, I continued to read from *Lost Treasure of the Jordan Valley!* Or what I had come to think of as—simply—the book.

Jerusalem, Christian Quarter, July 1878.

While his young daughter played nearby, the shop-keeper began the laborious task of transcribing the ancient writing. The texts became the entire focus of his life. He left the management of his shop to his assistants; his beloved family faded into the background. His work on the scrolls would not only bring great financial gain to provide for his wife and daughters. It would ensure him the station in life he longed for—to be seen not as a mere shopkeeper but as a scholar.

"God punishes those who would rise above their station," his wife warned.

But he knew the leather strips would make him someone in the world.

Reading these words, I at last felt a connection with that long-ago merchant and his estranged wife and daughters, one of whom would go on to write a book about her time in Jerusalem. For it is true that sometimes a man's family must pay a price for his greatness.

In that way, his destiny becomes theirs.

CHAPTER 25

Evan stared into the shadowed eyes of the young man who had just let himself into the car. Still clutching his phone in one hand, Evan lowered his satchel to the floor near his feet. He wanted the pistol inside the bag to be close. Just in case.

"Samad Rasheed, I presume," he said.

"My grandfather told me I could trust you." Sam nodded toward Evan's phone. "Please don't tell anyone I'm here."

"You were with Elizabeth the night she was murdered."

"I've come to tell you what I know. But I had nothing to do with her death! You have to believe me."

Evan placed the phone in the cup holder between the seats even as he kept his hand near his satchel. "I do."

Sam looked surprised. In the fading daylight, he also looked miserable—thin and unshaven, his eyes bloodshot. He gave off the smell of sour sweat and unwashed clothes, and Evan wondered when the kid had last eaten or slept.

Sam glanced at the side mirror. "There have been people following me. You should drive."

Evan nodded. "Buckle up," he said.

Sam barked a laugh but complied. Evan toed the satchel toward the driver's-side door, started the car, and pulled away from the curb.

"What happened that night?" he asked.

Sam thrust his hands between jittering knees. "I was delivering some papyri to Dr. El from Mr. Hassan. I work part-time for him. I asked her to meet me at my church."

"Your church?" Evan asked.

"St. Paul Coptic Orthodox in Logan Square. I had a big research paper due, and the church is near my university. I figured I would pick up the Moses papyri, drop them off with Dr. El, then head back to school."

"What went wrong?"

"Nothing! Mr. Hassan gave me the papyri, I took them to Dr. El, then I went to school. I spent the night researching and writing."

"Where?"

"Where? Like, for an alibi?"

"Exactly that."

Sam moaned. "I was at the library for a while. After it closed, I went to a friend's apartment near campus."

"Did anyone see you?"

"My friend. But that wasn't until, like, midnight." Another moan.

Which was right around the time when Elizabeth died. "It's all right, Sam. If you were in the library, there are probably cameras. Did you log in to a library computer?"

Sam nodded.

"Then you're golden."

"For real?" Sam puffed air. "Okay."

Without signaling, Evan turned sharply at the next corner. His gaze went to the rearview mirror, but no headlights followed them. "What about what was in the basket?"

Sam looked surprised. "It was a puppy for Dr. El. From Mr. Hassan. Why? Did something happen to the dog, too?"

"Why don't you tell me how you came to have the basket?"

"Mr. Hassan gave it to me to give to Dr. El."

"He handed it directly to you?"

Sam's brow creased. "No. It was Rana who gave it to me. Mr. Hassan's receptionist. She rushed it out to my car. She said it was a Norwegian Lundehund puppy that Mr. Hassan had forgotten to give me. I was to give the puppy to Dr. El. A promise for their future together."

"Did Rana tell you who brought it to her? Was it Hassan?"

"She didn't say. Why? Is it important?" His face grew paler. "Did it have something to do with Dr. El's death?"

"Someone wanted to frame you."

"It wasn't a puppy?"

Evan shook his head.

Sam reared back. "Then what—?"

"It was a murder weapon. A cobra."

Sam began to weep in long, silent sobs that shook his shoulders. Evan made another turn. And a few blocks later, another. Traffic picked up.

Rana. He'd circle back to her. "What do you know about Elizabeth's work?"

The young man—hardly more than a boy, Evan realized—pressed the heels of his palms against his eyes. He drew a deep breath.

"I knew some of what Dr. El was doing," he said. "She took an interest in me because of my grandfather. We met sometimes for dinner. The last time was a week before she—a week before. She told me Veritas had hired her to determine if any of their artifacts had been cataloged or were on display somewhere else before Veritas bought them. Do you know why that's important?"

Evan did. But he said, "Why don't you tell me."

"Because if you're forging provenance for an illegal artifact, it would be really bad to have a photo show up somewhere else, contradicting the history you're falsifying."

Evan pulled a U-turn on a quiet street and backtracked, still watching for pursuit. "Elizabeth agreed to do this kind of research?"

He nodded. "If the artifacts bought by Veritas hadn't appeared in a catalog or online before, then Elizabeth was supposed to create airtight provenances for them so that they could safely display them."

"Meaning Kelley or Chablain knew their artifacts were likely stolen?"

"That's what Dr. El thought."

"She was okay with that?"

"She pretended to be," Sam said. "The real reason she agreed to work with Veritas was to get access to their stored treasures and eventually expose their illegal purchases to the world."

And there it was. Elizabeth acting as a hero. Except to a man like Dawson. "Who do you think is following you?"

Sam sank farther down in the leather seat. "I don't know. Sometimes I see a dark SUV. I'm guessing it's whoever killed Dr. El. Or maybe someone thinks I have something of hers. A friend told me my apartment was torn apart. I haven't been back."

"What do they think you have?"

It seemed impossible, but Sam managed to sink even lower. He clenched his hands. "Have you heard of the Shapira Scrolls?"

"I have."

Sam outlined what Elizabeth had told him. She thought she had tracked the scrolls to a collection Mr. Watts had bought from a woman in England. The collection held books and journals, some antiquities, specimens of insects and plants, old coins, and a few other odds and ends. Mr. Watts had purchased the collection on a whim because the naturalist said the original owner was also an archaeology buff.

"Mr. Watts thought there might be something interesting mixed in with all the other stuff. But that's when he was starting to get sick, and he turned everything over to Dr. El to go through."

"The collection was at his house at that time?"

Sam shrugged. "I guess."

He continued. Elizabeth's clue was the natural-history items—the last known owner of the Shapira Scrolls was a British natural historian and amateur archaeologist. She found a piece of leather in an old manila envelope that someone had tossed in one of the boxes. She hoped that the scrap meant there were more pieces in the boxes Mr. Watts had purchased. But Dr. El had told Sam that the collection was large and disorganized.

"Bottom line, Dr. Wilding, I don't know if she found the scrolls or not. She told me that since I was interning with Hassan, the less I knew the better. She promised to fill me in later."

"But later never happened."

Sam wiped tears from his face. "Dr. El offered me a job at her institute once I finish my internship with Mr. Hassan. She'd have all of Mr. Watts's artifacts along with the money he'd set aside for her. She'd be able to help me pay off my student loans. But then Gerrit contested everything. And then Dr. El . . ."

His voice trailed off, and he looked out a window. "My grandfather always said wishes are as useful as a pocketful of air."

"Who do *you* think killed her?"

"Me?" Sam looked back. "The police won't care what I think, but my top candidates are Timothée Chablain, Gerrit Watts, or Mark Dawson. I'm guessing all of them figured out about the scrolls. And they all want them."

Evan thought of Addie's last words to him—that Chablain was missing.

"What about Rana?"

Sam looked perplexed. "Rana?"

"She gave you the basket with the cobra. Could she have anything to do with Elizabeth's death?"

Sam's mouth dropped open. "Rana is like me. She is working for Hassan only to get some experience, to make contacts. She has a PhD in

Egyptology from the American University in Cairo. She's worked with Zahi Hawass in the Nile Delta. Why would she throw away everything?"

Seemed like a good point, Evan silently conceded. "What about Hassan? Any reason he'd want Elizabeth dead?"

Sam blinked at him, then shook his head. "He thought Elizabeth was on his side. She was going to be his conduit to both the Watts collection and to Veritas. Killing her wouldn't make sense."

"Did you see anyone else in Hassan's gallery when you were there to pick up the papyri? Someone who might have given the basket to Rana?"

Sam closed his eyes, but soon opened them and shook his head. "I don't remember."

"Why do you suspect Chablain?"

"Dr. El told me he was secretly selling off artifacts owned by Veritas that Kelley said weren't to be put on display. Stuff they can't or won't put out for the public."

"And Dawson?" Evan asked, not revealing his own thoughts.

"Dawson was working with Gerrit."

"Dawson, not Chablain?"

Sam nodded. "Dawson was buying items from Mr. Watts's collection for Veritas. I mean, I think it was Chablain at first. But Dawson convinced Gerrit that Chablain was cheating him. He offered to take over."

"Hard to find a trustworthy thief these days. Was Dawson purchasing items with Kelley's approval?"

"Maybe. Dr. El told me that Kelley treated Dawson like a son. But a son who had to earn his keep."

"Sam, did Elizabeth ever mention an inventory of the Watts collection?"

For the first time, Sam smiled. A small triumphant smile. "She didn't just mention it. She gave me a copy."

Evan shot a look at the young man. "Where is it?"

"I put it in a safe-deposit box at a bank as soon as I heard about Dr. El. I knew someone from Veritas would want it."

"Smart man," Evan said. He took a breath. "Sam, I believe that you had nothing to do with Elizabeth's death."

"But the basket—"

"Not deliberately. But the safest thing for us to do is drive to the police station where Detective Bisset works. She's been handling Elizabeth's case, so she'll be very interested in what you have to say. She's a cop, yes, but she's also a friend."

"No police," Sam said. "Maybe after you find the killer, then I'll talk to your friend. But not now. What if they say I'm a—what do you call it—an accessory because I brought the basket to her?"

"The police don't shoot the messenger," Evan said. "You were as innocent as Elizabeth."

But Sam kept shaking his head. "I don't trust cops."

Evan was half-surprised when he glanced out and saw the domed windows of St. Paul Coptic Orthodox Church. He must have unconsciously been thinking of Elizabeth's last meeting with Sam and wondering when and how Dawson had gotten into her car and forced her to drive to the dirt lot.

He played the events of that night in his mind while he circled the block. The pieces, for so long disjointed, began to slide into place.

Sam arrived and gave Elizabeth the papyri, placed the basket in the back seat, then rushed away to work on his research paper.

Elizabeth, relieved that the sting operation was in full swing, reached into the back seat to free a puppy from a basket. A gift from a friend. When she lifted the lid, the snake struck.

She reared back, striking the dome light and causing the scalp injury. But she wouldn't have panicked. Not Elizabeth. As soon as the snake was no longer an immediate threat, she would have called for help and driven to an emergency room.

Instead, Dawson had appeared from the shadows. He'd opened the back door and subdued the cobra, probably sedating it. That could explain why the serpent had remained in the car until Elizabeth's body was found. At that point, less than a minute after the cobra strike, Elizabeth might have already begun failing. Dawson would have urged her into the passenger seat and taken over the car. She must have thought he was helping her. He probably pretended to call for an ambulance even as he promised he was driving her to a hospital.

Perhaps some time passed before she understood he intended her to die.

When she realized her error, she would have tried to fight back. But she was an older woman, sick with cancer and with cobra venom coursing through her veins. What chance did she have against a much younger man who believed he was doing the work of God?

When the deed was done, when Elizabeth's body had yielded to the venom, Dawson parked, dragged her back into the driver's seat, and left her as a sacrifice at the future site of the Moses Museum. In his twisted thinking, it had been God's will that the historian die. God's will, because there had been choices. Maybe Rana wouldn't deliver the basket. Maybe Elizabeth wouldn't open it. Maybe the snake wouldn't strike. Maybe the bite wouldn't be fatal.

But God had delivered Elizabeth to her death.

Dawson's role had been to provide the snake. Then to escort the historian across the divide. Nothing more.

Evan shook himself and came to a stop at a traffic light. A text from Addie flashed across his screen, and he read it quickly.

"What's that about?" Sam asked, alarm in his voice. He groped for the door handle.

"It's not about you," Evan said. "I promise you, Sam. The cops will understand."

But Sam threw open the passenger door and leapt out of the car. Evan yanked the Jaguar toward the curb. From behind came the sound of an engine accelerating. Headlights blazed through the rear window. Brakes shrieked and a door opened. "Stop!" a woman shouted at Sam. "Hands up! Turn around!"

Sam froze.

"Agent Holliday," Evan cried out with relief, squinting into the glare. He threw open his own door and stepped onto the sidewalk. "Wait!"

Holliday was silhouetted by the headlights, her gun aimed at the young man. The few drivers on the street sped past. Maybe they'd phone in a carjacking to the police. Maybe they thought this *was* police action.

"You're making a mistake," Evan called.

But Holliday shouted again. "Stop! Now!"

As Sam complied, raising his hands and slowly turning, the woman stepped clear of the lights and spared a glance for Evan.

"You, too, little man," she said to him. "Hands up."

That was when Evan realized his mistake. The woman wasn't Agent Holliday.

It was Miriam Fuller.

CHAPTER 26

Miriam directed Evan and Sam toward the cavernous shadows alongside the church. She wore all black. Black jeans, black sweater, black coat. But in the church's outdoor lights, Evan caught the gleam from the suppressor on her pistol as she waved them into a deeply recessed alcove.

As soon as they were out of view of the street, she ordered them to stand against the wall and then quickly and efficiently frisked them, removing their cell phones and keys. Her face was pale and tight.

"You're a pro," Evan commented as she pocketed their phones.

Miriam ignored him and kept her focus on Sam. She told the young man to unzip his coat and hold it open. She searched him again, coming up empty.

She frowned.

"I don't know where you've stashed them," she said, "but hand them over."

Sam straightened his shoulders. "Hand what over?" he asked bravely.

"Stop the bullshit. I followed you into the bank this afternoon, watched as you were escorted into the vault. Give them to me."

"You're right I went to the bank. But I didn't take anything." He looked defiant.

Defiant was the wrong tack to take.

She struck his face with the gun. Blood spurted from his nose, and his knees sagged. Evan moved to help him, but she ordered him back against the wall.

"The scrolls," she said to Sam. "Now."

Sam's earlier show of courage melted. Tears mixed with the blood streaming from his nose. "I never had them."

Miriam looked as if a cashier had just told her they were out of her favorite cigarettes. Peeved and momentarily inconvenienced. "Come on, kid. Are some scraps of leather really more important to you than your life? If I must, I'll search your corpse. But I'd rather avoid getting your blood on everything."

He wiped at his face with his sleeve. "I don't—I don't have them. I really don't."

Hoping to buy time, Evan said, "Isn't it the Moses papyri you want?"

But she shrugged off his attempted diversion. "Why would I care about some fakes?"

"How did you know?"

Disdain flooded her face. She was beautiful, Evan noticed. Behind the anger and coldness. Behind the scorn. Who had she been before she changed?

She said, "After Elizabeth died, Mark brought the papyri to the house, and I spent two days in the lab with them. Expertly done, but still fakes. Ancient papyri, modern ink. I tore them apart."

"Mark Dawson is your husband," Evan said with sudden realization.

Her eyes cut to him. "Soon-to-be ex-husband. But we're still a team. Especially when it comes to the Shapira Scrolls. He started the search. Now I'm going to finish it. Then we'll ride off into the sunset. Not together, maybe, but both of us rich."

Evan pulled the scattered shards together. Mark Dawson and Miriam Fuller. Estranged husband and wife. The contemptuous look the two had exchanged in the David Museum. The whitened skin on Miriam's ring finger. The photo in Dawson's office of him and a woman.

Not Leah. Miriam.

"He's a killer," Evan said. "Your soon-to-be ex-husband."

"There are larger forces at work. He did what was necessary."

"And so did you. You tracked the Shapira Scrolls by getting close to everyone involved. You befriended Gerrit and Hassan. Chablain, of course. They all trusted you. Especially Chablain, who gave you a job. You figured one of them would lead you to the scrolls."

She smiled, and the night turned colder. "And, eventually, one of them did. But when I started, not one of those men believed in the authenticity of the scrolls. Not even Mark. Chablain had the nerve to laugh at me. But I wouldn't give up. I suspected Elizabeth was three steps ahead of me, that she'd already managed to narrow the search to the Watts Collection. Which meant I needed to get there first. After the men realized I was onto something, they all wanted a piece of it."

"What did you do?"

He was stalling. And for what? The church was closed, the sidewalks deserted. No one knew he and Sam were spending the evening in the company of an armed and angry woman.

But Miriam seemed pleased to have someone serve as witness for her cleverness.

"It was easy to cut out Chablain by telling Gerrit that the Frenchman was cheating him," she said. "And Gerrit was desperate for money, so he was more than happy to sell me anything I wanted as long as his wife didn't catch wind of it. Hassan agreed to handle the deal, and Mark went to Kelley for the money. But when Gerrit and Mark couldn't find the scrolls, I knew Elizabeth must have already taken them. When this stupid kid went from Elizabeth's institute to the bank not long before she died, I realized she'd given them to him. Or that he'd taken them for himself."

"Why would she give them to me?" Sam protested. "Why would I steal them?"

She sighed. "Maybe you'll get smarter after you're dead."

"Is it the glory you care about, Miriam?" Evan asked. "Or is it the money?"

The full focus of her gaze fell on him as if it were a thing with weight. In the dim-yellow glow from the light above a nearby door, he saw the conviction in her eyes. Her expression revealed a madness utterly different from her husband's. Hers was the madness of greed. Of deep, raw avarice. A madness she shared with thousands of people.

"It's the money," he said, seeing it clearly.

Her smile widened. Then she pivoted back to Sam. Her finger moved to the trigger. "Last chance. A bullet in your head won't harm the texts. I can't say the same for you."

"But I'm telling the truth! I don't—"

"They're in the car," Evan said. "Under the passenger seat. Sam hid them there."

She pivoted back and studied him, looking for the lie.

"That is," he said, "they might be under the seat."

"I don't like games, little man." Her eyes glittered dangerously. "Which is it?"

He mentally pulled up Addie's text and pressed on. "A few minutes ago, I received word from Chicago PD. Mark boarded a flight to Amman, Jordan, two hours ago. No checked luggage, just a carry-on. He must have been in a rush. If I were to hazard a guess, I'd say he stole the Shapira Scrolls from Elizabeth. A few days before he killed her, he gained access to a lockbox she planned to deliver to her attorney for safekeeping. What do you think was in that box, Miriam?"

The smile faded. "Mark would never cut me out. Not after everything I did for him. For us. After he sells the scrolls to Kelley, we'll split the money."

"And Kelley will bury them. Maybe even destroy them."

Her shrug said she didn't care about the fate of the scrolls.

He forced aside the sorrow at the thought that Moses Shapira might never be vindicated. "Then let's go to the car and retrieve whatever it is Sam picked up at the bank. We'll see if it's the Shapira Scrolls. Or if Mark has them now."

His heart was beating hard enough he could feel it in his teeth. If he could just get to his satchel. And the gun. He felt Sam's eyes on him and sent a silent prayer that the young man would remain quiet.

Miriam said, "You've got something up your sleeve."

Evan forced a laugh. "As you can see, it's a very short sleeve. If it makes you more comfortable, stay with Sam and watch me from here. If I do anything but open the driver's door and remove Sam's bag, you can shoot me, then shoot Sam and be gone before anyone is the wiser."

Sam made a low sound in his throat.

Miriam held the gun steady as she considered.

"We'll go together," she said after a moment. "You will get the scrolls. Then he"—she nodded toward Sam—"will drive my vehicle."

"Where?" Sam asked in a dry whisper.

Her voice sounded brittle enough to shatter. "That will depend on what you do during the next few minutes."

She gestured with the gun again, directing Sam and Evan back toward the street. The neighborhood was as quiet as—Evan held his shudder—the proverbial tomb.

As they neared the end of the path that led into the alcove, Sam's body language shifted. Sensing the change, Miriam nudged him.

"Don't be stupid," she said. "Stupid makes you dead."

But Sam shouted "Run!" to Evan as he drove an elbow back into Miriam. He struck her midsection and took off at a sprint. Evan lunged for Miriam. She dodged his grasp and ran five or six yards before she planted her feet and raised her weapon. The pistol gave a throaty *whomp* through the suppressor.

Sam kept running.

"I have the scrolls!" Evan yelled at Miriam. "Let him go!"

She fired a warning shot in Evan's direction. The bullet struck the ground near his feet, forcing him back. Again, she took aim at Sam.

And fired.

Across the church's lawn, Sam stumbled and dropped. Miriam squinted through the pistol's sights for another shot.

Evan ran toward her, still yelling. Hoping to distract her. Hoping to knock her down before she fired.

Something.

A third shot sizzled through the purple twilight, this one from a different direction, a white-hot blast close enough he could hear the bullet's sharp crack as it went by.

The boom echoed against the backdrop of the church.

Miriam jerked and staggered backward. She looked down at blood seeping from a wound in her chest, then raised her chin and stared in shock at Evan.

"How?" she whispered.

The world shrank to her pale face and the wet, dark blood on her coat; its scarlet heat seemed to fill the night.

Sacred ground, thought Evan. *Now violated.* Or sanctified, depending on your beliefs.

Miriam swayed. Then straightened. She lifted her gun.

Once more, from somewhere close by, a shot blasted the night apart.

Miriam took a single step, then crumpled onto the grass. She didn't move again.

"Addie?" Evan called. But the only answer that came back was that of retreating footsteps.

The echo from the gunshot faded.

Once more, the night lay utterly silent.

CHAPTER 27

It seemed to take hours for Sam to rise to his feet and stagger toward Evan.

Hours for the police and an ambulance to arrive.

Hours for Addie and Patrick to pull up to the curb in Addie's Cherokee and take charge of the scene.

Hours while Miriam, curled on the ground, stared lifelessly at the church.

Sam was unharmed. At Miriam's first shot, he'd dropped to the ground. Later, crime-scene techs would dig two nine-millimeter slugs out of an ash tree on the church grounds. For now, the patrol officers had separated Sam and Evan. Evan watched as Sam, his face white, pointed toward the church as he gave his story to a cop. Evan gave his own story to a second cop after the officer had confiscated his gun from his car, bagged his hands so that they could check for gunshot residue, then slapped plastic handcuffs on to keep the bags in place— or so she said.

Later—minutes, hours—Addie found Evan sitting, still hand-cuffed, on the church steps, shivering in the cold. She said something to the officer standing nearby, who freed Evan's wrists but left the bags on.

Addie sat next to him. "Did you fire your weapon?"

"No. But if I'd had it with me, I would have."

She put an arm around him.

"Who did?" she asked.

Evan had his theories, but he wasn't going to share. Not even with Addie. He shook his head, and she seemed to accept it. No doubt the patrol officer had already filled her and Patrick in. A kidnapping. A dead woman. An anonymous shooter.

"Did I ever mention how much I hate guns?" he said.

"They have their uses." Addie's voice was dry. "Given Miriam's apparent willingness to kill you and Sam, do you still believe she isn't our killer? That it's her husband?"

Evan nodded wearily. "Mark Dawson killed Elizabeth and Hassan."

"We found Chablain," she said. "In a manner of speaking."

"Alive?"

"He fled to Russia within a day of our visit to Veritas. The story about him being at the hospital with his ill wife was just that. A story."

"And he went to a country that doesn't have an extradition agreement with the US. I imagine he took a few goodies with him."

"The Shapira Scrolls?"

"I don't think so. I think Dawson has them. If anyone does."

They sat quietly for a time, watching Addie's three-ring circus in blue. The ME knelt next to Miriam. Techs poured over the church grounds. A man dressed in long robes, presumably the church's priest, arrived. He gestured wildly toward the church, then back at himself, then again at the church. Patrick stepped outside the crime-scene tape to talk with him.

"Gerrit Watts is cooling his heels in an interview room," Addie said.

"Not Kelley?"

"Oh, we'll have a little chat with him. But unless things change, our conversation will be nice and civil and in the comfort of his office. There are a few degrees of separation here. It will be hard to convince anyone that Kelley has blood on his hands. You got my text about Dawson fleeing the country?"

Evan nodded. "It came just in time. I'm not sure I would have thought to make that up for Miriam's benefit."

"He won't be free for long. With the Jordanian authorities alerted and Interpol involved, they'll grab him as soon as he steps off the plane."

But Evan wasn't so sure. He suspected Dawson had cultivated friends in high places while working for the Veritas Foundation. Perhaps Yosef Khalil was one of them. Maybe they'd struck a deal before Dawson had even gotten on the plane. Giving Dawson his freedom in exchange for the scrolls would keep the leather fragments in Jordan and avoid a protracted battle for ownership between the two countries. England would probably also get into the mix, since Shapira had hoped to sell the scrolls to the British Museum. Maybe Germany as well; Shapira had gone there first.

If Dawson miraculously escaped custody, Khalil could shrug and shake his head and bemoan the loss of both man and scrolls.

Evan said as much to Addie.

"Maybe." She asked, "So you think Dawson has the scrolls?"

"If not, he probably has something else with which to buy his freedom. But I hope he has them. Otherwise . . ." His voice trailed off as his hand went to touch the outline of the journal stashed inside his zipped coat. Sam's copy of Elizabeth's inventory, which he'd handed to Evan before the police arrived. Miriam had been right about one thing—Sam had been to the bank that day. But it had been the inventory, not the scrolls, that he'd left with, hiding the notebook in an inside pocket of his coat. Miriam's fingers might have brushed against it. But she'd been looking for leather scrolls, not a student's notebook.

Evan was half-afraid to look at the inventory. Afraid of what it might contain. Stolen artifacts, looted treasures. And what might not be there—anything beyond a faint arrow that might—just might—point toward the Shapira Scrolls.

Elizabeth's dream, perhaps forever out of reach.

"Otherwise . . . ," he said again.

Addie nudged him. "Otherwise, what?"

Patrick walked over and leaned against the railing beside them.

Evan said, "This all began with the Shapira Scrolls. Two people murdered, a killer on the loose, a country fighting to get its antiquities back . . ."

"And?" Patrick prodded.

"And it's entirely possible the scrolls were never part of this. So many people have been hunting for them, but for all we know, they never resurfaced after disappearing more than a century ago."

A patrol cop hollered Patrick's name. Patrick held up his hand in acknowledgment.

"It's kind of like that movie, you know?" he said. "*Brigadoon.* The village in Scotland that disappeared into the mist."

Evan and Addie waited.

Patrick nodded. "Those Shapira Scrolls. It's like they never were." A patrol cop called to him, and he strolled away, whistling under his breath.

Evan was suddenly very tired. He looked at Addie fully for the first time. "Were you eating dinner while I was fighting for my life?"

"While you were getting yourself kidnapped, Patrick and I were grabbing Philly cheesesteaks. Why?"

"You have grease on your chin."

She reached into her coat pocket for a tissue and dabbed her face. "Better?" she asked.

"Better."

"What friends are for," she said softly, and smiled at him.

His heart melted.

"I'm very glad you're alive," she said.

He considered speaking his truth to her right then and there, with his hands trapped in white polyethylene bags and Miriam's blood on his coat. But before he could work up his courage, Addie stood and pulled him to his feet.

"Let's get this over with," she said. "I'll try to get you home before dawn."

~~~

They took Evan in for gunshot-residue testing, then to a conference room, where he spent hours going over what had happened at the church for the benefit of Addie, Patrick, other detectives, and the occasional brass. Sam endured the same fate in another room. Pizza was brought in and consumed, the cardboard boxes whisked away. Someone showed up with coffee. Empty soda cans filled the trash can. An assortment of pastries was quickly devoured.

At one point, the video recorder broke, allowing Evan a bathroom break while a tech came to fix it.

The police, of course, were especially interested in who had fired the shots that killed Miriam Fuller. The detectives parsed his story, turning his words over and over in their hunt for clues. While officers searched the church and surrounding blocks, and others scrolled through traffic footage, Evan rehashed his story. He knew that Sam had nothing to offer, and he himself was unwilling to speculate beyond saying that the antiquities business was dangerous, and a lot of people wanted what Miriam and her husband had desired—the Shapira Scrolls.

"Tell us again about these scrolls," said a lieutenant.

Someone crushed a soda can, and Evan winced. Exhaustion turned every sound into a gunshot. The scrape of chair legs on tile. The door closing, opening, closing again. Snatches of sound leaking in from the warren of offices outside. The fluorescent lights buzzed, and the room was weirdly bright, a place without shadows.

He shook off his weariness.

"It's possible Dawson has taken them to Jordan," Evan said. "Or maybe Chablain carried them to Russia. Or maybe they never existed—at least, not in the Watts collection."

Patrick set down his coffee and palmed the back of his head. "Consider me a beat cop who long ago got promoted too far up the ladder—"

"I usually do," Addie jumped in.

"Good one. But didn't Dawson kill Elizabeth to *get* the scrolls?"

Evan shook his head. "It seems like a good motive. But if the scrolls had surfaced—and we may never know the truth—I suspect they were in Elizabeth's lockbox, which Dawson accessed before he murdered her."

Patrick sighed. "It's like trying to make a complete picture out of a bunch of swiss cheese. Bottom line, we don't know if he got the scrolls. Maybe he didn't have *anything* in that little carry-on he took with him to Jordan. All we do know is that he stole the Moses papyri from Elizabeth. And they turned out to be fakes."

"Which Miriam destroyed." Evan picked at the Styrofoam cup on the table in front of him. "And while the scrolls and the papyri are a big part of the story, they aren't all of it. Dawson was obsessed with treachery. He learned that Elizabeth was going to betray the Veritas Foundation and his boss, William Kelley. Murdering her seemed like an appropriate response."

"What about Hassan?"

"Hassan's death is trickier. Dawson might have deemed him a traitor because I suspect the Egyptian was purchasing items from Gerrit Watts and undercutting Veritas. Whatever it was, in that final meeting with Hassan, Dawson's rage at the Egyptian's perceived betrayal reached a boiling point." He picked up the partially shredded cup. Set it back down. "That is my official guess."

Patrick sighed. "A guess might be as good as we get. Well, that and the news that just came in. Soon as we learned Dawson fled the country, we got a warrant for DNA samples from his house and car. Techs found blood on the steering wheel of his Mazda. We also got samples from his toothbrush, which he must have been in too big of a hurry to pack. We'll know soon if it's all a match for the DNA found in Elizabeth's car. But if I were a betting man, I'd say it's going to point right at Mark Dawson. Especially given that his vehicle shows up on cameras near St. Paul's the night of the murder."

Evan nodded, glad for the near proof. And unsurprised.

"So, in the end," Patrick said, his faded-blue eyes ringed with his own exhaustion, "we don't know if Elizabeth ever found these scrolls. We don't know if they were in the Watts collection. We don't know if Gerrit was selling them off, in bulk or one at a time, or at all. We don't know if Dawson has carried them to Jordan or if Chablain took them to Russia. We pretty much know shit. Am I getting this right?"

"See," Evan said. "You deserved your promotion."

The lieutenant cleared his throat. "Why did our mystery shooter kill Miriam Fuller and not you?"

Evan shrugged. "The shooter aimed high."

"A friggin' mess," Patrick said. "Only one glimmer of good in the whole thing."

"What's that?" the lieutenant asked.

Patrick smiled. "None of the players were Irish."

After an hour or two, they brought in Hassan's receptionist. Rana confirmed Dawson had been in the gallery that evening, and it was he who gave her the basket, claiming it was from Hassan.

"It's starting to come together," Addie said.

Patrick laughed. "Optimist."

During the darkest depths of the night, they finally cut Evan loose. A patrol unit dropped him off at his car, still parked next to the church. When he got behind the wheel, he found that his hands were shaking as he tried to insert the key in the ignition. Classic post-adrenaline response. He waited until the worst of it had passed, then picked up his phone. Christina didn't live all that far away. He hated to wake her, but the short drive to her condo might be safer than going home.

She picked up immediately. "I just heard on the news that shots were fired near a church and a little person was involved."

"Word travels fast." He filled her in on some of what had happened—more would come clear in the following days.

"Are you okay?" she asked.

"A little shaky."

"I'm sorry."

When she didn't say anything else, he asked if she wanted to come to his place for nightcaps. There was a long, pregnant pause.

"Is it Avraham?" Evan asked when the silence had lengthened to infinity.

Christina released a sigh. *Here it comes,* Evan thought. In truth, it had been so long since someone had broken up with him—as opposed to a mutually friendly separation or his own restless need for freedom— that he had forgotten how much it hurt.

He felt a flash of pity for Miriam Fuller.

"It's true that I find Avraham appealing," Christina said. "I won't lie about that. I might even want to explore a relationship with him. But it's more than that."

Or less than that. Evan hated when he felt sorry for himself. But this was promising to be one of those moments when he thought he'd make any kind of bargain with any kind of devil to gain a foot of height.

Maybe he and Mark Dawson weren't so different after all.

"It's not your height," she said, as if she'd read his mind. "Please don't tell me that's the first place you go when a woman breaks up with you."

"I'm only being rational. I'm a good cook, a great conversationalist, and terrific in bed. Not to mention, handsome and erudite. Plus, I live in a grand house and fly a hawk. And I only rarely leave the toilet seat up. Really, Christina. What else *could* it be?"

It felt good when they both laughed.

"You forgot your profound modesty," she said, and their laughter deepened.

After a moment, when their mirth had faded, Christina said, "It's Addie."

Even in the dark of his car, a flush crept up Evan's face as Christina went on to explain that she'd known from the first time Evan mentioned Addie's name that he was in love with her. "And Simon told me—"

"Simon is a rat."

"Simon is a good friend to us both. He told me that you'd never be fully committed to a relationship until you'd gotten Addie out of your system."

"He makes her sound like a disease."

"Love is like that. Infectious, sometimes deadly, and out of our control." Christina's tone was wry. "Anyway, being with you has proven one thing to me—I'm close to being ready to settle down. My biological clock is ticking. But I won't play second fiddle to another woman."

Evan opened his mouth to plead his case. Addie was a beloved friend. Which was a lot. But nothing more than that.

Then he closed his mouth without speaking.

"What do you think of Avraham?" she asked him.

A memory flashed of the shots so recently fired. Miriam's body in the grass.

"I would—I'd consider—he's—"

"Now there's a ringing endorsement."

"I like Avraham," Evan said honestly. "But you might want to ask him a lot of questions before you leap in."

"Questions about what?"

"Ask him where he spent the last ten years. Better yet, ask him what he does at the Office."

"The office?"

"With a capital *O*. Ask him exactly like that. And wink when you do it. You'll get him to talk."

"I'm confused."

"You won't be."

"I'll leave you with a final thought," she said.

"That sounds very . . . final."

She laughed softly. "I'll always be fond of you, Evan."

He felt himself nodding in the dark. "And I of you, Christina."

After they hung up, Evan considered abandoning his car and calling an Uber. He recalled how well that had gone last time and decided to simply sit and chill until he felt like himself again. Just as he finally gathered himself enough to drive, his phone rang. He ignored it. All he wanted was a hot shower, a little time with Ginny and Perro, and a good night's sleep.

The phone rang again. With a sigh, he answered using the car's Bluetooth.

"It's me," came Avraham's now-familiar voice. "I'm in your kitchen. I wanted you to know so you wouldn't shoot me when you come in."

What did you expect from a Mossad agent?

CHAPTER 28

Perro greeted Evan at the door to the garage with full-on Pembroke Welsh corgi enthusiasm, then escorted him to the kitchen.

Avraham had made himself quite at home. He'd placed the remains of the cassoulet in the oven and poured two glasses of wine from the second of the two bottles Christina had brought over. Had it been only three days ago? Evan looked at his watch. Four days ago.

"Nice place," Avraham said.

"I like it better when no one breaks in. It was you at the church, wasn't it?"

Avraham studied Evan. "Do you really want an answer to that question?"

Evan thought about it. The repercussions for himself and Avraham. The potential fallout between nations. The idea of throwing Elizabeth's friend under the bus for having saved his life and Sam's.

He said, "It's comforting to know spies are good at keeping secrets."

"As are professors." Avraham smiled and clinked his glass against Evan's, and they each took a swallow.

"Have you tried Israeli wine?" Avraham asked.

"Years ago. Quite good, as I recall."

"It's excellent, much of it." Avraham turned the wineglass in his hand, appearing to admire the legs. "But this isn't bad."

"You and Christina share a taste in wine, too. Look, it's not that I'm not glad to see you. Actually, I'm not totally clear on whether I'm glad to see you or not." Evan waved a hand. "But I'd like a few questions answered."

Avraham tipped his head. "I'll answer reasonable ones."

"A prince among men. Do you know if Elizabeth found the Shapira Scrolls? And if so, who has them?"

"No on both counts. I wish I did."

"Where did you go after you chased Polo Shirt—Kevin Grady?"

"It was time to vanish. I knew Simon wasn't hurt too badly, but that he'd have to call the police. It seemed prudent to disappear. But Grady and I had a couple of chats, and I got this off him."

Avraham reached inside his coat and removed a manila envelope. Evan recognized it as the one he'd found in Elizabeth's coat, with *MS? See Finch* written on the outside.

"How . . . ," Evan began.

"I simply pointed out to Grady that it didn't belong to him. It is now yours. Elizabeth would have wanted it that way."

Evan stared at the envelope. He reached out and brushed it with his fingertips, wondering what—if anything—they'd learn from this small bit of ancient history. For the first time in hours, he felt something akin to pleasure. "Thank you."

"You're welcome."

Evan looked up. "What about your relationship with Agent Holliday?" he asked.

"It's good, professionally speaking, even though we've never met face-to-face. Which is why I failed to recognize her at Boonoon's. Our relationship will remain congenial as long as we keep my name out of what's happened these last few days. Do you want to know what brought Holliday to your fair city?"

"It had crossed my mind," Evan said.

Avraham removed the cassoulet from the oven. He filled a plate and offered it to Evan, who declined. They moved to the kitchen table.

"Over a year ago," Avraham said, "while she was working to break up an international ring, she posed as a buyer and ensnared Hassan, who was conducting multiple illegal sales. She convinced him to turn by offering him 'work-off time' against his own likely conviction. It wasn't hard, apparently. Hassan was deeply unhappy that he hadn't been getting the respect he deserved from his associates."

"If Dawson got wind of Hassan's deal, he would definitely consider him a traitor."

"Indeed."

"But does Holliday really believe Elizabeth was involved with the bad guys?"

The Israeli gave a faint smile. "Not anymore."

"Ah." Evan drained his wineglass. "Did you find your prime minister's stolen treasure?"

Avraham paused with a forkful of the casserole near his lips. "This is quite good."

"Meaning you'd rather not say." Evan was thinking of the storage vault holding Theodore Watts's collection. If Avraham was intent on finding a stolen treasure, Elizabeth had no doubt been willing to help. Maybe she'd even given him a key.

Avraham said nothing.

"I suppose you've considered that you and Agent Holliday might have common cause regarding William Kelley," Evan said. "Perhaps even enough evidence to justify a raid on Veritas."

"I believe the formidable Holliday will manage just fine without me." He tipped his wineglass as if in a silent salute to the Homeland Security agent. "Are you done? Is it my turn?"

"Why not? As long as your questioning doesn't involve pliers and klieg lights."

"We shadow workers tend more toward truth serum and bribes these days. Anyway, I only have one question. Are you going to accept your inheritance?"

"Elizabeth told you?"

"She and I didn't have many secrets."

Evan closed his eyes and imagined Elizabeth standing in her office at the institute. Her joy at finally making the institute a reality.

And then her death before she could see it through.

It was a glorious thing, the Chicago Institute of Middle Eastern Antiquities. What had given Elizabeth the faith that he could succeed in continuing her dream? His background wasn't lacking, he supposed. And there was the fact that he didn't have a family to distract him. He was as alone in the world as Elizabeth had been after the death of her son. Friends aplenty. But only a few blood kin, and those too far away.

He opened his eyes, looked at Avraham. "I'd like to say yes. Give Elizabeth what might have been her final wish. But I don't have an answer for you. Not yet."

"If you do, consider hiring Sam. Elizabeth wasn't fond of many people, as you know. But she cared for Sam."

Evan nodded.

Outside the windows, the sky turned milky white with the coming dawn. Evan finished the wine. It was, as Sandra Yee had pointed out, five o'clock somewhere.

Avraham stood. "It's about time for me to fade back into the shadows."

Evan also rose. "Your story about being an archaeologist—was that a lie?"

"Not at all. But it's been years since I've been in the field. I miss it."

Evan walked with him to the front door. Perro trotted after them, then stopped at Evan's feet while Avraham stepped out onto the porch.

"About Christina," the Israeli began.

Evan shook his head. "I don't hold a grudge."

Avraham considered this. "I won't insult you by denying my attraction for her. She is very—"

"Appealing. I know. No need to rub it in. Just don't lie to her about what you do."

"Heard and accepted." He looked down at his hands, flexed his fingers, then looked up again. His smile was tight. His eyes weren't unkind.

"What?" Evan asked.

"I want you to know—the Jordanians won't arrest Dawson. Or, if they do, they won't extradite him to the US. They will honor whatever arrangement they made with him—a deal likely struck before Dawson proved himself a killer."

"I figured as much."

"But . . ." Avraham's jaw tightened. "You should also know this. The tip of the spear never misses."

Evan hesitated, then nodded. "Heard and accepted."

Close by, a lark's trill spilled into the dawning day.

The Israeli reached into the inside breast pocket of his leather jacket and handed Evan a photograph. Then he shook Evan's hand and turned away, walking quickly down the drive, changing from man to mere silhouette against the brightening sky.

Evan watched him until he was out of sight. Only then did he hold up the photo.

Elizabeth, standing alone in the desert. She was young, strong, her eyes narrowed against the sun, a trowel in her hand. Unaware of the triumphs and tragedies that lay ahead of her. Unaware of how her dreams would, in the end, be snatched away.

In the moment of the photo—and thus forever—she was radiantly happy.

Evan stared at the photo until he felt his smile match hers. Any given moment is all we ever have. All we are granted.

He turned and went into the house.

POSTLUDE

On the plane, seated in first class with a highball of bourbon and a blessedly dozing seatmate, I stared out at the blackness and smiled.

I'd escaped.

Wily like a fox, one of the teachers from Teen Confront whispered in my ear.

I raised my drink in a toast to the memory of those I'd left behind at a place that had at first been a prison, then shown me my path in life.

"Cunning," I said softly. "That's me."

The stranger dozing next to me stirred, and I fell silent.

The night Miriam told me she was certain she'd located the treasure was when my mind opened. I understood that the treasure did, in fact, exist. That it wasn't a forgery. That it was the reason I'd been led to the book in the Jerusalem shop. And that it was my task to hide the treasure. Or destroy it.

The subsequent actions I'd taken were not without personal sacrifice. The sacrifice of my ambition. The sacrifice of my future as a free man in America. But also, the idea of sacrifice as offering—the offering I had made to God. Elizabeth, who intended to share the heretical scrolls with the world, had to end up somewhere. The future site of a place commemorating God's glory was right and true.

Sacrificial sites become sacred.

I was confident that once I reached Jordan, their officials would honor my agreement with Yosef Khalil. They would hide the scrolls in a private collection. And they would pay well for the opportunity, providing me with enough money to continue my work.

A flight attendant came by to ask if I needed anything. I accepted another miniature of bourbon. In a few minutes, I would unfold the leather scrolls I'd taken from Elizabeth's metal box and examine them as closely as I could without benefit of a lab. I'd soon know if the leather strips were likely the lost treasure of Jordan, or if they were another artifact she'd taken from the Watts Collection.

For now, I pulled down the window shade and opened the book a final time. I wanted to know how the story ended.

London, August 1883.

"It is an obscene and impudent forgery," declared the well-respected scholar. "The method used is quite clear. The lines of text are nonsense—scrambled letters copied from the famous Moabite Stone. The leather was cut from an old synagogue scroll and aged with the use of chemical agents. It is preposterous to expect the queen's scholars to be fooled by such a rude fraud."

Not long after his thrashing in the papers and the utter destruction of his hope to rise above the label of shopkeeper, Moses Shapira left London for good. As his name was dragged through the mud across Europe and even on the other side of the ocean in America, he spent some weeks in Berlin, then Amsterdam, trying unsuccessfully to find his way back from ruin.

Nearly seven months after the debacle in London, Moses Wilhelm Shapira's body was found in a hotel room.

He lay silent, dead by his own hand.

I closed the book and shut off the overhead light. The cabin turned dim around me. Suicide was a fitting end for one such as Moses Shapira. He'd been nothing more than a heretic.

I poured more bourbon. A man came toward me down the aisle, headed back to his seat from the lavatory. Our eyes met, and when he reached my seat, he stopped and pointed at the book, now closed on my lap.

"You know the story of the Shapira Scrolls?" he asked in Hebrew.

"A little," I said. I rattled the ice in my glass.

"I'll tell you what *I* know." The man leaned across my sleeping seatmate until his face nearly touched mine. He spoke softly into my ear. "Everyone associated with the scrolls soon dies. Everyone. It's most tragic, is it not?"

And with that, I was no longer the fox.

He straightened and walked away. When I looked again, he'd vanished behind the curtain.

Unnerved, I tossed back the last of the whiskey and raised the window shade.

Outside lay only darkness.

Author's Note and Acknowledgments

The antiquities trade is what most people believe it to be—a tale of beautiful artifacts discovered by archaeologists and purchased at great cost for museums to share with the world.

But that is only a small part of the story.

Certainly, the wealth is there. Many who own antiquities are billionaires. Theirs is a world of glorious estates, offshore trusts, and the rarefied air of the über-wealthy.

But beneath the glitter lies a darker world. One of international criminality, terrorism, and the destruction of humanity's past. For the antiquities trade is also about tomb raiders, smugglers, and those who would rob a country of its history and culture.

If you are concerned with the fate of the world's treasures—that they might vanish into a rich person's private collection or be used to fund terrorism—then I suggest you look into the work being done by the Antiquities Coalition. Find them at theantiquitiescoalition.org.

Dark of Night is a work of fiction. Any resemblance to businesses, foundations, institutions, corporations, or actual persons, living or dead, is coincidental. The exception to this fictionalization is the Shapira Scrolls, an actual discovery made by Moses Wilhelm Shapira. The scrolls disappeared—as mentioned in this book—after their last public display on March 8, 1889. Their fate has never been determined, and I have allowed my imagination free rein to speculate on their current whereabouts. Those wishing to know more may look at *The Moses Scroll: Reopening the Most Controversial Case in the History of Biblical Scholarship* by Ross K. Nichols, *The Shapira Affair* by John M. Allegro, and *The Lost Book of Moses: The Hunt for the World's Oldest Bible* by Chanan Tigay.

I am deeply indebted to the following people. Mistakes and creative liberties are purely my own.

Kevin R. Hancock, attorney-at-law, for graciously sharing his wisdom on trusts, the contesting of trusts, and probate issues—all of which helped me navigate the trusts of Theodore Watts and Elizabeth Lawrence.

The Homeland Security Investigations New York Field Office Cultural Property, Arts, and Antiquities Unit. Thank you, gentlemen, for taking the time to answer my many questions and share your knowledge. My immense gratitude not only for your help but for the work you do.

Retired Denver detective Ron Gabel, who tirelessly answered my investigation-related questions as well as offering his unflagging support for my work.

Lisa Anne Rothstein, whose knowledge of Chicago graces these pages.

Once again, I thank my fellow authors for their help. Mike Bateman, who brainstormed this novel with me. Mike offered his brilliant insights on the story and gave invaluable comments on the manuscript. Mike Shepherd, who understands my characters and story better than I do and who bravely waded into the manuscript, making it better line by line. And Chris Mandeville, who added her insights. Chris excels—as she always does—with her own marvelous take on things.

To Bob Spiller, who has taught me a lot—not just about writing, but about life.

To Pat Coleman, who kept me company at restaurants and coffee shops while we worked on our novels. The companionship of writers is ever to be wished for.

Thank you to my sister-friends—Cathy Noakes, Deborah Coonts, Lori Dominquez, Maria Faulconer, and Pat Coleman. You have cared for my heart in ways friends shouldn't have to. I'm eternally grateful.

My gratitude to the team at Thomas & Mercer is unbounded. Thank you—all of you—for what you do. To my editor and lifeline, Liz Pearsons; the amazing Sarah Shaw, who solves problems big and small; and Gracie Doyle, who brought me into the Thomas & Mercer world and continues to support me.

I am fortunate to have a gifted developmental editor. Thank you, Charlotte Herscher, for guiding my book from rough to polished. And for doing so with insight, grace, and kindness.

And to my agent, Christina Hogrebe. I look forward to a long and fruitful relationship.

Thanks most of all to Steve and Amanda for being in my life. And to Kyle, whose love and presence still shine through.

ABOUT THE AUTHOR

Photo © Trystan Photography

Barbara Nickless is the *Wall Street Journal* and Amazon Charts bestselling author of *At First Light* in the Dr. Evan Wilding series as well as the Sydney Rose Parnell series, which includes *Blood on the Tracks*, a *Suspense Magazine* Best of 2016 selection and winner of the Colorado Book Award and the Daphne du Maurier Award for Excellence; *Dead Stop*, winner of the Colorado Book Award and nominee for the Daphne du Maurier Award for Excellence; *Ambush*; and *Gone to Darkness*. Her essays and short stories have appeared in *Writer's Digest* and on Criminal Element, among other markets. She lives in Colorado, where she loves to cave, snowshoe, hike, and drink single malt Scotch—usually not at the same time. Connect with her at www.barbaranickless.com.